# HISTORIC
## OF
# EXILE

| Cryssa Bazos | Amy Maroney |
| Anna Belfrage | Alison Morton |
| Elizabeth Chadwick | Charlene Newcomb |
| Cathie Dunn | Elizabeth St.John |
| J.G. Harlond | Marian L Thorpe |
| Helen Hollick | Annie Whitehead |
| Loretta Livingstone | |

*With an introduction by Deborah Swift*

TAW RIVER
PRESS

**HISTORICAL STORIES of EXILE**
by
Cryssa Bazos, Anna Belfrage, Elizabeth Chadwick, Cathie Dunn, J.G.
Harlond, Helen Hollick, Loretta Livingstone, Amy Maroney Alison
Morton, Charlene Newcomb, Elizabeth St.John, Marian L Thorpe,
Annie Whitehead.
With an introduction by Deborah Swift
Copyright © 2023

Cover Design © Cathy Helms Avalon Graphics 2023

ISBN: 978-1-7392720-1-2 (paperback)
ISBN: 978-1-8381318-9-0 (ebook)

Published by Taw River Press
https://www.tawriverpress.co.uk

# CONTENTS
## HISTORICAL STORIES of EXILE

## INTRODUCTION
### by Deborah Swift

'Only the misfortune of exile can provide the in-depth understanding and the overview into the realities of the world' – Stefan Zweig (author of *The Grand Budapest Hotel*, exiled from Austria during Nazi occupation).

The verb 'exile' comes from the Old French word *essillier*, meaning to banish, expel, or drive off. In the past to go into exile was often a punishment, though now people sometimes live in exile voluntarily – or because life at home has become too dangerous or difficult. Alison Morton's story *My Sister*, Cathie Dunn's *Exile* and Elizabeth St.John's story *Into the Light* emphasize this tug between the familiar world that has become unsafe, and the lure of a place where life might be lived in more freedom.

But exile is always a step into the unknown, and often holds no possibility of return. Each of us at some time in our lives has probably experienced the feeling of being an exile – of not quite fitting in to societal norms, and as in the story *Into the Light* the dislocation is often an internal one, as well as an external one.

Historically, leaders of countries were often sent into exile when a new leader, or new king, invaded or conquered the territory, or because someone feared they might be a threat to the new order. Exiled men were mostly members of political elites, or in the case of women, pawns to the men playing these games of 'King of the Castle'.

This kind of banishment is harder to achieve now, as with modern technology a person can still access their home and their circle of family and friends via the internet. As a punishment, exile has become impractical, though a political leader in exile can still be considered a danger, and no doubt it is harder to deal with them in a different territory with different laws. But the past was a different land, and this collection exploits this to the full.

Exile as a theme for a story collection has all the ingredients you might need for good fiction. The falling in love between a prisoner and his jailor's daughter, the tearing away of the familiar environment, the gulf between the self and its true home, and the arrival in an often hostile place, is a big feature of these stories. The exile need not even be to another country; Elizabeth Chadwick's story *Coming Home* features a woman exiled to the Tower of London, a gilded cage but exile nonetheless. Helen Hollick's story exploits the idea of removal from London to the remote countryside of Exmoor, and as her character St Croix says; 'he saw the sense of honourable exile over pointless execution.'

In earlier historical periods when travel was harder, and might involve treacherous sea crossings, or traversing inhospitable landscapes on foot, the person in exile often wondered if they would ever be re-united with their roots, leading to a permanent scar of sorrow at their loss. Today's war-torn world is full of people in exile – refugees fleeing persecution.

In many stories, and in many of these in this collection, it is the families ripped apart that take the heaviest toll; a mother separated from her child, or a wife from her husband. This is well expressed in the heart-breaking stories *Unwanted Prince* by Anna Belfrage and *Wadan Wraeclastas (Tread the Path of Exile)* by Annie Whitehead.

When Victor Hugo was exiled from France, in 1851, he did not know if he would ever see his country again. He didn't return until nineteen years later, after the Franco-Prussian war. During all that time he was unable to visit the grave of his eldest daughter Léopoldine. For a number of years after her death, Hugo had made annual pilgrimage to her grave. In this poem written during his exile, *To the One Who Stayed Behind in France*, Hugo wrote,

> *She knows, doesn't she? that it hasn't been my fault.*
> *If, these four years that have passed away so soon,*
> *I haven't gone and prayed at the foot of her tomb!*

The anguish of being parted from your ancestry, the place where the bones of your family lie, and of having to give up your history, looms large too in this collection. Once exiled, the person must build a new life to survive. If returning home, then in one sense the exile will never return to the place they knew. Their old life has moved on and can never be the same. The separation has formed a chasm between the old and new lives. In this collection, the time-slip tale *The Past, My Future* by Loretta Livingstone explores this sense of dislocation, and is a lovely way to highlight societal differences between the past and the present.

The stories in this book span many worlds, from 11$^{th}$-century Wales, to Iceland, to Greece, to the forests of Robin Hood and even the suburban house of an enemy alien in WWII. Each story is a little jewel of time and place, and so I recommend that you take time to savour each one. I'm sure you will find much to enjoy in this excellently written selection.

© Deborah Swift
   *Lancashire, 2023*

## ABOUT DEBORAH SWIFT

Deborah is a delver into archives, drinks too much tea, and loves antiques and old buildings. Her sturdy, stone-built house used to be the village primary school, and from her window she has a view of a few 17$^{th}$-century cottages, and behind those, green fields dotted with grazing sheep.

As a child she loved the Victorian classics such as *Jane Eyre, Little Women, Lorna Doone* and *Wuthering Heights.* Before becoming a writer Deborah used to work as a set and costume designer for theatre and TV, so historical fiction was a natural choice because she enjoyed the research aspect of her job. She has always loved poking about in archives and museums, not to mention the attraction of boned bodices and the excuse to visit old and interesting houses!

In her books Deborah likes to write about extraordinary characters set against the background of real historical events. Her first novel was **The Lady's Slipper** which was shortlisted for the Impress Prize, and her book **The Poison Keeper,** about the Renaissance poisoner Giulia Tofana, won the BookViral Millennium Award. She has written eighteen novels to date including two series set in WWII – her latest, *The Shadow Network* is due for release in early 2024.

She lives in England on the edge of the Lake District, a beautiful area made famous by the Romantic Poets such as Wordsworth and Coleridge, and when not writing, she enjoys exploring the mountainous landscapes and interesting coastline near her home.

"Her characters are so real that they linger in the mind long after the book is back on the shelf"'
*The Historical Novels Review.*

🕊 🕊 🕊

Website: **https://deborahswift.com/**
Buy Deborah's books on Amazon:
**http://author.to/DeborahSwift**
or Harper Collins
(Also available from other online stores or order from any bookshop.)

## READERS - PLEASE NOTE:

These are adult stories intended for adults and/or older teenagers, and may contain coarse language, or mild scenes of an intimate or sensitive nature.

# 1

## WADAN WRÆCLASTAS (TREAD THE PATH OF EXILE)

### BY ANNIE WHITEHEAD

**RHUDDLAN, NORTH WALES, SEPTEMBER 1057**

The early morning September mist hung low over the river. The grass beneath the horses' feet was pebbled with dew and the sun had begun its climb, promising to burn away the low clouds and offering the prospect of a bright day. It seemed irreligious to be sad on such a beautiful morning. Ealdgyth shivered, pulled her cloak a little tighter over her shoulders, and fought the urge to turn her horse and run away. Behind her, where the rising eastern sun would surely obscure the view, was the only land she'd ever known, but she needed no blinding morning rays to tell her that her home was already long out of sight.

Her father brought his horse alongside hers, and spoke softly. "See beyond the murk?" He pointed beyond the bend in the river to a natural mound with a building on it. "That's Twthill, and his hall, which the Welsh call a *llys*. He has many residences, just as our king does, but this is the one he prefers."

"Just as our king does," she murmured. He talked as if everything in Wales was the same as in England.

The truth of it was that here they spoke a different language, everyday life would not be the same, beyond the basics, and the only similarity was that both kings would now have an English wife called Ealdgyth. Yet Edith Godwineson, as she once was known, had not had to leave her homeland when she wed King Edward.

Her father squeezed her arm. "I sense that you are wary, but it's not as if he is a stranger to you."

"No, indeed not." Gruffudd of Wales had been an ally of her father's against the might of the Godwinesons for many years, even before her father inherited the earldom of Mercia, and she had met him on a few occasions, but that did not mean she wished to wed him.

He was old. Not as old as her father, but old enough to *be* her father. As the Mercians entered the hall, he stood up, moved away from his chair and walked to greet her. His beard was flecked with grey and his countenance seemed stern, but as he moved to stand in front of her, he smiled, the creases on his brow smoothed, and she wondered if he had been as nervous as she but no, she soon realised, it was that he knew how scared she was. Taking her arm, he led her to the dais, made sure that she was comfortable, and thereafter no need, no want of hers, went unattended. Her father was a tried and tested warrior yet was gentle as a lamb with his kin; why had she thought that Gruffudd would be any different? It was immediately clear that Gruffudd was a rich man. Items of gold and silver adorned the room, the king himself was dressed in an expensive, purple-dyed tunic edged with gold fabric, and he presented her with a gift, a brooch made from a lucrative nearby silver workings. It was exquisitely wrought, with delicate filigree turned and coiled into the shape of a wolf-like creature, and she was moved that he did not pin it to her silk overdress himself, but allowed her to do it, even though her hands were shaking. She felt it move with every breath, a symbol not of ownership, but of welcome, and protection. There was a lavish wedding feast of trout caught from the river, fresh leeks, the first of the apple crop and the last of the fresh summer cheeses, and Gruffudd ensured that her plate was kept full, her ale cup filled up. Music was provided by a bard with a harp, instead of a scop with a lyre as it would be in Mercia, but it was as lovely and lilting. That night, when they were alone, Gruffudd said, "I will not hurt you." Five words that eased her mind and soothed her fears.

The next day before her father left with the other Mercians, Gruffudd addressed him. "She will be safe with me, Lord Ælfgar. On that you have my word."

"I have no doubt. And long may our friendship continue." Her father turned to her, hugged her to him and spoke softly in her ear. "Can you make a life here?"

Over his shoulder, she saw the people of Gruffudd's *llys* smiling at her, and their king looking at her with affection. "Yes, Father, I think I will be able to make a home here."

Within a year, her daughter Nest came into her world. Ealdgyth recalled when her younger brothers, Edwin and Morcar, were born. She had still been a child herself, but old enough to help her mother, and she quickly learned to soothe the fractious babes. Nest was different; she slept for long periods, woke in a cheerful mood, smiled at most people and always at her mother. Ealdgyth gained enough Welsh to get by, Gruffudd continued to be an attentive and thoughtful husband, and Ealdgyth knew that for one such as she – noblewomen who, whilst in theory and in English law had the right to marry where and whom they chose, often had no say in choosing a husband – life was better than she might have hoped. The warm smell of her baby's skin and the feeling it evoked seemed the very essence of love, and she was content.

In England, there was only one king, but it had not always been so. Once, the rulers of Mercia, and Wessex, of East Anglia, and Northumbria, were kings, not earls. Their leaders were ambitious, powerful men, even now. In Wales, she discovered, it was a similar story, where Gruffudd fought to unite all the territories under his rule, and had no love for an English king wishing to expand his territories westward. No wonder he and her father were staunch allies.

Ælfgar had been exiled when the disgraced Godwinesons found favour once more with King Edward, accusing Ælfgar of treason and causing his banishment, and Ealdgyth recalled how her father went to Ireland, bought ships, and then asked for Gruffudd's help. Together they attacked Hereford and Ælfgar got his lands back. Not long after Nest was born Ælfgar had needed Gruffudd's help once more, for now King Edward's brother-in-law Harold Godwineson was not only earl of Wessex, but administrator of Hereford, so dangerously close to Ælfgar's lands, and to the Welsh border, and had caused Ælfgar to be banished once more. They fought back again, and won. Ealdgyth had worried, of course she had, but indulging grown-up concerns for loved ones at war was a luxury that a baby would not allow, and her attention was focused daily on her little child, a helpless babe with endless demands, and a smile more potent than any charm. In her mother and child cocoon, Ealdgyth was content.

Not all was well with Gruffudd though, for he had enemies within Wales, too, but he was careful never to bring his worries to their chamber. She heard a few details from others at the court, how the other leaders of Wales resented him and his sometimes brutal tactics. She'd long thought that his accumulated wealth had a story of violence behind it, but this was the way of kings and it neither impressed nor repelled her. What mattered was how he treated her and, if she had one regret, it was that Gruffudd, in striving to keep her free from care, had none to share his burdens. Instead, it was he who comforted her when the news came of Ælfgar's death, five years almost to the day that he had given her in marriage. Now Mercia was ruled by her brother Edwin, a lad whose voice had barely broken.

### RHUDDLAN, NORTH WALES, CHRISTMAS 1062

Gruffudd was in jovial mood, but Ealdgyth knew him well enough to sense that he was masking some uneasiness. He applauded his bard enthusiastically, made sure his guests were well fed, gave her solicitous looks knowing that she still grieved for her father, but he glanced at the door more than was usual. Occasionally he would catch the eye of one of his *teulu*, the extended family group of warriors who served him and rode with him in battle, and they would nod almost imperceptibly, or give a tiny shake of the head. When Ealdgyth rose to take Nest from her nurse and put her to bed, he placed a hand on her shoulder, not gripping with his fingers, but exerting enough pressure with his palm to ensure that she knew to take his command seriously. "She is tired, Husband. Should I ask the nurse to take her? Only I do like to settle her myself."

"I know you do, but you must not leave the hall. Not yet." He was looking again at the door, and when Rhodri, his most trusted deputy, opened it and came inside, Gruffudd let go of his wife's shoulder and instead pulled her gently to her feet. "Take the child, go to Rhodri, and do exactly what he says."

Rhodri came forward, brushing fast melting snow from his cloak. He bowed briefly, and spoke in a flurry of Welsh. The only words she caught were *gyda mi*: with me. His meaning was clear enough and, clutching the sleepy but curious Nest to her chest, she followed him. A backward glance at Gruffudd showed him marshalling the rest of the household, pointing to the door at the rear of the hall, and she willed him to look at her, but he did not.

Later, much later, she heard; in the mountain hideaway, deep in Gwynedd, the tale came to them eventually. Harold Godwineson, emboldened after the death of Ælfgar and not fearing the young beardless Edwin, had launched an attack. Gruffudd had discovered the plan, and sent his household overland in one direction, his wife and child in another, while he escaped by boat. The *llys* was burned to the ground, the remaining ships torched. For months Gruffudd hid but, at the end of the summer, a campaign by Harold and his brother Tostig saw him trapped, betrayed by his Welsh enemies and killed. His head was sent to Harold.

"Lady, it is no longer safe for you here," said Rhodri. "We will take you back to your brother, to your kin." And then, while she was still numb from the news of Gruffudd's death, he told her the worst of it.

In the autumn, a time of year she had begun to despise, Ealdgyth returned to Mercia. She should have been glad to be home, but any notion of home as a place had been shattered when she was told that she must leave Nest, a valuable Welsh princess, behind.

## WORCESTER, MERCIA, APRIL 1066

How did any mother recover from the wrench? Ealdgyth was comforted by her grandmother, Godiva, and made herself as busy as she could. She had been gone for much of her brothers' lives and she tried to get to know Edwin again, learning his ways and of their boyish exploits – stories of carefree days when they would climb trees and splash each other in the river, stories that made her heart constrict when she thought of all she would miss of Nest's girlhood – and realising with sadness that the weight of responsibility was like a lead cloak upon his shoulders. Edwin and Morcar were still young, but after a rebellion in the north, Morcar was now earl of Northumbria in place of Tostig Godwineson, and the Mercian family was powerful, but separated once more. Ealdgyth again had something in common with Edith Godwineson: they were both widows. King Edward had died not long after Yule, and it was said that Edith was bereft. But she had no children. Ealdgyth drew no comfort from knowing that another queen was in mourning. Her own heart was as a ball of twine, pulled daily from her very innards as it was tugged across the miles to Wales, to Nest.

It was Eastertide, a time of joy in the Church year, but Edwin was not smiling. Nor had he done, really, since Harold Godwineson became king upon the death of Edward. Grandmother Godiva tapped her stick as if squashing ants in anger wherever she walked, muttering about the Godwines and how they had stolen everything, including the kingship. *And broken my heart,* Ealdgyth wanted to add, but she never did.

Edwin came to her outside the chapel. Despite the growing strength of the sun at that time of year, any breeze that blew was chilling, and he put his arm around her, rubbing her shoulder as she had done to him when he was a small child and complained of the cold. His words, though, when they came, froze her veins. "King Harold wishes to wed you. And I have agreed."

Blood rushed to her ears, pounding there until all she could hear was her own heartbeat. But no, her heart was still in her chest, hammering as if it would break through her ribs and burst upon the ground. Ground which was swaying, refusing to hold her steady. She took a calming breath.

"Have I not endured enough? Have I not been a loyal sister? Why must I wed the man who killed my husband, who took my child from me?"

So this was how it felt, to be in the eye of a storm. Godiva shouted and waved her stick, flinging her words like barbs at Edwin: traitor, wretch, cruel. Edwin responded: no other way, but if one brother-in-law of a king could take the throne, then so, in future, could another. Ealdgyth, the most noble of all England's noblewomen, deserved another crown. "One day," he said, "I will be stronger, but for now I have no choice but to pretend friendship." And all the while, Ealdgyth shed her tears and prepared to leave home once more.

The walls of Worcester retreated until they were no bigger than sticks, and as they travelled east, the burhs and villages became less familiar. Folk, busy in the fields and tending the hedgerows, bowed their heads but no longer waved in recognition. London was the biggest settlement she had ever seen. Worcester, Gloucester, Tamworth, all of them fortified burhs, were like farm steadings compared with this place. Ealdgyth shrank with every roll of the cartwheels, until she felt no bigger than a mouse, soon to be dropped into a nest of adders.

They had travelled much of the way along Watling Street and now came to the site of the folk moot at St Paul's. This, she was told, was where the portreeve, who collected taxes and revenues for the king, also relayed the details of royal decrees to the people of London. Ealdgyth had spoken to many reeves in her lifetime, but had never heard of a portreeve. Nor had she seen such a busy river, where merchants in vessels called keels and hulks brought silks, gold, wine, oil pressed from olives, ivory and bronze, as well as the everyday timber, cloth, and farm produce. There was a king's hall nearby but, after a brief conversation, the party was informed that they were to turn and head to the late king's new hall at the West Minster.

They proceeded to an island where the river Tyburn flowed into the Thames and there, next to the new church, was the hall. The procession of riders and carts stopped. Standing on the steps of the biggest building Ealdgyth had ever seen was not her future husband, but a woman of middling height, who kept her chin high as she descended all but one of the steps. There she stood, dainty soft leather slippers peeping from below her gown, foot tapping, waiting for Ealdgyth to come to her, and there she still stood, one step above the ground, waiting for Ealdgyth to bow her head.

"I am Edith. The queen."

Five words. All that was needed to tell the newcomer her place.

Ealdgyth would not cry. Her throat tightened and

her eyes burned, but she would not cry. Near the doorway another lady was standing, small children either side of her, children who were looking intently at the new arrival. The woman was dressed as elaborately as the dowager queen, in a floor-length gown made from cloth dyed bright blue and with impractically long sleeves. Her head cloth was haphazardly arranged though, as if to show off her long and delicate neck. As Ealdgyth drew level, she smiled at her, but before words could be exchanged, Edith swept past. "And that is my brother's handfast woman; those are some of their children."

More than a hundred years since Mercia ceased to be an independent kingdom, tensions still existed. For comfort, Ealdgyth touched her beloved brooch, pinned, as always, to her kirtle, but the metal was cold against her finger. There was to be no welcome here for her among the people of Wessex, and no offer of protection from her new husband, who already had a family and needed no other. Gruffudd had always hidden his worries; Harold looked like a haunted man. Her place at his side guaranteed the support of her brothers for his kingship but he had a habit, she noticed, of never directly meeting anyone's gaze. Looking back, she wondered if her memory of him was coloured by hindsight but no, that way he had of walking, like a stag being hunted, was there long before October 1066.

Ealdgyth, invisible except when pointedly ignored – the dowager queen insisted on being lady of the hall, serving Harold his drinks and keeping the keys firmly on her belt – watched the pageant play out. Tostig Godwineson, disgraced and deprived of his northern earldom, had fled over the sea, and now, in league with Hardrada of Norway, attacked. Tostig and Edith had always been close, and now Edith and Harold argued. The kinship faltered and Ealdgyth often found herself wishing that her grandmother and father could see the unravelling of the ties that bound the Godwines together.

But there was to be no smug satisfaction. Her own brothers held the fate of the north in their hands, and when news came of their defeat at a battle just outside York, she felt sick. Yes, the messenger assured her, they were unharmed, but Edwin and Morcar, so very young, had lost many of their men. Harold said nothing to Ealdgyth before he rode north, but Edith threw a stinging rebuke. "Your useless brothers have let him down. You were of no value here at all."

Ealdgyth wrapped her arms round her belly, warming herself since no one else would.

As the weeks went by, she busied herself by working. With the men away there was little in the way of feasting but the apples and pears from the orchard needed to be stored, and the recently-stacked bales of winter fodder needed to be checked for pests. Ealdgyth supervised this, as well as overseeing the drying and smoking of cheeses made from surplus summer milk. Yet still the days moved slowly, the sun taking an age to travel across the narrowed autumn sky. Then one day news came. It was as if the very wind had brought it, swirling around the folk of London who gathered at St Paul's, rippling their clothes with its breath and sending speed to the messenger who rode his horse at breakneck speed.

"King Harold has defeated the Norwegians, and the traitor Tostig Godwineson is dead."

Ealdgyth had once seen a man die, watched as the blood drained from his face, leaving behind only a deathly pallor. The queen dowager's cheeks now had the same hue, her eyes staring wide but seeing only darkness. Then she crumpled like discarded clothing and fell to the floor, sobbing.

Harold returned, his army exhausted. He stayed only seven nights in London, no time to rest, only to replenish, restock, regroup. William of Normandy, after long threatening to do so, had finally landed. Harold must march his army once more.

The brambles pricked her finger, and she put it to her mouth, sucking at the iron taste, musing that soon she would be bleeding much more than this. She reached out with her uninjured hand to tease some of the fruits from the plant, but they were starting to wizen and she reminded herself that Michaelmas had passed and the devil had spat on the berries. She gazed up at the heavy sky, full of rain, and wondered if she had always hated this time of year, or whether her loathing of it had begun with that journey away from her homeland to Wales, so many years ago.

Behind her, a commotion in the yard told of riders arriving. Ealdgyth pondered the possibilities; either Harold had won the day, and her life would be one of continuous misery until one of them died, or William was the victor, in which case...

"Ealdgyth!"

She turned at the familiar and yet somehow unknown voice. "Morcar?"

Falling into her brother's embrace, she saw Edwin coming up alongside. "We have fresh horses. They are being saddled as I speak. Come."

Morcar released his hold and looked Ealdgyth up and down. "Can you ride?"

"Of course I can. But why must I? Oh, it is so good to see you both. After your battle, I thought... But what does this mean? Did you join the king? Has he fought William?"

Edwin grasped her by the elbow, gently but with urgency, leading her towards the stables. "Yes, he has fought William. By the time we were able to gather more men and ride south, it was too late. Harold is dead, and we must get you away before..."

Before William comes. That was what he would not say. So, she was a widow once more, and homeless once more. She asked God in that moment for forgiveness, for she could not shed a tear for her late husband. Where could she go? The king from Normandy would not harm her, surely, but Ealdgyth carried a secret that could threaten her whole family.

They rode hard, overnighting in abbeys which, as soon as they were in Mercia, were loyal and would say nothing if Norman soldiers came asking questions. She wanted to spend time getting to know Morcar again, but urgency drove them, and her brothers were quiet, grim-faced. She held her tongue. They headed north, bypassing all the familiar settlements of their youth, pressing on until they reached the uppermost edge of Mercian territory. In Chester, at the minster, where Godiva's coin had paid for the church to be restored, they rested. "Journey's end," Edwin said, although she found him and Morcar preparing to depart the next morning.

"We have to go, sweet sister. Harold might have lost, but we will fight on. You will be safe here and we will not have to worry, knowing that you are back in your homeland."

But not home. Ealdgyth hugged her brothers so tightly that they feigned suffocation. Morcar wiped a tear from her cheek and she watched them ride away. Then she turned to the abbot. "Would you please arrange for passage on a ship?"

The abbot bowed his head. "To where, and for whom?"

Ealdgyth recalled that this was the place where her father had sent the Irish ships to be paid off, all those years ago. It had remained an important naval base for Ælfgar and his family. The abbot was waiting for an answer. "For me."

Let the rest of the monks in the scriptorium write their history, of men and the battles they fought that year. Of kingships won and lost, of lands transferred, of crops destroyed. They would not write of the women, who suffered in their own ways, who endured, who loved and lost and were moved by others as thoughtlessly as game pieces were moved on a board. Ealdgyth had spent her whole adult life being displaced, sent from her home, having her home taken from her. Now, she would remove herself, make a new home that no one would ever find. A new home for her, and the child she was carrying.

In an abbey in a sunlit corner of a foreign land, the monks prepare to welcome the new century which will arrive in just three months. A young novice has been sent out to the churchyard to tend the gravestones; he kneels down in the fading autumn light to pull weeds from the upright slabs, and brush fallen leaves from the grave markers. He thanks God for sending a cloudless sky which will keep dusk at bay long enough to complete his task. He hums while he works, knowing that out here, none will scold him for it. And he smiles when he reaches his favourite grave. There are no words carved upon the tombstone. Stories abound, in the village, of the woman who came from a foreign land, and lived quietly with her son. He, it was rumoured, went sailing on the high seas, but the mother stayed. She passed away on a day such as this, a bright crisp autumn day, and had asked for two things. "Bury me as close as you can to my home, and let none know my name."

© Annie Whitehead
*Cumbria, 2023*

**AUTHOR'S NOTE**

The Old English in the title of this story, *Wadan Wræclastas* (walk/ tread the path of exile), is taken from a poem called *The Wanderer*, which dates from the 10th century. Ealdgyth may not ever have read it, but she would have sympathised with the sentiments expressed in it. The named characters in this story were all real historical people with the exception of Rhodri (Ealdgyth's grandmother was the redoubtable Lady Godiva of legend), and all the events mentioned really happened. The dialogue and motivation are my own ideas, of course. The Michaelmas referred to in the story is Old Michaelmas, 10th October.

No one knows what happened to Ealdgyth after she got to Chester, but anything's possible, and my research into her fate is ongoing. Because Gruffudd was, unusually, styled king of Wales and not prince, Ealdgyth holds the unique record of having been queen of Wales *AND* England.

Ealdgyth and her family also feature in my story for the anthology *1066 Turned Upside Down*, as well as in my nonfiction books, and all of my books, fiction and nonfiction, feature Mercians and/or the fascinating women of the Anglo-Saxon era, including my novel about Æthelflæd, Lady of the Mercians: *To Be A Queen.*

## ABOUT ANNIE WHITEHEAD

Annie Whitehead is an author, historian, and elected Fellow of the Royal Historical Society, and has written four award-winning novels set in Anglo-Saxon England. She has contributed to fiction and nonfiction anthologies and written for various magazines, has twice been a prize winner in the Mail on Sunday Novel Writing Competition, and won First Prize in the 2012 New Writer Magazine's Prose and Poetry Competition. She was a finalist in the 2015 Tom Howard Prize for Nonfiction and was shortlisted for the Exeter Story Prize/Trisha Ashley Award 2021.

She was the winner of the inaugural Historical Writers' Association/Dorothy Dunnett Prize 2017 and is now a judge for that same competition. She has also been a judge for the HNS (Historical Novel Society) Short Story Competition.

Her nonfiction books are *Mercia: The Rise and Fall of a Kingdom* (Amberley Books) and *Women of Power in Anglo-Saxon England* (Pen & Sword). She has contributed to a new history of English Monarchs, *Kings and Queens: 1200 Years of English and British Monarchs* (Hodder & Stoughton) and has signed a contract to write her third nonfiction book, to be published by Amberley books in 2024.

'Annie Whitehead gets the balance of research and story exactly right. And what a story she tells!' *Glynn Young, author, reviewer and book blogger.*

Website: **https://anniewhiteheadauthor.co.uk/**
Buy Annie's books on Amazon:
**https://viewauthor.at/Annie-Whitehead**
(Also available from other online stores or order from
any bookshop.)

## 2

# VICTORY IN EXILE DAY

## BY J.G. HARLOND

### AN ENGLISH COUNTRY TOWN
### 7.40 P.M. on 7<sup>th</sup> MAY 1945

*'In accordance with arrangements between three great powers, tomorrow, Tuesday, will be treated as Victory in Europe Day…'*

A tea towel in one hand, a saucepan in the other, Eva paused and stared at the kitchen wireless set. She smiled, then laughed out loud and danced a polka around the big table with the saucepan.

Then she stopped and took a deep breath. This would change things on her own domestic front. Dropping the pan and cloth on the draining board, she walked down the long garden path to tell her husband, and enjoy her moment of relief, and triumph.

Bernard was by the rear fence beyond the orchard, as far from the house as he could get, pushing papers into a bonfire. Spring-cleaning his study, he'd said. *Purging it, more likely*, Eva thought.

As she crossed the long, damp grass, Bernard

swung around, thrusting a fireside poker like a sword in her direction. "Stay back! You are not needed here."

"It's definitely over!" Eva cried across the space between them. "Victory in Europe, they name it." Bernard glared at her and muttered something. "What?" she called.

"I said, I know! I'm a senior civil servant, you cretin."

"Sorry. I thought you would be pleased. That it is over. For us. In Europe."

Bernard made no reply. Taking a manila folder from a box-file at his feet he tipped its contents into the oil drum he was using as an incinerator. Flames leapt high into the air. A typed sheet of correspondence tried to escape. He grabbed it with a gloved hand, crushed it, and shoved it back in.

"Tomorrow is a national holiday," Eva said, edging closer to see what was in the box-file.

"That's nice," Bernard sneered. "Have fun."

"Oh, I will," Eva replied. "I will celebrate."

Trying to contain her anger, Eva returned to the house. As she stepped onto the kitchen doormat, she noticed a slip of flimsy blue paper caught under the back door jamb. It was an un-sent airmail letter in Bernard's forward-sloping handwriting, but signed in her name. Her real name: Hanna Bloch.

She hadn't signed anything in that name since coming to England ten years ago. It wasn't even on their marriage certificate.

She took the letter to the kitchen table, sat down and smoothed out the thin paper. Written in English, it was dated 1st May, 1945. The day after Hitler committed suicide.

*Dear Carla* – Eva didn't think she knew about a Carla – *regrettably I shall not be able to visit as planned, but I will keep you in my thoughts and remember all you told me. We will of course stay in touch. This is not the end of our friendship or endeavours...*

*This is not the end...*

"Please, no. Let it end here," Eva whispered to herself, staring at the signature on the paper. Had Bernard realised what she had been doing? Was this his revenge – to implicate her?

Or had he been sending coded messages in apparently innocent letters *in her name* for longer and she'd simply not seen them? If so, how much longer? Ten years? Or since the war began?

Unsure what to do, how to react, Eva went to Bernard's study to place the letter very visibly on his desk. The door was closed but not locked, which wasn't usual. She had a key hiding in plain sight on her keyring on the hall table but never used it when Bernard was in the house.

The study was very untidy; the waste basket full of torn envelopes. On impulse she stuffed the letter into her apron pocket, then ran a hand over the leather desk blotter for recent indentations. A small memo-style note was tucked under a corner. It was a single paragraph in a language she did not recognise. After travelling across Europe, living a few years here and there, Eva could make sense of various languages. There was no punctuation, no capital letters. It was a new cipher. Eva's skin went cold, her heart began to thump loudly. Bernard had twigged; she was being set up as the guilty party. A foreign woman with a fake identity living in wartime England... Bernard could so easily make *her* guilty of aiding the enemy. And she thought she'd been so clever helping the American.

Was her life in England about to crumble with the Third Reich? It had been stable enough in the beginning. An unconventional but explicable marriage: a middle-aged, well-heeled English bachelor meets an attractive foreigner in a Brussels hotel. She is young and pretty, beautiful, even. Naturally blonde hair arranged in a classic chignon; a lean figure (due to poor nutrition, but surprisingly good teeth), and a wide, genuine smile. She tells him her father, a Polish academic, was more interested in current social injustices than Ancient Rome (or his family's welfare); that he had been invited to leave his university post, then forced into a peripatetic exile. They, Eva as a small child and her parents, had moved from one university town to another until her father found himself teaching history in a Belgian secondary school. It was a plausible fabrication, she thought, and explained her apparent poverty. Her family had never lived in Poland, but Bernard didn't need to know that either.

Details and circumstances that Bernard may have suspected, he was no fool, but chose to overlook. Or so Eva believed at the time.

"Marry me," Bernard said. "I can provide a very decent home and safe passage to a better kind of life."

Bernard arranged a British passport for her, and after a hasty civil marriage brought her to The Cedars, a beautiful house in the green Sussex Downs. It had not been a happy marriage, but it was secure enough – until the American started visiting.

Even after that, she'd managed to keep up her deception. Right until now, in fact. But Bernard had known all along that her real name was Hanna Bloch; that she had been born in Cologne, not Warsaw.

She opened a drawer to see if his passport was still there. It was. She bit her lip, remembering how she had enjoyed the fairy tale Bernard had created to explain her foreign origins to his 'old family'. A story repeated so often, so convincingly, over drinks with his gullible American acquaintances and haw-hawing Civil Service associates she had come to believe herself. Everyone loved a love story. Which this was not, but truth be told Bernard *could* have married the daughter of a real-but-impoverished Polish count if he'd made the effort. Instead, he chose someone whose origins they both kept expertly vague. A girl with nowhere to go when she discovered his fastidious distaste to marital life, or how lonely she would be in a country that distrusted all foreign accents.

Eva turned her attention back to the small note in her hand: how long had he been using this cipher? Was it for his work in London? That, he told her at the beginning, meant he had secrets. What task, however, required Bernard to sign apparently personal correspondence in *her* name?

Eva's carefully constructed life in exile tottered on the brink of disaster. All she had tolerated: the lonely marriage with separate rooms; the true and truly appalling reason for his weekend house parties and toady-ing to what he called 'top brass'. She had thought her worst fears had been confirmed when an American officer named Major Farley had said, "Your husband is an informer, Mrs Madden-Fox." They were strolling around her lovely flower garden that evening. "Did *you* know that?" He'd asked quietly.

A heavily laden question. "Yes. I think I did," she answered. Thanks to the spare study key Bernard thought no longer existed. "But what can I do about it?"

Major Farley told her. Then a British Lieutenant-Colonel Metherall came to the house. It was a Monday afternoon; Bernard was in his London office. "I have a young colleague, a civilian, who visits Brighton," he said. "You might like to take tea with him and tell him your news." Eva had smiled. What choice did she have? "Shall we say the second Wednesday of the month?"

"All right."

"Good-o. His name is Laurence Oliver. Nice boy. Your English nephew, perhaps." The emphasis on nationality was relevant.

*So,* Eva thought, *I have exchanged one deal to stay in Britain for another. Or now I have two. And I'm caught right between them.*

It wasn't that she was blasé about the Allied cause, but the war against Hitler – the horror in Germany starting well before she met Bernard – had always been so very one-sided in her perception. Her parents, and their parents, had always been powerless victims... It had never occurred to her she might do something to confront Hitler's evil.

But if Bernard was using her identity as his cover... that put her in very grave jeopardy. Did Farley and Metherall know this? Is that why they had set her up, to see whose side she favoured? To see if she was working *with* Bernard? Or if *she* was the informer?

Her mind in a whirl, Eva didn't hear her husband cross the hall floor tiles.

"What are you doing in here?" he demanded at the study door, his sharp features, red from the bonfire, now puce with anger.

She lifted the note, wordless. He snatched it. Then slapped her hard across the face. "This is private," he hissed.

"Private?" She grabbed the letter from her pocket with her other hand. "And this? With *my name* on it!"

Bernard slapped her again, harder. Eva reeled back against the desk. Her left hand touched a sturdy crystal paperweight. Her fingers curled around it. Bernard raised his hand to smack her again. She deflected it with the paperweight, then swung her arm out and smashed the heavy crystal against his head. They were of a height. She was better fed now despite rationing;

stronger after five years of digging for victory, and left-handed. Bernard toppled backwards, hit the back of his skull on the corner of his filing cabinet. His body folded at the waist and he slumped to the floor.

Eva froze. Waited. Then, slowly, taking care to stay out of his reach, she bent over to see if he was still breathing. He was. She ran from the room, slamming the door behind her.

Back in the kitchen, Eva put a glass under the cold tap and gulped down water. When she was calmer, she went into the garden, picked up the remaining files, and stuffed them in the oil drum.

As she waited for the cardboard to shrivel in the heat, Eva turned and studied the beautiful house. And a horrible certainty crept into her mind: Bernard loved this house, too. He would do anything to keep it. Meaning, when he came round from his knock and realised the threat she posed, *she* would be offered to the relevant authority for *his* crimes. Or he would kill her.

She needed help. She needed people here. She needed to contact Farley or Metherall. How soon could they get here from London? She needed someone right now. Someone nearby. Who? For numerous personal reasons under-pinned by Bernard's wealth and social class in a small rural town, she had kept herself to herself. Eva had no friend to call on, and nowhere to go. Exactly as Bernard had wanted.

Calmer now but no less frightened, Eva returned to the house. To reach the stairs to her room meant passing the study door. Bernard hadn't moved.

Eva locked the door to her bedroom then removed her smoky garments, had a thorough wash then dabbed a thick layer of Max Factor Pan-cake powder over her left cheek. As she dressed again, in dark sweater and slacks, she considered her alternatives:

play the innocent and call the doctor for Bernard. That would bring somebody into the house. But how to explain her swollen cheek if – when – Bernard claimed she attacked him? Calling the doctor for a dubious 'accident' would involve a series of inquiries. The police might be called, which was not such a good thing if her name was on anything else in the study. The logical thing was to call Farley or Metherall right now – but then Bernard would know for certain what she had been doing. He might even convince them that she was a double agent, and that not only jeopardised her marriage, she'd lose the right to stay in England, and probably her life.

At odds with her dark thoughts, cheerful music filtered up from the wireless. Britain was celebrating. Could she use that as an excuse to get people here? An impromptu party at The Cedars? Why not?

Whatever happened in the next 24 hours, she needed to protect herself. Opening an underwear drawer, Eva removed a small pistol and a box of bullets. She loaded the pistol the way Farley had shown her.

With the gun tucked into her shoulder bag, Eva left the house on her bicycle, heading for the church hall. People from Meadow Lane were living there because they'd been bombed out. Eva had felt it at the time, but The Cedars, which was also in Meadow Lane, was spared, being safely up a long drive, well off the road.

The hall was full to bursting with local churchgoers and the Meadow Lane homeless, and full of fun. Bottles of beer were circulating, children ran around screaming with excitement, unchecked. When she was noticed, the noise died down. Curious eyes gazed at her in surprise. Resentful eyes. The Cedars hadn't suffered the war like they had. Extra food, extra comforts – everyone said so – and now un-bombed.

Eva forced a smile. "You have heard the news," she said. "We must celebrate. Come to my house. We have a party, no?" Nervous and embarrassed, her English failed her. Everyone noticed it: heard her clipped accent and assumed what they'd always assumed – and perhaps Bernard had reinforced through his obvious fictions – that she was a European. Probably a German.

If they only knew... Her family had suffered more from land-grabbing and ethnic politics during the past half-century than anyone in this green and pleasant land could imagine.

"Not tonight, then," she said. "You have a party here. I can see. Tomorrow, yes?" she offered to fill the silence. "Come in the morning, we make a big picnic together, for a garden party."

A few people mumbled 'thank you'. Eva gave them a quick wave of the hand and slowly cycled back to The Cedars, wondering if she'd be alive for a garden party the next day.

The hole that had been Ruth Lee's home had filled with water. "There's no point looking at it," she told herself. "It won't bring your house back."

There were no family treasures to find. A few of Joe's socks floating in the muddy scum, her peg basket, which by some needless miracle lay untouched beyond the crater, but not a pot or a plate, nor the toffee tin of carefully saved house-keeping set aside for a rainy day.

Ruth pulled the white collar of her brown Viyella dress to her throat and swallowed hard; her home had been buzz-bombed out of existence in broad daylight a fortnight before the war in Europe ended. Determined not to give in to tears, she reminded herself it wasn't the first time she'd lost everything. It just felt like it.

Joseph Lee had brought his happy bride to this quiet Sussex town to make a new life, to feel safe. She thought her heart had broken the day Joe's ship had gone down. But no, there was more to come. Hitler had finally located her and destroyed the last of all she held dear.

"I didn't realise it was so big," she said. Then remembered the hole also contained next door's house and winced with guilt. "I should have been nicer to her," she murmured. Her neighbour always said 'good morning'. Always wanted to pass the time of day.

But Ruth couldn't do that. Not because of the language, because what could she say that her chatty neighbour wouldn't gossip about?

"Words can't be unsaid," Ruth's mother used to say. "Best to keep yourself to yourself." What her mother meant was: "There's enough suspicion about us without you adding to it." People could – and did – twist the most innocent of comments to suit their prejudices.

Not that the Feldman family had anything anyone might envy. After walking across half of Poland, east to west, then the misery of northern Germany – where refugees joined their sad column of displaced exiles daily – pushing Ruth in a handcart laden with their few possessions, her mother knew what she was talking about.

They'd got to Rotterdam, eventually. It was as far as her ailing father could go. Ruth understood that. A piece of wonderful luck, and a deadly mistake. Joe Lee had found his 'dark-eyed beauty' serving coffee and cakes in a modest hotel there. Then Germans had flattened it to the ground. Along with the rest of the city, and her parents' final lodgings.

Compared to Rotterdam, Ruth thought, I'm lucky. I

just can't face another week in that church hall. But where else could she go?

"Over here! Over here, Mrs Lee!" Old Mrs Watts was beckoning to Ruth across the crowded church hall. "We're invited to the big house! Who'd have thought it!" The ageing grandmother's round face was alight with mischief. "Her ladyship is entertaining the peasants."

"The Mad Folks are havin' a *garden party* for us," freckle-faced young Tommy Watts explained in a la-di-dah voice.

"He means Mrs Madden-Fox," Mrs Watts explained, while Tommy sniggered at the other, ruder version of the surname.

"'Spect she thinks it's safe to come outside now," Joyce Watts, Tommy's mother, suggested. "I haven't seen her since Lor'-knows when."

"She's one of your lot, Mrs Lee. Did you know that?" the grandmother said.

Ruth frowned. "*My lot?*"

"Oh, sorry. No offence. What I mean is, that her husband brought her back with him. From foreign parts. Like you and Joe."

"Yeah, she's always cooking funny, smelly things with onions. I call in with the morning papers on my round. Sometimes she's boilin' beagles," Tommy added. "Poor little buggers, don't know where she gets 'em all."

"Beagles?" Ruth repeated. "*Beagles*? No! Not beagles: *bagels*!" Ruth laughed out loud for the first time in months. "Oh, but, bagels. How lovely."

28

Somebody was setting off fireworks as Eva pedalled back to The Cedars. Bright purple flares lit the sky. What fool kept fireworks in a house under an enemy flight path direct to London? She was laughing at the audacity and joy of it when she arrived at The Cedars' double gates.

There were no lights on. Had she left any lights on? Perhaps not. Dismounting the bicycle, Eva crunched up the gravel drive and propped it against the garage wall. A non-combatant rocket surged into the sky and showered her precious garden with light. Bernard was sitting on the stone seat by the front door, waiting for her.

Eva opened her bag as if to retrieve her keys.

"How long?" Bernard demanded. "How long have you been betraying me?"

"Betraying *you*? You have been betraying me since the day we were married. You're even using my name."

"Am I? Which name would that be?"

Eva swallowed hard. Fear curled around her.

"You, dear wife, are as fake as the name you signed on your marriage certificate."

Eva's mouth went dry. He knew. Had always known.

"And your *married* name," Bernard continued, whining like a playground bully, "will now be deleted. I am annulling this stupid marriage."

"Annulling?"

"Annulment. The legal termination of a marriage. Non-consummation: I foresee no difficulty in that, or indeed any embarrassment. I no longer need a wife. Certainly not a dirty rag from your heritage. And you wondered why I never came near your bed..."

Eva let the night engulf her. She was a nobody

without a home again. A nobody whose remaining family had almost certainly been exterminated.

Bernard leaned forward and started his sneering, hee-hawing laugh then put a hand to his head. "You nearly killed me," he said.

"I should have done," Eva replied, raising the pistol in her left hand and aiming it at his head as another firework rose gloriously into the sky to spread light and celebrate peace.

Bernard's body bounced backwards but remained upright.

It took Eva a few moments to calm down, then another few moments to accept that the person who had pulled the trigger was a Jewish woman named Hanna. Who had abandoned her family and her heritage to live in a fine house in another country.

The glamourous woman named Eva, who had schemed her way into The Cedars, might conceal her true feelings, but her inner Hanna had reclaimed her identity and integrity.

Hanna put the pistol back into her bag. "Now what?" she asked.

"We try to keep what we've got, girl," Eva replied.

Together, Eva and Hanna went to the old stable and pulled out a handcart. "Useful things these old carts," Eva said, levering her husband's body into it, "Hanna grew up in one."

Eva woke after a very restless night to the song of blackbirds in the orchard. After carefully selecting a soft white blouse and a bright dirndl skirt for the special day, she ran downstairs to the kitchen. Anxious to get busy, she drank her morning tea and began pulling all the edibles she could find from her marble pantry shelves. They'd need more bread. It was a national holiday but bakers rarely took a day off, so she grabbed her bicycle and set off for the bakery. It was a splendid day – whatever might happen later.

When she returned with a basket of warm loaves, the two Mrs Watts, junior and senior, were waiting in the drive with Tommy. A few women with young children soon joined them. Many in their Sunday best.

For the rest of the morning Eva stayed busy fielding nosy questions, nipping in and out of the pantry for bottled damsons and chutney, filling a laundry basket with tumblers and plates for a feast day locals would talk about for years to come. Not until Mrs Watts Junior asked directly did it occur to Eva anyone might expect Bernard to be there, or have seen him the previous day.

His absence was easily explained. Today was Tuesday; he only came down at weekends. They all knew that anyway.

Another woman Eva did not know arrived, looking nervous, as if her presence wasn't expected or welcome. "That's Mrs Lee," Tommy informed Eva. "She's a widder now. Don't say much, but she's alright, I reckon."

Eva invited Mrs Lee to find table cloths in the dining room and sent Tommy into the garden to wipe down the old teak table and chairs there. A few older couples began to arrive, some bringing their own delicacies hoarded for a special occasion: tins of salmon and pineapple chunks, a can of real ham.

Mrs Cook, her cleaning lady, was conspicuous by her absence, but Eva was happy about this. One less witness to her domestic life to worry about. The Cedars filled with joking and friendly teasing and laughter, and Eva joined in.

Then Tommy Watts ran into the kitchen and ruined it all. "There's a body in the shed!" Tommy shouted. "I think it's your husband, Mrs M. He's dead. Dead as a door knob."

Eva gulped and sat down on the nearest chair. Ruth Lee moved around the table to sit next to her. "Has he been ill?" Ruth asked.

Eva shook her head, bit her lower lip.

"Thought you said he wasn't here," Old Mrs Watts said, peering at her from the pantry door.

"Oh, I forgot. Normally he is not here. In the week. I mean, with all the celebration, I forgot. Today is a national holiday. Of course."

"'Spect he was getting the garden ready for us and it was too much for him," Mrs Watts Junior said, exchanging glances with her mother-in-law.

"Bad heart, probly," someone suggested.

"I'll say!" Tommy replied. "Looks like he's got a ruddy bullet in it."

There was a collective intake of breath. They made space for Eva to get to the back door, then followed her to a substantial garden shed.

"You better call the police, my dear," old Mrs Watts said quietly in the murky gloom.

Kneeling beside her late husband on the filthy wooden floor, her face in shadow, Eva gaped at her. "The police?"

"Well, the doctor, any rate. If he's had an accident with a gun."

"Ah, yes. Yes. That might explain it. Thank you," Eva said.

Ruth reached around the old woman and placed a hand on Eva's shoulder. "Have you got a telephone here, Mrs Madden-Fox? Shall I call the doctor for you?"

"No, no. I'll call the doctor and the police, of course. Except it must have been an accident. Unless he..." Eva heaved a deep breath. "Bernard has been under terrible pressure."

Leaving her busy-body visitors with those two thoughts, Eva went into the hall, alone, and made three telephone calls. The first was to a private number on a card that she kept in her purse.

PC Walters and Dr Haig arrived within the hour, neither too pleased to be called out on such a special day. Dr Haig confirmed it was a gunshot wound in Bernard's chest. PC Walters told everyone they had to stay at the house until they'd been questioned. Then, taking her aside, PC Walters asked Eva about the purpling bruise on her cheek.

Eva put her left hand to her face. "A silly accident in the garden," she said. "I tripped over a hoe, and – fell on a flower pot. It doesn't hurt. Thank you for asking." She gave him her best blue-eyed smile. "Would you like a cup of tea while you wait for your superiors?"

Dr Haig left. Eva's guests milled around the garden, gossiping excitedly in small groups, wringing out what little they knew about Bernard Madden-Fox. "And we're witnesses! Like in an Agatha Christie," someone said.

Eventually the women returned to the kitchen and the men began ferrying plates of sandwiches and bowls of tinned fruit to the garden tables. No point wasting good food. Not on a day like this.

Ruth Lee found herself sitting next to Eva by the window in the drawing room. Eva was silent, twisting a handkerchief in her hands although her eyes were quite dry.

"It'll be the shock," Ruth said. "I couldn't cry when our house got bombed. I was out shopping so I was all right but, oh, what a shock." And for some reason, Ruth found herself telling Eva how many times she and her parents had had to move on and find a new place to live, and why. "Meeting Joe was the best thing that ever happened to me," she said. "He was in the Merchant Navy. I died a little bit every day of this war with him at sea. And now he's not coming back ever again."

Ruth waited for Mrs Madden-Fox to respond with something about her own life and marriage. How she had come to live in their small Sussex town. "We met in Brussels," she said, and nothing more.

But then Mrs Madden-Fox perked up, jumped to her feet. A black car was coming up the drive. A tall American in a beautifully tailored uniform got out. Ruth followed as Mrs Madden-Fox dashed to the front door and led him around the house into the vast garden. Locals watched, silent for a few moments, then bent their heads together. "What's a Yank doing here?"

"There's something fishy going on, you mark my words," Old Mrs Watts declared, bustling her way down the crazy-paving to be nearer the action.

Everyone followed, gawping, until the shed door was shut on their prying eyes and speculation could start again. Ruth returned to the house, not wanting to be in the audience.

A few minutes later a police car arrived with two detectives dressed for a day off. Ruth led them around to the shed and knocked on the door. Eva and the American came out.

The American, a dashingly handsome man, and a senior army officer by the pips on his uniform, took an identity card from his jacket pocket. The detectives examined it and stepped aside to speak to each other in private. Then one of them said, "Thank you, Major Farley. We'll leave you to handle it, but you'll send us your report, won't you? We need that for our files."

"Of course, gentleman," Major Farley replied. "I'll get it to you as soon as I can."

Major Farley waited until the two detectives and PC Walters were out of earshot then led Eva into the apple orchard, where there was an old bench, where they could sit down and converse out of anyone's hearing.

Ruth returned to the kitchen again, and filled a kettle to make a fresh pot of tea. Tommy Watts came in. "They say as how we gotta go now. Suicide, they reckon. My gran doesn't think so, though. Can I have some of that lemonade?"

Tommy slurped down his beverage and headed for the door. "Aren't you coming?" he asked Ruth, his eyes narrowing like his grandmother's.

"Later. Mrs Madden-Fox needs someone here with her. For a while."

Men in uniform made Ruth uncomfortable. Army officers made her very nervous. But there was something happening that told her Mrs Madden-Fox needed a compassionate friend.

An hour or so later, a British army officer with a thick blond moustache and a swagger stick arrived. Then an undertaker's van.

When the body had been removed, the two tall, uniformed men followed Eva's neat, bright figure into Mr Madden-Fox's study.

Ruth was never quite sure at what point in the day Mrs Madden-Fox became Eva, but brief squeezes of the hand, and a whispered 'Please stay', kept Ruth at her side or hovering in the background awaiting instructions.

The Allied officers left much later that day, taking with them numerous box-files and bags of loose documents and papers. Ruth made tea and sandwiches and watched, saying nothing. The men treated her with the courtesy they would show to domestic help. Eva whispered her thanks and asked Ruth to stay again.

Once the two women were finally on their own, Eva propelled Ruth into the drawing room, where she poured two brimming schooners of sherry. As they sat on matching powder blue velvet chairs, Eva finally relaxed, and told Ruth her tale. The true version of how a young German woman re-invented herself and came to the notice of a British civil servant in 1935, and why she had stayed with him despite his character. And what she had been doing here at The Cedars for the past two years.

"They asked you to report on your husband?" Ruth gasped.

"Yes. Two years ago, almost to the day. I remember it very clearly. Major Farley told me his suspicions, then Lt-Col Metherall, he's in the British Security Service, asked me to make a verbal report to a colleague. Farley gave me a card with his number on it, for emergencies."

Ruth put a hand to her mouth. "You mean, it was you who –"

"Major Farley is a widower, you know. Very sad. He cared for his wife deeply. Perhaps, one day, he..." Eva sipped her sherry, her mind elsewhere. "It started in a curious way. We were walking in the garden one evening after drinks and I heard myself telling him, Farley, everything. About how I'd met Bernard and let him think he was marrying me out of convenience, him not being that way inclined – with anyone, I should add – and then, I suppose, Farley must have picked up on the fact that I knew how to keep my eyes open and my mouth closed. The next time he visited he told me why he kept coming to the house, and that it wasn't entirely for my pretty face. Well, partly, perhaps. It was quite exciting. Bit dangerous, of course. Bernard could be *very* nasty."

"So..." Ruth tried to marshal a dozen questions into order, "your husband was a German spy?"

"Actively helping the governing group in Berlin, yes. Except, thanks to Farley and Metherall and their contacts some of Bernard's reports were intercepted and re-worded with bits of wrong information. Not entirely wrong to make the people in Berlin suspect Bernard had been discovered, just wrong enough, often enough to lessen the damage. And somebody in Berlin – a *truly* courageous person – was monitoring who was getting Bernard's messages."

Ruth put down her sherry. "Eva, you are very brave."

"I am, aren't I?" Eva gave Ruth a glorious smile.

"But, did you shoot your husband?" Ruth's voice was barely whisper.

"Whatever gave you that idea!"

Ruth wanted to say, "You did," but didn't. She gave an apologetic wince. "Sorry."

"I do have a little gun, though," Eva said with a wink. "A small pistol. I kept it with my undies upstairs."

Ruth blinked. 'Kept it': past tense. An irregular verb. Very. Unsure how to respond and having no vocabulary for this type of conversation, Ruth nevertheless tried again. "But it wasn't suicide?"

"Well, yes, it was. In a manner of speaking. If Bernard hadn't chosen to betray his country to people intent on destroying the entire Jewish population of Europe, he wouldn't have died. So, if you look at it in that way, yes, Bernard killed himself."

Ruth began to unravel the scrambled logic, but the telephone jangled before she could ask anything more.

Eva went into the hall and returned, her eyes over-bright. "That was Lt-Col Metherall, the English officer. He says his wife has a vacant fisherman's cottage in a place called Porthferris, in Cornwall, that I should go there as soon as I can. In case..."

"In case what?"

"To keep an eye on me somewhere small and remote, I suppose," Eva gave a knowing tilt of the head. "Unless Farley wants me there, away from this house."

Ruth pulled the collar of her dress to her throat: they suspected Eva.

"I know what you are thinking, Ruth," Eva said, "and under the circumstances, considering that I have been living a double life and I'm a pretty good liar – especially to myself – I'd suspect me as well." Resuming her seat on the blue chair beside her new friend, Eva patted Ruth's arm, and looking her in the eye, continued, "Would you come with me? If I go. I mean, would you like to come with me?"

"To Cornwall? It's a long way, isn't it?"

"Yes, but it won't be forever. The Cedars will be mine now. When everything is sorted out."

"My husband, Joe, said we would go there for a holiday. But we never did." Ruth felt tears begin to well. It had been a stressful day, a traumatic few weeks, a truly frightening six years... Suddenly everything came together and became too much, and she sobbed and sobbed. "I shouldn't have left my parents."

"That's not very natural, or very healthy," Eva countered gently.

"We shouldn't have left Poland. It was our home."

"It was home for a few hundred thousand of us, most of whom have died horrible deaths there. Ruth, your parents did the right thing getting you to safety. Relative safety."

Ruth blew her nose, took a deep breath. "I know,

but now Joe's dead as well and I've got nothing left of any of them."

Eva had no answer for that so she sat back in her chair and picked up her sherry, waiting for Ruth to work through her sorrow.

"The thing is," Ruth said, trying to catch her breath, "I feel so guilty. That I've survived and they haven't."

"But listen, that is what they wanted for you, your parents. That surely is why your husband risked his life at sea."

"I suppose so."

"For which we should honour them. And not just by surviving. Eva thinks we should enjoy living. Live the best we can. My Hanna understands you, though. She knows exactly how you feel."

Ruth sat up, looked at the elegant woman named Eva and frowned. "Who's Hanna?"

Eva took a freshly laundered handkerchief from a pocket and handed it to Ruth. "Use this one now. Yours is too wet."

Ruth took the embroidered white square and dabbed her eyes. "Who's Hanna?" she repeated.

"Me, actually. The other me, inside me. It's hard to explain." Eva squeezed Ruth's arm again. "Come with me to Cornwall. Help me get my Hanna back."

Confused but calmer, Ruth said, "Would you really like me to come? You're not just saying it because I'm sad?"

"I would, yes. You need somewhere to live, and being selfish, you are the first person I have been able to talk to in England. Or anywhere to be honest. I've never had a proper friend."

"Me neither."

"I couldn't risk it, you see. Because I was trying to be Eva all the time."

Ruth examined the tiny violet on the handkerchief,

trying to ward off the fear that Eva Madden-Fox was mentally unstable. "So, what you're telling me," she ventured, "is that you are really called Hanna, not Eva?"

"Yes, and I would be so grateful if you would call me Hanna. Please? I don't want to be Eva any longer."

Ruth nodded. "All right. But you'll have to tell me why."

"Because my personal, secret, exile is over."

Ruth nodded. Exile she understood; the rest might take a little bit longer. Stroking the soft velvet fabric under her arm, she said, "I do like these chairs. It's a lovely shade of blue."

"Shall we take them with us?" Hanna laughed. "There's an old handcart in the garden. We can push them down to Cornwall."


© J.G. Harlond
*Málaga, 2023*


**AUTHOR'S NOTE**

The idea behind *Victory In Exile* originated with what happened to a good friend's mother and grandmother during the Second World War. The family, Roman Catholic academics, lost their home and livelihood in Warsaw and were forced into exile. The women *walked* from Warsaw to the Black Sea coast, then found their way via Turkey and Spain to London. The espionage aspect is based on bits of what one might call British secret history.

Characters mentioned in the story and other stranger-than-fiction real events can be found in my WWII historical crime series **Bob Robbins Home Front Mysteries** –

https://www.amazon.co.uk/dp/B08BP128T8
https://www.amazon.com/dp/B08BP128T8


Lesser-known and often surprising bits of European history also feature in **The Chosen Man Trilogy** about a 17th-century rogue named Ludo da Portovenere who acts as a secret agent for the Vatican and various European monarchs.


## ABOUT J.G. HARLOND

*Secret agents, skulduggery, and crime that crosses continents.*

British author of historical crime fiction, J.G. (Jane) Harlond writes award-winning, page-turning novels set in the mid-17th and mid-20th centuries. Each story weaves fictional characters into real events. She describes her WWII **Bob Robbins Home Front Mysteries** as 'cosy crime with a sinister twist'. Prior to becoming a full-time author, Jane taught English and World Literature in international colleges. She also wrote school text books for many years using her married name.

Jane is married to a retired Spanish naval officer and they have a large, grown-up family living in various parts of Europe and the USA. After travelling widely (she has lived in or visited most of the places that feature in her novels) they are now settled near Málaga in Spain.

J.G. Harlond is a member of the British Crime Writers Association and the Dorothy Dunnett Society.

'A gripping wartime mystery with an intricate web of characters and secrets, steeped in historical detail.' *Readers' Favorite Book Reviews*.

❧ ❧ ❧

Website: **https://www.jgharlond.com/**
Buy Jane's books on Amazon:
**http://author.to/JGHarlond**
(Also available from other online stores or order from any bookshop.)

# 3

# THE DOONES OF EXMOOR

## BY HELEN HOLLICK

## FOREWORD

Anyone who enjoys romantic historical fiction is probably aware of R.D. Blackmore's *Lorna Doone*, set on the wilds of Exmoor during the late 1600s. I have set my nautical adventure *Sea Witch Voyages* in the early 1700s – the tales are pirate based with an overlap into fantasy and supernatural, but as I live in Devon I brought my protagonists, Captain Jesamiah Acorne and his wife, Tiola, from the Caribbean to North Devon, Barnstaple and Bideford being major trading centres for the Colonial tobacco trade until the mid-1700s when the rivers Taw and Torridge began to silt up. (If you enjoyed the first *Pirates of the Caribbean* movie, you will enjoy *Sea Witch*.) Because it was fun to do so, I introduced some disreputable fictional characters into the stories, notably Sir Ailie Doone and his grandson, Ascham Doone – characters imagined as the kindred of Blackmore's outlaw clan.

· · ·

But did Blackmore's Doones originate from anything historical? One possibility was a claim by Ida M. Browne who wrote a pamphlet in 1901 for the *West Somerset Free Press*.

https://www.lerwill-life.org.uk/history/doones.htm

She claimed that Sir Ensor Doone was the twin brother of Sir James Stewart, the first Earl of Moray and lord of Doune Castle. Ensor was accused of his brother's murder and rather than face imprisonment, fled into exile from Scotland to Exmoor. The article gives dates, places and a brief family tree – and is almost certainly fictitious. The Scots earl and the murder in 1602 are factual, but the rest is undoubtedly untrue, so can be discounted. But, like any historical fiction writer, Blackmore used factual events, locations he was familiar with and local names for his characters, blending everything into a satisfying tale. My *Sea Witch Voyages* are historic events woven into a fictional story, with the names of a few, real, people entwined alongside the made-up ones – in this instance, the Doones.

Who were they? Where did they come from? How did they end up as outlaws mercilessly preying on vulnerable people travelling across Exmoor? I cannot know what Mr Blackmore imagined their 'history' to be, but here is my version of their origin...

## LONDON, NOVEMBER 1678 - SIR ENSOR DOONE

Sir Ensor's hand hovered over the hilt of his sword. The thought running through his mind that it could be less trouble to simply draw it and slice its razor-sharp blade across this upstart clodpoll's throat. The word 'could' made him hesitate. The result would be a bloody mess – and not just on the black and white tiled floor of the entrance hall to his grand London house.

"Sir, I would not be foolish were I you," the upstart advised, his hand curling tighter around the hilt of his own partially drawn rapier. "The king himself has requested your presence. It would be unwise for you to resist, although quicker for me to kill you now and save us all future concern."

"On what accusation am I to be arrested – or slain?" With great difficulty, Sir Ensor managed to keep the rising anger from scorching his reply.

"Arrest? Nay Master Doone, you are not arrested. King Charles, second of that name, merely requires that you provide some answers to some questions."

"What sort of questions?" Sir Ensor knew perfectly well what the loathsome toad meant, but he was not going to be amenable to the impertinence. He managed to ignore the direct insult of being called 'Master' Doone. By right of inheritance he was honoured with the title of earl, though his estranged Scots kindred had contested the claim. Even so, he was *Sir* Ensor – as this fellow well knew.

Sir Ensor could hear movement from above stairs. A door opening and closing, floorboards creaking. His wife, Lady Marjorie Doone, was up there, heavy with their sixth child. *Pray God it be another boy*, he thought. *What good are girls in these troubled times?*

The children would be abed and shielded from this

unwelcome intrusion. The youngest was but two years, a sickly boy who would not be long for this world. Joshlin, his third-born was twelve, the girls not above ten. Sir Ensor's eldest surviving son, eighteen-year-old Carver, and Ailie, his nephew and ward since the death of the lad's father, Sir Ensor's younger brother, was three years older than Carver. Both were out together... somewhere or other. Probably frequenting a Cheapside tavern or Southwark brothel if their usual evening haunts were being followed. If they had Renfic with them... Sir Ensor attempted to suppress an inward snarl of disapproval. Of course his other son, Renfic, was with them! At ten-and-six years of age he behaved like a besotted puppy, trotting, eager, at their heels.

The upstart intruder noted Sir Ensor's narrowed eyes, the pinched nostrils and the slight curl to the mouth; assumed his adversary might be about to protest against arrest. He tightened the grip on his rapier's hilt.

More movement from the floor above. Sir Ensor glanced up the oak staircase, took a pace towards the lowest step.

"I assure you," the captain of the king's guard said, not particularly convincingly, "your wife and family will come to no harm if you come quietly with me."

Ignoring the wretched man, Sir Ensor wondered whether his wife was faring well this night. Her confinement was uncomfortable and tedious, and more than once she had openly cursed her husband's marital needs. He had responded, as curtly, that a wife's obligation was her wedded duty. All the same, he hoped this would be the last child to cause such inconvenience. Hoped, too, that the babe would be a boy, although a girl could bring advantages of another sort, an advantage he intended to see the fulfilment of, when, if, he had chance to arrange suitable – and profitable – marriages of Catholic alliance for his daughters.

Not for the first time it ran through his mind that he might need to, quietly, look to Spain or Portugal for such agreement. With the way this unrest against those of the Catholic faith was heading, he had even considered relocating to one of those foreign countries, but his business matters were securely established in England, and unlike his wife, he spoke no Spanish or Portuguese. He was a Scotsman, born and bred in the family home near Stirling, the home that should have been his.

The upstart inspected the dirt beneath the fingernails of his left hand; from the odour emanating from his unwashed body, he would benefit from a thorough dowsing. He looked up, stared at Sir Ensor, an ominous and unpleasant smile creasing the corners of his thin mouth. "You asked what questions? Questions regarding your connection to the papist banker, William Staley."

Sir Ensor snorted impatience. Spoke the truth. "Never heard of him."

"He was drawn and quartered, screaming like a slaughtered hog. His head now decorates London Bridge."

Sir Ensor shrugged. "Poor man. My condolences to his family, but still I do not know him."

"Do you not know of Viscount Stafford? Or maybe the Marquess of Powys or Baron Arundell? Baron Petre, perhaps, or Baron Belasyse? All of them are Roman Catholics of Parliament's House of Lords."

Sir Ensor was finding it more difficult to keep his temper in check, but calm he had to remain if he were not to – literally – lose his head. "Captain, I am a wine merchant of note. My trade arrangements supply a good deal of the wine consumed in that place, so I know *of* these named men, as do most of London's reputable merchants. But personally? No, I do not know them, although I hear that they are condemned to the Tower for their apparent part in this ridiculous fiction of a popish plot to murder King Charles? They have my sympathy, the Tower is a damp, dismal place. But I, as did my father and uncle before me, God rest their souls, remain loyal to his majesty. Would I have fought as a lad of ten-and-seven years alongside our king and endured those unpleasant years of exile with him in France and the Netherlands if I were not?"

"The truth that Titus Oates has discovered is no fiction, Sir Ensor. And I would advise you to be careful. Such misplaced sympathies for the fate of papist traitors might find you in the Tower alongside them."

"I am no Catholic," Sir Ensor lied. He was well practised. Like his father before him during the years of civil war, the family had been careful to conceal their true faith, had securely hidden it since the day Cromwell's Protestants had sliced the first King Charles' head from his body, that bitterly cold Whitehall January morning in the year 1649.

"If I were a Catholic," Sir Ensor remonstrated, "I would not be here. Did not our king recently banish all of that persuasion from within twenty miles around London because of the panic following the murder of that Parliamentarian, Sir Edmund Berry Godfrey?" He forced a congenial smile. "Or are you accusing me of his death as well? I assure you, beyond tale of his sorry fate, I know not of that man either." That too, was a lie.

"He was strangled then mutilated with his own sword. No perpetrator has yet been found."

"Again, I cannot help you. But it seems to me that Oates seized on Godfrey's murder as proof that his claim about this fictional plot rings true."

"I have my orders, Sir Ensor. I am to escort you,

with or without your agreement. It is but a short walk to St James's Palace. Must I summon my men from where they wait outside to assist me? Or would you rather that I take you direct to the Tower?" Gesturing towards the door, he added, "I would advise leaving your sword. You will have no need of it."

Sir Ensor Doone considered his best option, given the circumstances. St James's Palace was preferable to being dragged, beaten and bloodied, to the Tower. He sighed and, deciding it best to comply, unbuckled his sword belt and scabbard. Handed both, solemnly, to his hovering servant. "Fetch my cloak, Greaves, and send word to Lady Marjorie that I am stepping out for a short while."

He knew that she would not approve of such a message, for he had pledged not to leave her alone in the house, being so close to the birthing, but then, did the woman truly expect him to sit beside the library fire with nothing but a book and wine for company, as if he were an aged old man with gout and the joint ache? He shrugged, and swung his outdoor fur-lined woollen cloak around his shoulders. Beyond loyal Greaves, other servants were at home – assuming not too many of them were drunk beyond reason, as most were on these long, winter nights.

The night outside was cold, with a drizzling rain buffeted by flurries of a chill, east wind that spitefully slapped at cheeks, and bit deep to the bone. Five uniformed men of the king's guard, their weapons at ease but well displayed, stamped to attention as their captain and Sir Ensor emerged from the house. One, a younger lad, carried a torch flaring tar and flame to light their way, two men fell in ahead, two behind, with the captain striding, irritatingly, beside Sir Ensor at their centre.

"You understand," the captain said, indicating his

men, "that we are not here as guards, but as protectors. The populace is not particularly tolerant of papists."

The dark streets were deserted. No sensible man would be braving the rain that was already falling heavier and steering towards icy sleet. A mangy, flea-riddled cat paused ahead of the small group of men, the tip of her tail flicking, eyes narrowed. She hissed, then slunk away into the detritus-strewn shadows of a narrow side alley.

Sir Ensor raised an eyebrow and pointed at her disappearing tail. "Does the cat count as one among the intolerant populace?"

The captain sullenly ignored the sarcasm.

No sensible man...? Six men emerged from an alley ahead, swords drawn, flintlock pistols primed and aimed. Sir Ensor was as surprised as his guards.

"Ho, and where would you fine folk be off to on this foul night?" one of the men, the eldest, by the look of him, taunted. "I'd wager that a flagon of ale before a blazing fire, or a bed warmed by a willing young whore, would be of greater comfort." Another four men, similarly armed and menacing in appearance, appeared behind the confused king's guard.

For a moment, not one of the escort moved, only their wary eyes flickered to meet the hard gaze of the cocksure stranger. Then the captain made the decision to fight and clumsily lunged forward, one fist bunched, the other hand fiddling with his rapier hilt. He was too late. A knife ripped, deep, through his throat. Within less than three heartbeats, the four guards and the young torch bearer lay dead beside him on the rain-glistening, blood slicked cobbles.

Unharmed, Sir Ensor stared, appalled, his face crumpled like God's revenge of wrath at the grinning men gathered around him. With an animal snarl of rage, he drew his right hand back and cracked his gloved knuckles across the cheek of one of the men.

"That," he snarled through clenched, gritted, teeth, "was the stupidest thing you could have done."

His nephew, Ailee Doone, ignored the reprimand and the sharp sting across his cheek that was immediately blooming into a dark bruise. Unrepentant, he glowered back at his father's brother.

"Would you, then, Uncle, rather that we'd left them to take you to the Tower? For them to burn your house to the ground with all in it – after the women and girls had been defiled, and aye, the men and boys alongside them?"

"We were heading for St James's. Not the Tower," Sir Ensor countered.

The eldest and leader of his rescuers bent to wipe his bloodied blade on the tunic of one of the dead. Sir Ensor knew him well; his friend and business partner, Charles St Croix, an Anglo-French bastard-born, with a Devonshire nobleman for a father, a king's spy for a mother – and the public persona of a trader of fine wines when he was not playing the more usual part of a smuggler, or sailing the seas as a privateer alongside Jamaica's governor, Henry Morgan. And an outright pirate for the rest of it.

He sheathed the sword, then stepped forward to lay a soothing hand on Sir Ensor's arm, jerked his head in a quick nod over his right shoulder. "Last I knew, Ensor, St James's Palace is west of here. This street leads east. You have been betrayed, my friend. Titus Oates has included you and your family in his false tale of popery. To where these men were taking you was a one-way excursion. By sunrise you would have been dangling from a rope at Tyburn." St Croix paused, smiled, then broadened his mouth into a wry grin. "If good fortune had favoured you with such a relatively quick death, that is."

"And you know of all this? How?" Sir Ensor asked. "Has King Charles forgiven your various misdemeanours against him? Taken you into his intimate favour?"

St Croix grinned wider. "I have my scuttling earwigs secreted near the places where discretions and whispered confidences might be exchanged between careless tongues. Few notice the presence of a child servant hovering unseen in a dark corner, or innocently pouring wine for drunken lovers. As for King Charles, he is often not as discreet as he thinks when it comes to romping with his bedmates. I pay all my earwigs well. In return, they burrow deep into hidden cracks and crevices, and listen to what I might want to hear."

"And you heard of my imminent arrest?"

Charles St Croix agreed. "I did, and I decided to value you more as a trade partner and friend than a rotting head decorating London Bridge."

"We must leave here. Now." Sir Ensor's eldest son, Carver, grasped his father's arm with a firm, urgent grip. He professed to be a hard and ruthless swordsman, but fear glittered within his eyes, a damp sheen glistened on his paled skin. "Papa, please, take heed of St Croix. I have no desire to watch my entrails burned before my eyes as they start to quarter me."

"As all of us will surely be executed," Ailie added, backing his cousin's urgency. "For our deed this night, and for the vile reporting by those that tattle these things of our Catholic faith. You, St Croix, are not the only one in this city to bribe earwigs to crawl around beneath the debris. Oates and his followers have their ears and eyes as well."

St Croix nodded, smiled reassuringly. "That they do, but they are not as adept as mine. However, I also favour haste." He indicated the way back along the street, gesturing for them all to start moving. "My men," he added, "are on their way to alert your wife. I suggest, Ensor, that we travel light. Take the minimum you need, with only your most trusted servants, three at most, or none if you can do without for now. My ship is anchored at Greenwich, I have paid trusted watermen to take us down river." He moved aside, paused as Sir Ensor made no reciprocal movement. "Sir, my friend, we cannot linger. Your life, the lives of your family – and of my men – are in danger. We must go."

"I am no coward, St Croix. I do not run."

"No, you are no coward," St Croix answered softly, "but nor are you a fool. Your namesake, your grandfather, Sir Ensor Doone the elder, knew that when, unjustly accused of murdering his own brother, he forfeited his earldom and fled Scotland with his son, daughter-by-law and you, their child, to begin a new life here in England. He saw the sense of honourable exile over pointless execution. As must you, my friend, as must you."

Sir Ensor looked at his friend, his legal – and illegal – trade partner, with a mixture of bewilderment and stubbornness. He heard what he was being told but did not want to absorb the meaning, then relented, saw sense and spreading his hands, said plaintively, "To where do we go, Charles? I care too deeply for my wife and children to force them into impoverished disgrace, to live in some God-forsaken peat hovel in Scotland – a place that means nothing to me." Desperate, and unashamed to show his anxiety, he added, "I care not for myself, you understand, but in exile what terrors might befall my wife and younger sons? My defenceless daughters?"

St Croix slapped his friend on the shoulder. "I know

the very place that will suit you well. I own land in the West Country – a modest valley leading to a sheltered, private cove. There are a handful of moorland folk who mind their own, and my, business as long as I make it worth their while to do so. I have been considering selling the valley to someone trustworthy who would be willing to expand," he shrugged, "let's say, the trade I've established there. The house needs attention, but it is habitable. It will, admitted, be exile from the pleasures of the comfortable life you have enjoyed here in London. Others may call you rogue and outlaw, but your life will be your own to govern. Though it will be up to you and yours to ensure it remains so; you will be as safe there as you care to make it."

Sir Ensor looked doubtful. Charles St Croix could be frugal with the truth when it suited him.

"Or would you rather meet with the hangman's noose and quartering knife on the morrow?" St Croix grimaced as he spoke.

Resigned, Sir Ensor sighed. "You are right, I accept your offer, though I suspect in the months to come, my lady wife, when we have been forced to suffer solitude, ostracism, hunger and poverty, will advocate that widowhood and my hanging would have been her preferred option."

## EXMOOR, OCTOBER 1685 - SIR AILIE DOONE

The path that meandered down into Doone Valley was long and steep, dropping precariously in places through knee-high clumps of heather and winding through fierce stands of thorny gorse. It was little more than a deer track, although the sheep and wild ponies also used it – along with men, for this was the only suitable way into the valley from the westward direction.

Two men crested the rise and halted to let their mounts catch their breath from the exertion of a steep climb. It had been a long ride up onto the moor from the busy town of Barnstaple. Loosening the reins, Sir Ailie Doone allowed his horse the freedom to graze for a moment and, resting his arm on the saddle pommel, looked down on his uncle's personal empire. Nestled to the west side of Badgeworthy Water, a modest river that formed the Exmoor border between Devonshire and Somerset, the Doones' residence presided over a small, rambling village of stone and cob-built cottages, constructed with, apparently, no regard for an arranged plan, but suiting the purposes of the people who lived there. Moorland folk who loyally served the Doones as sheep farmers, fishermen and other required necessities.

Those months, when they had first come here as the new owners of the valley, the Doones had worked hard to restore the house to, if not luxury, then at least a comfortable condition. It had soon become home: an old, Tudor, stone-built dwelling enclosed within a walled garden where banks of flowers bloomed in tended profusion, despite the intrusion of rabbits, stray sheep and the occasional deer.

The two men watched a woman come from the chapel, built to the eastern side of the garden wall. Sir Ailie smiled, recognising his aunt, Lady Marjorie Doone, even from this distance, for she was the only female within several miles – perhaps even further – who insisted on wearing expensive satins and froths of French lace at her neck and wrists. But the satin was no longer the bright colours that she had worn in London, it was now the deep black of mourning.

"Your aunt continues to grieve, then?" his companion observed, pointing with his riding whip at the lady as she made her way towards the house.

"Aye," Ailee Doone answered Charles St Croix, gathering up the reins and kicking his mount forward to walk on down the slope. "She lost her youngest boy some months after we came here, and we all grieve for the wasted slaughter of our brothers who died at Sedgemoor. For all who died there come to that, no matter which idiotic side they fought on."

He glanced over his shoulder at his companion following behind to ascertain if he showed any sign of disapproval. Seeing no visible reaction continued, "Lady Marjorie has her daughters, but I fear that the deaths of the men who perished because of Monmouth's rebellion may well prove to have been for a wasted cause. Already King James, second of that name, is reneging on promises he made to those of us of the Catholic persuasion."

"Sedgemoor? A bad business, ill thought out by both sides. Did Jeffreys bother you here on Exmoor?" St Croix replied.

Ailie barked a single guffaw. "He paid us the honour of a visit, aye, but not for Sedgemoor. We are firm supporters of King James, but Judge Jeffreys decided to disrupt our livelihood by intruding onto the moor to seek those who had supported Monmouth, hanging men, and women, by the hundreds. We were not accused, but with so many men prowling the coast our trade had to discontinue."

St Croix snorted. "Indeed! I had to divert to Cornwall. Risky; I know not that coast or the nature of the people there."

Ailie tightened his grip on the reins as his mare stumbled slightly, his body swaying easily with the unexpected movement. He patted the grey mare's neck as she regained her balance. "We might have escaped Jeffreys' interest in us personally, but for my cousin Carver's stupidity. He had been pursuing his own feud with the Ridds down by Oare way. A dispute over a woman, would you believe? Hatreds had flared, along with unchecked tempers. Jeffreys heard of the dispute, used it as an excuse to poke his nose where 'twere not wanted. Found nothing untoward, o'course, but his presence was, let us say, a nuisance." Ailie chuckled. "Funnily enough, it were Lady Marjorie's youngest daughter, Gabriella, who eased the situation with her infectious gaiety. The little maid's but a bairn, but she could charm the birds from the trees, were she to set her mind to it. She certainly charmed Jeffreys. The sour old goat was enchanted by her intelligent – and incessant chatter."

St Croix laughed and set his horse to a small stream; jumped neatly over the babbling water. "What happened to Carver?"

In his wake, Sir Ailie popped his mare over the stream. "He drowned; pushed his temper too far and stumbled into one of the bogs out on the moor. I can't say that I miss him. He was always hot tempered, which made him unreliable."

"But trade is now prospering again is it not? I have heard no reports of any difficulties this past month."

"If there were any such trouble, we would not have sent word to you. We manage to keep ourselves private. This valley, as you originally advised when you sold it to us, is not easy to reach by outsiders, and is therefore easy to protect. We keep prying eyes at bay when moonless nights require it."

St Croix nodded. "Strange, though, that you need the privacy. Law-abiding folk, from rich landowner to local parson or schoolmaster or apothecary, have no qualm of conscience when it comes to acquiring smuggled goods at tax-free cost. Strange how these same men condemn rogues and scoundrels – aye and those of the Catholic faith – yet regularly enquire when the next night tide will be favourable for me to bring *Mermaid* and her cargo close to shore again."

Sir Ailie agreed. "The legitimate cargoes of wine and tobacco that you ship openly into Bideford and Barnstaple are safe trades which require no hiding. We handle those for you with no trouble, but contraband has always been our main source of income."

"My crews have told me that you employ good men?"

"Aye. Most live in the village yonder. Fisherfolk, farmers and moorland men by day, tubmen and patrolling eyes and ears by night. Fifty men with their wives and children reside here. They know a good thing. They are men who value loyalty and a regular handful of silver over gossiped tattle-tittle. Men who care not whether we live here in exile from our previous life, whether we are Protestant or Catholic, or whether we live outside the law. They know were they to betray us they'd lose all – and not just their home but their lives and the lives of their family. Harsh punishment, but effective, and our security depends upon it."

St Croix slapped at a drowsy autumn horsefly on his horse's neck, the sound loud in the moorland stillness. "So exile suits you well, eh?"

"My Uncle Ensor tolerates it. My Aunt Marjorie suffers it, but for myself, I confess, exile suits me well. I have two daughters born and a son, although, alas, my wife died giving birth to him, but there are women in town should I have need of comfort now and again. Our legitimate trade, as we have discussed, brings good profit, and the extra? Well, who does not benefit from the contraband trade, eh? Ho! We have been spotted, though I would wager our approach was noted from several miles back. Come, my friend, we shall dine on roast venison this night, and I will broach a rather fine keg of Spanish brandy that your smuggling crew provided back in the spring. What say you to that?"

St Croix grinned. "I say aye, and say it with loud, good cheer!"

## EXMOOR, DECEMBER 1693 - MISTRESS GABRIELLA DOONE

Burying my mother, yesterday, broke my heart, but for her, death was a blessed relief. She had detested Exmoor and exile alike. I think a day had not passed when sorrowing tears had not brimmed in her eyes, although she had tried her best to keep her lonely sadness private.

I was born on the moor in an uncomfortable, cold and miserable coach which had become wedged aslant, axle-deep in the mire. A bitter wind had swirled flurries of snow through every possible, and impossible, crack and opening. The men had whipped and bullied the four exhausted horses, but the coach had refused to move, and as I had taken my first breath, the rear axle had sheared in half. My mother, Lady Marjorie Doone, had held no more strength to cry out. Apparently, or so Papa enjoyed reminding me, I had spent that first hour of my life wailing in unison with Mama's distraught maid.

Mother's labour had begun two hours after the hired coach had left Exeter. Under the captaincy of my father's friend, Charles St Croix, we had sailed by ship from London to Devonshire. To confuse our trail from any vengeful enemy, we – I say 'we', as unborn, I'd had no knowledge or awareness of anything – had disembarked at Exeter and taken overland transport to the remote north of the county. My mother, her maid and the younger children in the coach that Master St

Croix had hired; the men, and our two trusted manservants following in a carter's wagon, with the few London possessions they'd hastily gathered together before fleeing that city.

My mother named me Gabriella, meaning 'God is my strength'. We had both needed His strength that day, and for many of the days, weeks, months, years, to follow.

During that short time when James, second of that name, had reigned as king after the death of his childless brother, Charles, my mother had hoped that our exile might be ended. She loved her husband and her children, as all wives and mothers should, but she had resented our enforced exile. Papa, however, had soon discovered that he preferred life here on Exmoor. In London, Mama had thrived, or so she often told me as I grew from child to early womanhood. She told me stories of visiting the theatre with King Charles and Master Pepys, of taking tea with noble ladies – aye, including the queen, Catherine of Braganza. Mama spoke fluent Portuguese and they would often, or so she claimed, enjoy an intimate *tête-à-tête*.

But we had fled that life when the London populace, spurred on by the lies and defamatory slurs made by that wretched man, Titus Oates, had become too dangerous to ignore. Mama's yearning to return to London had ended when King James had abandoned England and left those of us of the Catholic faith to fend for ourselves. We were despised, condemned and persecuted, and with the Dutch butterball, William of Orange and his wife, James's Protestant daughter, Mary, reigning as king and queen, there came no hope for an end to our exile. Mama took that knowledge hard. I was too young to notice or care, and indeed, I had no desire for London or its gay society. Exmoor was my home, I loved its wild freedom, despite my loneliness.

Now, these fifteen years after my birthing, the tears had fallen, unchecked, down my wind-chilled face as we had committed my dear mother to rest in the quiet graveyard beside the winter-worn moorland chapel where we acknowledge God, the Virgin Mary, and Jesu Christ every Sunday. It is an old chapel, stone built, with no tower or steeple, but a thatched roof which needs new sedge reeds in places where the wind, rain and decay have done their worst. One window, its glass cracked and broken, is covered by the tanned and oiled skin of a red deer. It does little to keep out the cold when the wind roars in across the moor. There are no adornments to the plain, stone walls inside, apart from God's own contribution of natural patterning by moss and lichen where the damp has encroached. Upon the altar stands a single silver crucifix and two brass candlesticks. Nothing else. Papa has not entirely abandoned his faith, but his caring for God waned after my brothers were slaughtered at that battle on Sedgemoor. Or perhaps it was the betrayal by King James which had caused his faltering? He never said, and I never asked.

We now have no priest, for Father Damion also lies at rest in the graveyard. God took him from us a sennight since. Reading from his Bible, Papa had recited suitable words for Father Damion's burial, and he did so again for my mother. No other priest would dare venture up here onto the wild heath of Exmoor, not to our remote valley, anyway. No one comes to Doone Valley unless they have specific reason. We prefer it that way. Those of us who deal in the illicit trade of contraband value our privacy.

Snowflakes had drifted from the leaden sky as, one by one, we'd tossed a clod of earth thumping down onto my mother's coffin. There were not many of us standing there. At the head of the grave, my father, Sir Ensor Doone. Barely fifty and three years of age, he more often than not looks tired and haggard. Exile – and the harshness of remote Exmoor – has not worn well with his health, and my mother's passing has greatly grieved him. An accident, four years past began his ageing. A net full of brandy kegs slipped its rope as it had been hoisted up the cliff face of our little secluded cove, and it had crashed down onto the beach below. Two tubmen had been killed outright and my father's leg had been badly broke. He never walked straight again, and I know, though he hides it well, that the injury continues to pain him.

Next to him, had stood my cousin Ailie, *Sir* Ailie as he is properly titled. As Papa read God's word from the Bible, I am certain that, despite his bowed head, my cousin's suspicious gaze had studied the gathered mourners. To all effect he runs the trade business now. Papa keeps the book accounts, Sir Ailie manages the industrious side, the ships and the cargoes, legal and illegal. Nearing two score years of age, he will become head of the family when my father goes to God's good care. I dread that day, for my cousin plays by his own rules, and they can be as fickle as a southerly wind, and as cold as an easterly gale. He has only ever cared for the prospect of ruling our valley with his own command, and for the gaining of wealth, no matter how he comes by it.

His son, Winnard, is like his father where a stone heart and calculating mind takes precedence over compassion. He is adept at feigning grief. He stood at the graveside with his hat clutched in his hands a step or two in front of his mouse of a wife. She is heavy with their first child, despite Winnard being not long out of childhood himself. If a boy, the babe is to be called Ascham. No name has been chosen for a girl.

Both my older sisters, Mary and Ursula, are married. Papa disowned them on the day they had left Exmoor to be wed, their betrayal all the deeper for their treachery of conversion from the Catholic faith to their husbands' Protestant persuasion. They live in Bristol now, and they are, I believe, both well. They write me once a year, sending brief greetings for my birthing day. They had been, reluctantly, invited to attend our mother's funeral. They had not come.

On the other side of the grave, my father's friend and business partner had stood in solemn respect, hat in hand, head bowed, Charles St Croix – although for reasons I do not wholly understand, he calls himself Charles Mereno now. His wife had accompanied him. A Spanish lady, Señora Dona – something or other. A long name which I can neither remember nor pronounce. In the lady's arms, their newborn son, Jesamiah, a strong, bold, child. He had been mewling when first brought out into yesterday's bitter, penetrating wind, but I had noticed that his eyes, though he is but only two weeks old, had sparkled with interest as he'd watched the delicate lace-flutters of snow settling on the soft woollen shawl that had been tucked tight around him.

Until they had arrived here a few days past, I had not known Charles St Croix – Mereno – to have a wife. He had not spoken of her before, on those many nights when his ship, *Mermaid*, had dropped anchor in our cove below our valley. Those silent nights when he'd brought contraband in, with no one to witness his coming and going, save us Doones and our loyal men who benefit from the reward of smuggling.

They are our tubmen, the men who help transfer the contraband from ship to shore. They haul the kegs of brandy, rum or genever; the hogsheads of tobacco, the packets of tea, the slips of expensive lace and the casks of saffron, nutmeg and other sought-after spices, up the steep cliff, then load them onto the backs of our sturdy Exmoor-bred ponies.

Again, I say 'we', for I do my share when the boats come in. I am not tall or strong, but I know the ponies and handle them well. Once the goods are safe ashore, the tubmen carry their half-barrels, one on their chest, one on their back, and set off towards our clients in Lynton, Barnstaple, Porlock and Minehead. The packponies, loaded with a heavier burden, are taken further across the moor, following the deer tracks. Since the age of twelve I have gone with them, leading my string of four ponies, tied nose to tail. Apart from the dull sound of unshod hooves we move quietly, no talking or whispering, a caravan of contraband crossing the moor to drop down to the trustworthy village inns, delivering our secretive goods. We make use of the narrow cattle and sheep-droving lanes that are sheltered from wind, weather and prying eyes by their high-banked hedgerows. Then we ride home, equally as quiet, with the ponies as exhausted as are we, all of us eager to reach safety before the pink and gold fingers of dawn peep over the horizon.

Several of Captain Mereno's crew and our villagers had stood a little apart from the grave. We pay well for the loyal service of the village men and women. Not one would consider betrayal and risk forgoing the generous palmfuls of earned silver. They all admired and respected Mama, for although she was wary of their rough tongues and ways, she always treated them kindly, seeing to any sores or wounds, caring for their welfare by ensuring they had wood or peat for their fires, clothes for their backs, adequate food for their bellies. And a proper burial for their dead.

I expect this will be my responsibility now.

And thus we, the last of the Doones, residing in secluded exile here in the wilds of Exmoor, buried my mother. Our family of mourners, alongside a huddled group of house servants which include the foreigner, Maha'dun, a stranger who keeps his face covered and has a preference for hunting down unwelcome visitors during the hours of darkness. Our reputation for causing misery and danger to those who stray too close to our valley has spread wide across the moors. A reputation of murder, a reputation deliberately spread by us in order to keep inquisitive men away.

Poor Mama. How often had she wept for that reputation? She left behind, in London, her fine gowns, her beautiful furniture, her delicate blue and white Dutch porcelain – everything, except what she had quickly packed: a few gowns and her jewellery. She had been afeared of the wild moorland, cowed by the wide sweep of the open sky, and unsettled by the roar of the restless sea constantly pounding against the rocks below the cliffs. Save for visits to our chapel, she had rarely left the house or its garden; not once during all those years did she venture further than the village.

We know no one outside of those whom Papa and Sir Ailie trust. And they are few of number. Rarely does any visitor come to dine with us, or to pass a pleasant afternoon. Except for Captain Mereno. He visits often, bringing, along with the contraband, his laughter and tales of exotic lands. Tales of dangerous seas, gape-mouthed monsters and beautiful siren mermaids luring unwary sailors to their doom. Mama always, politely, welcomed him, but disliked his presence. She would resent him being at her burying, for she had blamed him for bringing us here to Exmoor.

I had glanced across her grave at him, and felt my wind-chilled cheeks redden. He is a handsome man, and despite my young age, I would have willingly given myself to him, no matter the loss of my innocence, but he has this new Spanish wife, and the child. They too, are exiled. He from his English father, his wife from her Spanish family.

Exile, it seems, follows in our wake. I have known no other life, and while I love to ride on the moors, glorying in the salt smell and wind-roar of the sea, witnessing, enchanted, the proud red deer stags rutting in the autumn, or to sit quiet, watching while an otter fishes in the river, my life is otherwise solitary. There is no escape for us, the Doones of Exmoor; no escape for me, for, beyond the confine of our valley, unless wanted for our smuggling trade we are unwelcome and disliked.

Although it pained me, I'd hoped, nay, I had prayed, as I stood beside Mama's snow-swept grave, that the babe this Spanish woman held in her arms would not grow to know the bitterness of exile. Not that I care for him or his black-haired, black-eyed mother, but misery is not a thing to pass on to another.

My tears, they thought, were for my mother's passing into Christ's loving hands, but how could they know the truth of it? Mama is now free, but, today, my tears still fall, and I continue to withstand my own form of exile. My only love, my only delight, beyond the freedom of the moors, comes on moonless nights into our cove and stays for but a day or two. That is hard enough to bear, but he has now gone again, gone back to his ship with his wife and child. Has gone, sailing back to his home in Virginia, and I know not when – if – he shall ever return.

I stand here, thinking these things at the edge of the cliff, staring out across the grey sea, my sight blurred by tears. I have loved that man ever since I had first known him. I weep my tears of grief. Not for my mother, but for my own exile. Charles St Croix Mereno, had never, would never, think of me as I think of him.

I must accept the truth of it. I am banished, forever. An exile from the realm of love.


© Helen Hollick
   *Devon, 2023*


You can read more about the characters in this story in the nautical adventure series *The Sea Witch Voyages.* The Doones first appear in Voyage Four, *Ripples in the Sand.*


## ABOUT HELEN HOLLICK

Helen Hollick and her husband and adult daughter moved from north-east London in January 2013 after finding an 18th-century North Devon farmhouse through being a 'victim' on BBC TV's popular *Escape to The Country* show. The thirteen-acre property was the first one she was shown – and it was love at first sight. She enjoys her new rural life, and has a variety of animals on the farm, including Exmoor ponies, dogs, cats, hens, ducks and geese and her daughter's string of show jumpers.


First accepted for publication by William Heinemann in 1993 – a week after her fortieth birthday – Helen then became a USA Today Bestseller with her historical novel, *The Forever Queen* (titled *A Hollow Crown* in the UK) with the sequel, *Harold the King* (US: *I Am the Chosen King*), novels that explore the events that led to the battle of Hastings in 1066. Her *Pendragon's Banner*

*Trilogy* is a 5th-century version of the Arthurian legend, and she also writes a pirate-based nautical adventure/fantasy series, *The Sea Witch Voyages*, where you can read more about Jesamiah Acorne, son of Charles St Croix – and the Doones.

Despite being impaired by the visual disorder of Glaucoma, she is also branching out into the quick read novella, 'Cosy Mystery' genre with the *Jan Christopher Mysteries*, set in the 1970s, with the first in the series, *A Mirror Murder* incorporating her, often hilarious, memories of working for thirteen years as a library assistant.

Her nonfiction books are *Pirates: Truth and Tale*s and *Life of a Smuggler* and she is planning on writing about the ghosts of North Devon (in particular, those who are resident in her house), and maybe something about famous horses: these might appear as published books or serialised on her blog. She also runs a news and events blog and a Facebook page for her village, and supports her daughter's passion for horses and showjumping.

'Helen Hollick has it all! She tells a great story, gets her history right, and writes consistently readable books.' *Bernard Cornwell.*

Website: **https://helenhollick.net/**
Buy Helen's books on Amazon:
**https://viewauthor.at/HelenHollick**
(Or order from any bookshop.)

## 4

# THE UNWANTED PRINCE

### A STORY OF A 16TH-CENTURY EXILE BY
### ANNA BELFRAGE

Buttons were hard. Gustav squinted down his front and concentrated on pushing the little silver disk through the corresponding hole.

"Let me help, clumsy-fingers." Sigrid batted away his hands.

"I can do it." After all, he was all of seven, and Madame Jeanne had told him all boys his age could dress themselves. The shirt, the hose and the puff breeches—all of that was easy. But the doublet was stiff and heavy, and there were thousands upon thousands of buttons.

"Silly. Twenty-two buttons, not thousands," Sigrid said, deftly buttoning up the last one. She frowned at him. "I think you have the hose on backwards."

Only on one leg. Gustav shrugged and hastily stomped his feet into his boots. Old and well-worn, they were beginning to pinch round his toes, but he hadn't said anything to Mamma, because lately whenever she saw him, her eyes filled with tears, and he didn't know what it was he was doing that made her so sad. He tried to be a good boy. He sat still and quiet in church, he ate his food without protesting even if he hated cabbage, he did his lessons and did his best to be polite to everyone. Even Sigrid. Well, only when Mamma was close. When they were alone, he saw no reason to be polite to his big sister – after all, she was never polite to him.

"Will we ever see Pappa again?" he asked Sigrid as they made their way down to the hall. The stairs were steep and dark, and he did not protest when she took him by the hand.

"You must stop asking that," Sigrid said with a frown. "It makes Mamma sad when you talk about Pappa."

He never did. "I only ask you," he said.

Sigrid sighed, her hold on his hand tightening. "I do not think we will," she said. "I do not think Uncle Johan wants us to."

"Do you think he misses us?" He had fragmented memories of his father, of all those months they'd lived together in one castle or the other. He knew his father had been king once, but in his memories, his father was a sad man kept under constant guard. Some of those guards had been nice; one of them had even taught Gustav to ride. Most of the guards had been gruff and surly, even if it was hard to be surly with Mamma.

"I think he misses Mamma," Sigrid said.

"Not us?" For some odd reason, that made his chest ache.

"Us too," Sigrid amended. "But mostly Mamma." She smiled. "She used to sing to him a lot. He said it made his headaches go away."

Gustav nodded. His father had a lot of headaches.

"I like it when Mamma sings," he said. Even if he didn't have any headaches. When Mamma sang, it was as if the entire world stopped to listen, and he'd rest his head on her lap while she combed her fingers through his hair.

*"Rida, rida, ranka,"* she'd sing. *"Hästen heter Blanka."*
And he'd fall asleep as she sang of little boys who won
their spurs and lost their childhood, of men who
became kings and lost their peace of mind.

Sometimes, he wondered if that was what had
happened to Pappa: he became king, and then he
had all those terrible, terrible headaches, and one day
the headache was so bad he had even killed
someone. He hadn't told Mamma about that. She
wouldn't like to know that Pappa had stabbed
someone to death. He hadn't even told Sigrid. He
only knew because he'd heard one of their guards
tell one of their new servants about it. But if Pappa
had killed someone, that person probably deserved
it.

Sigrid shoved the door open and ducked under the
heavy tapestry that covered it. For warmth, Mamma
said, complaining the door that led to their private
apartments was too thin to keep the cold out. The hall
was draped in shadows – except for the one corner in
which Mamma sat, her face turned up to the light that
fell in through the unshuttered window. She was
wearing blue today. He peeked down at his doublet
and puffed out his chest. He too was in blue.

Mamma held out her arms and hand in hand they
ran towards her. He was faster than Sigrid but he let
her set the pace.

"Did you sleep well?" Mamma asked, gesturing for
one of the serving wenches.

"Yes." Gustav sighed at the bowl of porridge.
Always porridge.

"Eat up." Mamma's hands were in his hair,
smoothing down his fair curls. Moments later, she was

adjusting the lace of his collar and cuffs. "We are expecting visitors."

"We are?" Sigrid asked.

"A royal emissary," Mamma said, her mouth flattening. "The emissary of a usurper," she muttered, and Gustav was just about to ask what a usurper was when Mamma shook herself and smiled. "And I have a surprise for you," she added, winking at him.

"For me?"

"For you."

"And me?" Sigrid asked.

"Not this time," Mamma said and Sigrid scowled. "Sigrid," Mamma admonished, and Sigrid flushed.

"We can share my surprise," Gustav whispered, sneaking his hand into Sigrid's.

A commotion in the yard outside had Mamma standing up. She gestured for them to stand beside her, and Gustav stood as tall and straight as he could when the large outer door swung open, bringing with it a blast of icy March air and two men.

Gustav gawked at their elegant attire. Richly embroidered doublets, starched ruffles in their collars and cuffs, the two men looked rich – almost as rich as Uncle Johan had looked the single time he'd met him. Both carried swords – rapiers – the basket guards decorated in gold and silver.

"Mistress Karin," one of the men said, offering Mamma a slight bow. The other man merely nodded, staring straight at Gustav. The look in his eyes made him want to hide behind Mamma's skirts, but he was too big to act like a babe. So Gustav took a deep breath and remained where he was, happy for the comfort of Mamma's hand on his shoulder.

"We come from the king," the one with the icy eyes said.

"May God bless him and keep him safe," Mamma said, which had both men giving her a surprised look. "I am a loyal subject of our king," Mamma told them.

"Of course, of course," the smaller of the men said. He bowed yet again in Mamma's direction. "No one has ever suggested otherwise."

Sigrid's hand had tightened round Gustav's.

"We have matters to discuss – important matters related to the realm's security," the other man said. He looked down his nose first at Mamma, then at Gustav. "It is time, Mistress."

Mamma swallowed loudly. "Please." She gestured at the table before nudging Gustav and Sigrid towards the door. "Go on," she said. "It is a fine day outside."

They did not go outside. Instead, Sigrid had them scurrying round the old manor house to the kitchen entrance. From there, they made for the stairs that led not only to the hall but to the old solar and the nursery on the upper floor. Sigrid pressed her ear to the door behind the tapestry. Gustav followed suit. He heard the low rumble of male voices, and then there was Mamma.

"No!" she exclaimed. "No, you cannot do this! This is not what he said. He promised…"

More low rumbling.

"Have some mercy," Mamma said. "He's a child! What danger can a child be?"

"Come." Sigrid tugged at him. "Let us go outside."

"What child?" Gustav asked.

"I don't know." Sigrid looked uncommonly pale. "We should not have eavesdropped."

"That was your idea," he protested.

"I know." Her mouth wobbled, and for an instant he worried she was about to weep.

"You can tell Mamma it was my idea," he therefore said. "It's alright, Sigrid. I can take the punishment." Not that Mamma was ever particularly harsh, but to judge from Sigrid's countenance, eavesdropping was a very, very bad thing to do.

"Oh, Gustav!" Sigrid hugged him. He squirmed until she released him, leaping back to glare at her while he wiped away all that silly girl stuff from his garments.

"Let's go and look at the puppies," he said. "And no more yucky hugs!"

It was gone noon when Mamma came to find them. Gustav studied her carefully. She'd been weeping, and he had only seen her weep once before, the day they'd been taken away from Pappa. Oh, how she'd wept that day, how she'd clung to Pappa who clung just as hard to her.

"Were they mean to you?" Gustav asked.

"Hmm?"

"Those men, the royal memsirs."

"Emissaries," Mamma corrected. She smoothed her hand over his hair, looking so, so sad.

Daylight had already waned when Gustav recalled he had never had his surprise. He stirred his soup and looked at Mamma from under his lashes. Should he remind her? But she was weeping again, silent tears rolling down her cheeks, and it made all of him itch, so he decided not to ask.

After their meal, Mamma ordered up a bath.

"For me?" Gustav was not entirely fond of baths.

"For you." Mamma was already busy with the buttons he'd struggled with previously. "And then I'm going to put you to bed and sing your favourite song."

Gustav drew back. "Am I sick?" Why else would she fuss so over him?

She laughed, but her eyes were shiny with tears. "No, my sweet boy, you are not sick. But sometimes, a mother just wants to coddle her children."

"You could coddle Sigrid instead," he said.

"I'll do that tomorrow," Mamma said. "Tonight is all about you."

An hour or so later, he was in his bed, all of him drowsy and warm. He held Mamma's hand as she sang.

*"Rida, rida ranka,*
*Hästen heter Blanka,*
*Liten riddare så rar,*
*Ännu inga sporrar har,*
*När han dem har vunnit,*
*barndomsro försvunnit."*

Over and over she sang, and Gustav smiled as he slipped into the land of dreams.

Next morning, he was shaken awake. Mamma looked grey and haggard.

"Here," she said, helping him into thick hose and breeches, a woollen vest over his shirt and a new doublet in brown. She showed him two gold coins before slipping them into the little pocket in his doublet. "Don't tell them about the coins," she said.

Gustav wasn't quite awake yet, but Mamma's haste

and her expression had his innards turning and twisting. "Tell who?" he asked. "Sigrid?"

"No, sweeting." She kissed his brow. "Do not tell anyone. Those coins are for you. Only for you."

"Is it my surprise?" Maybe he could buy a horse with the coins. He'd like a horse of his own.

"Yes, my heart. It is your surprise. Dearest boy, I wish I had more to give you, that I could spare you..." Now she was weeping again, and Gustav didn't like it when Mamma cried.

Dawn was a faint streak of pink along the eastern horizon when he was hustled out into the yard. The two men from yesterday were already there, both astride horses.

"Mamma?" he asked, backing away.

"I am so, so sorry." She fell to her knees before him. She swallowed. "I love you so much, my son. You are a good boy and today you have to be a brave boy as well."

"Brave?" He bit his lip to stop it from wobbling. What was going on? All of this reminded him of that day when they'd left Pappa. He looked at the two men, one of them studying him with obvious dislike, the other seemingly incapable to look at him and Mamma.

Mamma inhaled. "They're here for you." She tried to smile. "Our king has plans for you. As he should, my little prince." But her tears kept on flowing, and that smile was more of a grimace. Gustav's heart thudded hard against his ribs.

"No." He shook his head. "I want to stay here. Tell them to go away."

"There is no choice, my beautiful boy." She cupped his face and kissed him everywhere.

"Sigrid!" he yelled. "Help me, Sigrid!" But his sister was nowhere close.

"Oh, Gustav!" Mamma squished him to her chest.

"We cannot do anything to help you," she whispered. "What can we possibly do when your uncle, the king, wills it so?"

"What will happen to me?" he whispered back.

"You are to ride with Sir Erik." Mamma gestured at the less forbidding of the two men. "He will ensure you are well cared for."

"But I don't want to." Gustav held onto her. "I want to stay here, with you."

"Time is up!" the taller of the men said.

"For God's sake, Knut," the other – Sir Erik – said. "Give the woman the time she needs. It's not as if she'll be seeing..." He broke off.

Mamma sat back on her heels. "Know this," she said. "Know that wherever you are I love you. You are my precious Gustav, and I will love you until the day I die."

Gustav could no longer hold back the tears. "Mamma, please."

"There is nothing I can do," Mamma said. She wheeled to stare at the men. "He's a cruel man to take vengeance on the innocent."

"Innocent for now. Not in twenty years' time," the taller man replied with a shrug. "A king must do as he must." He urged his horse into motion, leaned over and suddenly Gustav was hoisted into the air.

"Mamma!" he yelled. "Mamma!"

"Gustav!" Out of the manor came Sigrid, making as if to charge the man holding him. Mamma grabbed hold of her, sinking to her knees in the yard.

"Mamma!" Gustav screamed.

"Shut your mouth," the man said, slapping him hard over the head. From Sigrid came a loud shriek and Mamma was up on her feet running towards them brandishing her eating knife.

"No!" Sir Erik barked. "Do not even try it, Mistress

Karin. And you, you oaf, stop it," he added, glaring at the man who'd hit Gustav. He rode over and lifted Gustav over to his horse. "We must go."

"No!" Gustav fought. "Mamma! Sigrid!"

The horse beneath him broke into a canter, but he could still hear his mother and sister calling his name. "Mamma," he moaned, and he didn't understand any of this. Sir Erik swept his thick cloak round both himself and Gustav.

"I'm sorry, lad," he muttered. "I wish this did not need to happen, but what the king wants, the king gets. There, there," he added, a strong arm holding Gustav close. "Weep if you need to lad. There's no shame in tears when your entire life has been ripped from you."

An hour or so later, they arrived in Åbo. The small town was a thriving place, dominated by the royal castle in which Gustav had stayed several times with his mamma and sister. Other than the castle and the church, most of the buildings were low, squat things lining the streets that led to the harbour and the tall Hansa warehouses that sat along the quays. Despite everything, Gustav sat up straight. He loved visiting the harbour, a magical place filled with men and ships, with heaps of goods recently unloaded or about to be loaded.

"How long will it take her to find out where her precious whelp ended up?" the taller of the men – Knut – said.

"Hush," Sir Erik said.

"Hush? It wasn't me who spun that silly web of lies, promising her the lad would grow up well cared for in your household."

79

Gustav did not like the sound of this. "What is going to happen to me?" he squeaked.

"Had it been up to me, you'd be dead," Knut sneered.

"Dead?" He shrank back against Sir Erik. "Why?"

"Why?" Knut shook his head. "What sort of a fool are you? You're a Vasa, damn it. Some would say you have a better right to the throne than your uncle does."

"I do?"

"No you don't!" Knut hissed. "You are the son of an insane fool who wed a woman so lowborn she should be scrubbing floors in the kitchen, not living the life of a lady."

"Knut, that's enough," Sir Erik said.

"My mamma is a good lady." Gustav bristled. "She is kind to everyone. Not like you." He wiped at his eyes. "I don't want to leave," he said. "Please, good sirs, can't you just take me back home?"

"No, Gustav, we cannot do that. The king would be mightily displeased." Sir Erik sounded tired.

"But why? I do not want to be king. I just want to be with Sigrid and Mamma."

"There's the ship." Knut pointed in the direction of a creaking vessel. "Make haste, or we'll miss it."

It did not help how he protested, or how he tried to kick free. When the ship slipped its moorings, Gustav was aboard, that horrible man Knut telling him he'd tie him up and throw him in the hold if he didn't behave. Gustav had been on ships before. Many times, actually. Usually, he liked being on the sea, but this time he stared as the familiar outline of Åbo castle receded into the distance.

Sir Erik and Knut left him alone, beyond Sir Erik

handing him some bread. Neither of them had told him where they were going, but Gustav asked one of the sailors who said they were destined for Poland. Gustav bit into the bread. He'd never been to Poland. Mayhap this could turn out to be some sort of adventure. The bread in his mouth swelled. He did not want an adventure. He wanted Mamma. He clung to the railings and closed his eyes, hoping this was some sort of terrible dream, one he would very soon wake from.

He must have fallen asleep huddled on the deck, because he woke to strong arms carrying him into the relative warmth of a small cabin.

"Why bother?" Knut said. "Might have been best for everyone if he just died out there."

"He's a child," Sir Erik said.

Late next day, they arrived at a place called Braunsberg. Yet another busy harbour, and everywhere Gustav saw the pennants of the Hanseatic league. He followed Sir Erik and Knut off the ship, hurrying after them as they strode through the thronged streets. They reached a large square over which loomed a church that was much, much bigger than the one in Åbo. The two men argued heatedly. Gustav was distracted by a handsome horse and when he turned to look for Sir Erik, he was gone. Only Knut remained, looking as grim as always.

"Come on," he barked and set off into a maze of alleys and small streets. Gustav did his best to keep up, but evening was falling and the shadows made it hard to see where Knut went.

Gustav's stomach growled. He was hungry and he was cold, and it seemed to him Knut was walking faster.

"Wait!" Gustav called out. "Wait for me."

Knut turned a corner.

By the time Gustav reached it, Knut was gone.

Gustav ran. Up one street, down the other. He skidded down steep alleys, he ran and ran, hoping that at some point he would see Knut, easily recognisable by his height.

"Mamma," he moaned, but that wouldn't help – he realised that. He tried to find his way back to the harbour, even tried to ask someone, but no one understood Swedish, and he could not speak Polish. One man just shoved him aside, and Gustav landed on his backside in a puddle.

It was dark by the time he gave up. His feet hurt, his boots pinching his toes. He was cold and wet and he was utterly alone. Where before the streets had been full of people, now they were almost deserted, people preparing for night and curfew.

A bell tolled. It tolled again, and Gustav shivered in his doublet. He'd torn the sleeve, and his hose was dirty. Mamma would not be pleased. She'd nag at him, telling him he had to be careful of the few garments he had. "We have to be thrifty," she'd say, going on to explain that she did not have much coin. Coins. He stuck his fingers into the tight little pocket. He had coins. Maybe he could buy something to eat, find somewhere to sleep.

Hesitantly, he made his way towards what looked like a tavern. Warm light spilled from the door when someone opened it, releasing the mouthwatering scents of meat and bread. Gustav inched closer. He was so, so hungry!

Next time the door opened, he scurried inside.

There were men everywhere, men seated at tables and drinking beer and eating thick slices of what smelled like roasted ham. A woman approached him, hands on her hips. She said something.

"I do not understand," he said. He held up one of his coins. "Food, I want food."

The woman snatched the coin out of his hand. Moments later, she'd thrown him outside, saying something in a loud angry voice. He huddled together under her anger and yet again he wept. The tone of her voice changed. He scrubbed at his eyes with knuckled hands and tried to stop himself from blubbering like a silly girl.

The woman disappeared inside.

Gustav remained where he was, too tired to even try moving.

The woman reappeared and handed him a thick wedge of bread with a slice of ham. Gustav inhaled. Food. She shooed at him, her voice becoming angry again when at first he didn't move. A kick to his leg had him hurrying off as fast as he could.

Some time later, he snuck into the narrow alley beside the church and slid down to sit with his back against one of the massive walls. He curled up as tight as he could, trying to find some warmth. He yawned, his eyes drooping. If Mamma was here she'd sing and he'd fall asleep to her voice. But she wasn't here. No one was here. Not even Sigrid.

"For fuck's sake! Damnation, Knut, are there no limits to your cruelty?"

Gustav stirred awake.

"Lad, are you alright?" Sir Erik crouched before him.

83

Gustav wet his lips with his tongue. He was stiff with cold.

Sir Erik cursed and swept him up in his arms.

"I want to go home," Gustav whispered. "I do not want an adventure. I want my mamma."

"I know," Sir Erik whispered back. "But that is not going to happen." He cleared his throat and turned to glare at Knut. "How could you just abandon him?"

Knut shrugged. "That's what we're supposed to do, isn't it?"

"Not like that!" Sir Erik bellowed. "Damn it man, can you feel no compassion?"

Knut's mouth twisted into a sneer, but then his shoulders slumped. "Of course I can. I am no monster."

"No?" Sir Erik strode off, still with Gustav in his arms. "And yet you left a child of seven utterly alone in an unfamiliar place."

"That's what we're here to do!" Knut yelled. "He may not have said as much, but you know exactly what King Johan wants. He wants the whelp d..."

"Not by my hand." Sir Erik set Gustav down in front of a large door. "I will not burden my immortal soul with something that heinous."

"Neither will I," Knut muttered. He looked at Gustav. "It is not personal, lad. We are but doing what we've been told to do."

Sir Erik snorted before using the huge iron clapper on the door. "Don't expect him to absolve you. I dare say not even God will absolve us."

Gustav's head hurt. Maybe he was getting one of those headaches Pappa had. Maybe all this was like one of Pappa's fevered dreams, and soon enough he'd wake to Mamma's soft touch, to Sigrid rolling her eyes and telling him he was a stupid little boy.

The door swung open. A man in dark robes stood

on the other side, and Gustav shied away. A Catholic priest! Dearest God, keep him safe!

"This is the best I can do," Sir Erik said, gently shoving him in the direction of the priest. He said something in what Gustav recognised as Latin. He was not good at Latin – Sigrid was much better – but he did recognise the word *puerulus*.

"I am not that little," he protested. The priest had hold of his arm, nodding at Sir Erik. "No, let me go!" Gustav squirmed like a hooked worm. "Sir Erik, please! Don't leave me here!"

"I am sorry, lad."

"I want to go home!" Gustav cried. "Please, take me home!"

"You cannot go home," Knut said harshly. "The moment you set foot on Swedish soil, your uncle will have you killed." He slid a finger over his throat.

"But why?"

"Because you're a threat to him and his son," Sir Erik said.

Gustav shook his head. He wasn't a threat. He was just a boy who liked horses.

"I just want to be with Mamma. And Sigrid," he said. "Please take me back."

Sir Erik looked about to weep. "We cannot. You will never see your mother again." He took a step backwards. "May God keep you," he muttered.

"No!" Gustav fought. Never in his entire life had he fought like he did at that moment, but the priest would not let him go, his voice low and soothing as he said things Gustav did not understand. The door banged shut and the passage was plunged into darkness.

"Mamma!" Gustav cried out. "I want Mamma!"

He was carried out of the passage. Up some winding stairs and into a small room with a window that showed a small patch of overcast sky, no more. The priest sat down on the pallet bed, still with Gustav in his arms, still speaking to him in that low voice, words Gustav did not understand or want to hear. Instead, he cried. He cried and cried in the arms of this stranger and at some point he was wrung dry of all tears, left exhausted and hurting all over – but mostly there was this huge ache in his chest.

Much later, he remained curled on the bed. He'd been fed and washed, that large priest – a Jesuit, he'd gathered – talking to him as if he were a spooked horse. The entire building was quiet, and he'd considered trying to escape, but he'd heard the lock click as the Jesuit left.

He wound his arms around himself. "*Rida, rida ranka,*" he sang softly. "*Hästen heter Blanka.*" If he closed his eyes, he could pretend that was Mamma's arms holding him, and she would smell of lavender and meadowsweet. "*Liten riddare så rar, ännu inga sporrar har.*" His voice broke. He had nothing here. Nothing. But as he lay in the unfamiliar bed, Gustav Erikson Vasa promised himself that one day he would see Mamma again. One day, she'd hold him and shush him as she sang about little knights and the lost joys of childhood. One day.

© Anna Belfrage
*Sweden, 2023*

## AUTHOR'S NOTE

Sadly, the story above is true. In 1575, Gustav Erikson Vasa's uncle Johan III – who'd effectively usurped the throne from the somewhat mentally unstable Erik XIV – separated Gustav from his mother, Karin Månsdotter, and dumped him alone in Poland. The seven-year-old was saved from dying by the local Jesuits, who also educated him. Gustav converted and grew up to be an impoverished vagrant – well, except for those few occasions when someone thought he could be useful in an attempt to destabilise Johan III. Gustav always refused to participate in any such plots.

In the 1580s, he managed to sneak into the royal compound in Krakow and spend some time with his sister, Sigrid, who was then a lady-in-waiting to her cousin, Johan III's daughter Anna. How the two siblings conversed with each other I do not know, because by then Gustav's Swedish was mostly forgotten. The single thing he asked his sister for was to help him see his mamma again.

In 1596, more than twenty years after he'd been ripped from his home, Gustav was finally allowed to see his mother in Reval (present day Tallin). It was an awkward meeting: she only spoke Swedish, he no longer did. Besides, she did not recognise her little boy in the gangly, much too thin man standing before her. But after being shown some distinctive birthmarks, Karin enfolded her son in her arms. I hope she sang to him. He sort of deserved it.

Gustav was to end up in Russia, an unwilling participant in yet another plot directed at destabilising Sweden. He refused and was kicked to the curb, living out the few years remaining to him as he'd lived most of his life: in destitution. In 1607, Gustav Erikson Vasa, rightful heir to the Swedish throne, died and was buried in Russia.

And as to that lullaby, it was probably not around when Gustav was a boy, but it is a much loved traditional Swedish lullaby.

You can find one version here:
**https://www.youtube.com/watch?v=Tgd-0TYBbW8**

### A ROUGH TRANSLATION OF THE LULLABY
*Ride, ride astride,*
*your horsey's name is Blanka*
*Little rider young and bright*
*has no worries, has no cares.*
*Once he's won the spurs of knighthood,*
*the peace of childhood days is gone.*

### ABOUT ANNA BELFRAGE

Had Anna been allowed to choose, she'd have become a time-traveller. As this was impossible, she became a financial professional with three absorbing interests: history, romance and writing. Anna always writes about love and has authored the acclaimed time travelling series *The Graham Saga*, set in 17th-century Scotland and Maryland, as well as the equally acclaimed medieval series *The King's Greatest Enemy* which is set in 14th-century England. Anna is presently hard at work with her other medieval series, *The Castilian Saga*, which is set against the conquest of Wales. The third installment, *Her Castilian Heart*, was published in 2022, and the fourth and final one will be out in 2024. She has recently released *Times of Turmoil*, a sequel to her time travel romance, *The Whirlpools of Time.*

   'A master storyteller. This is what all historical fiction should be like. Superb.'

Website: **www.annabelfrage.com**
Buy Anna's books on Amazon:
**http://Author.to/ABG**
or
**http://amazon.com/author/anna_belfrage**

# 5

# COMING HOME

## BY ELIZABETH CHADWICK

## THE TOWER OF LONDON, JULY 1189

Tense with excitement and anticipation, Isabelle waited for her mother's arrival. It had been five months since their last meeting on a grey February day with snow patching the ground and the Thames washing past the Tower's walls in muddy-grey spate. Today was one of bright sun and occasional shadows under a blue sky patched with swift white clouds.

Catching her mood, her small silvery hound, Damask, whined and gave her a moist nudge with her nose. Isabelle stroked her pet's sleek head and murmured a distracted endearment.

In the four years she had dwelt in exile in the Tower of London, Isabelle had grown accustomed to its confines. She had her own chamber and two maids provided. She could walk the grounds freely and had made friends with many of the other young heiresses dwelling here in the same situation as herself – marriage prizes, their fathers dead, their mothers widowed. Girls too valuable to live unguarded in a world of voracious self-seeking men. She understood why these thick walls protected her but knew bitter irony that her status restricted her freedom. The seamstresses, the goose girls, the ale wives who came and went from the Tower had more liberty than she did. It was a powerless power indeed and she hated it. She knew she should be grateful because she had privilege, she had her life, and her cushioned existence. Her cage was gilded and her mother visited when she could. Isabelle had her life before her – unlike her brother who would never see the sky again, or eat fresh bread, or stand on Striguil's battlements and watch the peregrines soar over the Wye.

Thinking about Gilbert as she often did, she picked up the carved wooden knight that stood in a little niche at her bedside. It had been his favourite toy and had sparked many an imaginative adventure. Her lively red-haired brother and partner in play – suddenly dead at twelve years old, thrown from his spirited new mount while they were visiting Haverford. He had died there in the courtyard of a broken neck, in their mother's arms, blown out by a single breath of God. Isabelle's stomach still lurched when she remembered those moments. The shock, the disbelief, and then the terrible numbness of utter grief.

Her childhood companion, snatched from her in an instant had made her realise with new pain, the preciousness of life and how swiftly it could be taken away. She had lost her father from an infected foot when she was six years old, and then Gilbert and for a while too her mother, who had descended into a dark pit of bitter despair. Isabelle's nature, a combination of her mother's determination to survive blended with her father's steady composure had brought her through, but an aching sadness like hunger still remained in her heart.

King Henry had commanded her to be brought here

to the Tower, for she was now the sole heiress to Striguil on the Welsh border, to fertile lands in Southern Ireland, and to castles and estates in Normandy. Being thirteen years old and of marriageable age, her importance as a prize had risen to a point where she had to be taken into a custody more secure than that which her mother, and a Welsh border castle could provide.

Turning the wooden toy in her hands, feeling the marks of the carver's knife, she remembered the day they had sent for her. It was at Striguil, four months after Gilbert's death and her mother, Aoife still in deep mourning. She had been weaving a length of braid on a small loom in the women's chamber, with its glimpses of the meandering Wye. She had seen a seal fishing for salmon in the river this morning, and was even smiling a little as she worked.

A messenger had arrived bearing a letter from the king and as her mother read it, she caught her breath and pressed her fist to her midriff. Isabelle's tenuous happiness had evaporated on the instant. "What is it Mama?"

Aoife had turned, her fine features drawn tight and frown lines scoring her brow. "Leave that," she said with a terse gesture at the weaving. "I have something important to tell you."

Isabelle carefully set her work aside, precise in her movements, centring herself.

"The king commands you to go to London. You are to be lodged in the Tower with other heiresses in his wardship."

Isabelle's stomach lurched. "But why? I don't understand!"

"Do you not?" Aoife demanded, almost in accusation. "Well, you should. It is because you are an heiress to great lands. It is because you are of marriageable age. It is because your brother is dead."

Isabelle stared at her and Aoife said angrily, "We have to go and pack the things you will need. Do not just sit there like a cow chewing the cud!"

Isabelle had understood her mother's moods and her pain, and had understood that she was angry at the situation, not her. She had watched her cope with the death of her father that had brought them from their royal Irish homeland to the Marches of Wales, and then, eight years later, the loss of Gilbert. She was damaged, surviving against the odds and battling to hold their position steady and stop their family ship from sinking amid a storm of political ambition.

Her mother began sorting through the coffers and cupboards, yanking out fabric, veils, ribbons and trinkets. "You can't take this veil; the edge is frayed. Use that one instead. And have that bolt of blue cloth for a new gown. You are growing so fast. You need more laces and ribbons. I was hoping to buy some next month in Bristol. I thought... I thought we had more time." Her mother abruptly stopped, and swallowing, stared at the heap on the bed in front of her as if it were a mountain impossible to climb.

Isabelle still remembered the grief and the fear. All she had ever known as a constant in her life was her mother and the thought of parting from her had made her feel sick and afraid. Everyone she loved went away – her father, her brother. All the people she had known in her Irish homeland.

Aoife had jerked herself back into the moment and reached for her. "Oh, come here!" Grabbing Isabelle, she had pulled her into her body and hugged her hard while they both wept together.

Eventually she had wiped her eyes and turning to the

clothes, had begun folding them. "Your father left us in a difficult condition when he was taken untimely from the world," she said. "We have to fend for ourselves as women, you no more than me. This is not my doing; I hope you understand. This is the doing of men." Her expression hardened. "Do not ever, my daughter, depend upon a man, for he will let you down. Do not let yourself be beguiled; it is all falseness and wit until it comes to the moment of truth – and then they push you off a cliff."

Isabelle felt as though she had been thrown into a lake of icy water and could only gaze at her mother in bewildered distress. Aoife had ceased her folding, embraced her again, and drawn her to sit before the hearth.

"You are still very young," she said, stroking her hair, "but I was barely older than you when I came to England for the first time and made a betrothal with your father at the behest of my own father. We had been exiled from Ireland by your grandsire's enemies and we needed help, and I was the price to secure that help – tasty bait to lure the fine, red-haired Norman lord onto our hook, so that we might go home. You do not yet understand the machinations of men, but you must learn swiftly. To them you look like a little fish to be gobbled up off the table, and they all wish to have you. You stand in the stead of your father and all that he once was and all that he owned. It has come down to you and it is your burden to bear and to face down anyone who would take it from you. King Henry seeks to draw you into his enclave of so-called protection and we must bear with it for he is the king and there is nothing we can do. If we fled, we would be hunted down. I cannot be with you every day – it hurts me that we shall be separated. But I will come to you whenever I can, and I will make that same king mindful of his pledge. I will protect you until my dying breath. We are mother and daughter and part of each other for ever. We must be brave and tread this path, even if it is not the one we would have chosen."

Isabelle still hadn't fully understood, but she was able to take the words inside her and with them, her mother's formidable strength. There might be unpleasantness ahead, but she would show no weakness.

Three days later she had left Striguil, for a deeper exile, further from Ireland, further from Wales. Climbing into the travelling cart, leaving her mother and everything she had known, heading for a foreign horizon. Her mother had grasped her hand for a final moment and she could still recall the look in her eyes and her fierce expression.

"You are a princess in my stead and you are born from royalty," she had said. "You are the one to bear it forward. Show no weakness to the world and honour me and our forebears. I will come to you as soon as I can and I miss you already. I will send you gifts and letters more often than I can afford." Her voice had caught and her eyes shone with tears. "I will not let you down my daughter, my precious girl. I love you more than the earth I walk upon. My heart is torn, but I shall not show it to the world, and you must do the same, whatever happens. Remember who you are and where you come from."

The cart had picked up the pace, their hands had parted and she had been borne away to her new life in a cage of stone and gold.

Surfacing from her memories, Isabelle gently set the little horseman back in his niche and wiped away the tears running down her face. Irish rain her mother was wont to call them in her gentler moments – which were not often. Isabelle always wept when she thought about Gilbert and her life

95

before coming here. She had left Leinster as a tiny girl and remembered little of it, but the rain and the greenery, and the misty image of a copper-haired man who had carried her in his arms and loved her were engraved on her soul. If the Tower was engraved, it was for different reasons. Four years of exile. Four years of journeying from child to young woman in a world where the future was uncertain beyond marriage to a Norman stranger, and her anchors were all in the past.

For the moment the king was preoccupied with his campaigns across the Narrow Sea. She had heard he was seriously ailing, but it was all rumours – on which the Tower community thrived. The trick was separating truth from lies.

One of her attendant women put her head around the door. "Your lady mother is here," she said.

Isabelle thanked her politely, giving nothing away. She had learned to guard herself because everything was reported. She sent the woman to bring two cups and a flagon and sat down to wait.

Her mother arrived, escorted by Ranulf de Glanville, who had overall custody of the heiresses in the Tower. Isabelle had no liking for the man and neither did her mother, for he was not of their affinity and not to be trusted. However, her mother was always courteous and brought him gifts of money or jewels or fine cloth to satisfy his avid desire for such things – as she said, it served to open doors.

Aoife thanked de Glanville with charm but made it clear she wished to be alone with Isabelle. He gave her a wary look, born of experience but bowed and left, a fat pouch of silver tied to his belt.

"Mother!" Isabelle rose and the women embraced each other tightly.

"Ah," Aoife said. "You are taller than me now – you have your father's height, aye, and his eyes – all the colours of the sea my beautiful girl – now a woman." A look of pain crossed her mother's face. "Are they treating you well?" She stared round the chamber at the furnishings and as her gaze lit on the wooden horse in its niche, her jaw tightened.

Isabelle saw the look. Her mother had endured the struggle, sorrow and dark, debilitating bitterness. At times she had sought oblivion in the wine jug. Her world had turned black when she lost Gilbert. She had emerged from that grief scoured to the bone, living for the fight, staying strong and indomitable. And Isabelle had witnessed it all and sworn never to be like that.

"I have everything I need," Isabelle said. "Master Glanville is kind."

Her mother raised her brows. "You should not mistake duty for kindness," she said, "and you should not trust Master Glanville because he can be bought. You have everything you need except your freedom and the execution of will."

"Yes Mama," Isabelle said, and saw her mother's eyes narrow. She quickly poured her a cup of wine. Aoife set it on the coffer after a single sip, and folded her hands. "I am returning to Ireland until the autumn," she said. "It is a long time since I saw our Irish kin, and I need to discover what is happening, but before I go, I have to speak of your marriage."

Isabelle's eyes widened with a mingling of surprise and fear. Ireland was so far from London and even if she and her mother had been separated, it had never been by long distances and oceans. And marriage, although it had always loomed like a shadow, it had been some time in the future – until now.

"The king has written to me with details of the men he is considering," Aoife said. "I can do nothing to influence him and I do not know any of these men well, even the ones I have met at court." She set her lips. "I have to be glad that he has even seen fit to inform me, for it is often his way not to do so on such matters. I have no notion of who they truly are. Whoever is chosen, you must depend only on yourself, not them – for they will let you down. They always do."

"What does the king say?" Isabelle asked, and bit her lip.

Aoife picked up her wine again. "He writes to assure me he will do his best for you – as he thinks. Hah!" She took a large swallow.

"Who is he considering?" *Dear God, not some old man with coarse whiskers and sour breath.*

"Andrew de Chauvigny," her mother said. "A man of high birth, Queen Alienor's cousin, and supposedly a strong soldier, but he is of Poitou." She waved her hand dismissively.

Isabelle shook her head. "I do not know him." She most certainly did not want to go and dwell in Poitou.

"William fitz Reinfred." Her mother shrugged impatiently. "He is not of sufficient standing for you. You are a jewel, not to be bestowed lightly for reward. I have always made that clear to the king."

"I do not know him either, Mama."

"Then there is the king's own son, John, Count of Mortain."

Isabelle drew back in revulsion. "No!"

"He is lord of Ireland and heir to the throne after Richard," Aoife said shrewdly. "You should think on him well. It may be that such a match will allow you to return to your homeland."

"No," Isabelle said again and shuddered. "He... he has visited us in the Tower – the heiresses that is. He

98

touches us when he thinks no one is looking and presses himself against us. If I married him, I would sleep with a knife under my pillow I swear. He may be the king's son, but he is not worthy and the price is too high." She looked at her mother who was regarding her with her head on one side and a thoughtful look on her face. "Surely you do not think I would be well-matched with him!"

Aoife pursed her lips. "His father has designated him to rule Ireland," she said. "And you cannot rise higher than wedding a prince. I had to marry your father in order to secure his aid for my father, and I did my duty."

"But you loved my father..." Isabelle gave her mother a hard stare, fearful that she would reply in the negative, but still having to say the words.

"At times," Aoife said. "And look where it got me. He was like all men and it was what he wanted that mattered – and that will be true whoever you wed."

"Well, I pray that it will not be the king's son, John," Isabelle said, "and I hope that even with the practical reasons for such a match, you would not push me to it."

Her mother gave her a considering look. "No," she said at length, "I would not, but I ask you still to consider it, for it may well come to be."

Isabelle shivered. "Is there anyone else you want to add to that list, or is that it?"

"William the Marshal," her mother said with a dismissive shrug. "He has little land to speak of – a small estate in the north, but he is an accomplished courtier and soldier. I met him at court when your father was alive. I do not know why the king would choose him except for his loyal service and military skill. He is not your match in bloodline and estates."

"I thought he was going to wed Heloise of

Lancaster," Isabelle replied. "I met him when he came to escort her to her lands in Kendal."

"Well clearly he has his eyes on a bigger prize than that." Her mother's green eyes sharpened. "You are blushing," she said. "Beware of ambitious men, my girl, especially the ones with reputations at court. You are worth far more than a means to an end for some soldier climbing fortune's ladder."

"I know that, Mama."

"I shall write to the king, reminding him of obligation and friendship. He will not act until he returns to England, but we must be diligent, and you must know your worth, my daughter. Ask what these men have to offer in return for their right to have you and your land. What do they bring of value to the marriage? What lands do they have? What wealth and ties of influence? Are they worthy of your attention? What gain is there to yourself? And you must phrase your questions in ways acceptable to the king so it does not seem that you are challenging him."

"Yes, Mama," Isabelle said, recognising anew what a formidable woman her mother was, and of course, she was right.

Aoife gave her a penetrating look. "Might your husband be trusted with such high status? Might his character be weak or flawed so that he fails to protect you and your estates? You need someone who has power enough to fulfil his office and serve you but not one who will take it into his own hands and use it as a weapon against you. He should be in his prime and give you strong, healthy children for your succession."

Isabelle's flush deepened and Aoife nodded. "Yes, you must consider that too. It will be your duty to lie with him and bear children from his seed and yours. We need to provide heirs who will be trustworthy in the eyes of the king. That too must be emphasised, for not all sons are loyal to their fathers – including his own – and it is a relevant issue for him. Use it to your utmost but in a reasonable way. Smile and be gentle in your speech but hold firm – use the assets God gave you. You are a rare beauty, but let your mind be rarer still." Aoife slipped a pearl and crystal ring from her finger and presented it to Isabelle. "The king gave this to me in token of his willingness to protect us, and I give it to you now for safekeeping while I am gone."

Isabelle slid the ring onto the middle finger of her left hand. She remembered being a child, sitting in the middle of her mother's bed, trying it on and watching it slide round with a huge gap, but now it was a perfect fit. "I will do as you ask, Mama, and I will take great care," she said seriously.

Aoife embraced her and drew back, a tearful glint in her eyes. "No man will ever be good enough for you," she said, "not even if he is the greatest knight in Christendom. I would keep you with me, that is my wish, but it cannot be. Keep well, I shall write to you when I reach Kilkenny, and you must write to me."

Her mother departed at sunset. She kissed Isabelle tenderly and left in her care meticulous copies of all the documents pertaining to her lands. "Every stick and stitch, every mill, every cow and calf," she said. "This is what you have and I want you to learn it by heart." She pressed a hefty pouch of silver into Isabelle's hand. "This is yours too, from your manors. Show none of your women; keep it well hidden."

Isabelle bade her mother farewell, her heart filled with love and gratitude, and sadness at their parting, but with a kernel of relief too. She needed solitude and time to digest everything Aoife had said. Whatever the future held, she was determined to live up to her mother's courage and strength, her honour and sacrifice.

She paced to her chamber window, still thinking of Ireland. The colours and the memories were dappled green and grey, mossy and soft as light summer rain: the smell of turf fires, the hearts of the Bards in the dark winter halls, and the long summer nights of May and June. She remembered her father swinging her up in his arms and of his beard tickling against her neck while she squealed. And then she blinked to clear her eyes and turned from the window. It was in the past, long gone. Even if she returned, like her mother, it would never be the same, for then she had been a small child running in her smock, and now by her very status she was not allowed to run anywhere.

A few weeks later, Isabelle was sitting at her sewing when the constable's nephew, Theobald Walter, came to visit her in her chamber, and bowed to her with impeccable manners. "My lady, I have come to fetch you to a visitor, who unfortunately cannot climb the stairs at this time."

She regarded him warily. At one time a couple of years ago, he too had been a possible suitor for her hand in marriage, and the constable, Rannulph de Glanville, still harboured that intent. Theobald Walter was in his late prime and handsome with fair curls, cut sternly short. Isabelle knew and liked him, but that did not mean she desired to be his wife. But who knew what the new sovereign had in mind? King Henry had recently died and although his heir, Richard, was still in Normandy, changes were afoot.

"Who is this visitor?" she asked. The person must be important, otherwise an ordinary attendant would have borne the news. Surely not the old king's other son, John, Count of Mortain, although she knew

Theobald Walter was his friend. Why couldn't this visitor climb the stairs? Her mind raced through the various older men who might have reason to visit her in the Tower, but could think of no one.

Theobald Walter's mouth tightened. "Sir William Marshal has arrived with letters from King Richard and Queen Alienor," he said. "Doubtless he will explain himself why he is here."

William Marshal. Isabelle's stomach swirled with emotion. She had met him three years ago when he had come to take her heiress friend Heloise of Kendal to her holdings in the north of England, having been granted her wardship. Isabelle had expected him to marry her, but he hadn't. And now he was here. She thought back on what her mother had said, and it did not ease her anxiety.

Her maids in tow, Isabelle followed Theobald Walter from her quarters to a public chamber. Her heart was pounding but there was no time to compose herself. The door was already open and she was ushered straight into the presence of William Marshal. He was leaning against a trestle table but he pushed himself upright as she entered the room. Vaguely she took in the detail that he had two squires with him, a couple of knights, and a clerk. Feeling acute apprehension, she met his composed dark stare.

"If I were you, Marshal, I would be quick about the matter," said Theobald Walter. "My uncle is about his business elsewhere this morning, but he will soon return, and may prove reluctant to release the lady into your keeping, even with the orders you bear."

The knight's calm gaze left Isabelle's and focused on Theobald Walter. "Is that by way of threat, or just friendly advice?" he enquired.

Theobald Walter shrugged, his gaze equally unruffled. "You do not know me well, my lord, or you would not ask such a question. It is not my way to threaten, and I have no quarrel with you. My uncle's ambition brought me to court and as you know, a man has to make the best of the opportunities he is given, but I am not a fool to go against the will of a king." An acerbic smile curved his lips. "And especially not the will of a queen. I do not believe my uncle Ranulf will go against it either, but it would still be wise not to linger." He nodded in salutation, went to the door, and on the threshold turned. "I hope you will remember my goodwill in times to come. I wish you both well."

Isabelle looked at William, feeling shaky. If Theobald Walter was wishing them well, then it could only be for one reason.

"My lady," he said. "Will you be seated?" He indicated one of the benches at the side of the room.

His assumption that she needed to be seated made Isabelle feel contrary. "Thank you, messire," she said, "but I would rather stand and face you."

"Then perhaps we should both sit. It would certainly be more comfortable for me." He limped heavily to the bench. "An accident while boarding the ship for England," he said with a wave of his hand. "I may be an old warhorse, but I am usually sound of wind and limb." He eased himself carefully down and she saw his eyes tighten with pain.

Since it would have been ungracious to continue standing, Isabel reluctantly followed suit, glad that the full skirts of her gown prevented him from seeing that her own legs were trembling. She made herself meet his gaze. Fine lines were etched at the corners of his eyes as if he smiled a lot. Their colour was that of a dark, winter sea.

"My lady, I do not know if you remember me; my visit to the Tower was brief then, and we met for a few minutes only."

"Yes, I do remember," Isabelle said. "You came for Heloise, and I thought you were going to marry her."

"I thought so too, but matters changed."

He had a pleasant voice, neither high nor deep, but well-modulated and without any particular accent unlike her own which bore the cadences of her Irish childhood and her life among the Welsh. "Heloise wrote to me and said that you were not of a mind to wed her."

"Did she?" He raised an eyebrow but did not seem particularly disturbed. "I know that she wrote to you; she told me herself, but I never asked what she had the scribe write. It seemed to me that she was entitled to a little privacy."

Isabelle eyed him, uncertain whether to approve or feel slighted. Giving a little privacy sounded suspiciously like placating a potentially fractious child with a sweetmeat, yet, having lived without privacy of late, such a gesture felt like consideration beyond price.

"I dare say if I had married her, we would have tolerated each other's failings – either that or driven each other mad and settled for different households once our heirs were begotten. I'm still fond of her and I hope she remembers me with a smile too." He studied Isabelle. "In truth, for some time, my mind has been set on a greater prize."

Isabelle stiffened. "Heloise's northern lands must pale in comparison to the estates that come through me," she said.

"I was offered Denise de Chateauroux instead of the lady Heloise, but I refused because I knew what I wanted, and had wanted ever since I laid eyes on you."

Her face grew hot. He was a courtier; such words came easily to him. Any landless knight would desire her for the lands and prestige she brought, irrespective of her person. "And if Heloise had been the lady of Striguil?" she asked.

He spread his hands and she noticed that his fingernails were clean and that he wore more rings than a soldier, but fewer than a court dandy. "Then we would have learned to live with each other. I may have a few romantic bones in my body, but not enough to overthrow reason – however one always hopes for the best of both worlds."

"And what of me?" Isabelle asked. "What choice do I have?"

"How pragmatic are your own bones my lady? You have no choice in the matter of your marriage, even if the church pays lip service to the fact that you do. Your lands and yourself have been entrusted into my keeping. You can make the best of matters, or shroud yourself in martyrdom."

Isabelle returned his stare and then lowered her lids. The offer was better than remaining here and, as he said, she had no choice in the matter. "I do not know you," she said, "nor you me."

"That is a remedy for which I have no cure except time, my lady. I swear to you that I will treat you with all the honour and deference due to your rank, if you will do the same for me as your husband."

Isabelle tried to steady her panic by breathing slowly. "I do not know how pragmatic my own bones are," she said, "but I will try."

He was careful to exhale without making a sound, but she saw the long movement of his chest and realised that he too was under considerable strain, although he was better at concealing it. "Thank you," he said, and, pushing to his feet reached his hand to her. She saw the beads of sweat on his brow and the way he held himself. She didn't want to put her hand in his, for then he would know how frightened she was, and her mother said that one should never show fear in the face of challenge. Soon it would be more than just the joining of hands. Thinking swiftly, she laid her hand on his sleeve instead, in the manner of the court, and saw his eyelids tighten, but whether in amusement or displeasure was hard to tell.

"I have a boat waiting; we can go now."

"What about my household and my baggage?"

"How great a household do you have?"

Isabelle pursed her lips. "Two ladies, a chaplain, and a scribe – although they are all in lord Glanville's employ, not mine."

He nodded. "Do you wish to keep them?"

She shook her head. "Not if I can have the choosing of others."

"It is for you to say and order your own household as you desire."

Isabelle felt a stirring in her solar plexus as if some part of her that had gone to sleep in chains was now awakening and discovering that its fetters had vanished. "Then I will have new people of my own," she said. "My baggage will fit in one coffer."

"Then let it be forwarded."

"Is such haste necessary? Am I truly in danger?"

"Not you, my lady, no," William said, "but I would be happier to be away from this place and among friends. If you have no objection to leaving immediately, then I would like us to be on our way."

It was a command couched as a polite and deferential request. Isabel noted it and wondered what would happen if she baulked and said that she wanted to supervise her own packing and that she was going nowhere with him. Not that she had any intention of doing so. She was the key to his wealth and status, but he was her key to freedom from this place.

"No," she said, lifting her chin. "I have no objection."

William handed Isabel down into the barge. The weedy smell of the river was strong in her nostrils and the water lapped against the vessel's sides in small green tongues that occasionally burst in a white saliva of spray. He had lent her his cloak, for although it was a bright summer's day, the wind off the river was stiff. She seated herself on one of the benches along the barge's side and watched him gingerly do the same. Behind them, the Tower was a great lime-washed bulwark and it was the sight of the massive walls rather than the breeze of the water that made her shiver and hug the cloak around her body.

"Cold?" he asked solicitously.

Isabelle stroked Damask, who had curled at her feet, and shook her head. "Some walls protect, and some imprison," she said. "I have dwelt here for more than four years, but it has never been my home – I have been in exile."

"So have I, for the longest time." He looked at her. "There are always places of the heart, but if we journey well together, we need never have to be in exile again."

A piece of waterlogged wood bobbed away from them on the opaque water. Isabel eyed it and thought that she could drift aimlessly and let fate take her where it would, or she could be a passenger in a boat with this man and steer a true course in partnership, and it would be her choice to do so. Neither of them need be ruled by their past and the experience of others, but they could make their own way. When you had a water-tight ship, you could sail anywhere.

She returned his look. "Then let us go home," she said.

❧ ❧ ❧

Read about Aoife in *The Irish Princess* and more about Isabelle and William Marshal in *The Scarlet Lion*, by Elizabeth Chadwick.

*The Irish Princess:*
UK Amazon:
https://www.amazon.co.uk/gp/product/B07JN2RW2X/
US Amazon:
**https://www.amazon.com/Irish-Princess-Elizabeth-Chadwick/dp/0751565016/**
*The Scarlet Lion:*
UK Amazon:
**https://www.amazon.co.uk/gp/product/B002TXZT48/**
US Amazon:
**https://www.amazon.com/Scarlet-Lion-William-Marshal-Book-ebook/dp/B0039VH38O?**

## ABOUT ELIZABETH CHADWICK

New York Times bestselling author Elizabeth Chadwick lives in a cottage in the Vale of Belvoir in Nottinghamshire with her husband and their four terriers, Pip, Jack, Billy and Little Ted. Her first novel, *The Wild Hunt*, won a Betty Trask Award and *To Defy a King* won the RNA's 2011 Historical Novel Prize. She was also shortlisted for the Romantic Novelists' Award in 1998 for *The Champion*, in 2001 for **Lords of the White Castle**, **in 2002 for *The Winter Mantle* and in 2003 for *The Falcons of Montabard*.** Her sixteenth novel, *The Scarlet Lion*, was nominated by Richard Lee, founder of the Historical Novel Society, as one of the top ten historical novels of the last decade. She often lectures at conferences and historical venues, has been consulted for television documentaries and is a member of the Royal Historical Society.

"An author who makes history come gloriously alive."
*The Times*

≁ ≁ ≁

Website: **https://elizabethchadwick.com/**
Book list: **https://elizabethchadwick.com/books-list/**
(Available from Amazon and other online stores or order from any bookshop.)

## 6

# THE PAST, MY FUTURE

## BY LORETTA LIVINGSTONE

**JULY 2042**

In sight of the ruins of Sparnstow Abbey stood a huge, spreading beech tree. Dawn was a mere glimmer on the horizon, dimly outlining the man who stood in the dark shadows of its branches. He was in his early fifties by appearance, brown beard, grizzled with red and grey, head covered with a cap. He wore a tunic of forest green, some kind of brown leggings, and a grey woollen cloak and looked out of place for the time he was in. Next to him, a covered cart harnessed to a sturdy mule which they were lucky to have been able to buy. There weren't many around, apart from those belonging to folks who had gone back to the old ways and lived off grid. Beyond him, three women stood close; two around middle-age, the third much older. One of the younger women wore a pair of worn cargo pants and a dark t-shirt while the other two wore long dresses in muted shades, their hair caught up into single braids.

"My darling Chloe, I'm going to miss you." There was a catch in the oldest woman's voice as she embraced the woman in cargo pants. A tear slid, unheeded, down her face.

"Me, too, Mum. More than I can say. But at least, at Sparnstow, I'll know you're alive!"

The third woman hugged her sister. "Chlo, are you sure? Won't you come with us?"

Chloe shook her head. "I can't, Shan. It's not my world. It's never going to be. And I want my world back. Ray and I, we're going to fight to make it right again. You know that."

"But it's not safe."

"Safer for me than you three. Mum can't stay, anyway, and neither can you. I'd rather know you're alive back in those times than Mum dead and you and Craig in a punishment block. And," Chloe sniffed, wiping her eyes on the back of her hand, "at least we can stay in touch. Well, as long as that tree of yours works. Your portal to the past."

"I suppose."

The older woman chimed in, "It will. It worked for years before. Can you not hear the buzzing? It's started already."

Chloe disentangled herself and gave the other two a gentle shove. "Go on, then. I must get back before I'm missed. Stay safe. Write! If you can find something to write on. You can push it through the tree. I'll check around the roots once a month on a Sunday at ten if I'm able. You did pack paper?"

The older woman nodded and gave her another hug, then Shan – Shannon – tugged her away, gave her sister one last embrace, and turned towards the man by the beech. Both women pulled on head coverings, enveloping their hair and necks, and hastily pinned veils to them. Shannon reached for her mother's hand, took her husband's, and with Craig leading the mule, they walked towards the tree. Craig had stiffened his back and trod purposefully, but the steps of the two women lagged a little as though their feet were reluctant to take them further.

As they moved away, the mother called back to Chloe, "If it all goes wrong... Try to join us. I'm sure it will work for you, too. It seems to recognise our family."

Chloe nodded, dashing away the tears that would not stop. As the trio reached the tree, a buzzing filled her head, gnawing at her teeth, her eyes, her tongue. She put her hands to her ears, never taking her gaze from the three figures and the mule in front of her. As she watched, they walked into the tree, one by one, each turning, hands upraised in farewell, faded, and were gone.

She held her breath, waiting to see if the cart would follow them through. Would it fit? It did. As it disappeared, she dropped to the ground, overcome with loss and pain, great wrenching sobs racking her body, control momentarily lost. But she didn't have the luxury to fall apart. She took a deep breath to calm herself, then got slowly to her feet and walked away.

## JULY 1227

Just after dawn, three travellers, a merchant and his wife accompanied by an older woman, approached the gates of Sparnstow Abbey. The man halted the mule he was leading, and the younger woman reached for him, her fingers twitching convulsively as they clasped at his tunic sleeve. He placed his arm around her shoulders and gratefully, she shrank into his solid comfort.

"I'm scared, Craig – I mean Will. What if there's no one here who remembers me?"

"*You're* scared?" He gave her a reassuring grin. "I'm

the one who should be scared. You've done this before." He turned to the older woman. "You too, Marion. I'm the novice here."

Shannon shook her head. "Not like this. Last time, it was no more than a game. I had safety nets. This time it matters. And don't forget to call me Rohese, not Shannon. Even in your thoughts. Shannon and Craig are gone. We always have to think Will and Rohese, otherwise we'll slip up. Last time, it didn't matter if I made mistakes. This time, it could cost us dear."

"Well, it's done now... *Rohese*. Come on, let's get it over with." He raised his hand to knock.

Marion caught his sleeve. "Not your hand. Use your staff."

He nodded and struck it against the thick oak. Beside him, Rohese winced at the hollow noise. A grille opened in the wicket set within the gates.

"That's new," Rohese murmured as a pair of eyes peered out at them.

"Who seeks entry?" The voice demanded, yet Rohese sensed the speaker was smiling.

"The merchant, William of the Bolohoveni, his wife, Rohese, and her mother, Marion."

Craig's – no, Will! She must get this right. Will's voice sounded confident as he answered, probably more confident than he really felt. The face at the grille disappeared and the wicket creaked on its hinges as it swung open. A robust middle-aged nun stood before them, beaming a snaggle-toothed welcome.

"Oh, you have a wain. I'm sorry, I didn't see. Wait and I'll open the gates. It won't fit through here."

Before either Will or Rohese could say anything, she'd disappeared back inside and unlatched the gates, pushing them wide. "Enter and be welcome. Have you come far? I'm Sister Bertrade. Come in, come in. Brother Anselm!" She waited a moment, then raised her voice. "Brother Anselm? Where is that man? Oh, I'll take your mule. Help me unhitch the beast."

Bemused, Rohese stood back and let Will unhitch the mule. This was not quite the Sparnstow she'd known when Hildegarde was abbess, but although the grille and the wicket were new, the atmosphere seemed the same. Her shoulders relaxed as the tension drained out of them.

As Sister Bertrade turned to lead the mule away, a stout brother came bustling up, his habit awry, the wispy grey hair around his tonsure sticking out like dandelion fluff. "Sister, let me take the mule."

Sister Bertrade faced him, hands on hips. "And where were you when I needed you, Brother?"

"Just in the stable. I could hear you perfectly well. Come now, calm yourself, Sister. You look less like a nun and more like an alewife when you bristle up like that."

Sister Bertrade made a noise that could have been a snort and turned back to Will. "If you'll wait while I close these gates, I'll take you to the guest quarters."

Before Rohese could open her mouth, Marion asked the question that she'd been about to frame. "Who is the abbess here now?"

Sister Bertrade studied her with an interested air. "You've been here before, then, Mistress?"

"Yes, but not in your time. Sister Berthe was porteress back then."

"Sister Berthe? That's many a year ago, Mistress. Back in the lady Hildegarde's day, of blessed memory. Lady Etheldreda is our abbess now."

"Etheldreda." Rohese's voice was a gasp of relief. "Oh, I hope she'll remember me."

Bertrade's mouth turned up into a grin, her eyes creased into mere slits. "Abbess Etheldreda remembers everything, as many a novice has discovered to her dismay. She'll remember you if she's once met you. Forget the guest quarters, they can wait. If you know her, I can take you straight to her. Come, Master, Dames." She held her hand out, gesturing them to follow her, and led them through the abbey grounds.

As they passed through the infirmary herb garden, if that's what it still was, several nuns picking flowerheads and leaves paused, watching the newcomers. One of them, a thin woman with bright eyes and a smiling face suddenly darted towards Rohese and stood gazing at her, head on one side, eyes studying her intently. A vague sense of recognition tugged at her mind; surely, she knew that face? But thirty years wreak many changes.

The nun stared a moment longer, then exclaimed and caught Rohese's hands in her thin fingers. "My lady Rohese, can it truly be you?" Her face shone with an almost unearthly radiance, and she dropped Rohese's hands, lifting her own in a gesture of praise as she cried out, "Oh, thanks be to God. Thanks be to our blessed Saviour and His dear Mother for answering my prayers!"

Rohese gaped in astonishment. She couldn't be Sister Aldith, could she? The features were the same, although older, more wrinkled, but transformed by an inner luminosity she certainly hadn't possessed before. Gone the tight lips, the piously lowered eyes and judgemental frown. Here was a woman who glowed. But even as recognition was dawning, Aldith's face crumpled, and two large tears began welling in her eyes before brimming over.

Taken aback, Rohese was still speechless when Aldith knelt before her laughing and crying at the same time, grasping her hands and kissing them. Rohese was appalled. Too self-conscious to tug her hands away, aware of the startled faces of her family and the other nuns, she felt herself burn with embarrassment before pity took over. Falling to her own knees, she put her arms around the sobbing nun. "Sister Aldith, what ails you? What have I done?"

The nun raised her face. Joy radiated from her. "My lady, for thirty years I have asked our dear Lord and His blessed Mother to allow me to beg your forgiveness for the way I wronged you. And see, He has brought you to me at last. Oh, praise His name."

Rohese, uncomfortable and confused, fidgeted, and cast her gaze around; a dumpy nun with eyes the colour of forget-me-nots and a rosy face but stern expression came bustling over. Unlike the other nuns, she wore a large, silver pectoral cross – a symbol of authority. The newcomer's lips quivered slightly for a moment as she watched the tableau playing out before her, eyes widening in surprise, before she appeared to recover herself.

Shooing away the other nuns, who were beginning to cluster about them murmuring to each other, she raised Sister Aldith to her feet, saying in brisk tones, "Yes, indeed, Sister, a true miracle. However, I think it best if you continue this in private. You may use my chambers. Come." And sweeping them all inexorably before her, she chivvied them inside to her suite of rooms and bustled them through the door.

Rohese, still speechless, was unable to think of anything Aldith had done to her. Once inside, Marion held her hands out to the abbess, saying uncertainly, "Etheldreda? Is it really you? This is better than I could have hoped."

The abbess enveloped Marion in a warm embrace before stepping back, eyeing the visitors with disbelief. She gazed at them for a long moment, then, satisfied, her eyes twinkled. "Marion! And Rohese? Truly?" She covered her heart with her hands as though to still it. "Can I really believe what I see?"

She turned to Will, "And you are, good Master?"

He gave her an awkward little bow. "I'm William of the Bolohoveni, my lady. Husband to Rohese."

"Sweet Mary!" The abbess sat down with a bump on a chair beside a large desk, face frozen in an expression of part shock, part pleasure.

Aldith, still glowing, indicated to the others to be seated on the long settle against the wall which Rohese remembered so well, pulled up a stool and sat before her, and for a moment, there was an awed silence. Aldith was the only one who seemed to take everything in her stride.

At last, Rohese managed to find her voice. "But I don't understand. What did you do?"

"My lady, I used you most shamefully. At first, I judged you. Your strange arrival, your different speech and customs. And then the squire, Adam his name was, drew me to one side."

*Adam?* Rohese cringed.

Aldith flushed to the top of her wimple. "He told me he had received a divine visitation from our blessed Virgin. He said she had laid her hands upon his head and told him she had sent you to be a bride to him." She shook her head, her face crimson. "Little fool that I was, I believed him. I cannot understand why I should have, but, ah, he was so handsome."

Rohese shot an embarrassed glance at Will, who was grinning at her discomfort, and Aldith continued.

"And so convincing. He told me of the times our Lord's Mother had come to him and described his future wife. I must have been out of my senses, but God forgive me, I did believe him."

Rohese took Aldith's hands. "But that was Adam all over. He was convincing. Where I come from, we'd have called him a conman – a trickster – amongst other things."

"But it was worse than that," Aldith said. "I aided him in his pursuit of you."

Ah! Now it made sense. That explained why Adam had been able to find her each time she'd been alone and to slip away seconds before anyone discovered them. "But, Sister Aldith, you are so much changed. I never would have recognised you."

Aldith smiled. "That is both to my joy and to my shame, my lady. I was in despair after your abduction, and I begged our dear Abbess Hildegarde to beat me and imprison me."

She paused as though gathering her thoughts. "I had been a bride of Christ for several years, but I still did not understand His grace and kindness. Abbess Hildegarde taught me that repentance cannot be whipped into us. She showed me the only way to find true forgiveness was to offer up my sin to Him and believe that He had cleansed me. And, oh, the joy when I came to know Him more perfectly. Now, I feel His love more strongly in me every day. All my petty jealousies, my unkind judgements, my meanness – I lay them on His altar daily, and I allow Him to fill me with His great love."

If her face had been radiant before, now something shone from her so strongly, Rohese could almost see light emanating from her. If she'd ever had her doubts about God, seeing the change in this nun would have convinced her.

A discreet cough came from Etheldreda. "Yes, indeed, Sister Aldith, a true miracle, it seems." She shook her head as Aldith gave her a slightly reproachful look. "No, not the change in you, Sister, dear, although we certainly rejoiced in that. But that Marion and Rohese have come back to us." She put her head on one side, eyeing them like a bright robin. "But why, might I ask? And for how long? For this is not entirely unexpected; although, I confess, I did not honestly believe it would happen. But Abbess Hildegarde, of blessed memory, foresaw it."

Marion nodded. "I know. She sent me a note." She fumbled in the pouch that hung at her waist and pulled out a worn page of parchment plus a second, smaller piece. "Hildegarde wrote this to me and enclosed a copy in your own scribing for you. She said you'd not be able to read the version she wrote for me. Here." She held out the larger of the two.

Etheldreda, with a hand that trembled slightly, took it, cleared her throat, and with a voice that was not quite steady read aloud.

*"Dearest Marion,*

*When you receive this, you will know King John has gone. It is also most likely that I, myself, will have passed into the hereafter, for I do not think I will long outlive him. Know that to have spent time with you and Rohese, or Shannon as she is in your time, was an unlooked for and most treasured gift for which I daily thank our Lord.*

*I know not why I write the next words – haply it is merely the wandering wits of the old woman I have become. And yet, there may be cause. I feel our Lord has impressed on me that, before the end of your own natural years, a danger may come to your time – a danger which may threaten you and your family. I urge you, if that should happen, to consider whether your future may lie in the past.*

*If my words have any resonance in your heart, it may be wise to prepare yourself in any way you deem best. Whether or no, dear child, I pray we shall meet again one day in the presence of Him to whom my heart belongs. Make wise decisions and pray often, my dear, and know I have done my best to ensure you will find both welcome and succour at the abbey when you use my name.*

*I remain your loving cousin, for I know you have discovered our relationship by now.*

*Hildegarde (Doreen Suttoner)"*

Again, a silence fell, and more than one hand surreptitiously wiped away a tear. Etheldreda was the first to find her voice.

"Our dear abbess told me a little of this before she passed. I took a sacred vow that you would always find a welcome and a sanctuary with us."

She looked down, but not before Rohese had seen the sparkle of moisture on her face. After a moment, she raised her head, smiling. "And a joy and a privilege it is for me to meet you both again. And, of course, your husband, Rohese." She inclined her head towards Will who looked as though he'd swallowed his tongue. "I trust you will come to know us as well as your wife and her mother do. We have no entire guest houses available; however, we do have a large room. I assume you would wish to stay together until a guest house becomes available?"

Will nodded, awkward in this company of religious women. Etheldreda picked up a small handbell and went to the door, ringing it vigorously; a nun came hurrying to her summons.

"Ah, Sister Felice, ask Sister Hospitaller to prepare our largest chamber, please, but wait an instant." She turned back to Will. "You brought your goods with you? I believe I saw Brother Anselm with a cart?"

He nodded again.

"Then, should you wish to help him offload your belongings?" Without waiting for an answer, she said, "Sister, you will please take Master William to Brother Anselm. He will help transfer their belongings to the guest chamber."

The nun smiled at Will, indicating he should follow her, and Etheldreda closed the door, saying with a knowing look, "I think your husband will be more comfortable if we find him something to do, do you not, Rohese?"

Marion chuckled as Rohese answered. "Thank you, Abbess. He looked like a spare part standing there."

"What can you expect, Rohese? You've brought him to a nunnery." Marion grinned at Etheldreda's puzzled expression. "She means out of place," she said to the abbess, whose eyes twinkled at the explanation.

"An apt description. I find men are often taken that way in a women's domain. Now, let us settle you into your quarters, and then, you can tell me your story and why you are here."


## MAY 1228

Somewhere, a bell was ringing. Marion opened her eyes to an unfathomable darkness, pierced only by a few candles in places where shadowy figures were rising from their cots, yawning.

Although she loved the companionship of the sisters, communal sleeping was not so easy to adjust to, especially for a light sleeper. Feeling as though she'd only just dozed off, she waited for the fog to clear from her brain. It took longer, these days, to remember where she was and why, and she lay motionless as her world settled. The sad truth: one day, she would not remember at all. It was why she had urged Will and Rohese to move from the abbey and make lives for themselves. Thank God she had met Giles de Soutenay all those years ago and discovered he was kin to them. And thank God, too, that Rohese had made her own separate journey to the past and established her relationship with him and his wife, Isabella. It had given them a place to start from, kin to give them a background and home. Such a relief that Rohese had been able to birth her babe safely. That had been their biggest fear, given her age, but what had been the alternative? They couldn't have stayed in their own time. How on earth she'd even fallen pregnant so late in her life was a wonder.

Marion heaved a sigh of distress. One day, likely she would not remember them, either. But for now... Ah, for now, she would see them often, enjoy the babe and enjoy her work here at the abbey. For the time being, she could keep the demon of dementia at bay. It was barely noticeable, yet she knew it lurked like a spectre in the background. Whether she would take her vows, she did not yet know. She could remain at the cott assigned to her if she preferred, but it was lonely there now Will and Rohese were gone, and she liked being with the lay sisters. It made her feel useful, gave her a sense of family. Not yet a postulant but helping in any way she could – and there were many ways she could assist them – Etheldreda had taken the unusual step of letting her share the lay sisters' dormitory.

One of the figures approached and touched her lightly on the shoulder. "Marion? Marion? Are you awake? Time for Matins."

Marion focused her eyes on the pale oval face that peered down at her and recognition flickered. Sister Amicia, the most senior of the lay sisters. Marion sat up and swung her legs over the side of her low bed, pushing her feet into her soft, wool night boots, and reached for her loose over-garment and veil that the sisters wore for their night-time prayer.

Amicia waited as she stood, then held her candle out and moved ahead, lighting the way to the night stairs huddled in the corner of the dortoir which led down to the abbey. Marion caught up another freshly lit candle and followed.

During Matins, as the voices of the nuns in the quire rose in pure notes – all except for the flat tones of Sister Agnes, who, fortunately, sang quiet enough to barely be heard – Marion's sleep-tousled mind began to wander. She pinched herself to stay alert and awake. What time would it be? Two? Three in the morning? Would she ever get used to these nocturnal sessions? When the service of worship at last drew to a close, she followed the other sisters back to the dortoir, tumbled into her bed and slept until dawn.

Later that day, on a rare trip out of the abbey to the stream nearby, which had been partly diverted to feed the fish pools, Marion creaked herself upright, pushing her fists against her aching back muscles as she gazed around her. Aldith was busy supervising the young nuns harvesting watercress for the abbey's nostrums. Aldith might be the infirmeress now, but from what Marion had heard when they'd arrived, it seemed her past had been somewhat chequered.

She must have changed much since then; she exuded wisdom and good sense now. And how could Marion hold it against Aldith when Rohese should never have come here in the first place? But oh, thank God she had or maybe Hildegarde would have forgotten about them. And thank God for the letter Hildegarde had managed to get to her to assure her of welcome.

Most of the water flowed briskly, swirling around her feet before it burbled its way downstream, but in a spot just ahead of her, there was a place where it stilled. Out of curiosity, Marion waded over and peered into the calm surface; she'd not seen her face reflected in a mirror for months. A stranger eyed her solemnly back – an old woman, skin puckered around her lips, no make-up, hair scraped back beneath the severe wimple she wore. *At least I'll have no more bad hair days.* She suppressed a giggle.

What was she doing here? She wiggled a loose tooth with her tongue. How long before she lost it? There were no dentists here, and no dentures or floss, either; although, she'd brought some cotton thread to use. And oh, how she longed for Tom, her husband. An inadvertent whimper escaped her, and she cuffed roughly at eyes gone suddenly moist.

Oh, but she was a fool. Tom was no more; killed 'legally' by a government gone mad, his only crime that he had lived past the seventy years allotted by law. And if she'd not escaped, she'd have been dead by now, too. Much as she hated looking her age, it was better to be a living old crone here than a corpse there. And here, Rohese's babe would have a chance to be brought up in relative freedom, always assuming the prevailing diseases spared the child.

And how glad she was Chloe had joined them at last. The fear of her daughter dying in the future while the remainder of the family were in the past had haunted her. Although, of course, she must remember to call her Eleanor. But Eleanor's sadness, the loss of her husband, was hard for Marion herself to bear, too.

Someone nudged her, and she half turned to see Aldith regarding her with a worried air.

"Are you wearied, Marion? Should you like to sit and rest yourself?"

"Maybe for just a short while, Sister. My back aches, but I'm glad I came." She gestured towards where a beech tree had, until recently, stood alone in a clearing. She climbed out of the clear chalk stream and sat on the bank, her feet still in the water, her basket resting on her lap.

Aldith perched beside her, her own basket almost overflowing with watercress.

"It seems so long ago when I first travelled to this time. I never dreamed I'd end up dwelling here."

The infirmeress smiled and nodded. "We can never know where God, in His mercy, will take us. But you are happy here, Marion? Was your decision to stay with us the right one?"

"Mostly. There are things I miss. Things I can't believe I could survive without." She gave a wry grin before adding, "But here, I can live out my life." Marion put her head on one side, considering. "And here, too, like Abbess Hildegarde, I've found a peace I never expected."

"You didn't want to stay with Rohese and Will?"

Marion shook her head. "And when I lose my mind, as we both know will happen, burden them with my care? No, I want them to be free from that. The adjustment is hard enough for them."

Sister Aldith tilted her head. "Was it so very different where you came from? Forgive me if I probe too much, but I cannot imagine how your life must have been."

Marion smiled, her eyes still fixed on the site of the beech tree. "I can't begin to explain. It would sound like paradise, yet it had become a hell. We had food you couldn't dream of, medicines to treat so many ailments that will kill you here, fruits from all over the world. We could travel to other lands in hours, not weeks. We had such easy bathing facilities. And tea and chocolate. Oh, how I miss those. But it all turned sour. Everything went horribly wrong with the whole world. We'd abused it for so long. Weather patterns changed – floods and famines, terrible temperature changes, droughts."

Aldith wrinkled her brow. "But Marion, we have all these things here."

"You do, yes, but not like we had in the future. Our world, there, is dying."

Aldith gaped, seemingly lost for words. Marion noted it but continued. "And on top of that, we were outside of the law, not because we'd done wrong but because the law turned against us. Here, they can't find us; we're safe. And somehow, it feels as though it was always meant to be."

"And Eleanor? Do you think she will decide to take her vows?"

For a moment, Marion's brow furrowed, then she said, "Oh, Eleanor. I still forget that's what she calls herself now. I still think of her as Chloe most of the time." She saw the concern in Aldith's expression. "No, that's not the dementia, Sister. I knew her for most of her life as Chloe. Rohese was always Shannon to me, of course, but I've had longer to get used to her new name. But I used their original names for nigh on fifty years. Is it any wonder I sometimes forget?"

Aldith laughed. "I suppose not. And Eleanor may return from visiting her sister soon. It will be your blessing to have her here to care for you."

Marion grimaced. "It will not! What mother wants their child to watch their deterioration? I'd rather she met someone else while she stays with Rohese and found the chance to marry again."

She saw pity cross Aldith's face once more as the nun hesitated, then spoke. "It's unlikely, Marion. A woman of her age with no connections and no fortune..."

"I know it. But maybe she'll meet a nice widower.

He doesn't have to be a knight. A craftsman or farmer would do once she's over the loss of her Raymond."

"God's will be done." Aldith looked at the sky. "It grows late. Come, Marion, it's time to return to the abbey. I must gather our young sisters." She rose and turned to give Marion a hand.

Marion leaned heavily on Aldith as she struggled to rise. Dratted arthritis. She hooked her basket over her arm, then caught Aldith's sleeve. "Before we go, do you mind if I wander over there?" She pointed in the direction where the beech tree had once stood.

Aldith's eyes widened. "You're not...?"

Marion laughed. "Don't worry, Sister Aldith. I don't think I could, even if I wanted to. Not now it's been destroyed."

"Then go, by all means. I will wait for you here."

Marion nodded and set off past the copse to the site where, for so many centuries, the old beech had stood alone. Her limbs had loosened again now she was on flat ground, and walking always eased her back. As she approached, she trod more warily, for there had been magic here, of a sort. She could not afford to be whisked back to her old life.

But all was silent. There was no buzz, no vibration, just a blackened stump. She stood, lost in thought, gazing into the distance of her old life, more than eight hundred years in the future.

She jumped as an arm crept round her waist and she turned her head to see her eldest daughter, Eleanor. "You're back! I thought you'd be away much longer."

Eleanor kissed her. "It was lovely seeing Rohese and Will, but I've made my decision."

Marion's mouth drooped. "You're sure? Really? This is what you want?"

"*Mm hmm.* I've done too much and seen too much. And now, I just want peace."

Marion stifled a sigh. "Well, if that's what you really want."

"It is." Eleanor smiled, softening the brevity of her words, and the pair of them looked at the stump of the old tree. "What do you suppose happened to it?"

"I don't know. Caught up in the bombing back there, maybe? I feel as though I've lost a friend. But I suppose it doesn't really matter. For us, there was no going back, anyway. Not ever."

"Well, I don't want to. I can be happy here, and I think you can, too. You know, just before I came here, I wrote a poem."

"A poem? You?" Marion's eyes widened.

"Ray had been killed. I was on their wanted list. I'd done my share of killing, too. I had a lot on my mind and no one to tell it to. Want to hear it?"

Marion nodded. Eleanor blushed and cleared her throat "Well, here goes. It's not very good." She paused, took a breath:

> "I must move on, though my soul yearns,
>     for... oh, that hope is vain,
>     to have the life I had once more,
>     but never will again.
>     I gaze upon the distance
>     with many a sigh and tear.
>     The more I want the past, the more
>     the future here seems drear.
>     So, I will turn my gaze away,
>     and weep and sigh no more,
>     but turn my hope to what's beyond
>     and move t'wards that; for sure
>     the past I had is done and gone,
>     and I can only vow
>     to make a thousand times more joy
>     and live life in the now."

Her voice choked on the last words, but the smile she turned towards her mother was radiant.

Marion's eyes blurred with tears. "Chloe, that's beautiful."

Eleanor turned deeper pink, but she didn't say anything else. She held her arm out to Marion, and arm in arm and without looking behind them, the two exiles headed back towards the stream where Aldith and the others waited.

They hadn't noticed that a sapling had started to spring up from the stump of the old tree. And alone in its clearing, had they been listening, they would have heard the faint hum of invisible bees.

© Loretta Livingstone
*Hertfordshire, 2023*

You can read more about the characters in this story in *Out Of Time*, *A Promise to Keep* and *Blossom on the Thorn*.

## ABOUT LORETTA LIVINGSTONE

Loretta had no intention of writing anything but short stories or poetry, and especially not historical fiction. She stated it quite clearly on social media, only to suddenly find herself writing... historical fiction. Her debut novel, *Out Of Time*, set in the mythical Sparnstow Abbey, was shortlisted for the Historical Novel Society Indie Award in 2016, which stunned and elated her in equal measures.

It was supposed to be a one-off. It wasn't. She went on to write two more standalone novels in the series: *A Promise to Keep* and **Blossom on the Thorn**. She had plans for more but has had ME for many years, and ill health has temporarily reined in her gallop. However, she intends to write again soon...

Her other books include short story collections and poetry, and can be found on Amazon.

'The medieval world is nicely described, well researched and the characters, especially the abbess, are entirely believable.' *Discovering Diamonds Reviews.*

Loretta doesn't have a website but find her on Facebook:
**https://www.facebook.com/groups/217686418294125**

Buy Loretta's books on Amazon: **https://geni.us/4621**

## 7

# INTO THE LIGHT

## BY ELIZABETH ST.JOHN

## BOSTON, ENGLAND, SPRING 1636

February's thaw was in full flow, filling the brimming ditches of Lincolnshire's fenlands. Water-laden clouds brooded over the land, spawning a marsh-tainted mist that sank into Boston's alleys and swathed cottage gardens. Today was another grey day; yet as Elizabeth walked the mile from the rectory in Skirbeck to Boston's market, she discovered beauty in the luminous surprise of snowdrops hidden in a tree root's pocket, and the first thrush of the year warbled a piercingly exquisite song of hope. Spring was just around the corner.

Even in the bustling marketplace, the centre of Lincolnshire's thriving wool and leather trade, she found joyful distraction at the herb and curatives stall. Enticed by the aromas, Elizabeth glimpsed fresh ginger and horseradish roots, pungent and tender. She bargained satisfactorily for two starts of each – one to plant and one to cook – until a pealing from St. Botolph's steeple warned her she was late.

Elizabeth counted out precious coin, for a minister's

wife had little housekeeping money, and, clutching her purchases, carefully negotiated the slippery cobbles towards Market Street and the school. The master had expressed horror when she first told him of her desire to formally educate the community's girls, starting with her own seven-year-old stepdaughter. He had been avoiding her since. Only her husband's intervention had secured Elizabeth this meeting to win the schoolmaster's approval and a classroom corner.

A sudden sharp sting on her brow made Elizabeth stumble. An ancient flint arrowhead lay at her feet, pointing accusingly towards her. She was familiar with its chiselled silvery-grey profile, for she loved to collect these old stones that were strewn across East Anglia, remnants of those who had come before. But this was the first time one had struck her. As she stooped to pick it up and fling it back at the sender, returning a taste of their own medicine, a volley of words halted her.

"Zealot!"

"Devil's handmaid!"

"Puritan!"

Jeers from a group of women gathered by the cloth stall inflamed Elizabeth's reaction. Blood now ran down from a cut above her right brow, trickled into the corner of her eye.

Dear God. She may as well be wearing a crown of thorns, such was the copious amount of red on her kerchief as she mopped her forehead. Had Jesus suffered so at the hands of those about to crucify him? And then she scolded herself silently for her blasphemy, comparing her station, a simple preacher's wife, to God's son and man's saviour.

"What did you say? How dare you!" Elizabeth cried out to the women. There was Goodwife Barley and Mistress Robinson, Lady Edgecombe's housekeeper. Women she knew from the congregation. Women she prayed alongside, shared charity in baking bread for the poor together. "How dare you taunt me with these slurs?"

She kicked the stone aside and, pressing the scrap of lace to her bleeding face, strode towards the women. They silently stood their ground, defiant in numbers, as black-clad and threatening as a murder of crows.

"What has made you taunt me so?" Elizabeth repeated. "When only this past week we sat together in my husband's church, mourned for the soul of your baby, Goodwife Barley."

She knew the answer. She just wanted to make them say it. If they had the courage.

"Your husband preaches a gospel of nonconformity. This past Sunday he went far beyond that of the Church's approval." A booted and bonneted woman stepped forward, her fine Suffolk cloak proclaiming her wool merchant husband's riches. "We know you are his amanuensis, scribing his words and making fair copies for distribution. There is no doubt they are your beliefs too."

"And since when is a desire to spread the pure word of God a sin, Mistress Susannah Johnson?" retorted Elizabeth. "Especially if it means disregarding the papist tracts that put priests and preachers ahead of God."

"But you now reject our Anglican ways," the woman replied.

"There is too much *Rome* in our *Anglican* ways." Elizabeth knew this argument of old, for the doctrine of nonconformity was one she'd defended often. But it was the first time someone had struck her for her beliefs. She wiped her brow again, wincing at the torn flesh. "And now, excuse me."

Elizabeth's opponent blocked her path. The woman

was breathing heavily, her stout figure a square block under her expensive cloak.

"'Tis one thing to preach God's word without Rome's influence," said Mistress Johnson. She jabbed her forefinger at Elizabeth, her cheeks reddened and aflame with her passion. "And quite another to stir people to question the authority of England's reformed Church."

The marketplace of Boston was no place to conduct a theological discussion, and on this, of all days, Elizabeth was in no mood to take on the assembled women. She was already anticipating a fight with Schoolmaster Thorn. This dispute only served to stir her up more.

"We do not encourage our congregation to rebel against the Church," Elizabeth replied shortly, torn between hurrying to her appointment and defending her faith. "But we do believe in educating everyone in our community to read for themselves the word of God."

"We! I knew it. You talk as if you are equal to your husband," the woman said triumphantly. "He has no place here. We have heard that he was dismissed from his position in Lynn for his sermons, taking the living at Skirbeck's church as an outcast, relying on his family here in Boston to protect him."

"That is not true," Elizabeth cried. "Samuel's brother may be mayor, but we ask for no special favours."

Susannah Johnson ignored her. "My children do not need to hear his blasphemy. If we speak to our husbands, they will cast him from here too. And then you will be without sponsors, exiled from the community."

"My husband is a truth-teller. Samuel Whiting will always find a pulpit to deliver the word of God."

Elizabeth stared at the woman who had drawn her into this unwanted argument, who until now she had counted as one of her friends. How quickly people turned when fear and ignorance crept like ivy into their minds, choking reason and reckoning.

"A pulpit? Or a prison? Your husband is dangerously close to exchanging one for the other."

Elizabeth snapped. "I regret you fear his words, Susannah Johnson. Does he hold a mirror up to your soul that clouds the glass with your sins of self-deceit? Look to yourself first before you blame others for your deficiencies."

Susannah blinked, and Elizabeth stepped around her, ignoring an indrawn hiss from the other women.

"Puritan." The insult pierced the mist, hovered in the air before her.

Enough.

"Don't you dare question my devotion to God," she shouted as she marched past them towards the schoolmaster's house. "And don't you ever threaten my husband and me again with your passive ignorance and your clumsy stoning. It will take a lot more than your contempt to quell my words."

There. That should quieten their tongues for a bit. Until the next sermon, at least.

She must talk to Samuel before a twisted account of this argument reached him. Her husband would understand she had to defend their beliefs. It was her education as an earl's granddaughter, on par with his Cambridge tutoring, which devised the context of his sermons. But of late, the lectures Samuel preached seemed to stir more dispute than agreement. Perhaps Skirbeck wasn't the haven they had believed it to be.

Elizabeth took a deep breath and prepared for her next battle.

The rhythmic thump of an axe splitting wood echoed from behind the rectory as Elizabeth hurried home. Her pace was also driven by another layer of anger – this time fuelled by the infuriating conversation with the schoolmaster. As she had anticipated, he was completely opposed to girls receiving any formal education other than learning to sew or cook and knowing their letters so they could sign their name. When she had laid before him her dream of a school for young women, equipping them with an education far beyond that of copying the alphabet into their hornbooks, he had shrunk away from her. If he could have had the courage to lift his fingers in the old sign to stave off witches, he would have.

What an ignorant and petty man.

Pulling the ribbons on her bonnet, she ripped it off as soon as she ran through the gate, letting it dangle from her fingers, not caring that it caught on the rosemary hedge that lined the path. She tugged the pins from her hair and gingerly shook it loose, relieving the pain that the combined aggravations of Boston's citizens had induced. Between the welt on her forehead and the injury to her pride, Elizabeth was eager to leave the morning behind.

Her husband was in his sleeves, his cream linen shirt clinging to his chest as he swung the axe on the stump of the old apple tree he was felling. His leather britches moulded to his muscular thighs, and his shoulder-length dark hair was tied back from his face – except for one thick lock that fell over his brow.

Samuel looked, she thought, like a young lord of the manor, with his fine features and athletic body. No one would have guessed he was a book-learned preacher who shared her passion for rhetoric and logic, Latin and Greek. When she had fallen in love with him, his sharp intellect and his devotion to God had been as attractive as his physicality. What had her brother Oliver said? *"You have a man's mind in a woman's body, Lizzie. Use it well, and do not let it be lost in the mires of convention and society."*

"Elizabeth." Samuel smiled as he stopped and leaned on the axe hilt, drawing his forearm across his forehead. "You look flustered, my love. Here, come and let me kiss you better."

She stood a quarter turn away for a moment, seeking her calm, for she did not want to upset him with her injured head. His first reaction was always to fight for what was right, and if she presented her indignation as anger, he would respond with further fuel. Elizabeth did not need her beloved, hot-headed husband creating more havoc amongst his congregation. She stepped into his arms and relaxed as he closed them around her in a reassuring embrace. They stood together for several minutes until she felt the anxiety run from her and lifted her head to kiss him deeply.

"That's better." Samuel grinned as he smoothed the hair from her forehead, and then he gasped. "What happened here?"

Elizabeth took a deep breath. It was important she kept composed. "A misunderstanding," she replied. "I stood in the way of a stone that was perhaps intended only to frighten me, not hit me."

"You were stoned?" Samuel's eyes narrowed. "Where? By whom?"

"No, not stoned. It was one flint that hit me by mistake. It made more of a cut than expected." She took a deep breath. "In Boston market."

"By whom?" he demanded again.

Elizabeth remained silent. Sharing this news would indicate a different path in life than that which they had planned. She knew Samuel had encountered resistance from his congregations before they were married. He had been ousted from Lynn for preaching a nonconformist text. But they believed themselves safe in Boston, their living in Skirbeck protected by centuries of family ties with the ancient borough. Today's incident in the market proved different.

"Elizabeth. You must tell me, or I shall find out for myself." Samuel was already reaching for the jacket he'd tossed across the hedge.

"Some women. From our congregation..."

"*Our* congregation?"

Elizabeth nodded and committed to the truth. "Samuel, they threatened to force you from town. They said your sermons contravene the word of God."

"And that was the reason they threw stones at you?" He pushed his arm into his jacket, struggling because his hand was clenched as a fist and caught in the fabric of his cuff. Impatiently, he tugged at it, almost tore the cloth. "This is completely intolerable."

"Just one stone," Elizabeth repeated. "And I don't think she intended it to hit me. Please, my love, don't make the situation worse."

"So you will just accept this?" Samuel was buttoning his jacket, searching for his hat, which Elizabeth could see was hanging from the branch of another tree in the budding orchard. Beneath the gnarled trees, the daffodils' green spikes pushed from rich loamy soil, and a robin hopped along a branch, searching for insects. How peaceful this scene, how disturbing their conversation. Elizabeth struggled to equate the two.

"We need to talk," she said quietly. "I fear this foretells of something much deeper than just one arrowhead or confrontation."

He paused then, quirked his head to one side. "What do you mean?"

Elizabeth put her hands on his shoulders, drew close to him so he could see the serious intent in her eyes. "Your sermons are no longer acceptable to the small-minded people in Skirbeck."

"I will not change," Samuel said abruptly. "I will not preach a different message."

"Then, my love," she responded, "we may need to find a different congregation."

What she didn't know was where. Or how. For the worry of being ousted was one that had been hidden so deep in her heart that she didn't realise it until just now.

The following Sunday's sermon passed without incident until they left by the great north door of St. Nicholas's Church. This week, as she and Samuel had prepared the sermon and she had developed some suggestions, Elizabeth had intentionally tempered the directness of Samuel's rhetoric within the subtleties of her prose. Between her concepts and his charisma, their sermons had always been highly regarded. Surely the congregation would be satisfied that the Reverend Whiting had heeded their concerns. As she and Samuel walked slowly home along the yew-lined path, the dark trees casting deeper shadows under the slate-grey sky, a figure detached itself from the bosky depths and blocked their passage.

"Susannah," Elizabeth greeted cautiously. She would start this friendship afresh.

Mistress Johnson flicked a look of contempt and turned her attention to Samuel. "Reverend Whiting," she said. "A moment, if you please."

Samuel inclined his head politely, oblivious to the awkwardness between the two women. Elizabeth had not told him which of his congregation had confronted her in the marketplace, refusing to prejudice him in his relationship with his flock. She moved closer to her husband and protectively placed her hand on his arm.

"Mistress Johnson," he replied courteously. "Is there something I may help you with?"

"A simple matter," the woman responded. Elizabeth held her breath. Surely her amendments to Samuel's sermon had quieted the congregation, placated them. "But one that is quite urgent."

Samuel smiled, his handsome face open and encouraging. "Yes, of course. What is it you need to tell me?" He glanced behind her and to the left and right of the path. They were the only ones in the churchyard. "Is your husband not here too?"

Susannah lifted her face so that the shade of her bonnet did not obscure her eyes. "My husband meets with the other men of the congregation even now," she replied. "And for the sake of the friendship I once had with Elizabeth" – Elizabeth blanched at the past tense of her words – "I will tell you they discuss your position here in Skirbeck as the leader of our church and review the content of your sermons."

Samuel nodded encouragingly. "I am glad to hear it. I always welcome the opinions of my congregation."

Elizabeth glanced at him sharply, tightening the pressure on his arm. Surely he had not forgotten her encounter in the market. But then she realised because she did not tell him of Susannah's role, he did not connect deed and word.

"These are not mere opinions," replied Susannah. "I warned your wife last week that your sermons have crossed the border into the dangerous world of nonconformity. You follow the path of those before you, which led them into the darkness of exile. The men meet today to start the process of ousting you from this parish." She looked quickly at Elizabeth, pulled her bonnet down over her face again. "I'm sorry," she muttered. "I warned you."

Mistress Johnson hurried away, fading into the gloom of the yew shadows until she passed through the crooked lychgate and disappeared.

Elizabeth turned to Samuel. "It has come sooner than I thought," she said softly.

Samuel's face was thunderous. "They mean nothing by this. It is just words."

"So are your sermons. But the word of God can move people in powerful ways. They can become twisted, intolerant. This does not bode well."

Her husband clenched his mouth, and she took advantage of his shock.

"It is time I went to talk to Oliver. We need my brother's lawyerly intellect, his worldly Puritan learnings."

"I'll go with you."

"No," Elizabeth replied. "They could misconstrue that you are already running away..."

"Never," Samuel interrupted. "We have made this our home. I would never leave."

"But the congregation do not wish you here." Elizabeth took her husband's arm, walked him slowly back towards their rectory home. The low stone building was humble but warm and welcoming. Samuel's daughter, Dorothy, the new babe, Sammy, and a fragrant Sunday dinner awaited them. "Remember how your predecessor, John Cotton, was hunted into hiding until he boarded a ship and sailed to the New World?"

"Yes, of course." Samuel stopped dead on the path, gripped Elizabeth's arm. "They will not cast me out from England. I will not leave behind all that I love.

This country is in my blood. I would rather die than desert it."

"We shall find a way forward, my darling." She kissed her husband, held him close to her. "I will leave early tomorrow morning. It is a two-day ride to Bletsoe. My brother has powerful friends. Just as the earl of Lincoln intervened in Lynn on your behalf, I will ask Oliver to approach him again. He should be able to refer you to a new parish. The sooner we can solicit Oliver's help, the quicker we can resolve this situation."

❧ ❧ ❧

"Lizzie, I fear this is not an easy situation to resolve." Oliver's words stung, a flurry of further arrowheads piercing her heart. "England is dividing over religious views, even here in East Anglia. What was once countenanced is now outlawed. And so are the men who preach it."

"Samuel's lectures have not changed," she protested.

"But his congregation have," responded her brother. "All over the country, we are hearing of bishops restricting the words of the preachers. And even in the hidden villages of Norfolk and Bedfordshire, Suffolk and Essex, rectors are being judged and persecuted for their eagerness to conform to the king's will. Or not."

This hour was so poignantly familiar, walking at her brother's side through the neat lanes and tidy pastures of their Bedfordshire home. How often had they paced, heads down into the prevailing easterly, words whipped from their mouths by a sea-wind flying unchecked across the exposed landscape?

In times past, their talk had been academic, competing to recite the longest Latin passage, debating philosophy in Greek, pitching Oliver's university training against Elizabeth's intellect. Now, this conversation was about her future. And the present. And how she could possibly save Samuel's living at Skirbeck.

"He will not change his sermon, bend his knee to the bishop, no matter what is threatened," Elizabeth shouted against the gale. "This is more than a simple lecture, more than just words, Oliver. This is our souls, our destiny."

Oliver put his arm around her, hugged her close as a particularly strong gust of wind caught her skirts and threatened to blow her into the ditch bordering the track. In summer, the channel was full of dandelions and cow parsley, a fertile bed providing sustenance to the flourishing wildlife. Today, February's rains and the seeping of the fen had filled it to the brim with brackish water, darkly hiding its depths. A metaphor for her life, she thought briefly. And yet still she loved this land's ancient beauty, the arc of its limitless skies.

"Have you considered what you might do?" Oliver steadied her and continued marching forward. Across the fields, Bletsoe's curled brick chimney pots propped up the heavy grey clouds, and wisps of smoke promised a cheerful fire and mulled wine. The manor was more a fortified mansion than a castle, a mellow long house with fruitful gardens and thriving fishponds. Elizabeth matched her brother, step for step, each familiar oak they passed marking welcome boundaries and leading her home.

"Can you not suggest another congregation we might go to?" she asked breathlessly, out of practice with country walking, her pace being confined to towns in the past few years. "Do your patrons not require a rector to preach in their manors? The earl of Lincoln intervened for Samuel before, when he was cast out of Lynn, and was most helpful to John Cotton and other preachers. Is he not still your sponsor?"

As they reached the boundary to Home Farm, Oliver swung open the wooden barred gate and helped Elizabeth across the rutted and muddy ground left by the cow herd. "Not anymore," replied her brother. "I am now his partner."

Elizabeth splashed ankle deep through the muck, concentrating on avoiding the slick pools that pitted the ground. "Well, that's good," she said. "Really, Oliver, could we not have taken the lane?"

"You're a country girl," Oliver laughed. "You should be used to this. Or has urban living replaced your love for nature's splendour?"

Just to prove him wrong, Elizabeth hopped over a wide puddle and, grasping her skirts in her fist, climbed over the gate that led to the gardens. "I will always love the land," she called to Oliver. *"Ab imo pectore."*

He laughed. *"From the bottom of your heart*? And so now you quote Julius Caesar to me?"

"Just keeping you on your toes, brother," she rejoined. Reaching the gravelled path, she took his proffered arm. Together they arrived home and pushed open the side door, both craving the welcome of their childhood haven. "What do you mean, you are partner to the earl of Lincoln?"

"I am now a member of the Providence Island Company," Oliver replied. "We are investing in the New World. We could think about..."

"Samuel would not think about it at all," Elizabeth interrupted. "He loves England with a fierceness born of his long heritage here. He could never leave."

"Perhaps not voluntarily." Oliver took her damp cloak, led her to the fireplace and removed her muddy boots. His tenderness reminded her of all the times he had done this for her when she was a little girl, when his adventurous shortcuts had steered them into sudden marshes and sodden fields. "But, Elizabeth, I want you to be prepared. No longer can I be certain of protecting Samuel for any length of time, keeping you from harm. If you cannot find a middle ground here, you may have no other choice but to find fresh pastures in New England."

Oliver's warning rang in Elizabeth's head as she rode home to Skirbeck. Far from returning with the promise of a new congregation in England, perhaps deep in Norfolk, where even Archbishop Laud's henchmen would not find them, Oliver's solemn words had brought home the precariousness of their situation.

Elizabeth and Samuel had lived within the bubble of Skirbeck's relative safety, protected by Oliver's patron and Samuel's family name. But over the past three years, not only had Laud taken on the crusade of eradicating nonconformity within the Church, but he had also enlisted King Charles's support in prosecuting those curates who delivered exactly the kind of sermons that Samuel was called by God to preach. In recent months, no longer were warnings or fines being issued; men were being rounded up and imprisoned, their families turned out of houses and cast out of communities.

Worse, Oliver had confided that he feared this was just the beginning of a devastating new era in England's politics.

"The confrontation between the king and Parliament is set on an inevitable course of conflict," he had said soberly as they sat together late the previous night. "We are not just going to fight over freedom to practise our religion, Lizzie. The king's illegal requisitioning of ship money and undue taxation will be the ignition point for a fire that will consume us all."

"What do you mean, Oliver?" Elizabeth knew her brother held the confidence of many of England's most influential parliamentarians. His recent appointment to examine the legality of the king's insistence on ship money taxes had secured his reputation as a first-rate lawyer. "What ignition point?"

"War," he'd replied shortly. "This could lead to war, Elizabeth."

"Never," she'd gasped. "England has not been at war with itself for centuries. And never between the king and Parliament."

Oliver had just leaned forward, poked at the dying embers in the fire until a flame briefly flared and then dwindled. "These are different times," he had replied. "England has never tasted this kind of freedom of expression before either."

As she approached Skirbeck, the events of the past two weeks replayed in Elizabeth's mind. Susannah's betrayal, the hostility of the women in the marketplace, even the contempt of the mealymouthed schoolmaster. Was this a world that she wanted to live in? More so, was this a world for Dorothy and little Sammy?

No, in a word.

She was trapped as a cony in a warren, the bishops yipping like hounds at the entrance. She was forever resigned to her place, her role in life. Mother, wife, dutiful and obedient. The only time to use her Latin was when reading her L'Obel's herbal. And if the opportunity to collaborate on Samuel's sermons were taken away from her, she feared she would go mad.

And yet... and yet, despite Oliver's dire predictions and the failure of her mission to secure a new living for Samuel, there was a tiny glimmer of excitement that bubbled in her chest, threatened to rise in her throat.

Of all the words that Oliver had said, for together they had analysed Elizabeth's life as thoroughly as studying for matriculation, of all the words, two echoed in her head.

New England. *New* England. New *England*.

She rolled the name around her tongue, tasted the freedom that this simplest of all phrases promised. A chance to leave behind the old, the decrepit, the bonds and boundaries of a society hewn from the stone of centuries of tradition and convention.

An opportunity where nonconformity was welcome. Where the old rules didn't apply anymore.

Perhaps – and here she gasped aloud at the thought, and her mare's ears twitched at the sound – even a world where women had a voice. An educated voice.

From that simple idea came a tumbling forth of all that she could dream of in this new frontier until the spire of St. Nicholas's Church proclaimed she was almost home. Tamping down her elation to an ember glowing in her belly, Elizabeth walked her horse into the stable yard and dismounted, relieved that Samuel had not come out of the house to greet her. If he saw her in this heightened state of excitement, he would demand to know the reason. And would never be able to share her enthusiasm.

No. She had to take a deep breath, remind herself that Samuel's concern was that of ministering to his congregation, ensuring that she and the children were safe. Running into the house and announcing that she thought a move to New England was the best solution would absolutely stun him. And his famous obstinacy would throw enough water on her flame to drown it forever.

Elizabeth composed herself, walked slowly and deliberately into the house, quietly laid her bonnet and gloves on the table. Samuel was in his study, his dark head bowed over his desk, intent on writing. He had not even heard her arrive. As she entered the room, he looked up, and she saw her sombre expression mirrored in his face.

"Oliver could not help us?" he asked quietly.

"Not now," she replied, speaking honestly in the omission of detail. "But perhaps in the future. He will think about what is best."

"Then I shall continue with my lectures and sermons," said Samuel. "And put my trust in God's will that He find us a home for His word."

"God's will," Elizabeth agreed.

*"And mine too,"* she added silently, lowering her eyes piously so Samuel could not see the flame.

By March, when the crows were repopulating the rookery in the trees at the end of the garden, cawing and squabbling for precedence in the bare branches, they had thought the threat had passed. The congregation seemed settled; Samuel's sermons had been tempered with Elizabeth's judicious editing.

"We are still welcome here," announced Samuel as the eighth week had passed since the stoning. "You see, Elizabeth, it's just a matter of finding the right words. Reverend Cotton taught me that. He is a master of preaching nonconformity and yet escaped being designated a separatist."

"Until he could no longer fool the bishops," Elizabeth responded. "And had to flee through the underground Puritan network." Cross with herself for doubting her husband's faith, she laid her hand on his shoulder as she looked over his desk at his writings.

"What will be your topic this week, my love?"

"I thought I should speak of the concept of exile," Samuel replied. "The Bible mentions it frequently. From Adam and Eve to the Israelites, God's children have wandered from pillar to post."

"And what message do you wish to convey?" Elizabeth asked. This subject could get touchy.

"That even an exile lost in the desert can have hope," he replied. "That we should consider those who have been cast out of their livings and welcome them back to their homes."

Elizabeth's heart sank. "Samuel, this sounds a little too pointed for our congregation," she began. "The preaching of the Nonconformists still burns their ears. The last thing they want to do is welcome them back into their communities."

"And you don't think I can deliver this message with grace and subtlety?"

"It's not that," she rushed to reassure him. "It's that I don't think they are quite ready to face those truths."

"Well, I am ready to tell them so." He pushed back from the table and paused at the door to go outside. "I am sorry you don't have the confidence in me that I can preach a sermon that both gets its point across and does not antagonise my congregation." She could tell that he was wrestling with his own conscience, needed to clear his head.

"Samuel, I..." But he had already left. And later, when Elizabeth returned to him in his study to help with the final draft of his sermon, he politely and firmly turned her away.

"I write with God's fire in my heart, Elizabeth," he

said. "No need for you to douse my words or disguise my intent."

After the sermon, they sat in the kitchen, sharing a simple supper and talking about the day, as they always did.

"I think it went well, my love." Samuel finished his wine, ready to bank the fire. "No one confronted us after I preached."

"No one stopped to speak to us either," replied Elizabeth. She started to gather their plates, paused in thought. "The congregation was too silent, avoided us almost." It was too quiet, too still.

A single lantern on the table cast a puddle of light, the deeply inset windows reflecting a shimmering in the thick glass. A gust of wind rattled the door, as it always did when blowing from the east.

And then rattled harder. And harder.

Great thumps resounded on the wall of the rectory, as if it was being pounded by a hundred sticks. Shouting echoed in the garden, split the dark night with a frightening intensity.

Samuel jumped up; Elizabeth ran to the window and bit back a scream. Flaring torches cast orange flames into the blackness, brandished by a dozen cloaked and hooded men. As one, they roared in anger against Samuel's blasphemy; as one, they clattered staves on the door.

A brick flew through the window, showering Elizabeth with brutal shards.

"Get down!" yelled Samuel.

"Zealots! Dissenters!" the mob shouted. "We oust you. WE OUST YOU!"

From the bedroom, Dorothy and Sammy cried out,

and Elizabeth crawled on her hands and knees along the kitchen floor to get to them, not caring that she knelt on glass, that her palms were bleeding.

Samuel stood to the side of the broken window, shouted into the darkness. "Be gone. Be gone! In God's name, go home."

Suddenly, the pounding of footsteps and shouts from the watch echoed into the rectory, chasing away those who had dared to oust Skirbeck's nonconformist minister.

Silence fell upon them again.

Elizabeth huddled on the bedroom floor, holding the children tightly in her arms, rocking them back and forth. "Hush," she whispered as she looked up at Samuel, standing white-faced in the doorway. "Hush, you are safe... tonight."

It took only two days for Archbishop Laud's men to arrive on their doorstep with a summons to appear before the bishop of Lincoln. Samuel was charged with preaching a sermon that did not conform to the tenets of the Anglican Church, spreading sedition, encouraging disobedience, and inciting people who trusted his education and wisdom to stray from the rightful path of God.

"It has happened again." Samuel looked up at Elizabeth from his desk, the order lying neatly before him as if it were another sermon awaiting her review. "I trusted the leaders of our community. I thought we had found a way forward together. I thought they had accepted me. They did not speak of what remained in their hearts."

"Susannah made it clear to me. And there was no mistaking their mood on Sunday," Elizabeth replied grimly. The arrowhead in the marketplace had pointed to their destiny. The mob at their house had confirmed it. She and Samuel had just prolonged the moment of truth. Elizabeth crossed to stand beside him, leaned over, and put her arm around his shoulder as she read the order.

"You are commanded before the bishop of Lincoln," she said. "And he is now under Laud's direction. This certainly means fines that will break us, imprisonment that will tear us apart. Some men, I hear, are even being executed." Her voice broke, and she steadied herself. "What will you do?"

"Fight."

In his one word, Elizabeth realised their perilous future as if through a necromancer's glass. She berated herself silently for her turning first to the old country magic, not God's word. Sometimes her superstitions overpowered her faith.

"If you fight, you will lose," she said carefully.

"Do I have a choice?" Samuel looked up at her, and she caught the uncertainty in his eyes, behind the clear gaze of the truth of his godly convictions.

"Yes," said Elizabeth. "We have a choice."

The moment had come sooner than she thought. But the mob had really shaken her. And while Oliver's predictions were fresh in her mind, she must speak. "Listen to me." She drew him to his feet so they stood equal. She laid her hands on his broad chest, drawing his attention to her and only her. "Oliver warned me this could, *would* happen. And I have made provision."

"So have I." Samuel smoothed her hair in his familiar way, gently touched the scar on her brow. "And I would take on the burden of defending our faith, Elizabeth, not you. I will send you and the children to Bletsoe, remain here to face Laud's men. This is not your battle."

For a moment, she believed him. Imagined their son brought up as an English gentleman, Dorothy receiving the same education she had enjoyed. And then Oliver's prediction of terrible conflict between the king and Parliament rang in her mind. It would be no safer for them at Bletsoe if her brother were to be proven right.

"It may not be my battle, but this is our war," she replied. "I tell you, Oliver and I have made provision, and we will not let this enemy in Archbishop Laud prevent you from preaching the true word of God."

"What do you mean, Elizabeth?" Samuel searched her eyes with his. "Did your brother find us another living? In Norfolk, perhaps, or Suffolk, where we can safely..." Her husband's voice trailed off as he realised she was not acknowledging his last hopes.

"No, my love," she replied gently. "There is no safety in England anymore. Not for the words you wish to preach, the life I wish to live, the future we've dreamed of for our children."

"I cannot go to Amsterdam," he replied quickly. "I have no stomach for the structure and strictures of the Calvinists."

She was silent. Better that he reached his own understanding, uttered the words himself. She waited. A clock ticked. A clatter of pots in the kitchen, where their cook was preparing dinner. The children's laughter. A dog barking. All sounds of home, unremarkable, until home was about to be taken away.

"I'd heard," Samuel said slowly, "I'd heard that Oliver is now investing in a partnership with the earl of Lincoln."

"Yes," she said. "So he told me."

"Commerce that is trading across the world."

She waited.

"In... New England."

There. He'd said it. She nodded.

"New England." Samuel's voice cracked. "That is the provision you have made. Oliver would send us to New England. Leave our home, our land, our families, all that is familiar to us."

"But not our God, my love," she said softly. "We are not leaving our God."

He looked at her questioningly. She was the one now who was leading the fight against Laud and the bishops, showing him a different path to evade their foe.

"We are going to a place where we can become closer to God. Where we can worship as we choose, live as we wish." She cupped his cheek in her hand, and for a second he closed his eyes, tilted his head to her palm.

"What say you, Samuel?" she asked quietly.

"So, like the Lord, I am called into the wilderness." He fell silent, his gaze travelling from his desk, the fine furniture, the comfortable chair, the warm hangings by the window, the apple trees budding through the glass. "I am called to join others to be as a city upon a hill."

Elizabeth nodded, acknowledging the words of John Winthrop, answering in like. "'So therefore, let us choose life.'"

"I thought my life was in England." The anguish in Samuel's voice relayed the pain in his soul.

"Would you rather submit to the bishops? Subjugate your soul for the sake of their rules? Be cast into prison and lose your family, possibly your life?" Elizabeth took a deep breath, willed him to look at her now so he could see the promise in her face. "Or would you travel with us freely to New England and leave this prison behind?"

This time he did not hesitate, did not survey what he would leave.

"Yes," he whispered, his eyes fixed on hers as if

swearing an oath to her and her alone. "Yes. I would give up everything here that imprisons me, to live a life of freedom with you there."

The ship moored alongside the wharf at King's Lynn was a large three-masted vessel with ample deck space and sails that unfurled even as she stood with Dorothy's hand in hers. The boundless Norfolk skies were anchored by streaks of ochre and silver clouds framing the ship's profile. On the quay, there was frenzied activity, provisions being loaded, other emigrants standing in small groups, comforting weeping relatives they were leaving behind. No one came to bid goodbye to Samuel and Elizabeth; they had told only Oliver, who had hidden them upon their flight from Skirbeck and arranged their passage, for fear of endangering other members of their family. Archbishop Laud would not be merciful to anyone who helped a nonconformer escape orders to appear before the bishop of Lincoln.

"Time to board, my love." Samuel held Sammy in his arms, the babe wrapped warmly in his winter jacket, even on this bonny April morning. He took Dorothy's hand, smiled at Elizabeth. "Come."

Elizabeth could not move her feet. She was fixed, rooted to this English soil, tears burning her eyes. With every step she walked toward the ship, she was walking away from the land she loved.

"One moment more," she whispered. "Just a moment more."

Samuel nodded, stood with their children at the edge of the gangplank. A curlew set up a plaintive cry, and the sun filtered through mackerel clouds, shining a pathway across the estuary, shimmering and dancing within the prism of her tears. Never had she seen this country look more beautiful. Where had her courage gone?

She could not leave. She could not place her family in such unknown danger.

*Into the wilderness.*

Into a wild and alien world.

She was the one who had cast them into the unknown, not the bishops, not the king. She was the one who had arranged their exile, blithely and with excitement, until this final moment arrived.

Oh, God help her, what had she done?

Samuel sent Dorothy the few paces to her so he could carry Sammy firmly in both arms as he strode up the gangplank. "Do not despair, Elizabeth," he called. "We can always come home again."

The sun slipped behind the land, silver turning to grey, gold to a dull bronze. Soon the luminescence would fade, night flood the estuary. There was no more reason to look to the familiar shoreline. It had disappeared. On deck, glowing in the darkness, a ship's lantern illuminated the excitement in Samuel's face as he hugged their boy close and beckoned for her to join them.

*Into the light.*

Elizabeth stepped forward, holding Dorothy's hand. No, she thought. This will change us. We may return, but we can never come home again.

© Elizabeth St.John
*California, 2023*

## AUTHOR'S NOTE

The Rev. Samuel Whiting, D.D., and his wife, Elizabeth St.John, along with their two young children sailed to New England and arrived in Boston Harbor on 26 May 1636. After recovering from a terrible voyage, they settled in Saugus, Massachusetts, which was renamed Lynn in Sam's honour as its first official minister. Elizabeth's brother, Sir Oliver St.John, remained in England and led the 'Ship Money' case in parliament, which contributed to the outbreak of the English Civil War. He subsequently became Lord Chief Justice.

You can read more about the characters in this story and other ancestral adventures on Elizabeth St.John's website at: **www.elizabethjstjohn.com**

## ABOUT ELIZABETH ST.JOHN

Elizabeth St.John's critically acclaimed historical fiction novels tell the stories of her ancestors: extraordinary women whose intriguing kinship with England's kings and queens brings an intimately unique perspective to Medieval, Tudor, and Stuart times.

Inspired by family archives and residences from Lydiard Park to the Tower of London, Elizabeth spends much of her time exploring ancestral portraits, diaries, and lost gardens. And encountering the occasional ghost. But that's another story.

Living between California, England, and the past, Elizabeth is the International Ambassador for The Friends of Lydiard Park, an English charity dedicated to conserving and enhancing this beautiful centuries-old country house and park. As a curator for The Lydiard Archives, she is constantly looking for an undiscovered treasure to inspire her next novel.

Elizabeth's books include her trilogy, *The Lydiard Chronicles*, set in 17th-century England during the Civil War, and her medieval novel, *The Godmother's Secret*, which explores the mystery of the missing princes in the Tower of London.

*From Elizabeth:*

*"I was brought up in England and my research has taken me to family memoirs and letters at Nottingham Castle, the British Library, the Tower of London, Yale University and, of course, the family seat of Lydiard Park. From these fragments the St.Johns emerge, leaving a portrait, a sentence, a deed that seats them with us, telling of their hopes and dreams. As I researched, my voice became a conduit for their stories, recounting a passion for the England of my childhood where they once walked, where their portraits still hang, where they lived, loved, and found redemption. We do not know my family first hand, but the more we read their words, we feel their passions. Across the ages, we understand their fears and successes, losses and loves. We are not so very different from them."*

'Her world and characters are so real I wanted to remain there. *The Lydiard Chronicles* are now on my list

of all-time favourite historical novels. A fantastic read.'
*Editor's Choice, Historical Novel Society.*

Buy Elizabeth's books on Amazon:
**https://geni.us/AmazonElizabethStJohn**
(Also available from other online stores or order from any bookshop.)

## 8

## MY SISTER
### BY ALISON MORTON

*A group of Roman families is preparing to go into voluntary exile and found a new colony in the mountains of Noricum. But how can Marcellus Varus broach this to the most awkward sister in all Rome?*

## ROME, SUMMER AD 395

"Have the *maniae* entered your mind and destroyed it?"

My sister, pale skin flushed and eyes blazing, was a change from her usual whingeing persona. She shook her head so fiercely that several strands of her curly hair became unpinned.

"No, Flavola, and if the mad spirits had entered my head, it would make no difference. We're going and that's it."

"You can go on your own then, Marcellus."

"Fair enough."

She stuck her chin out in the way a recalcitrant mule did.

"It's only a dinner and poetry recital," I said. "Maelia Mitela will not eat you."

"She's snooty and ignores me. Take that time I told

you about at the baths. She and Apulius's daughter – the middle one – just gave me a curt nod, then she turned her back to me and went off to the *caldarium* arm in arm with the girl and didn't say another word to me. She thinks that just because the Miteli have more consuls in their ancestors that she's above me. She's certainly above herself considering her husband was a traitor and she had to sell up to pay the fine."

"That's an old story, and none of it was her fault. She just caught the brunt of it."

I wasn't about to disclose the efforts I'd made at the time to negotiate total confiscation of Maelia's late husband's estate down to a large fine. Flavola did *not* need to know that.

"Are you still sweet on her?"

"Don't be ridiculous. We're old friends and I advise her from time to time about property."

I fixed my eyes on the red and gold patterns at the top of the far wall. They gleamed in the light of the afternoon sun and the dancing gods and their flute boys seemed about to step down into the room. Frankly, any diversion would be welcome at this instant.

"Is that all?" Flavola's eyes narrowed though she didn't quite sneer at me.

"Maelia Mitela is devoted to her family and does not think of another marriage."

"She rejected you? Ha! Good thing. I couldn't stand her coming to live here. And take over the household keys."

I was sure Maelia would rather be torn apart in the arena than live under the same roof as Flavola.

The Mitelus *domus* sat on the summit of the Mons Cispius, part of the Esquiline, so it wasn't too far away. Flavola had appeared, decked out in a bright yellow *dalmatica* with orange embroidery and stripes which made her look like a basket of citrus fruit. It clashed with my late mother's carnelian and gold necklace from which hung a heavy gold pendant. I remember being upset when my father had given it to Flavola's mother when he'd married her as I always regarded it as belonging to my mother. Flavola would have an aching neck by the end of the evening which would do nothing for her mood. She stepped into the litter, pulled the curtains shut and didn't say a word. I sighed, more to myself than out loud.

Flavola was my sister, so obviously I cared for her and protected her. But she had such a prickly manner that she'd seen off any number of suitors despite the size of the portion that she would take into her marriage. She had few women friends as she quarrelled with them with almost indecent haste after she'd met them. She was now twenty-two and I had no idea what to do with her.

Honorina Mitela, Maelia's late aunt, said Flavola needed to keep a civil tongue in her head and not assume the world was against her. Her mother was my father's second wife and had been very young, barely sixteen, when Flavola was born, and had probably transmitted her own nervousness and desperate need for recognition to her daughter.

Flavola had recovered her temper by the time we arrived at the *domus* Mitela and deigned to take my hand to step down from the litter. Inside, the steward ushered us through to the atrium where Maelia waited to receive us. Flavola took in an audible breath, then set her lips in a tight smile.

"Welcome, Marcellus and Flavola. Please come and meet our other guests," Maelia said smoothly and smiled.

I nodded to Lucius Apulius standing behind her, a fellow senator and leader of our little group. I hadn't explained to Flavola exactly what lay behind this evening; getting her here was struggle enough. Lucius's daughter, Galla, came forward and took Flavola off to talk to some of the other women while Lucius himself and that scamp Gaius Mitelus drew me aside.

"How are your plans progressing, Marcellus?" Lucius was a serious man who wore a solemn expression every time I met him. Maelia said he had never recovered from the death of his wife more than a dozen years ago. Now he was planning an expedition of the most ambitious sort involving hundreds of people and the gods knew how much stock and baggage. I could see an endless procession of carts and carriages disappearing into a distant cloud of dust in my mind's eye. A migration north to Noricum that would be permanent and a rupture from everything we knew. However, up to now, I had fought shy of informing Flavola and I was scratching my head about how to broach it with her.

"I've sold most of my property portfolio which has been tricky with all the disruption going on," I replied. "*Magister militum* Stilicho is supposed to be ruling on behalf of that boy emperor Honorius, but he's buggered off to Greece chasing after that turncoat Alaric. Now we're left with Stilicho's wife Serena who is supposedly keeping an eye on us here in Rome, but the Senate has never forgiven her since she stole the goddess's necklace from the Temple of Vesta last year. Few outside her court will even give her the time of day, but they're all worried about how Stilicho will take it if they don't cooperate with her, so they're all feeling jittery."

"Well, you're more in contact with the Senate than I am these days," Lucius said. He glanced round. "I've sold my remaining property and sent the proceeds to my father-in-law Bacausus in Noricum by confidential messenger."

"Sure it's safe?"

"Yes. Bacausus sent him from Virunum to help us. Cuso's the grandson of the man who escorted my late wife from Noricum to Rome. And he has a couple of my father-in-law's tribesmen to accompany him. One's a former ironsmith with shoulders you wouldn't believe. The other is one of those wiry mountain men who move almost too quickly to be seen."

"Well, my steward at Arretium has been busy buying up oxen and mules. He thinks I'm losing it, but I told him to do what I say and get on with it."

"How's your sister taking it?" Gaius asked me, nodding to the group of women where Flavola stood with a sullen expression.

"Ah. Well, I..."

"What?"

"I haven't exactly told her yet."

Lucius looked at me in disbelief. Gaius collapsed laughing. The group of women turned and stared at the outburst of noise. Even the dozen or so other men at the back of the atrium sent puzzled looks at us. After a heartbeat, they returned to their talking. Maelia looked across the room and frowned at us. Lucius took my arm and hustled me into a side room. Gaius followed, still chuckling.

Lucius pushed me down onto a stool.

"Are you seriously saying that you haven't told Flavola you're uprooting her from Rome, from all she knows, and going into voluntary exile?"

"Look," I said, "it was hard enough to get her here tonight. She doesn't get on with Maelia."

"You're wrong, Marcellus," Gaius said. "She doesn't get on with *anybody*."

"Don't poke at my sister, Gaius. You're not the easiest piece in the pack."

He took a step towards me. Lucius laid a hand on his chest.

"Enough. We're going in eight weeks' time. We need your estate at Arretium as a harbouring place, but if you haven't organised your household by then, Marcellus, we'll be forced to leave without you. We can't stay here any longer than absolutely necessary." The expression on his face drew together and he looked across at the far wall but I knew he wasn't admiring the pipes of the dancing Maenads his father had had painted there.

"What's happened?"

Lucius shook his head.

"Tell me," I commanded.

"One of the kitchen girls... She went to the market two days ago. I sent one of the men with her, just in case. If nothing else, he could carry anything heavy. She never came back and he's in his room covered in bruises, with a broken leg and only one eye. He was dumped outside my door yesterday with that fish sign carved across his chest."

"Gods!"

"He won't make it, the physician says. The housekeeper who found him is still in hysterics."

"And the girl?"

"We sent out our own people to look for her as soon as we realised she was missing. Nothing yet. I reported it to the urban prefect's office, of course, and they're searching, including the brothels. She was born on our estate, so she's a country girl and came here only recently. She's probably no virgin, but she doesn't deserve that bleak fate."

"Poor little tart if she's been shut up in one of those places," I said in a low voice.

Gaius looked at me with the most solemn face I've ever seen on him.

"I'm doing the rounds and have also put out a few feelers among my contacts around the city," he said.

"I have to hope that it's an isolated incident by somebody afflicted by the gods, or by their god," Lucius added. "Attacking servants is unpardonable. They should come after me, not innocents."

"Well, I've only had the odd snide comment, but one of my potential buyers related the pleasure he'd had in buying up the stone and marble from a demolished temple. He was going to grind up the statues of the gods to make mortar, apparently. I made a remark about ground up bones being more effective, then he shut up."

"I think it's only a few fanatics going to these extremes. Most of the Christos followers appear gentle enough," Lucius said.

"Most of 'em don't care one way or another," I replied. "They follow that religion because the emperor does and because not following blocks their careers. I'll be glad to be rid of it all quite frankly, even if you make me scrabble around in the mud to grow my food, Lucius."

"It won't come to that, my friend. But we will have to do things we're not used to. It won't just be exile from Rome, but from the life we have led until now."

"All I have to do now is convince Flavola."

"Did you enjoy the evening?" I attempted to sound casual.

"I suppose so." Flavola shrugged as she cut a minuscule piece from the large cheese the slave had placed on the table.

"That much?" I reached out for more bread and tore a piece off the loaf. I took my time dipping it in the oil before putting it in my mouth.

167

"They're all so trite, chattering on about hairstyles, possible lovers, or children's ailments, if they have any. But Lucius Apulius's daughter Galla was polite enough, even friendly. At least she included me in everything and invited me to sit next to her at dinner."

"High praise indeed." Galla must have exercised the patience and wisdom of Minerva to put Flavola at such ease. "I find Galla to be a very pleasant young woman and wise beyond what one would expect at her age," I added.

"She's helping her father with an important scheme which she says will change all their lives. I suppose as Apulius has no son, these things fall on her as the eldest daughter. I probed, but she wouldn't tell me what it was." She took a long draught of her watered wine. "I'm intrigued. For her sake, I hope it's not something that's going to get her father into trouble as happened with the Miteli."

"How many times must I tell you that the Miteli did not get themselves into trouble?"

Flavola shrugged.

"Whatever you say, brother."

I threw her a hard look, sighed and left her to it. My study beckoned. It was a great deal more attractive than sparring with Flavola. Rome was becoming difficult as Lucius illustrated with that story of his kitchen slave. I hoped they would find the poor girl soon, not only because she was valuable property, but for her own sake.

"Is it true?" Flavola flew at me as soon as I entered the house.

"Is what true?" I replied.

She'd been at Galla Apulia's house this morning

and I thought she would still be there. Her eyes narrowed and she attempted a smile.

"Come, Marcellus, surely we don't keep secrets from each other, do we?"

"Of course we do. If I told you all my clients' business, it would be all over Rome."

"Gods! You really are a pig. I wouldn't gossip about your wretched clients. I couldn't think of anything more boring."

"Never stopped you in the past."

She flounced off in the direction of her sleeping room. At least she hadn't asked me any further questions. This was a ridiculous state of affairs. I was one of the sharpest lawyers in Rome – a specialist in land transactions. Thus, I knew exactly who was selling what property, who was marrying whom and transferring property into a marriage, and who had property to dispose of after the death of a relative. My social connections were solid and nobody had sued me for breach of confidentiality. But I had avoided telling my sister that I was selling up and we were moving into the mountains – far more important in our lives than mere clients.

However uneasy I felt about approaching the subject – and it did bring me out in a sweat when I thought about it – any remaining peace was shattered the next day at the second hour. An almighty thump on the door was followed by a group of six soldiers of the urban cohorts barging their way in.

"Marcellus Varus, you are summoned before the urban prefect. You will come with us immediately."

What in Hades did Florentinus want with me? The last time we'd met was for a pleasant dinner among friends to discuss the latest letter he'd received from Symmachus. Surely, he would have sent a polite message, not six sweating hulks with beef for brains.

As we made our way to the office on the Mons Oppius, I tried to fathom the cause for the urgent, and very publicly escorted, summons. Florentinus was a busy man. He supervised trade guilds and corporations, was ultimately responsible for keeping the city provided with grain – all hell broke out if the grain dole was interrupted – and kept the officials responsible for the drainage of the Tiber and maintaining the city's sewers and water supply on their toes. He was also the ultimate legal authority as the emperors had deserted Rome for Mediolanum and he pretty much ran the city as his independent fiefdom with the urban cohorts to enforce his will. Not a man to cross.

It wasn't that far from my house in the Carinae to the prefect's office, but on the way, I heard several shouts of 'idolator', and 'pagan' with several rude suggestions for me. The squad commander said and did nothing to quell the insults, so I smiled to myself when he caught one poorly aimed gob of spittle. While they were unsettling, the violent curses didn't frighten me – I'd heard worse in court – but such open, almost systematic, shouting was unusual. And it was becoming worse. Mostly, it started with one of their preachers ranting to a small crowd clustered round him and cursing everybody else who was passing by. I didn't give them the satisfaction of reacting.

As we entered the prefect's office, the shouting faded away. We sailed past the desks of secretaries, wound round corridors, past beautiful walls and even more beautiful statues, vases and couches until we stopped in front of a pair of tall, gilded doors guarded by a ferocious couple of urbans. The pug-faced one looked as if he would eat his mother. The other merely sneered. I had studied the patterns of the gilt inlay on the doors in some detail before one door eventually opened. A secretary ushered me in.

"Ah, Varus." Florentinus looked up from a codex he was reading. "Come in. Sit yourself down. I won't be a moment." He scrutinised a piece of vellum to the side, signed it and nodded at the secretary who whipped it away and left the room. We were alone. Well, unless somebody was listening discreetly from behind the screens at the back of the room. I was aware he kept a couch there for an afternoon nap, but who knew who was skulking there now?

"Well, my dear fellow, I'm sorry to pull you in here so publicly, but I have to look as if I'm doing something about you."

I said nothing. He looked away, sniffed, then glanced down at his desk. He looked distinctly awkward, but I let him sweat, and waited. He raised his eyes to me. They were red-rimmed. He liked his drink, so perhaps he was hung-over.

"Look, this is most awkward, but I can't ignore it. I've had enough reprimands from the Divine Honorius already. Well, from one of his secretaries, if I'm honest."

*Which he wasn't.*

"This comes from the top," he continued. "Well, effectively from the top."

What in Hades was he talking about? I didn't have all day and I really didn't want to watch him squirm like this.

"What is it, Florentinus?"

"You've been denounced."

"What?" I was thunderstruck and couldn't speak for a moment. Then I gathered my brains together. Somebody who disliked or envied me was trying to harm me in order to gain something or some influence. In my mind, I skimmed through recent events and clients and couldn't immediately think of anything.

Some clients were unhappy at the outcome of their cases – that was standard – but I couldn't recall anyone going this far. "What is my perceived wrongdoing?" I frowned at Florentinus.

"The most noble lady Serena has received information that you have sacrificed a calf to the gods. I mean the pagan idols," he added hastily. "She has instructed me to investigate." He glanced to the side, then at me, then backwards over his shoulder. So we were being listened to. Florentinus was in a difficult bind. Back in ninety-three, he'd supported the reinstatement of the Altar of Victory; now he served convinced Christos followers, *magister militum* Stilicho and his wife Serena, the de facto rulers of the western provinces. I wouldn't be surprised if he went and mumbled prayers in one of their *ecclesiae* every Sunday just to keep his job. But Serena was involved. And she was a vindictive bitch.

"Sacrifices are illegal," I said. "They stopped years ago." I knew some people furtively sacrificed a chicken or two in the country, but I'd seen and heard very little in Rome these days. "When was this supposed offence said to have taken place?"

Florentinus buried his head in a sheaf of parchment.

"Five days ago."

I burst out laughing. I couldn't help it.

Florentinus looked at me, his mouth hanging open. I wiped my eyes with the back of my hand.

"Whoever told you that is a fool," I said. "We roasted a calf for eating. I invited a few friends and their families to take their meal with us. My cook has butchery skills, so it was all prepared at home. Being thrifty, he caught the blood in a bowl to make *lucanica* sausages – a favourite of mine."

"No ritual or priestly blessing?"

172

"No. As I said before, that sort of thing has been stopped."

"On your word of honour?"

"What do you take me for, Florentinus? Of course, on my word of honour, if you need me to say it." I sighed. "Now you can tell me who has spread this appalling untruth so that I can sue them."

"Ah, well, I'd rather not say as the matter is now cleared up. There's obviously been a mistake." His eyes held what I could only take as a pleading expression. I took the hint and stood up.

"Very well, we'll leave it there. But I'd appreciate a note another time rather than a detachment of squaddies upsetting my household for no good reason."

"Of course, of course. But you do understand that pagan practices of any kind are illegal and taken seriously. Instant exile or even the death penalty can be invoked."

"I understand that this is the law as proclaimed by the Divine Theodosius and reinforced by his son, the equally Divine Honorius." I couldn't keep the ripple of sarcasm out of my voice.

Florentinus shot me a querying look. I gave him the blandest smile in return, then left.

"What a disgrace," Lucius Apulius said later as we met in the *caldarium* of the Baths of Diocletian. I'd needed to sweat my anger out and as I strode into the entrance, I'd sent a boy with a message inviting Apulius to join me. "But a sign of the times," he added. The *caldarium* was more than spacious and we'd found a secluded corner where we wouldn't be overheard. Still, we kept our voices low.

"I'm sure there was something else going on there. Florentinus obviously couldn't speak freely and the only person in Stilicho's absence who has any authority to pull over him is Serena. I wish she'd shove off back to Mediolanum."

"She's supposed to be keeping an eye on us pagans," Lucius replied with a rare hint of humour.

"We're such a threat, aren't we?"

"Given much of the Senate and many of the older families refuse to convert to the Christos, I suppose that's how they see us. They are so sure of themselves and the story of their god."

"Well, I must have upset her or somebody in her circle. I'll try and get Florentinus on his own somewhere and see if I can squeeze it out of him. In the meantime, be warned."

"It won't matter either way as we're going in two months." Sweat ran down from his raised eyebrow.

"Agreed, but if they accelerate it through the courts and call it *exsilium* or formal deportation, I'd lose every penny and my citizenship," I retorted. "No, thanks. *Relegatio* would save both but as *that's* for sexual offences then I'd be branded an adulterer or worse, a procurer. Also, no thanks."

Lucius bent closer and whispered.

"If I were you, Marcellus, I'd start sending your gold and best silver north to your estate at Arretium. Perhaps I can ask my father-in-law to provide secure passage for it to go on to Noricum. If they do try and come after you again at least some of your wealth will be safe."

I stared at him, letting these thoughts roll round in my head. Sometimes Lucius Apulius was less naive than I thought.

Calmer, I went home straight into my office. Unlike the earlier fashion for an open room set between atrium and peristyle, my grandfather had amalgamated the traditional *tablinum* with an empty room at the side and inserted a door. As a child I'd been forbidden access and only after Father became the *paterfamilias* on Grandfather's death was I admitted. I had no sooner dropped onto my padded stool than my clerk shot through the door as fast as a damned Greek panther and started shuffling tablets in front of me. I'd scarcely read the first one when the door was thrust open and Flavola burst in.

"What was all that about this morning?" she cried. "The steward was spluttering something about the prefect arresting you."

I glanced at my clerk, who placed the remaining tablets carefully on my desk and withdrew, hardly making a sound as he closed the door behind him.

"Flavola, I've told you before not to interrupt me when I'm in my office. Please leave."

"Not until you tell me what's going on."

"We'll discuss this later when I've finished here."

She threw me a look worthy of a Hun and crossed her arms.

"No."

"Yes, or I will tell you nothing."

She huffed, then gave a most unladylike snort. I appreciated her courage, but not such defiance.

"Go away, Flavola. Unless you want a whipping."

"You wouldn't!"

"If I were you, I wouldn't gamble on whether to find out." I gave her a hard look and eventually she moved to the door and put her hand on the latch. Then she turned her head and glared at me over her shoulder.

"You'd better tell me the whole story then. I want to

know how much trouble we're in and where to hide my jewellery when the confiscators come to take our possessions," she offered as her Parthian shot.

I did tell her what had happened, but I left one essential part out. A germ of an idea was growing in my mind.

Florentinus was a hard man to pin down, but I managed to speak to him two weeks later on one of his visits to the Senate when he was reading out the latest dispatch from Honorius's court at Mediolanum. His attendant tried to insert himself between us, but Florentinus waved him aside.

"Walk outside with me, Varus," he commanded. He flicked his embroidered cloak back over his shoulder. I was surprised that he seemed willing to talk to me and be seen to be speaking to me. "Look as if I'm reprimanding you," he said in a low tone. "I'm truly sorry about arresting you the other week. You probably realised that I was under pressure and sharp as you are, you probably worked out who was sitting behind my screen."

I nodded as if contrite.

"That particular person is very keen to squash some of the more influential movers here in the city and confiscate their wealth. Somebody was persuaded, let us say, or even bribed to inform against you. I couldn't go against her. It's bloody irritating to have to bow to her wishes, but we must keep in mind who her husband is, that she's the niece of the late emperor and the fact that her daughter is betrothed to *this* emperor."

"I understand, Florentinus." I bowed my head as if being submissive but shot him a fierce look.

"I'm going to tell her that I need to investigate

further but that I've threatened you with exile. That should keep her off your back."

"Oh, thanks – that's comforting," I retorted.

"Don't take that tone with me, Varus. I'm doing my best. I'll spin it out and try to drop it quietly."

And I had no option but to accept it. The man might like to act the genial colleague but it would be utmost folly to forget that he held the power of life and death in Rome.

"I *am* grateful, Florentinus," I said. "I appreciate you're in a tight spot. Perhaps I'll go and rusticate for a few weeks at my estate."

"Good man," he said, patting me on the shoulder, then turned away to talk to other senators vying for his attention.

"Perfect," said Lucius with a gleam in his eye. "A neat solution. Will Flavola swallow it?"

"I think she'll move to Arretium without too much trouble." I was still worried about informing Flavola we would be going much further north to Noricum, but I wasn't going to confess to Lucius Apulius that I *still* hadn't informed her. I coughed to cover the gap in our conversation. "She likes the country and bossing the farmworkers about. She'll find a long list of tasks that need to be carried out. Everybody will be miserable, but she *will* get things done. She's bored here and needs an occupation of some kind. Impossible, of course."

"Don't rule anything out, Marcellus. When we move to the Norican mountains, we'll need every hand in our new colony, even bossy organising ones, whether they come from a man or a woman."

Over the next two weeks, I moved our best furniture to the estate at Arretium. Hidden in discreet lockers under the boards of every cart, the proceeds of my recent land sales went with it. With a heavy guard, the wagons should be safe along the Via Cassia which was reasonably well maintained and a busy route with a fair number of troops using it. If I were one of these damned bandits that seem to infest us these days, it wouldn't be my first choice of target.

"Are we moving permanently?" Flavola asked archly one evening at *cena*. "Everything seems to be disappearing, even my second-best bed covering."

"Things have been very uncertain since Eugenius and Arbogastes went under at the Frigidus River and Serena and Stilicho seem to have it in for Senate members. Look at that accusation of animal sacrifice levelled at me. Florentinus is still hanging the threat of exile or even execution over me, mostly at *her* instigation."

"Execution?" she shrieked. "He wouldn't dare!"

"Nothing is out of play these days. I think we're best out of Rome for a while."

"What about your clients?"

"They'll manage. Plenty of other legal sharks in the pool."

"I can't believe you're so offhand about them."

"Well, of course, I haven't left them dangling! What do you think I am?"

She said nothing but munched on the remains of a bowl of nuts. She glanced around the room. Apart from the wall paintings and the table where the remains of our dinner were spread out, very little of our furnishings remained.

"Well, then, I'd better start packing," she said, wiping her fingers on a piece of linen the slave handed her. But as she left, I caught a little smile on her lips. What in Hades was that about?

On the day we moved north – a three-day journey on horseback to Arretium, but at Flavola's carriage pace five if we were lucky – I was surprised to see her up and ready at the first hour. And she was dressed for riding, not for lounging on down-stuffed cushions in the travelling carriage. Moreover, she was wearing boots, a short tunic and close-fitting *femoralia* on her legs.

"Why are you wearing men's riding dress?" I said. "I've ordered the carriage for you." It was early in the day, but I didn't want anybody to see my sister riding through the suburbs of Rome in barbarian get-up, especially in such revealing trousers.

"Because if you think I'm going to be cooped up in a carriage for weeks on end, you're mistaken."

"What do you mean? It's only a few days to the estate at Arretium."

"Oh, do grow up, Marcellus! Do you think I'm that stupid? I know what you, Apulius and Mitelus have been hatching. It's hilarious how you've convinced yourselves that I couldn't possibly have worked it out. All those boys' meetings and huddling together and little clues from the other women's chit-chat. Even the perfect Galla let a few things drop, no doubt without realising. Did you think I wouldn't question all those property sales?"

I swallowed hard. Had our plan been discovered generally? It wasn't illegal and we'd obtained, mostly through bribery, a permit necessary to establish a new settlement, but we didn't want any sudden confiscations or arrests on spurious charges.

"I'm not sure I follow you," I temporised. I knew Flavola was clever, but was she this sharp-witted?

She stamped her foot on the mosaic of Mercury's head – not a good omen for a journey.

"If we're going to push north and found a new

colony in the mountains near Apulius's father-in-law, I suggest you mount your horse now."

© Alison Morton
*France, 2023*

You can read more about some of the characters in this story in Alison Morton's *Roma Nova first Foundation* story **https://books2read.com/JULIAPRIMA** which will be followed in early 2024 by a sequel *Exsilium* when we will meet Marcellus Varus and Flavola again.

## ABOUT ALISON MORTON

Alison Morton writes award-winning thrillers featuring tough but compassionate heroines. Her ten-book *Roma Nova* series is set in an imaginary European country where a remnant of the ancient Roman Empire has survived into the 21$^{st}$ century and is ruled by women who face conspiracy, revolution and heartache but use a sharp line in dialogue. Several of her novels have hit #1 in Amazon US, UK, Canada and Australia. The latest, *Julia Prima*, plunges us back to AD 370 when the founders of Roma Nova met.

She blends her fascination for Ancient Rome with six years' military service and a life of reading crime, historical and thriller fiction. On the way, she collected a BA in modern languages and an MA in history.

Alison now lives in Poitou in France, the home of Mélisende, the heroine of her two contemporary thrillers, *Double Identity* and *Double Pursuit*. Oh, and she's writing the next *Roma Nova* story.

'This is a stunning historical novel set in the 4$^{th}$ century. Morton's descriptions of the countryside on

Julia's journey are magnificent, and you feel as if you are traveling along with her.' *Historical Novel Society - Editors' Choice.* (**Julia Prima**.)

❧ ❧ ❧

Website: **https://www.alison-morton.com/**
Buy Alison's books on Amazon:
**https://author.to/AlisonMortonAmazon**
(Also available from other online stores or order from any bookshop.)

## 9

# A KING'S MAN NO MORE

## BY CHARLENE NEWCOMB

**FRANCE, 2nd APRIL 1199**

"I know you were to leave for England on the morrow, Robin." It was well past dusk when Queen Eleanor had summoned me. Fire crackled in the hearth of her solar at Fontevraud Abbey, but cold gripped me. An hour earlier I had learned her son, my liege lord King Richard, lay dying more than one hundred miles away at Chalus-Chabrol.

I had only returned from Paris two days past as her envoy to the French king. I had made that journey in secret many times the past three months, and this was to have been the last – but that is a story for another day.

Eleanor stood dry-eyed, her tears shed before I arrived. Still, I had known her long enough to see pain in her creased brow. Her dark crimson gown was plain and unadorned, more suitable for riding rather than entertaining her usual visitors. She was prepared for the long, hard ride – day and night – to be with Richard.

"I have rarely asked more of any man, but I have one last request."

*I should be home with Marian and our children since Christmas. Three long years. How I miss them...*

I held my disappointment and tried to make light of her words. "When is a request from you not an order, madam?"

Eleanor would have teased me with her own rebuke, but not this time. She didn't smile. "John is at the Breton court."

My throat tightened, like the queen mother had set a noose round my neck. I expected her to ask me to accompany her to see Richard. I couldn't speak. But John?

"You must get to him." Eleanor's words came haltingly. "Before they learn Richard is not long for this world. You must get John safely away before..."

"Me?" I protested. She had any number of household knights who could see to that task. I'd served in John's camp as Richard's spy. Beaten, tossed in the dungeon, nearly died at John's hands. Richard knew this, Eleanor knew it. How could she ask me to help him now? "John wants my head."

"And Arthur and his barons will have *his* head if the Bretons get news of Richard." She sat by the fire, folding her hands through the fabric of her gown.

With a clenched jaw, I nodded. Many – especially in the Angevin continental domains – would rally around twelve-year-old Duke Arthur and support his right to the English throne, including Richard's long-time adversary, the king of France. Arthur was King Richard's nephew, Eleanor's grandson. Lines of succession in England were decided by the wishes of barons and prelates.

If Arthur was crowned to rule England, he would be nothing more than a pawn of the French king. John might be Richard's brother and a legitimate contender for the crown, but few had fond memories of him. Some might support him. Better the enemy you know rather than the stranger you do not.

Eleanor's hands shook. "You have infiltrated Paris and more strongholds than I could name. You can get to John unnoticed where no others could." She looked unapologetically at me. "I trust few men. John will see what faith I place in you. You must get him out of Brittany. For me, Robin. For the crown."

~ ~ ~

Woodsmoke drifted through the air. Duke Arthur's banner rippled above the palace in the breeze. He was in residence, and with him his retinue.

I had been here before, but this was the first time I needed to slip inside unobserved. Torches illuminated the lush garden surrounding the courtyard and a stand of evergreens shielded a postern gate, which meant my approach from the thick wood beyond shouldn't be noticed. The great hall overlooked it all, its windows shuttered to ward off the cool April evening.

Sweat beaded on my brow. One guard stood near the courtyard door. I collected a handful of rocks I could use to distract him. If that didn't work, I would take him if I must.

As I stole closer, movement off to my left caught the guard's eye.

*John.*

And in fine form – usual form. John's hands roughly caressed a woman dressed in fine silks. I lowered my head, disgusted, though John would admit he couldn't care less whether he had an audience or not.

There was no escape from the lustful moans, grunts,

and thrusts that ended when he climaxed with a groan. No whispers of love. No promises. For a minute they hung against the wall unmoving. He finally pecked her cheek, pinched her buttocks, and pulled away, tucking his flaccid cock into his braies and adjusting his hose.

"Hawise," John said.

"My name is Millesant."

"I was thinking of Hawise, one of the court whores at Rouen."

Millesant slapped John. "Bastard."

John rubbed his cheek. "She was a much better garden fuck than you, dear lady."

Her hand shot out again, but John seized it. His fingers hooked Millesant's neck and he dragged her close, forcing his tongue into her mouth. She wrenched away from him and stalked toward the courtyard door.

My gut churned. John was as cruel and cold as ever. *You must get him safely away...*

I would. For Queen Eleanor. For England. I had spent near a score of years fighting the French. I would not see them take England.

Shaking my head, I approached John quietly. He'd retreated to a stone bench and gulped down wine, nearly choking when he saw me emerge from the shadows. I offered him the sealed messages from the king and Eleanor.

John read the words, his face intent. "I am his heir. I am the king," he said wistfully, and then cleared his throat. "As it should be."

We did not even know if Richard was dead, but gangrene was a merciless, aggressive killer. I had seen it rack a man's body and take him in two days. A week had passed since that bolt struck Richard down. Time enough that he could be at St. Peter's gate. I almost smiled, envisioning that audience. Ever the diplomat, Richard would negotiate for admittance.

Convincing John to leave required no coaxing. He understood the danger should his nephew's men learn the king was dying.

John had untied the horses and mounted one I'd left tied outside the postern gate. As I pulled it shut, voices rang through the garden. Millesant. "He was there – near the fountain." Pebbles stirred beneath heavy boots.

John wheeled his bay around and shot down the path. Guards bolted toward the gate. I wasn't a praying man, but at that moment I asked for God's help. So close to turning for England, for Marian – I could not get caught now.

My stallion had started for the deep wood, but a quick whistle brought him back. I sprang into the saddle as two men charged through the gate. Fer reared, forcing them back. But the whole of the Breton court would know the news if that woman had heard our conversation.

I spurred my horse after John. We didn't slow for several miles and when we did John was quick to condemn his brother's careless ways. The shock of the news had dimmed and was now buried behind a cold façade. "The great warrior takes a bolt whilst walking through his own camp. God can be spiteful I would say."

He needn't remind me. I'd seen King Richard cheat death in the Holy Land, and from Normandy to Aquitaine. I could only imagine how pissed he must be, not struck down in the midst of battle.

"Richard wants to be buried at our father's feet at Fontevraud. Ironic, isn't it? He drove the man to his death, fighting him until the end." John scoffed.

"Their relationship had its failings. Not unlike yours. But King Richard had great respect for your father."

John's eyes narrowed. I could have reminded him he had deserted his dying father but kept my tongue. The list of John's offenses against his family, including his attempt to usurp Richard's throne, was as long as I was tall.

"What of your father, Robin?"

The hair on my neck prickled. "We had our disagreements," I offered. "Is any father-son relationship without them?" It was more than I wanted to say. John knew my father had left our village in Lincolnshire, but we had covered those tracks well. There'd been no indication John or his spies knew I'd settled him in Yorkshire. And he knew nothing of Marian and our children, and I had to keep it that way.

John glanced sidelong at me with those piercing eyes. I dreaded there'd be more inquiries about my father. Fighting a biting fear, I stroked Fer's mane to calm my mind. I thought of Robert and Lucy, sending ripples of longing through my heart and soul. To be home with Marian. To watch the children grow...

John surprised me when he turned the conversation to himself. "Most of the barons will support me, here and in England." He reached for the wineskin hooked on his saddle.

"Support, yes – mayhap for a brief while. But trust? They still remember your actions against the king whilst he was on crusade and during his imprisonment. You have their support because they would not have a boy crowned who sits in the lap of the king of France."

John uncorked the wine and took a deep swallow. "And you feel the same way."

"You have repeatedly threatened me and the people I care for because I helped stop your treason."

A shadow fell across John's face.

Tugging at the neck of my tunic, I swallowed hard.

"I know I am only alive because of King Richard's grip on you, my lord."

The veins in John's neck rippled. "You kept me from the crown!" He sounded like a petulant child. "Richard's time is over, Robin. I will not forget... any of it."

~ ~ ~

We rode through the night. I just wanted to be rid of John, to get home to Marian.

*I will not forget.*

John sulked in silence. A good thing because if he opened his mouth I could not swear but I might leave him at the side of the road with a neck broken from a fall.

By mid-morning I delivered him safely across the Norman border to allies who would accompany him to Chinon. He would rendezvous with Queen Eleanor there.

I turned north, heading for the coast. Rain soaked the land and churning seas kept boats at the dock in Barfleur until the sixth day of April when I finally sailed for England.

From the galley I stared back toward the town. No bells, no chaos. I counted back the days. Eleven since that bolt struck King Richard. Surely Queen Eleanor's arrival in his camp would stir gossip. With John gathering men around him to secure the treasury, word would wash across the land – then across the sea. Mayhap it already infiltrated the lanes, but the quiet of Barfleur gave me hope I was one or more days ahead of the news.

As soon as it spread, John's men would hunt me down.

*I will not forget.*

Robin du Louviers, Robin Carpenter – must die.

~  ~  ~

It was late in the day and a breeze off the Leen chilled the air in Nottingham. Draped in the castle's shadows, Ye Olde Trip to Jerusalem was not astir with crowds. I'd been on the road from Southampton for four days. If news of the king's death had come this far north – for certainly the gangrene must have taken him by now – I was certain I'd see people gossiping in the streets, taverns overflowing, praying priests, and mayhap more soldiers.

Most shops on Castle Gate Road were shuttered, but one shopkeeper swept the step outside his door. He cast a curious look my way, and then nodded as I passed. Another moved leather goods from a cart into his shop. He studied me a moment. I wasn't dressed in the king's colors, but had a fine woolen cloak strapped behind my saddle. My leather chausses – a bit mud-splattered – were rich-looking. He spread his hands over his wares. A crucifix with an intricate ingrained design caught my eye. Mayhap a gift for Marian, but I shook my head. "Not today, friend." I didn't need to leave him any memory of a man wanting a gift for his wife.

I trotted through the wooden gatehouse at the castle unchallenged. Clangs echoed from the blacksmith shop, cows grazed in the field, and the tiltyard stood deserted.

Two guards tracked my movement toward the barbican of the middle bailey. Fer's hooves clattered on the stone bridge, and I reined in.

"What business, sir?" one shouted down at me from the tower.

I held tight on Fer's reins though I didn't feel a

hasty departure would be necessary. The portcullis was up. This was not a place preparing for siege or unrest, which bolstered my confidence. "I am Sir Robin du Louviers. I've a message for William FitzHenry, the castellan's clerk."

The other guard straightened – he recognized my name. John's words beat like a hammer in my mind. *I will not forget.* I blew out a breath, and held a straight face.

The guard gestured toward the keep. I nudged Fer through the barbican, trotted past the timber-framed buildings and chapel in the middle bailey, and crossed the bridge into the upper bailey.

A young squire came from the hall as I tethered my horse. "I'll take you to Sir William," he said when I announced my business. He turned back to the king's hall rather than the keep.

Known across Nottinghamshire as Sir William FitzHenry, the castellan clerk's true name was Allan a Dale. He had been my squire until King Richard appointed him to the position, and had let it be known Allan, er William, was the bastard son of his own late brother. No one would dare question the king.

Walking the length of the hall as the boy slipped into the adjoining solar, I admired the gold-threaded designs on the linen cloth on the table. Gilded candle holders, crimson-cushioned benches, and a sideboard replete with silver platters and cups and embossed flagons for wine lent the room an air of opulence. Allan had done well these past five years. Too bad it must end.

My palms began to sweat. *Get me away from this place.*

The boy returned with a servant who beckoned me into the solar. I was barely through the door as Allan approached, his face filled with the boyish mischievousness I remembered so well. He embraced me warmly. I held him a long while, our grips on other each tightening.

I was as proud of him as a father would be of a son, but couldn't help but tease. "You don't do your business in the keep?"

Allan pounded my back. "I am closer to the secret passages here. Easier to escape."

Pouring cups of wine, the servant tried to hide a chuckle. Allan, of course, was serious whether the older man knew it or not.

"My God, Robin," Allan said, "it is good to have a friendly face nearby. Does the king's business bring you?"

With his eyes on mine, Allan caught my subtle nod and dismissed his attendants. He grabbed a piece of cheese and dried apple from the desk as their footsteps faded. "What has happened?"

Stunned when I told him of Richard's mortal wound, Allan sat hard at his desk suddenly looking much older than his twenty-two summers. His green eyes misted. The high-backed chair seemed to swallow him. He guzzled his wine and stared past me. "He named John to be king?"

I gulped my drink, nodding. We both knew John would never allow Allan to retain his office. He would want Allan's head as much as mine. "You should leave Nottingham, today, tomorrow the latest."

A crooked smile curved the edges of his mouth. "I was tiring of this life. Was never one for finery, not after living on the streets of London and following the king's army to the Holy Land." He ran his hand along the fine oak desk, glanced from the sideboard laden with food to me, and then grinned. "I've had a pack ready for four years."

"There's a place for us at Castle l'Aigle."

Allan shook his head, pushing back the blond hair that fell across his eyes. "I've stockpiled food and coin. Mapped out a dozen tunnels."

"You've been busy."

Allan chuckled. "The Hood's work will go on. Some we've kept in the caves in Sherwood, but just as much in the undercroft here." He scrubbed his hands together. "Thanks to the sheriff and goodly travelers along the Old North Road we will not forsake the poor."

"Goodly travelers?" I laughed and feigned pulling back a bow string. "At the tip of an arrow they aren't so reluctant to hand over a coin or two."

Allan grabbed the flagon and refilled our cups. "We never leave them with empty pockets. That would be bad manners." He said he would take the news to our friends, and then took a long swallow of his drink, savoring it with a sigh. It wouldn't be his last – I imagine he had hidden plenty to replenish his needs, and those of his gang.

I warmed my hands at the brazier, studying everything Allan must leave behind. Trading this life for a life in the forest.

"You remember our motto?" Allan lifted his drink to me. "'Rob from the rich, give to the poor'."

I smiled. "I do like that turn of the phrase."

"We could use your help here."

"The cause is a good one, but Marian will want me to find a way to help that doesn't involve anything illegal."

Allan came around the desk. "I can't argue that it's well past time you gave yourself to your wife." He wrapped me in a brotherly embrace. "May we find peace and joy in our new lives. God be with you, Robin."

I rode out taking one last look at the keep. "Goodbye, Nottingham. May our paths never cross again."

Dark clouds loosed a torrent of rain as I crossed the open fields north of town. I pulled my woolen hood over my head and my cloak closer to ward off the stinging cold deluge.

I did not know how or when, but I would see Allan again. I admired him for choosing to stay in Nottingham, but I had tired of saying *goodbye* and *someday* to Marian. The thought of falling asleep with her in my arms sent ripples of pleasure down my spine. We would have a life at Castle l'Aigle, even if we must forever hold the secret of our family there.

Unplowed fields gave way to Sherwood Forest. I slowed Fer to a trot, wary of roots and ruts on the road. Birch and oak rose like an army around me. Bracken and evergreens carpeted the forest floor.

Allan's gang had eyes on the road for riders traveling alone like me no matter the weather. At close inspection, an outlaw might believe my purse was heavy with coin.

The rain dwindled to a drizzle. The *clop-clop* of Fer's hooves on fallen leaves and the song of woodlarks filled me with a peace I had not felt since learning of the king's lethal wound. Rest his soul.

Bushes half up a hill rustled, but not from a breeze. The outlaws were here. Watching. I reached for my wineskin, lifted it to them and then uncorked it to take a swallow. Would Allan's men know me?

I saw the archer from the corner of my eye. Then two more in plain sight, and a fourth man brandished a sword in the road ahead of me. Every one of them, including a boy who looked no older than fifteen summers, dressed in brown from head to toe. All but the boy were broad through the chest from years plying their skills with a bow.

I reined in, both hands held high to show I wasn't reaching for my blade.

"We'll have your coin, friend." The sword-brandishing outlaw was brash and confident.

I nodded, tossing my hood back and slowly resting my hands on the pommel of my saddle. "True on both counts."

That drew a frown, and I noticed the other men blink, confounded by my response.

I locked eyes with the outlaw, certain I could be as bold as him. I'd been accused of it, teased about it, often enough through the years by friends and foes. "I've just left our friend Allan packing his goods at the castle."

I'd have missed the slight tilt of the outlaw's head had I not been watching him.

Three more men with bows appeared at the edge of the road. I didn't recognize any of them but Allan trusted them, and so must I – at least to a point.

"I had a token engraved with a hooded falcon – do you know that sign?" Years earlier, we used the wooden token to signal friend. My mind on family, I'd forgotten to ask Allan if carrying that would give me safe passage through Sherwood. At least I knew the Hood gang wasn't in the habit of murdering travelers. "Or mayhap Allan exchanged it for another?"

The outlaw took a step towards me, his face no less stern. "He's packing you say?"

"King Richard was mortally wounded in Aquitaine. John, who will be king, has no kind thoughts of Allan or me." I brushed raindrops from my cloak. "I am – was – Robin du Louviers, and would ask you to forget my name."

My journey to York was only for me and my closest friends to know and I'd tell them no more. The old

Robin must disappear. For Marian and my children – it was the only way to keep them safe.

With a shrewd smile, the man eyed me. "King Richard's man. Tales of your exploits are near legend."

There were past times I would revel in that, but I cringed. I did not need my name waved over John's head.

The outlaw signaled one of his archers forward. I gave his gang a quick look. They stood firm, arrows trained from my head to hip. Did they believe me?

Exchanging his sword for the archer's bow, the outlaw nocked it and drew back the string. His men relaxed, some even grinned. "Prove you are who you say." He loosed the arrow, his shot penetrating an oak a hundred feet away.

*Too easy.*

The archer offered me an arrow. I shrugged, and then slid from the saddle. The outlaw handed over the bow. I tested the string, nocked and let fly. The arrow hissed through the air. And missed!

The outlaws raised their bows again.

"Well." I shook my head. "That doesn't happen very often." Rather than give back the bow, I extended my hand for a second arrow. I wasn't about to offer any excuses. "May I?"

The archer graciously pulled one from his quiver and passed it to me with a sly grin.

Nock, loose. Before the arrow struck a tree three times the distance from the first, I'd reached for a third arrow. Eyes wide, the outlaws gaped and then cheered as my shot split the second.

"Allan always speaks well of you," the outlaw said as I turned the bow over to the archer. "He says you're a friend."

I reached for the purse tied to my belt. Coins clinked. "I can offer two pennies now, and will send more when I'm settled." The man could insist on more, but half that could buy two chickens – though I suspected they'd a brood of their own somewhere in the forest.

Fingering the silver I tossed to him, he said, "Whoever you are, nameless old friend of Allan, we've a place not far to stay dry and rest for the night."

Fer grunted, head lowered. I gave a whistle and he sidled next to me. I was anxious to move on, but we both needed rest. "My thanks, friends."

Through the drizzle I could see the outlaw's eyes gleaming. "If you're headed north and need a friend, see the butcher in the shadow of Tickhill Castle. Name of William." He cocked his head toward a path through the bushes. "This way."

I followed the outlaw into the wood. Tickhill on the morrow. I'd find this butcher, always mindful of having friends, especially when many enemies could be watching.

I slept well and dry in a warm cave and, come morning, slurped down an egg poached in broth by one of Allan's men. The day's ride to Tickhill felt like it would never end, the sun a stranger, the rain cascading down from dark gray skies throughout the day. I stabled Fer in the village, tossed off my wet cloak, and started down the road past wattle and daub cottages. Candlelight flickered through shutters closed against the April chill.

Near the castle gatehouse, a few men gathered outside a tavern. Their conversation was lively, peppered with shouts and curses – something had roused their spirits. Excitement and curiosity filled every face.

"Was it one of de Camville's men?" one voice rang out.

All I wanted was a hot meal and a bed at the tavern and dreams of Marian, but those words turned my ear. I knew the name well. Gerard de Camville, former sheriff of Lincolnshire and castellan at Lincoln had long supported John. It had cost him his position whilst Richard was on crusade.

"He's ridden all day to deliver a message."

"Must be of great import."

"What do you suppose it might be?"

Lincoln was a day's ride to the east and on Ermine, an old Roman road connecting it to London and points north. This messenger... I closed my eyes a moment. It had to be news of King Richard's death. *God rest his soul.*

A bell began to peal from the chapel, its spire just visible above the stone curtain wall surrounding the castle. Guards lit torches on the gatehouse tower and the voices around me grew subdued. Three men appeared, one in a fur-trimmed cloak and hat. Whispered asides repeated, "Lord Thomas" or "The castellan."

"What news?" someone shouted above the clamor of the bell.

The castellan glanced toward the chapel, and a moment later the bell ceased ringing.

"The king is dead." His voice was like a hammer pounding steel, strong and steady. "Long live King John."

The quiet was palpable. Excitement and curiosity turned to shock and indifference or sorrow. Merchants and villeins felt the hand of their local lord more than a king few had ever seen. Around me, some of the folk signed themselves, and one man ran a hand along the sheath of his long dagger.

197

God's blood... A pity they'd never met the man I had served. *My* king, Richard. A brilliant tactician who knew when to fight, or when to be the diplomat.

A baby's cry broke the silence, and the castellan shouted, "May God keep King John. May he long rule."

Voices joined in chorus. "Long live King John! Long live King John!"

John might be my liege lord by right, but I would never kneel before the man and pledge my fealty. Never.

Deep breaths slowed my boiling blood. I pushed my way through the crowds and into the tavern before the place thronged with bodies. I had to eat, and would try to sleep a few hours before I took to the road again.

I had to get home. If Lincoln and Tickhill had the news, then York would know today, or mayhap by tomorrow. Marian held her concern close, the strongest woman I knew, not unlike Queen Eleanor. But she would worry when she heard, and she'd done that for far too many years. No more. *I'll be with you soon, my love.*

Rush torches on the tavern walls flickered illuminating faces around me. I sat across from the door. My name might be known, but I'd never had business in Tickhill and didn't fear being recognized. Not yet. *King* John was occupied across the Narrow Sea. He wouldn't have time to plaster my name and face across the land. Not yet.

Mayhap Queen Eleanor could convince him killing the man who'd saved him from Duke Arthur and the Bretons was reckless. It was a mad thought, and I shook my head.

Men strode through the door, none paying me much mind. I could eat in peace and listen. A young boy delivered ale, a trencher with a piece of chicken drenched in dark brown gravy, and wheaten bread warm from the oven. Two merchants closest to me laughed at others taking bets as to whether their new king would spend more time in England than his late brother. I could have reminded them Richard was defending his birthright across the Narrow Sea, ensuring his barons did not lose their own land to the French king. The men complained of their taxes to pay his ransom, to support a crusade called for by their Pope. I held my tongue.

The tavern door flew open and grating shouts came from the road. Several mail-clad knights cantered past.

Men in the tavern were on their feet. Racing outside, they nearly stumbled over each other. I wasn't going anywhere, determined to sup until my belly was full or the tavern started to burn down around me. The chicken was juicy and tender. I soaked my bread in the gravy and bit into it, savoring the first decent meal I'd had since crossing the Narrow Sea.

A stocky man wearing a blood-stained apron started past me. *Could it be...*

"William the butcher?" I called.

He stared down at me with a grizzled face and deep set eyes. "Do I know you?"

I looked around the room, which had nearly emptied. "Robin." I combed my fingers through my long wind and rain-soaked hair. "A friend of the Hoods."

William mulled over my words, his brow puckered.

"Allan's gang," I added, "who told me to make your acquaintance."

My mention of Allan met his approval. "A man who keeps good company then." He almost smiled.

I offered William my hand, but a curse from the tavern keeper distracted him. He stood at the door speaking to a mounted knight. William hurried to his side. "Soldiers," he called back to me. "Sighted just to the east."

*So it begins.*

William hurried outside. My jaw clenched. Men who'd lost land or titles during King Richard's reign would fight to take them back. Townsfolk would be at the mercy of fractious barons and soldiers. It was always the innocents who suffered.

My hand coiled into a fist. *My stallion...* If soldiers ravaged the village, Fer would be a great prize. I forgot about the rest of my food and bolted out the door.

From somewhere up the road came a roar of voices. The scent of burning wood whipped my nose as I ran. Townsfolk with clubs chased a man on a horse as black as a moonless sky. They cut him off, and forced him toward the gatehouse. I heard a cheer – a guard on the wall walk must have shot him through.

Hooves pounded the cobbled street and two mounted riders emerged from a shroud of smoke. Dressed in mail from head to foot, each knight brandished a blade in one hand, a blazing torch in the other. People scattered from their path. I grabbed my long dagger and unsheathed my sword. My hand melded round the hilt, the blade raised high above my head.

Teeth grinding so hard I swore I heard one crack, I ran at the riders. Spittle spewed from my mouth. "For King Richard," I shouted. I must have looked and sounded like a madman.

"Scum!" one of the knights shouted.

He brought his sword round in an arc that would take my head off. I wore only a thick-padded gambeson and it was too late to wish for a shield. Terror gripped me – fear is good – but only for a moment. I didn't duck and both horses shied, one veering up the road, leaving his companion to fend for himself.

My blade met the knight's in a thundering crash. The impact sent him reeling and ripples shot up my arm, my muscles tightening. I whirled around and wrenched him from the saddle.

As his palfrey bolted, the knight staggered to his feet like a man who'd had a few too many ales. Somehow, he'd managed to keep both sword and torch locked in his fists.

"You bastard!" With a grunt, he tossed the fiery weapon onto a thatched-roof cottage.

I blew out a breath. "Why did you do that?"

He stalked towards me, sword slicing the air. Smoke grew thick as fire spread from the cottage to another rooftop. *The stables...*

Flames burst out on another roof, shooting sparks into the sky.

*Must get to the stables.*

My blade arced high and downward and I threw off his strike, our weapons ringing. Sweat trickled down my back. I drove him back with one slash, then a second that slapped his hauberk.

Breaths steady, I lunged forward. My sword crackled against the mail on the knight's chest. I brought it round again and raked his arm. I swore I saw surprise in his eyes at my skill. He staggered back, sucking air through his teeth. He hacked down, up, but each blow was weaker than the last.

Our weapons locked. With a swift upward cut, I sent his sword into the air. It clattered to the cobbled stone as I pinned him against a wall, my blade at his neck. Ash whirled like heavy snow around us. Burning thatch fell at our feet, but I didn't care. He stared at me, defiant, but too worn to pull away. I could dispatch him to his Maker with a twist of my wrist. Had done that as King Richard's man more times than I would want to count.

Damn... We are both Englishmen. I should not have to fight him. But if John sent men for me or for my family, friends, the people I loved, I would do it. I would kill.

"Leave these people alone!" I pricked his throat with my blade, drawing a speck of blood. "They've done nothing to hurt you."

He glared at me. "Who are you?"

"No one!"

No amount of reasoning would keep the man from following his lord's orders, but mayhap he would stop and think, question. Englishmen against Englishmen – was I the only one who saw nothing good could come from it?

He leaned closer, trying to loose my grip on him, but it only pressed my blade deeper into his flesh. Blood trickled down his neck. I wouldn't kill him, but the townsfolk or castle guard would string him up if I left him unconscious.

Stepping back, I smashed his face with the hilt of my sword. He groaned, blood rushing from his nose.

"Son of a..."

"You're alive. Now get the hell out of here before I do worse."

The man took me at my word. He staggered up the road in the direction of the stables. "You're not getting my horse!" Waving my sword, I tore past him.

My heart sank with each step I took. Wind carried hot ash from one roof to another. How could the stables be spared?

Before I'd gained another hundred steps, curses erupted like the flames licking the air around me.

"God's blood, damn you!" William the butcher sliced through a rope securing a side of beef on a horse tethered outside his shop. A soldier stormed through the door, abandoning his second stolen slab to the ground.

William saw him charge. He grabbed a loose stone from the road, hardly a deadly weapon, but his aim struck true. "God take you!" he shouted as the rock ricocheted off the soldier's nose.

Face souring, the man unsheathed his weapon. William wrenched the beef from the horse. I bellowed the war cry of King Richard's troops. "*Dex aie!*" Running hard, I plowed towards them.

William swung the beef, blocking the downward slash of the soldier's blade. Before the man's second pass slit the butcher like a cut of meat, my sword swept across his neck. His weapon slid from his hands. He clasped his bloodied throat and collapsed to the ground.

William thanked me with a curt nod. Fire roared from a nearby roof, and he just shook his head.

I pointed up the road. "My horse..."

He waved me away knowing there was nothing I could help with here – little chance his shop would be spared. Smoke hid the stars and shrouded the moon in a gray blanket as I raced away.

Just ahead, the corral was empty. A man lay prone on the ground by the open stable doors, wounded or dead I couldn't tell. Shouts echoed nearby, but the street was deserted. I could only think the attackers had already plundered the stables. Fer – my last connection to Queen Eleanor – would be lost to me. I ran that much harder.

Suddenly, two mounted knights charged from the barn with a dozen horses on leads. Fer was near the back of the herd. Both knights had swords drawn, but there was no one to challenge them.

Not yet, I thought.

I rushed towards them. Perhaps I *was* mad.

Cursing under my breath, I decided another head-on confrontation against two mounted knights was more than mad. On my warhorse, or with bow, I wouldn't hesitate. On foot? And having lit off from the tavern and faced two already? My luck might have deserted me.

Slowing, I turned into a side street and cut through a narrow alley to intercept the thieves. Dark shadows closed around me as the knights cantered past. I sheathed my sword. Fists clenched at my side, I waited, blinking back sweat stinging my eyes. I counted hoofbeats, watched the horses pass until the last six moved directly in front of me and a wagon blocking the thieves line of sight.

With a whistle, I broke at a run from the alley. Fer's ears perked. I sprang into the back of the wagon, and then vaulted onto Fer's bare back with another low whistle.

Fer lifted his head when I grabbed his mane, my thighs clamping around him. "Good to see you, old friend." He snorted as if to say 'where have you been?'

One of the knights spotted me. Grasping the short dagger from my boot, I started to cut the rope looped over Fer's neck. Riding bareback was the easy part. But trying to sever the line and stay astride wasn't in my pocket of stunts.

The knight handed the lead to his companion. I carved deeper into the rope. The knight circled back to attack, his sword aimed for a swift cut. I seated the dagger in my mouth and grabbed Fer's mane with both hands. Waiting until the last possible second, I threw my leg over Fer's neck, twisted, and pivoted to the ground. The blade slashed the air, missing me. I whipped back onto Fer as the knight passed.

Mouth bloodied from the dagger, I worked all the harder to slice through the rope. My heart pounded like thunder in my ears.

The knight came up beside me. I twisted, driving my dagger into his gloved hand. Cursing, he brought the flat of his sword down across my arm, barely a whack. Fer widened the distance between us and I reached for my sword. But too late...

The knight's blade pierced my chausses ripping into my flesh just above the knee. Horrendous pain shuddered through me. Vision blurring, I lost my grip on Fer and the world went black around me.

※　※　※

"Marian!" *Legs clamped around a thick oak branch, I reached out for Marian. "Take my hand."*

*"It's no good..."*

*I touched her finger, leaned down further to slip my hand around hers.*

*"You waited too long..."*

*I lost my grip, and Marian fell into the mist.*

"No!"

I jerked upright, sweat pouring down my face. My eyes were pinched tight as I heaved convulsively. My leg burned, the pain enough to make me want to retch.

"Awake. Finally." A man grunted. "Some nightmares you've had."

That voice – I'd heard it before. The smells of raw meat assaulted my nose. The wave of pain faded, and I struggled to open my eyes. William the butcher stood over a huge trestle covered in blood, meat, and knives, saws, and cleavers.

"Was a damn fool thing you did," William said.

I swallowed back the bile in my throat. "How long?"

"Three days." William came to the bedside and held out a cup. "Tisane. From the surgeon."

Stomach churning, I swallowed the disgusting liquid and gagged. William offered me a flagon. "Ale. From me."

The drink soothed my parched throat and drowned the bitterness of the medicinal herb tea. "Thank you."

"Saved me from that bastard knight." William's voice was low, but he looked past the open door. "Friend of the Hood. It's the least I could do."

Trying to offer a smile, I grimaced. Even my face hurt. I tossed off the thin blanket covering me from the waist down and stared at the bloodied bandage on my leg. Chasing down thieves would have to wait.

"Couldn't get your horse," William said.

I gulped more ale. "Did anyone recognize them?"

William shook his head. "But they rode east, not that you'll be catching them up anytime too soon."

I'd find Fer some day. And when I did... My thoughts turned as dark as the stone on the walls around me. I blinked. Stone, not timber. This wasn't William's shop.

He saw my gaze flick from one end of the room to the other. "Nothing but ash, like half the town. We're in the castle."

My throat grew thick. "In the king's control?"

"Aye. The castellan has pledged his fealty to the new king."

"John?" I knew it, but asked anyway.

William nodded. "Nottingham, Lincoln, too, but we've heard little else."

*God's blood.* Would John have crossed to England by now? The days... how many days had passed? I couldn't think.

"John must not – no one must learn I've been here."

"Not from my lips." William crossed the room kicking up sawdust around the room. He glanced back at me. "The wheeler saw you jump from the wagon outside his shop."

"Christ." I rubbed a new ache in my temples. "Has he told the whole town by now?"

William chuckled. "He's telling about some madman who went after the horses, but he didn't see you fall. Lucky for you, those thieves cut right near me. That trick you pulled – never seen such a thing before. But I still say you're a damn fool."

"A fool whose head the king will have." I tried to move my leg and winced. It would be days before I could leave.

William studied me, his brows arched. "Whoever you are, whatever you did, do you want me to get word to our friend?"

I took a deep breath, scrubbing my chin. My close-cropped beard was thick, a bushy mess. "Messengers can be intercepted. You risk enough in whatever business you have with our friend. Don't up the odds."

I began to peel back the bandage. The flesh didn't smell and was only slightly red. I took hope no infection had set in, but when I shifted to lean against the wall, the throbbing in my leg took my breath away.

William retrieved a small bag from a meat hook and tossed it to me. "Clean wraps. Poultice for the wound." He grabbed his cleaver and hacked into a cut of meat. "Hungry?"

I felt like shite, but needed my strength back. My stomach rumbled.

Taking the noise for an *aye*, William said, "I'll get some pottage for you when I deliver this to the cook." He carved another chunk of beef with his bloodied cleaver.

I swallowed hard. The man could truss me up like a side of beef, turn me over to the castellan. I could think of reasons why he would – coin was enough for most men – and mayhap a handful more why he would not. He'd had three days to get rid of me and years to reveal Allan's association with the outlaws in Sherwood. Did it come down to trust? Hope? That, and doing what was right for the good of the people.

I would not forget William. Allies like him were priceless.

✤ ✤ ✤

Under William's good care, I paced his makeshift shop for what seemed like miles. My leg ached but improved each day. My strength trickled back.

Only once did he ask me where I was headed, what I would do.

"Exile." I said no more, and he did not ask again.

I was not good company, saying little, but while we supped, he spoke of what he'd learned on his daily deliveries to the castle kitchen. Some was just the chattering of cooks, clerks, carters, guards and the like, but other bits were from the castellan's mouth or his seconds'. It was much the same each day – clearing of rubble in the village, rebuilding, spring planting.

I hadn't ventured into the bailey, but William saw me watching the carts overflowing with hay or crates and barrels lumbering past his door.

"The castellan says we must prepare for siege."

I nodded, relieved Marian was behind the walls of Castle l'Aigle, and that Robert still trained with the baron there.

"The king?"

"Still no word that he's in England." William

tapped his mug. "Isn't it always the way, the king must be crowned at Westminster?"

"It is." I had been to Richard's coronation, but certainly would not be at John's.

"I hear it's not a long journey across the Narrow Sea."

Tipping my head side to side, I picked up my ale, and then took a drink. "Depends on the weather. Many a man never prays harder when a day's journey on the water feels like a month in Hell. The sea can be unforgiving."

"I won't ask what you know of Hell." William chuckled. "But you look like you've been there the last few days." He picked up his cutting knife and swept it toward my hairy face. "I'm good with this."

I combed my fingers through my shoulder length hair and scruffy beard. "Better?"

William laughed, pounding the trestle so hard his ale sloshed over the rim. He cleaned the spill with his bloodied apron, and we downed the brew before he returned to his work.

Four days later, William helped me acquire two palfreys. Dried meat, bread and cheese, and a flagon of watered wine in my pack, I left Tickhill behind.

It had been near a fortnight since I'd set foot on English soil. From Tickhill, I stayed off the Old North Road to avoid the small hamlets along the way. I passed peasants hunting for game – a crime in the king's forest – but kept my head down and spoke to no one.

*Marian.* Every step closer to my love raised my spirits.

Daydreams took me to times I'd held Marian's hand on a rocky outcrop at the river, our secret place deep in the wood. She was a princess to me in her emerald green dress and with small white flowers like a crown in her hair. I had kissed her eyelids, her nose, heard her sweet giggle. I could see her, hear her, plain as day. Her dark eyes and round face sent love and desire through my veins.

It was growing dark when I sighted the 'Old Man', an ancient tree on l'Aigle land. One of the l'Aigle brothers had drawn an eagle on it, burnt the edges with the tip of a heated sword. The creature's wings spanned more than a third of the massive trunk. I was close to home. To my family.

Spurring my horse to a gallop, my heart raced. The tree-lined road gave way to pastureland and I barely noticed the grazing sheep and their new offspring. The stone keep of Castle l'Aigle rose high on the motte, wind rippling the tower's blue and white banners emblazoned with a red eagle in flight.

It didn't matter that Marian wasn't standing on the wall walk and wouldn't hear me. I shouted her name. "Marian!"

I pricked spurs to my horse and charged like my life depended on it. Which it did. My life with Marian, the children – I would have it now. *King* John be damned. "Nothing will stop me."

Except the gate.

The portcullis was down.

A guard on the gatehouse tower watched me approach. He turned his back a time or two, perhaps speaking to someone I couldn't see.

Reining in, I waved to him. "I have a message for the Lady Marian."

The guard turned away again. Voices drifted from the tower and a second guard holding a lance peered down. "No one passes without the baron's consent. Who are you?"

"I am her husband Robin d–" I bit my lip, chiding myself for nearly revealing the name that must be buried. "Robin Fitzwilliam. Now, if you please, get Lord Gilbert."

The guards disappeared. The skies grew darker with each minute that passed – they'd never see me as the moon slid behind clouds. How could I be so close, yet barred from this place that would be home?

Finally there was movement atop the tower.

"Robin?"

I looked closer, smiled, and raised my hand to Lord Gilbert l'Aigle.

"Open the gate," he shouted.

Gil met me at the bottom of the stairs inside the bailey. Guards held their swords ready and stood to either side of him. I hung onto the pommel on my saddle and slid down cautiously, testing my injured leg before I put my weight down on it. It was stiff, aching, not necessarily improved from my last day at William's, but I had been astride since before dawn.

I turned to bow to the baron, but he grasped my shoulders before I could. "Is it you?" Gil studied my face, my scruffy beard, and then wrapped his arms around me.

Wobbling on my injured leg, I winced. "My lord." I pounded his back.

"You're hurt?" He shouted at someone to get the healer, and then turned back to me. "We've been so worried. Come, come." Gil started toward the keep, slowing when he noticed my limp. "You must be hungry. We'll have cook fix a platter."

"Marian first." I grinned. "Then food."

Gil laughed. "I just left the ladies – they'll be in the solar."

I wanted to run to my wife, but might fall headlong to the stone cobbles if I tried. When we entered the great hall with its soaring stone arches, the door from the solar opened. Gil's wife Bea rushed up to me. "Blessed be God, you're home safe." She kissed me on both cheeks, and then tipped her head toward the solar.

A fire in the hearth washed the room in a pale glow. Marian sat by the window with her embroidery on her lap.

"Bea, what...?" She looked up, and then shot to her feet. "Oh dear God. Robin!" Tossing her needlework aside, she ran to me.

A twinge racked my leg and I limped heavily, colliding with her near the middle of the room. "My love."

My lips found hers. Her arms went around my neck. I claimed her mouth, but her kisses were as fierce and needy as mine.

Breathless, Marian swept the hair from my brow. "What have you done now, Robin?" She touched my injured leg.

"I tried to stop a man stealing my horse."

"Is he the worse off?"

"I fear not."

Marian turned my sword hand over in her own soft ones. I shivered at her touch.

"What's this?" She pointed to another mark.

"Swipe of a dagger at Tickhill."

Her eyes widened.

I kissed her cheek. "If I could have a bath, I'll tell you about every new one, but *you* must promise to inspect me head to toe."

Marian cleared her throat. "I will do my best, but this..." She touched my beard. "This will not do." She combed her fingers through the bedraggled mess. "I have a blade..."

Intercepting her hand, I said, "Later." My lips found

hers again, and I kissed her deeply, long. Her hand was warm, and mine slid from her face, past her shoulders, to the small of her back. I pulled her closer, smelled her fresh skin. Just as I always remembered.

Marian pulled away from me, smiling. "This way," she said, taking my hand and leading me to our rooms.

I would never forget her touch though she hadn't been in my arms for near three years. Our clothes found the floor and we collapsed on the feather bed tangled in each other's need. Lying with her on this day drove me wild with yearning. My flesh hardened, and a low moan escaped her lips as I took her slow and gentle. "I love you."

Marian answered with her lips on mine, her body arching towards me, her hands pulling me deeper into her. We came in a rush of breaths and words of love. I pressed against her, feeling her heartbeat raging against mine.

Later, I watched her sleeping, her eyelashes brushing her cheeks, her mouth curled in a smile... I want this, want her, every day of my life. My eyes welled with tears.

"What's this?" Marian caught a tear on my cheek.

"Another scar I carry." I smiled wearily.

Marian batted my arm and kissed the tear away. "And this one." She pointed to rough flesh on my shoulder, kissed it. "And this." I trembled when her lips found their way to my chest. She threw the blanket off us. Staring at my still healing leg, she pursed her lips.

I caught hold of her arm, and then pulled her down to me.

"I love you, Robin." Marian's warm breath caressed my face.

"I have missed you so much, my love. Never a day passed, no matter where I was in the king's—"

"I watched messengers arrive, but none with word from you when we heard King Richard passed. Love should not hurt so much."

I brushed my hand across her cheek, my thumb along her lips. "I could not risk anyone discovering we've made a home and family here."

She leaned forward and kissed my cheek. "Knowing that has never made the days any easier."

"I love you so, Marian."

"Will you stay this time?" Her voice was a whisper.

"I exiled you here, and will gladly suffer this with you 'til the end of my days."

"I have you back in my arms." She kissed me again. "Let's not speak of an end."

"A new beginning then. Exile could never taste so good."

© Charlene Newcomb
*Louisiana, 2023*

## AUTHOR'S NOTE

The scenes with Queen Eleanor, John, and Allan are adapted and expanded from chapters of *Swords of the King*

## ABOUT CHARLENE NEWCOMB

Charlene Newcomb, aka Char, writes historical fiction and science fiction. Her award-winning **Battle Scars trilogy** is set in the 12th century during the reign of Richard the Lionheart. Her writing roots are in the *Star Wars Expanded Universe* (aka *Legends*) where she published ten short stories in the **Star Wars Adventure Journal**. Sci-Fi/Space Opera fans should check out

*Echoes of the Storm,* her original novel published in 2020. Char returned to medieval times with her novel *Rogue* in 2023.

'Newcomb [creates] a believable world of the bloody crusades: she captures brilliantly the twisted ideology of those religious wars whilst also narrating the personal traumas and passions of her main characters.'
*Dr. Christopher Monk.*

~ ~ ~

Website: **https://charlenenewcomb.com/**
Buy Charlene's books on Amazon:
**https://viewauthor.at/CharNewcomb**

## 10

# ON SHINING WINGS

### BY MARIAN L THORPE

## NORTHAMPTONSHIRE, 1265

"Tell us again," my oldest grandchild begs. Outside, the snow is falling, but it is tolerably warm close to the hearth. Winters are for stories, and while they've heard this one many a time, I'll do as he asks. He is English, this boy and his brothers and sisters. I am too, I suppose, but once I wasn't.

"The voyage came first," I begin. "Cold it was, and dangerous. Waves that drenched us, and wind so strong the oarsmen couldn't keep us on course."

"Were there sea monsters?" The middle boy's eyes are huge in the firelight.

"Ja, of a sort. *Hvalir*. Whales. Bigger than the ship." I spread my arms wide. "Enormous! And when they surfaced beside us, ahh, the smell of their breath!"

The children giggle as I pretend to gag. Across the hearth, my son smiles, but at his children's amusement. He's heard this story so many times he could tell it himself.

"It took us five days to reach Iceland." I resume the

story. "And more to travel along the coast to the north, where the falcons are."

In my mind I am there again, seventeen, thinking myself a man. My father chose me to accompany him on this task for King Haakon. I look up at the cliffs, hiding my fear. I have gone after eggs and chicks on the cliffs at home, but the seabirds aren't to be feared, even when they scream and peck. Although it's wise to keep your head turned away. Sometimes men have lost eyes to the jab of a beak. And these cliffs are higher. Much higher.

"In summer," I tell the rapt children, "it is light all the time. The sun is never high, but always there."

"How do you know when to sleep?" The oldest girl. Already concerned with the rhythms of the day, when to milk, when to gather eggs, when to eat.

"When you are tired," I tell her. "The body knows, ja?" I bring them back to the story. "Finally we reach the cliffs. We make a camp. There is a beach for the ship, and a place to build a fire and hang a cooking pot. We have fish stew to eat, and bread from home." Stale by then, hard, but soaked in the stew it is fine.

"And then?" The oldest is impatient. He pretends himself me, I think. He wants to imagine the danger. Play at it in his mind. I want him to learn something more.

"And then the next morning we climb up a long valley, to the top of the cliffs." Several hours' walk, it had been. The sun low, but the world is alive. The tundra is in flower, and there are insects and birds everywhere. We carry ropes and baskets with lids. Some men carry cooking equipment, others food. One or two have bows. We will sleep up here, on the clifftops, until we have what we came for.

It took a day to find the first nest, on a ledge maybe twenty man-heights below. My father flattens himself on his belly, peering over the cliffs. Gulls soar and scream. He watches. "Three chicks," he says. "Nearly fledged."

"Do we take them all?" I ask. I will be going over that cliff, harnessed like a pony and held by ropes, to bring up the birds. I am small, and still thin, so it will be easy for the men to handle the ropes. I will wear leather, even a cap to protect my head. These falcons are strong and fierce and huge.

"Always leave one. It will grow fat and strong. In a few years it will breed, so when we come back to fetch more for the king there will be chicks to be had." My father pushes himself up. The breeze is strong, enough to keep the biting insects away. "Time's wasting. Let's get you over, Olai."

I don the leather harness that is a belt around my waist and between my legs. The ropes are attached. I am given a bag to put the chicks in. Eyas is the proper term, I remember, for a hatchling falcon. I tell that to my grandchildren.

"Didn't the harness," – the oldest boy sniggers – "crush your balls?"

"Perrin!" his mother scolds. I laugh.

"Being as scared as I was shrivels them," I tell him. "They lowered me down, backwards. The first step's the hardest, over the edge. Then you hope the men have the rope fast, and keep going." Terrified, I was, for a minute, two. I prayed and prayed to God and the saints. Then a feeling of invincibility took over. If fate wanted me dead, I'd die. Otherwise, I was flying. I laughed, and pushed off and went down further in big leaps, soaring like an eagle. "Hold up!" my father shouted. "And look out!"

A shadow, and then talons too close to my face. I descended an arm's length further, steadying my feet against the rock. I reached for the chick. A glancing blow on my back made me rock. I cried out in fear, but I had a job to do. I took the first chick, cupping fingers over its wings like I'd learned to do with seabird chicks, and slid it into the bag. It didn't struggle. Neither did the second.

"Did you kill the big birds?" my smallest granddaughter asks. Her eyes are wide, wondering.

"No, no," I reassure her. They had circled and cried, but the hungry calls of their remaining chick had to be answered. Inside the bag there was no light, so the two I carried were silent. I clamber back up the cliff. Bits of rock fall from beneath my feet, but the ropes keep me safe, just as the bag keeps the two chicks safe.

Back on the flat ground, I took the chicks, one by one, from the bag. Into a wicker basket they went, the two together for warmth and familiarity. One is larger than the other, stronger. A female, my father told me. When he fed them later, she pecked at the other, trying to take all the food, until I took her out so the other could eat. I stroked her. She pecked at my finger, and I laughed. I dreamt of flying that night. When I woke to find myself on the ground, I nearly cried. I would have, except the men would have laughed at me.

"The food is ready," my son's wife announces. "Come and eat. The story can wait." She is a good, strong woman who has borne my son four children. So far all have lived. She is pregnant again. It is growing colder here, in this place called Northamptonshire where the English king mews his ger-falcons. Each winter now is worse than the last. I wonder if this new babe will live, born as it will be early in the year of Our Lord 1265, into the cold and snow of Fill-Dyke month.

Prayers are said before the food. I lead them, as befits the oldest of the house. I follow all the priests say, fast when I should, stay away from strong drink and women, now my wife is dead. Heaven is in the sky, the priests say. So I must go, because if I am in the sky will I not be flying? Perhaps I will have wings.

We were in Iceland over two summers. That first year I took eight eyas from their nests, some barely fledged, some nearly ready to fly. There are scars on my back from where the adult ger-falcons struck, fighting for their young ones. I bled for my king and those falcons, but I regret none of it.

When I wasn't on the cliffs I helped feed the birds. The hunters brought back grouse, and we took the auklets from the cliffs, for us and for the young falcons. For much of the day they lived in the baskets, covered and quiet, but we took them out, stroked them, talked to them. We were accustoming them to being handled by men, taming them. The first eyas I took, the big female, grew quickly. Soon she had her own basket, the biggest. She was in my charge, and I made sure she thrived.

At night, I dreamt I flew. I felt the wings that sprouted from my back. I soared with the gulls and the falcons. In that half-dreamworld just at waking, I believed for a moment that the scars on my back were from when my wings were taken. I spoke of this to no one mortal, but sometimes I whispered of it to St Michael, first among the angels. Surely an angel would understand?

After the meal we return to the fire. It is nearly coals now, so it is time to sleep. The oldest boy wants more stories. "Tell us about coming to England," he begs. But his father sends him and his brothers to their bed. The girls are helping their mother. My son banks the fire, so it will smoulder over the night and burn bright again in the morning with a little encouragement.

Later I lie on my bed, under a thick blanket. My lord de Hauville has treated me well, as he should. He is one of the king's falconers. He mews the birds when they are not hunted; he takes them across the water to France, if King Henry is minded to fly them there. But it is I who care for them, treats eye infections, notes their mutes for colour and whether they are too liquid or too firm, removes lice, all the time talking to them. I feed them, and sometimes my lord de Hauville will tell me to fly them for exercise, if he is too busy.

I dream of flying more often in this last year. I think I know what that means. In my solitary bed, sometimes I let tears creep down my cheeks when the longing rends me. At church on Sundays and feast days, the priest speaks of the yearning for paradise we should all feel, the paradise closed to us because Eve listened to the serpent. I think that what I feel at dawn, after these dreams, is the longing of an exile too.

In the morning I take the oldest boy to the mews with me. The sky is still grey, heavy with snow. He will begin his formal apprenticeship next year, but for now he sweeps snow from the paths as I cut up food for the falcons, chickens and partridge and rabbits. Six are mewed here, including the king's favourite. My lord de Hauville is given 2d a day by the king for their food. It is more than I am paid.

My hands are cold, wielding the knife and wet with blood. The dogs that guard the mews sit at my feet, waiting for scraps. My grandson finishes clearing the snow. We had to push hard on the gate this morning to gain entry into the enclosure where the mews stand. Snow had drifted against it, and the dogs had been curled together on its doorstep. "You had snow all the time at home," he says to me.

"Ja." Does he want a story about skiing? But something else is on his mind.

"Do the falcons miss it?" my grandson asks. "Snow, and the cliffs, and the sea?" He looks up at me, and I see something new in his eyes. "Do you?"

My king sent me here, I tell him. When we finished in Iceland I was nineteen. Two years of cold and danger, men dead, two falcons dead too. A waste. But we brought back thirteen all in all. Ten were grey, but three were the most valuable white birds. In flight their wings shine like those of angels.

I grew adept at handling the birds, in those two years. So King Haakon sent me from Norway to England with the falcons. I was not unhappy to come, I tell my grandson, and it is true, at least at first. Another adventure, and there was no girl waiting for me. The one I had my eye on had married another while I was gone. I had risked my life for those birds, and I did not want to leave them to the care of another. They knew me. My voice calmed them. I knew how to stroke each bird with a feather to steady them. I even knew how to tell their cries apart. One, I loved fiercely, even though she was to belong to the king of England.

It was I who readied the birds for their presentation to King Henry. In a mews at the White Tower on the great river of London. I smoothed feathers and washed legs and feet, before attaching the jesses of fine leather. And for my favourite, my white lady, I took special care, so that this English king would see how fine she was.

"Did you see the king?" My grandson has propped the broom against the wall of the mews, and has bent to warm his hands in a dog's fur.

"Not that day. But, ja, since then. I have spoken to him once."

"To the king?" His eyes are bright with curiosity. This is not a story I tell, but it is a strong memory. And this boy will succeed me in these mews in a few years. He should know.

"Ja." It is time for our midday food. Usually I eat outside, on a bench against the wall, but not today. It is too cold. I rinse blood from my hands, and beckon to the boy. The dogs crowd in behind him. I let them. Inside it is dim, but warmer, out of the wind. The space smells of old meat and mutes and the dusty scent of the birds. I hand the boy a piece of bread. There are onions too.

My lord de Hauville will come to see the falcons soon. Maybe I will be told to fly the birds today. They will see only snow and rock and ice, and perhaps not recognize where they fly. I will need to be careful. If I lose a bird, I will lose my position. At least. Regardless of what the king said to me years before.

"When did you speak to the king?" my grandson asks, crunching an onion. He is like a terrier after a rat, this one.

"Many years past," I say. We had travelled for several days that March, to the eastern marshes. We were to hunt cranes and herons, birds that only the ger-falcons, large and strong, could take. Best at this was my special falcon, the one I loved. Of the thirteen King Haakon had sent, I doubt he would have parted with her, had he known what she would become. She was pure white, and larger than even the other females. Englene, her name was now. In the French spoken by the king and his lords, it means 'Angel', and when she was high in the sky it was easy to see why. I have seen women drop to their knees and cross themselves when Englene passed over them, her white wings gleaming.

That day in the marshes the ground was a mire, what ground there was. Much was water, with islands covered with sparse trees or turf cropped short by sheep, and vast areas of reed. Not bog like I knew from home, but a place neither lake nor land, where men and women lived in huts on the islands and travelled more by boat than on the occasional paths of logs laid down. The waters teemed with waterfowl and fish, and herons' nests weighed down thin branches. A strange land, and one I did not understand. It made me long for my own land of forest and rock.

There had been much rain that spring; dykes filled in February were overflowing in March. Even on the higher ground, the horses slipped and struggled, mud coating them to their bellies. But King Henry would have his sport, although the water was deep and one packhorse had broken a leg, falling. Henry was no older than me, and I was just twenty. What cares have young men for danger, even when they are kings?

So we led the horses to an island over a causeway of logs. The king of course did not dismount. Englene sat on the king's fist, where her magnificence belonged. God had made Henry a king, so he should fly the angel-bird, ja?

"Do angels kill?" We have finished eating, and should resume our work. I set the boy to sweeping the straw from under the falcons' perches.

"Don't you listen to the priests?" I ask. "St. Michael is the highest angel of all, and does he not have a sword?" It is to fierce Michael I pray, not God. I cannot understand God, the priests say, and I agree, but maybe I can understand the archangel just a little. He has wings, and he kills.

My grandson makes a face. He does not listen to the priests, not as I do, but he is eleven. "So," I say. "That day, the dogs were sent out into the reeds, to make the cranes rise. They feed on drier patches among the reeds, and do not fly unless disturbed," I explain. "The reeds hide them, ja? Even though they are tall birds, as tall as you."

He holds a hand to the top of his head, then extends his arm, judging the height. "Really?" he asks. I hear the doubt, and laugh.

"Really. Only a ger-falcon can take them, and it is dangerous even for them." I am going in and out, fetching the cut-up meat for the feeding, dividing it among the boards. "It was not long before the cry of cranes could be heard, and three rose from within the reeds. King Henry loosed Englene. She flew like an arrow towards the cranes, and came down to strike with her talons." I show him with my hands, my fingers curved. "But the crane turned in the air, jabbing with its beak. It struck Englene." I pause. My grandson has stopped sweeping. In the dim light of the mews his eyes are huge.

"She was a brave bird, as well as strong," I say, remembering. "She righted herself and struck again, and together the crane and Englene fell. The crane was still fighting, ja? Twisting and flapping its long wings. But Englene did not let go. She held on, driving the crane towards the earth. Except..." I stop, the memory of how horror welled up from my gut that day making my mouth dry, even now. "It was water beneath them. And Englene did not release her prey."

The king had shouted, but even before he did I had dropped the reins of the pony I was holding and was running, running, and then the water was to my waist and I plunged, swimming. Cold it was, but unmoving. This was nothing. I had swum in the swelling seas of Norway all my life. My arms reached, my legs kicked, and then I was with the struggling, soaked birds. Both were fighting, tumbling in the water, battling for life.

Blood streaked Englene's breast. The crane's neck twisted like a dragon's, striking out.

"What did you do?" Said almost breathlessly.

"What God or the angels told me to." I dived, and from under the water I grabbed the thrashing crane's head and held it below the surface while it twisted and fought – and then weakened. Its body stilled, the neck fell straight. I let go. Treading water, I reached an arm out for Englene. I had no glove or leather wristlet, but what did that matter?

She did not move. Her feathers dripped water, and blood still flowed from the wound. Her eyes were dulled, the white membrane of the inner eyelid half covering them. My heart clenched with fear.

There were voices now, the splash of oars. I touched Englene, stroking, murmuring, feeling tremors running through her. Loosened first one foot from the crane's back, then the other, to bring her onto my arm. She clutched, but her talons did not break my skin.

The boat was beside us, hands reaching down. "Olai! Olai, give me the bird." My lord de Hauville. I obeyed, of course. When he had taken her, arms pulled me into the boat. Others retrieved the dead crane. Someone wrapped a cloak around my shoulders.

On the island, the king awaited us. He had dismounted, and when my lord de Hauville carried Englene up to him he examined her closely, his face worried. "Will she live?" I heard him ask. "Will she fly again?" His concern was real. I liked seeing that, although who was I to pass judgement on a king?

My lord de Hauville was careful with his words. "With good care and prayers, I have hope, my lord king," he replied. He hooded Englene to quiet her, although she was not moving.

"She needs to be kept warm," I said. I took off the cloak I had been given, held it out. To speak, or even to act without orders in front of the king was not my place. He looked at me, frowning. "Until the wound can be cleaned and stitched, my lords. Or the cold will kill her."

"Who is this?" King Henry demanded.

"Olai, my lord king. One of the men who came from Norway with the falcons. He is a mews servant now."

I knelt, as I should have before.

"I am grateful to you, Olai," the king said. My eyes were downcast, but I saw movement, the cloak being folded around the bird.

"She is a brave falcon, my lord king," I said. "Since I took her from the nest, she was always the bravest and most beautiful." I should have said nothing, but from his worry I thought this young king loved Englene too.

"You took her from the nest?" His voice sounded interested. "King Haakon wrote to me when he sent the birds. He told me it took two years to find them, and the voyage was long and dangerous, so that I must consider them more valuable than gold or silver."

"Ja," I said, and then, "Yes, my lord king."

"So," the king said, "today is not the first time you have risked your life for Englene. What reward would you like, Olai?" My lord de Hauville started to speak, but the king held up a hand.

Today, in these flat, wet, strange lands, my heart had cried out for cliffs and forest and sea, the crash of waves on the rocks and the lights that played in the night skies. "I would like to go home to Norway, my lord king." But as I said the words, my gut tightened.

"I am sure your lord will release you, if that is what you truly want." My lord de Hauville still held Englene, but now she was under the cloak, and held close to his body. He was frowning, but he could not gainsay the king.

How could I leave Englene? She was the first I took

from the nests, the first day I flew myself, the day I felt wings on my back. She was a king's bird, first King Haakon's, then King Henry's. But she was mine, too.

*St Michael*, I prayed silently, *what do I do*?

*What will gain you heaven*, I heard inside me.

I took a breath. "I will stay to care for Englene. If she dies, I will go home, if my lord allows. But I swear on my own life, lord king, that I will do my best to heal her."

The king's brow rose. He looked at my master. "If anyone can," my lord de Hauville said, "it is Olai."

"Is that so," King Henry said quietly. Then, "If you do, Olai, you will never need to look for other work. There will be a place for you with my falcons for all your life."

My grandson is quiet when I am done. "You stayed," he says finally. "So you saved her life?"

"Ja. She lived another fifteen years, and brought the king much pleasure in the field."

"Why didn't you go home when she died?"

I chuckle. "I had a wife and children, ja? Your father, and your uncle and aunts. They were English, and so I was too. And my work is here."

He considers this. "I'm glad you stayed."

I nod. "Today you can help me feed the birds. It is time you began to learn how." Soon I will teach him how to soothe them, the stroked feather or finger. I will have a small glove made for him, and wristlets.

I glance outside, to where the snow has flattened this land even more. I will dream of flying tonight, I think, over forest and sea, soaring on wings of white. I will never see cliffs again, or the *hvalir* amongst the waves, unless from heaven I can see all the world below me. As a falcon must do, as she spirals upward.

We are all in exile, the priests say. Eve defied God's orders, and sent us from paradise, but it can be regained by those who obey and pray. I have done both. I served first one king and now another, both anointed by God, and I served an angel. Surely my exile will end when I am taken up to heaven on shining wings?

## AUTHOR'S NOTE

The title *On Shining Wings* is taken from the song *King of Rome* by Dave Sudbury. If you don't know it, it's about another working man and the bird he loves – in his case a homing pigeon. A true story, while it didn't inspire my story here, it shaped how it was told, and it's well worth listening to.

## ABOUT MARIAN L THORPE

Taught to read at the age of three, words have been central to Marian's life for as long as she can remember. A novelist, poet, and essayist, Marian has several degrees, none of which are related to writing. After two careers as a research scientist and an educator, she retired from salaried work and returned to writing things that weren't research papers or reports.

Marian's first published work was poetry, in small journals; her first novel was released in 2015. Her award-winning *Empire's Legacy* series is historical fiction of another world, based to some extent on northern Europe after the decline of Rome.

In addition to her novels, Marian has read poetry, short stories, and nonfiction work at writers' festivals and other juried venues.

Her other two passions in life are birding and landscape history, both of which are reflected in her books. Birding has taken her and her husband to all seven continents, but these days she's mostly content to move between Canada and the UK.

'This is (alternative) historical fiction at its best; a credible story, believable characters and a superb consistency of setting and action.' *Northern Reader Reviews.*

~ ~ ~

Website: **https://marianlthorpe.com/**
Buy Marian's books on Amazon:
**https://relinks.me/MarianLThorpe**
(Also available from other online stores or order from any bookshop.)

# 11

# LAST HOPE FOR A QUEEN

## BY AMY MARONEY

## ISLAND OF RHODES, GREECE, AUTUMN 1461

Queen Charlotta strode down the broad corridor leading to the grand master's great receiving hall, sweeping past guards and other attendants with barely a glance, her mind fixed on the challenge ahead.

*No matter what happens, you're here to save your crown.*

She halted in front of the double doors and drew in a long breath. Her translator, Estelle de Montavon, leaned close.

"You are the queen of Cyprus." The Frenchwoman's calm voice was reassuring, as always. "The knights will give you the respect you're due."

"I must have the truth. Don't try to protect me."

Estelle held her gaze. "Never. I always give you the words as I hear them, not as I wish them to be."

Charlotta glanced down at the gold-and-ruby ring on her hand. She gave it a quick polish with the hem of her headpiece, then said a silent prayer to all the saints.

*For my kingdom. For my people.*

The massive doors swung open. Charlotta forged ahead, followed by Estelle and two personal guards, their footsteps muted by the soft plushness of hand-hooked woolen rugs. Eight high-ranking members of the Knights Hospitaller sat in a semicircle on the dais. The men studied her in silence, the pale eight-pointed stars on their black tunics gleaming in the sunlight that streamed through the windows.

Glancing at the crowd gathered along the wood-paneled walls, the queen recognized diplomats, various servants of the Order, and leading members of families who had been closely allied with the knights ever since they seized control of Rhodes centuries ago.

Uneasiness surged up her spine as she searched in vain for another female figure.

*So be it. As I've done many times before, I shall draw strength from Estelle.*

Her eyes slipped to the empty chair in the center of the dais, the grand master's seat. The Catalan who now held the office of grand master had been called away suddenly to Aragon, something she'd not anticipated. Now she could not make her plea to the man who held most of the power here. To her horror, a sob rose unbidden in her chest, nearly choking her. She swallowed hard, forcing it away.

*Lord de Milly, that was and will always be your chair. How could you leave me when I needed you most? How will I do this without you?*

Her heart began to beat faster.

One of the council members, a Catalan who served as the absent grand master's second-in-command, cleared his throat.

When the man spoke, Estelle quietly translated the French to Greek. Charlotta thanked God that French remained the organization's common language despite the fact that Catalans ruled the Order now.

"Thank you for your kind welcome and your generous hospitality, members of the council." The queen recited the French words from memory as Estelle had taught her, doing her best to soften the harsh edges of her Greek accent. "The Knights Hospitaller of the Order of St. John honor me with this audience."

The Catalan held up a hand. "Your Grace, if I understand correctly, you are here to ask, yet again, for our support in your bid to save your throne. Despite all the support you have received from the Order in recent months."

His tone was condescending. When Estelle translated the words, Charlotta bristled, fighting the urge to reprimand him. Lord de Milly never would have allowed such rudeness in his council meetings, especially not to a queen. She forced herself to speak with slow consideration.

"The challenges my kingdom faces grow by the day. By the hour, my lord." She brandished her husband Louis's latest letter, describing the deplorable conditions in their fortress on the coast of Cyprus. "My husband the king now eats rats to survive. Meanwhile, my half-brother parades around our kingdom, murdering my friends, spending plundered ducats to raise armies that should rightly be mine! Jacco is not the true heir, my lords. He's a bastard, the child of a whore..."

The Catalan grunted. "We've heard all of this before. And we have always answered your call, Queen Charlotta. When earlier this summer you declared you would return to Kyrenia fortress and die alongside your husband, we gave you not one, but two galleys. Not satisfied, you asked for guns with ammunition, which we supplied. Then you changed your mind in favor of sailing to Italy and seeking the support of the pope. We provided you with an escort and a substantial loan." His eyes came to rest on the Order's senior treasurer. "The exact amount escapes me."

"It was one thousand golden ducats, my lord," the man said quickly.

"Which brings me to a troubling question, Your Grace." The Catalan stared at her with narrowed eyes. "Why are you still in Rhodes?"

Charlotta's chest tightened. Any illusion she'd maintained that the Catalan branch of the Order would harbor the same generous spirit displayed toward her by Lord de Milly vanished in that instant.

"I had hoped that, with time and reflection, the new grand master would look favorably upon my cause. I did not realize he would leave Rhodes so soon after his election."

"I must be frank, Your Grace. If you demand yet more gold, more ships, more men, more weapons – well our answer is no. There are too many other pressing needs we must attend to."

She clenched her hands, hidden in the folds of her long black gown. She'd worn mourning clothes since Lord de Milly's death. Had it truly been just weeks since he died? The days had passed in a blur of grief and worry, the nights torturously long. If only she could sleep more, keep a clear mind...

*Speak. Don't think.*

"My lords, I and all of my kingdom's people are eminently grateful for the generosity shown us by the Order. I do not request more gold, ships, men, or any other thing. I only beseech you to offer me wise counsel." She regarded each man on the dais, meeting the gaze of every knight. "I simply wish to ask you one question: what should I do?"

Estelle's clear voice translated the Greek to French, the final words hanging in the air with the crisp precision of a chiming bell.

Quiet settled over the chamber for a long, agonizing

moment. A French knight who had been close to Lord de Milly broke the silence.

"That is between you and God, Your Grace. It is a decision the council cannot make for you, I regret to say." His voice was kind, even if his words did nothing to soothe her desperate thoughts.

Several of the other council members nodded in agreement.

The Catalan shifted in his seat. "Please inform us as to your plans as soon as possible, Your Grace. The Order cannot continue providing for you and your household indefinitely."

"I am aware of the costs associated with our stay here, my lord, and I am deeply grateful for all the Order has done to ensure we are well housed and fed."

Charlotta turned to leave. The haunting call of a peacock drifted in through the windows overlooking the gardens. She sped her step, longing to eclipse the peacock's cry with an earth-shattering roar of fury.

As she and Estelle moved through the corridor, followed by their guards, a pair of Italian knights walked past them. One of the men tossed a curious glance her way, then muttered something to his companion.

Charlotta looked sidelong at Estelle. "You speak Italian. What did he say?"

Estelle's cheeks colored. "I – oh, Your Grace, I..."

"The truth, Estelle. Always!"

"Very well. He said, 'Poor exiled queen.'."

Charlotta's cheeks burned. She wanted to slap the knight across the face for his insolence.

"Exiled?" she said tightly. "What a fool. He knows nothing, that knight."

But for a moment, she stood frozen, seized by a powerful wave of inadequacy. The weight of responsibility for her kingdom's future was a cloak of iron she could never shed.

"Your Grace," Estelle's gentle voice broke through her despair.

"Let's away to the courtyard," the queen ordered, not looking Estelle in the eye.

She could not bear sympathy at this moment. It might break her.

As they hurried toward the staircase, someone behind them called out in a deep voice tinged with a Venetian accent. A powerfully built man approached, the swish of his silk tunic whispering through the air. Smiling, he exposed even white teeth that shone brightly against his dark beard.

"I am Admiral Capello of the Venetian navy." His Greek was smooth and fluent. "I'm a guest of the Order and a great admirer of Your Majesty. I heard how you commanded a fleet that retook the Castle of Paphos from your brother..." He paused, studying her with a speculative gaze. "They say he refers to himself as the king of Cyprus now, but perhaps that is simply gossip."

"His proper titles are Usurper, Pretender, and Bastard." Her bitter words sliced the air like daggers. "Call Jacco any of those things. But do not call him the king. As long as my husband, Louis, lives, he will be the one true king of Cyprus."

"I would never honor Jacco with a title he does not deserve. I only wish to share some information with you. There is a new sultan in Egypt, I'm sure you are aware..."

She nodded, impatient. "Yes. What of it, Admiral?"

"Jacco could not have raised an army and driven your court into Kyrenia fortress last year without the Mamluk Sultanate's support. Things have changed, though. Our envoys to Alexandria tell me the new sultan has rebuffed your brother's attempts to gain his favor."

Charlotta contemplated him with an assessing gaze. "What is your motive in telling me this news, I wonder?"

"Lord de Milly would have given you wise counsel, even though his brethren refused. It's no secret that you were close to him, as I was. I have no such consideration for the Catalans, nor do I place great faith in their grand master."

She nodded. Who knew what transpired on the seas between Venetians and Catalans? Piracy was rampant, and though Venetian military fleets dominated the Mediterranean, the Catalans were known to be ruthless and cunning seamen, with vast trade networks throughout Europe, Asia, and Africa.

Admiral Capello's tone sharpened. "The Order will not offer you more aid in your hour of greatest need – but perhaps Egypt's new sultan will."

When they descended the stairs and entered the vast central courtyard, Charlotta put a hand on Estelle's arm and pitched her voice low.

"The admiral confirmed what I've already heard from several reliable sources. I'd placed all my hopes in the Order, but the generosity this organization once showed me no longer exists. We'll sail for Alexandria in a week's time, and I shall get an audience with the new sultan. This is my opportunity, and I must seize it."

"With all respect, Your Grace..." Estelle bit her lip, hesitating.

"Say it, without fear. Go on."

"Jacco bought the prior Sultanate's favor with a

tribute of eight thousand ducats. How will you ever match that?"

Several guards marched around the perimeter of the courtyard, the slap of their boots on the cobblestones echoing overhead. They were far away, yet Charlotta put her lips to Estelle's ear.

"It's true, I cannot raise that much coin. But I have an object of exquisite value, something the Sultan will want – a treasure Lord de Milly bequeathed to me in his will."

Estelle's troubled look deepened. "Still, there is much at risk in a journey to Alexandria. Pirates, for instance."

"We would encounter the same risks on a voyage to Rome or Cyprus. Danger will follow us no matter where we go." Though it was high summer and the sun beat down upon her brow, a cold sensation struck Charlotta, unfurling in her veins like the tentacles of an octopus. "The truth is, we've no other choice. These knights have forsaken my cause."

Gulls wheeled over the sparkling waters of Rhodes harbor, their shrill cries mingling with the shouts of crewmen on the galleys anchored there. The long wooden blades of the windmills along the massive stone seawalls turned ponderously in the breeze. Trumpeters on the city walls blared a complex signal of welcome to merchant ships fast approaching from the sea.

Charlotta stood in the sun on the galley's well-scrubbed deck, studying the moored vessels of their fleet with care. Her own captain, who had traveled with her from Kyrenia fortress in Cyprus, was a seasoned seaman and soldier. She had no qualms about his mastery of sailing, of managing an armed fleet, or of defending his ship against pirates. This galley was sound and swift, with two iron swivel guns mounted to the gunwales.

*All well and good. But where do Captain de Naves's loyalties truly lie?*

She shook her head to banish the unsettling question, sweeping her gaze over the other galleys again. The familiar banner of a Scots privateer caught her eye. A fleeting sensation of relief relaxed the tension in her chest.

"Estelle." She gestured the Frenchwoman forward. "I believe I have you to thank for ensuring Captain Fordun's presence in our fleet."

Estelle drew closer. "I can't claim to hold much influence with him, but his wife is my dearest friend. Any thanks should, by rights, go to her."

"The Scot was close to Lord de Milly, I've learned. The grand master bequeathed a garden outside the walls of Rhodes Town to him in his will."

"Indeed." Estelle's tone grew languid and dreamy. "It's a lovely refuge."

"You've been there?" The queen smiled slyly. "Is it a favorite haunt of a certain falconer, too?"

A sheepish expression crept over Estelle's face, and her cheeks colored. "Perhaps."

"It's unfortunate your Gabriel has already left Rhodes. We could have used his language skills on this journey. And wasn't his mother born in Alexandria?"

"Yes, but she was taken captive by Christian knights as a child. She never returned to Egypt."

Charlotta pointed at the deck boards under her feet.

"The Mamluk captives in the hold will help ensure that the sultan's heart warms to my cause. With luck and a bit of persuading, perhaps he'll see the value in gifting me Christian captives in exchange."

239

She clasped her hands at her waist, thinking of the special treasure she carried for the sultan. Instead of giving her comfort, the thought made her even more uneasy.

"Estelle! Your Grace!" Etienne de Montavon approached, outlined by the sun. His golden-brown eyes, exact copies of Estelle's, shone with anticipation. "What is this talk of Christian captives?"

The queen regarded Estelle's brother with a measure of sympathy. Not so long ago, he and a group of other Savoyard knights had been captives, too, and she could only imagine the terror they'd experienced.

"Don't worry, Etienne," Estelle reassured him. "The only captives on this ship are Mamluks. They're heading home to Egypt to be ransomed or perhaps traded for Christians."

"An enslaved man can never be certain of his fate. If there is an opportunity to escape, the Mamluks will take it."

Etienne stopped Captain de Naves, who was hurrying by with his navigator.

The captain gave the queen a shallow bow. "Your Grace."

One hand over his heart, the navigator bowed deeply to her. "Your Majesty," he said with reverence.

She inclined her head at him, then fixed Captain de Naves with a sharp look. "Captain, are the prisoners closely guarded below decks?"

"I doubled my usual roster of guards. I'll take no chances with that lot. We secured everything just as you commanded, Your Grace."

She lifted her chin, leveling her gaze at him.

*Including your loyalty?*

The words flared in her mind like glowing embers. She tried to douse them with cold rationality. Captain de Naves had served her for many years. Then, with her support, he'd made a pretense of betraying her to serve Jacco. He'd held fast to their plan, tricking her half-brother with false promises about supplies and men. The soldiers and goods he'd transported across the sea from Syria had been delivered to her at Kyrenia fortress instead.

And yet – and yet. How long would Captain de Naves maintain his loyalty? Too many men who'd sworn their fealty to her were now Jacco's servants. Most of her closest advisors had abandoned her for him, tempted by his lavish promises of gold and property. The endless betrayals she'd endured poisoned her from within, eroding her ability to trust anyone. The loneliness she suffered as a result made her feel as if she could never quite fill her lungs with enough air to breathe properly.

Her gaze settled on Captain de Naves's inscrutable brown eyes. Even now, he could be concealing in his purse a written offer of lands, titles, and gold sent by her bastard half-brother on the latest merchant fleet from Cyprus.

*Stop tormenting yourself. You have no choice but to trust him.*

With effort, she blocked out the disturbing thoughts.

"Captain, this is Etienne de Montavon, knight of Savoy. He will inspect the goods, crew, and captives below decks at regular intervals during the voyage and report back to me."

The captain bowed to her, then gave a clipped nod to Etienne. "Follow me below, monsieur. You can perform your first inspection before we leave the harbor."

Oars dipped and flashed in the sun as the fleet passed through the gap in the stone walls, heading for the open sea. Idly, Charlotta wondered if the old tale was true: had a bronze colossus once straddled these walls, looming over the harbor as ships passed beneath his towering form?

Below decks, the overseer's shouts to his rowers rang out with deep authority. The queen's eyes lingered on the waves ahead, churned by wind and tides into foaming whitecaps. An unsettling current of exhilaration and dread swept through her body at the sight. The Mediterranean Sea was benignly beautiful one moment, terrible in its destructive powers the next. What lay ahead? Calm seas, a constant wind? Or storms, lightning, the snapping jaws of sea monsters?

*Santa Maria, guide and protector of seafarers, lead us safely to Alexandria, I beseech you.*

To calm herself, she silently reviewed the factors that had guided her decision to leave today, of all days, on this critically important voyage.

She had consulted astrologers in the grand master's library and enlisted the services of a fortune teller before leaving Rhodes Town. Guided by the charts, she had chosen the eighth of September for their departure, as it was believed to be the day of Santa Maria's birth. In addition, the new moon had begun on the fourth of September. The moon would be waxing for the entire journey, boding well for the acquisition of wealth, influence, and allies.

She'd visited the fortune teller with trepidation. Hidden in her palm had been a miniature portrait of her first husband, a young prince of Portugal. She'd been barely fourteen when they wed. They'd visited a fortune teller in Nicosia often during those golden early days of their marriage, before the Cypriot court destroyed him. Since his death, whenever she sought the counsel of a fortune teller, Charlotta had carried his portrait and said a prayer for his soul.

*He would have made a wise king, a bold king, a leader strong enough to destroy Jacco.*

She crushed the dark thoughts, trapped them in an imaginary net, and cast them into the sea.

The fortune teller she'd visited – Greek, for Charlotta wanted to hear the words in her own native tongue – had made a strange pronouncement. The queen turned it over in her mind now, for what must have been the hundredth time.

*The gold you seek, like the sun, beckons from the east at dawn,* the woman had said. *But when evening comes, you'll find better fortune in the west.*

Several crewmen startled her as they swarmed over the decks, unfurling sails and securing ropes. Soon sails tugged at their riggings, aided by a bountiful wind from the north. With cries of relief, the rowers withdrew their oars from the water in a disorderly fashion. Their overseer's harsh commands grated on Charlotta's ears.

She knew the rowers had all been conscripted into serving as oarsmen, and they weren't being paid much for their service. There was not enough coin to go around these days. If the sultan came to her aid, she would ensure every man in the fleet got an extra portion.

"Your Grace." Estelle appeared, grasping the gunwale with both hands. "Do you wish to retire to the stern and take refreshment? We have a long voyage ahead."

The galley crested on a swell, and Charlotta clutched at Estelle's arm for support. "If this gets worse, I suspect my appetite will not return until we land in Alexandria."

"Captain de Naves told me these northerly winds

will push us south all afternoon, but we'll find calmer waters once evening comes." As always, Estelle's melodious voice and steady gaze were comforting.

For a moment, Charlotta's eyes stung with tears.

*So many have abandoned me, betrayed me, rejected my calls for aid. Estelle's loyalty has never wavered, even when my faith in her was so shaken I threw her to the wolves.*

She drew in a long breath, profoundly grateful for the Frenchwoman's consistent presence in her life.

"Thank you, Estelle. At sunset, I'll take refreshment."

The sun slid gracefully into the sapphire waves, and the winds grew stronger. The white sails of the other ships in the fleet gleamed like pearls in the distance. The hours since the galleys left Rhodes harbor had felt monotonous in their sameness. The only diversion was the fleeting excitement of a pod of dolphins keeping pace with them a while, their sleek dark bodies bursting from the waves with astonishing power.

A blast of trumpets shattered the queen's reverie. Captain de Naves shouted from the stern, and several crewmen ran past her in their haste to reach him. Etienne de Montavon hurried to her side.

"The Mamluk captives are quiet, and all is well below," he reported. "But ships approach from the west."

"A merchant fleet? War galleys?" She squinted against the sun, studying the horizon. "I see nothing."

"It's best that you go below, Your Grace."

The galley shuddered as it tipped into a wave's trough. A sour feeling churned in Charlotta's stomach. She took Etienne's proffered arm, trying to ignore her queasiness.

"Let me speak to the captain first."

Captain de Naves and his navigator were having a heated exchange near the ship's wheel. As she and Etienne approached, they fell silent.

"What is your plan, Captain?" the queen asked crisply.

He cleared his throat. "If it's a merchant fleet, we'll stay the course. If we determine the ships pose a threat, we'll try to outrun them."

"How?"

"We'll deploy all the sails and put the oarsmen back to work."

"Why are the other ships in our fleet so far away?" She directed this question to the navigator.

He bowed, an apologetic look on his face. "Your Majesty, the winds are coming from two directions, and the gusts are unpredictable. It's very difficult for ships to stay together in such conditions."

"Please, Your Grace, go below," the captain said. "My cabin is yours for the voyage. Make use of it, I beg you."

"What if this is no merchant fleet on our tail?" she persisted. "Who else might it be?"

His expression betrayed impatience. "Not likely Turks, for they come from the wrong direction. Perhaps pirates, but I think not because pirates rarely travel in a fleet. Could be Genoese, could be Venetians." He paused, his brown eyes narrowing. "With you on board, I can't afford to take any risks – especially with our fleet scattered by the wind."

Charlotta's mind went to the Venetian admiral she had met at the grand master's palace.

*Oh, Santa Maria, let it be him. Let it be Admiral Capello's fleet.*

"Very well." The queen gave one decisive nod. "I shall retreat to your cabin." She turned to Etienne.

"You'll be stationed at the door. And Estelle will be at my side. There's no safer place for her."

Charlotta sank down in Captain de Naves's chair for an instant, then sprang up and paced around the cramped space. The shouts of men, thumping of footsteps, and ominous creaks and bangs from the deck overhead created a disturbing blend of sounds that reminded her all too acutely of war.

Estelle stood at the door and spoke to her brother, who was stationed outside. "Etienne, what news?"

His muffled voice seeped through gaps in the planks. "Our lookout spied the banners of Venice on the lead ship. Our own fleet remains dispersed, too far away to hear our call for aid."

"We're alone in the sea with a fleet of Venetian warships bearing down upon us?" Estelle gasped. "Where is Captain Fordun's galley? His is faster than the rest."

Charlotta hastened to Estelle's side. "We're not at war with Venice! There's no need for alarm."

The rowers' overseer bellowed to his men. A series of splashes sounded outside, like stones being tossed into the waves, as the oars were lowered.

"The captain is going to try to outrun them," Estelle said.

The words sparked outrage in Charlotta's blood. What foolishness was this? When the Venetians saw the blue-and-gold banner of the kingdom of Cyprus, they would show no aggression. Venice had long been an ally of her court. On several occasions in recent years, when her royal coffers had run dangerously low, Venetians had provided critically needed funds to keep the kingdom solvent.

"Tell the captain to await their approach," she told Etienne.

"The captain's orders cannot be overruled, Your Grace." Etienne's measured voice made her even more furious. "That is the law of the sea."

"Let me out, then!" Her voice rose, shrill with anger. She fumbled with the latch, but the door was blocked from the outside. "Let him defy me to my face!"

"Forgive me, Your Grace. I cannot. It is for your own safety."

She glared sidelong at Estelle. "Tell your brother to obey me, by God!"

"He's following the captain's orders, Your Grace." Estelle met her gaze. "He won't follow mine."

"I know something about the laws of the sea, too. If a ship overtakes a hostile vessel, it is permitted for the crew to enter the premises and take what they desire." The queen pounded on the door for emphasis. "Trying to outrun the Venetians will only signal our unfriendliness and make them think we've something to hide."

"But you do have something to hide," Estelle pointed out. "Something of great value, you said."

Reflexively, Charlotta's hands went to her waist. She folded them together as if in prayer, her pulse surging. "The Venetians are not our enemies. We have no reason to flee!"

She pressed her head against the door, willing her fury to subside. Unless she discovered an axe in this cabin and used it to splinter the door, they were trapped in here, powerless, awaiting an uncertain fate.

Shouts rose like a runaway wave, first low and distant, then seeping into the cabin from every direction. A tremendous crash sounded from somewhere else in the hold, followed by a series of victorious shrieks and whoops. Outside the door, a man cried out in pain.

"That was Etienne!" Estelle's face was pale, her eyes wild. "They'll come for us next."

Working quickly, they dragged the captain's chair and battered table across the floorboards, then wedged the furniture against the door.

Charlotta unlatched a cabinet next to the captain's bed, hoping to find weapons. A flagon of wine, two ceramic cups. Some rolled-up scrolls. Nothing useful.

When she turned, Estelle was brandishing a dagger, facing the door.

"Stay behind me, Your Grace." The Frenchwoman's voice was steady, but the blade trembled in her outstretched hand. "Hide your ring."

Papa's ring shone with a mellow luster, its central ruby shimmering with mysterious crimson fire. The queen had intended to give it to Louis after they wed and he was proclaimed the one true king of Cyprus.

But Louis had proved to be a disappointment both as a husband and a king, more interested in chess, hawking, and milk-fed veal than battles and diplomatic matters. The ring had stayed on her finger through her darkest hours, providing her more comfort than her husband ever could. She would not relinquish it now.

Carefully, Charlotta drew her small dagger from the sheath at her waist. It felt awkward in her hand. Why had she not practiced using it? Her palm was slippery with sweat.

The bellows and roars of fighting men grew louder. She swallowed. Her mouth was dry as dust.

The door burst open, scattering the furniture, and a group of Mamluk men in turbans and long cotton tunics pushed inside.

*Dear God, the captives have escaped.*

"How dare you!" Estelle cried. "Leave at once!"

The men ignored her.

"Which one is the queen?" a man asked in heavily accented Greek.

Estelle bravely stepped forward. "Me."

A pair of the attackers reached for her, but someone at the back of the group spoke up. "That's not her! It's the other one. Look at her ring. And her gown – see all the gold thread?"

As one, the Mamluks turned in the queen's direction.

She stiffened.

One man shoved Estelle out of his way, toppling her to the floor, and snatched at Charlotta's arm. She struck out fiercely with the dagger, nicking his flesh. He yelped in pain, relinquishing her. Another man dove for her blade, but she feinted, twisting away. A third fellow darted forward and threw his arms around her, his teeth bared, like a leopard seizing its prey. The dagger slipped from her grasp. A scream tore from deep in her chest, scraping her throat raw.

"The queen is our captive!" her captor crowed, his grip so tight she feared he would crack her bones.

She writhed and screamed, fighting with every ounce of her strength. He hooked an arm around her midriff and dragged her toward the open door.

Then he abruptly released her.

"She's got something under her dress," he reported to the others. "Something hard – like metal."

He took her dagger and sliced at her silk bodice, tearing it to shreds. Another man ripped the ruined cloth away, exposing her underclothes.

Charlotta struggled, cursing them in a torrent of Greek.

A hush descended as the item encasing her waist was revealed.

The queen slumped over, tried to shield the priceless golden belt from the men's gaze. But it was no use. The belt glinted softly in the muted light, its embedded jewels glowing, each link of gold inscribed with Arabic words. It had been taken by Christian knights during a raid on Damascus decades ago and gifted to Jacques de Milly. He'd bequeathed it to her, hoping she could use it to negotiate support with the Mamluks.

Two of the men tore it off her, praising Allah for their good fortune.

*Forgive me, Lord de Milly. The belt is in Mamluk hands, but the wrong ones.*

She fought to keep her mind clear, her despair deepening.

"Your ring!" one of the men snapped. "Take it off!"

Slowly, she lifted her head, met the man's gaze.

"No."

Her defiant word rippled around the packed cabin, resonating overhead.

Before anyone could react, guns fired outside and iron thudded against wood. The clatter of weaponry and strident voices shouting in Italian filled the air. The Mamluks wheeled to face a contingent of heavily armed Venetians crowding the open doorway, at their center Admiral Capello.

He pushed inside, followed by two valets.

"I'll take that." He snatched the golden belt with one decisive motion.

Relief cascaded over Charlotta, and she held out a shaking hand to receive the recovered treasure from him.

*The Venetians will right this wrong. The Mamluks will pay with their lives, by God.*

And then the unthinkable happened.

"Take these Mamluk captives to our ship," the

admiral commanded his men, stuffing the belt in his purse. "And all the valuables you can find."

"What's the meaning of this, Admiral?" Charlotta clenched her fists, molten fury rushing through her veins. "You are looting my ship? I thought you were my ally."

He looked at her with cool, unreadable eyes. "We are at sea. Alliances made on land do not always survive on the water. An unfortunate truth." He looked her up and down, assessing her bedraggled state, then removed his short cape and flung it over her shoulders. "I am sorry for your trouble. I assure you, we've tried to avoid bloodshed, but this ship is crawling with mutineers, Your Grace. It seems your oarsmen fled their posts and cut down the sails. You'd best wait for your fleet to catch up to you, then turn back to Rhodes."

"I curse you!" Charlotta raged in Greek at his receding back. "May you grow horns, and may the devil take you to hell for all eternity!"

"Where is my brother?" Estelle scrambled to her feet and rushed through the doorway, then let out a sharp cry.

Charlotta hastened out to find the Frenchman sprawled on the floorboards, completely still.

"Is he...?" She could not bring herself to finish the sentence.

Estelle dropped to her knees and pressed her head against Etienne's heart. "He's alive, thank God."

"Let's move him to the bed," Charlotta said, grasping one of his arms.

As they dragged him slowly through the doorway, heavy footsteps sounded behind them.

"Your Grace! In the name of Santa Maria, let me help." Captain de Naves's navigator advanced through the gloom, his boots and leather armor stained by seawater, a bloody scrape vivid on his cheek.

All three of them carefully laid the Frenchman on the narrow bed.

"That's a nasty bump on his forehead," the navigator mused, examining Etienne with concern. "He'll have a terrible headache when he awakes, but God willing, nothing worse."

"Thank you, sir," Estelle said shakily.

He examined Charlotta with a concerned frown. "Are you hurt, Your Majesty? Did those bastards harm you?"

A powerful desire to weep swept over her. She closed her eyes a moment, warding it off. The anger that had carried her through the confrontation with the Mamluk captives transformed into something else entirely – a rush of sorrow.

Somehow, she summoned the ability to speak calmly. "I am quite well, but I fear the admiral's men took everything of value from this ship."

"They did. The sails are in tatters, and the crew is standing guard over the rowers to keep them from mutinying again. Our captain bleeds on the deck. A physician is attending to him now."

Charlotta took in his words with wide eyes, struck by remorse. She had wished for those Venetians to overtake them. She'd wanted to defy Captain de Naves's orders. What a fool she'd been. He had only thought of her safety.

*You trusted the wrong man. Yet again.*

"I must speak to the captain. Will you take me to him, sir? I'll have the physician sent down to examine Etienne, too."

"Wear my dress, Your Grace," Estelle said, rising. "Your clothes are ruined."

"What's happened?" Etienne's voice rose from the bed, raspy and faint. "Are we in Alexandria?"

"No," Charlotta said with glum finality. Her left knee buckled. She widened her stance, determined to remain upright. "I fear we will not be visiting Alexandria after all."

❧ ❧ ❧

The captain lay in the shelter of a waxed canvas shade in the galley's stern, surrounded by attendants. The sight of the loyal crewmen tending to their leader made Charlotta's heart glad. And deepened her remorse.

She approached, the men parting around her like water around a rock.

"Captain." She took his hand between both of hers. His head was bandaged, as were both of his upper arms. He blinked up at her groggily, too disoriented to respond.

"He should make a full recovery, Your Grace," the physician said from across the cot. "He insisted on bustling about, checking on his men, even with blood leaking from his injuries. I gave him milk of the poppy so he would rest. I suppose every captain would behave similarly, considering the circumstances."

The physician gestured overhead at the shredded ribbons of sail flapping in the breeze. Charlotta followed his gaze, then studied the other sails in turn. All of them were ruined.

"The oarsmen did a thorough job of destruction," she said wryly. "I see nothing salvageable up there."

"The masts are in good shape, Your Majesty," the navigator said. "And reinforcements are coming."

He pointed off the starboard side of the ship at an

approaching galley. The queen recognized the familiar banner of Captain Fordun, and nearly wept with relief.

She stayed at Captain de Naves's side, wiping his brow with a damp cloth and offering him sips of wine, until Master Fordun's galley drew alongside them and two dozen of its crewmen boarded their ship.

Greeting Master Fordun in the waning light of evening, Charlotta led him to the mounted swivel gun on the bow deck.

"You've always been a trusted ally of my court, and Lord de Milly thought highly of you. Everything of value I'd hoped to present to the sultan was stolen, and my ship is in ruins. It seems obvious that this journey is doomed. But I'm no master of the sea. What is your advice, Captain Fordun?"

He peered down at her with a look of surprise on his sun-browned face, then cast an assessing gaze around the galley's deck.

"I've brought aboard several replacements for the sails." He pointed at three wooden trunks arrayed along the gunwale. "The crew will get them rigged, and this ship will be back in prime condition by tomorrow. There's no significant damage to the hull, the crew tells me." His green eyes met hers. "It's still possible to voyage to Alexandria."

She let out a short, bitter laugh. "What would be the use? I've lost my tribute payment, the gift I'd intended to present to the sultan, and everything else of value we carried. The safest course – the most logical course – is to return to Rhodes."

Her mind seized on an image of Rhodes harbor and the grand master's palace. The thought of returning to those familiar waters, throwing herself on the mercy of the Knights Hospitaller once more, made her limbs heavy with despair.

*Poor exiled queen,* the Italian knight had said. His words now circled her mind relentlessly.

Whispers about her powerlessness, her failure to preserve her throne – they would follow her everywhere in the streets of Rhodes Town, a poisonous mist drifting in her wake.

"But we shall not return to Rhodes, Master Fordun," she said definitively.

The Scot regarded her with an air of expectation. "Where, then?"

What was the alternative? Kyrenia? No. It was impossible to feed every soul in the massive Cypriot fortress already – bringing a fleet of ships and all their crew into such a desperate situation would be madness. And tending to her husband's petty desires and grievances would grind what was left of her patience into dust.

She gulped the briny air, watched the foam-capped waves surge. A thousand glimmering stars shone down as the sun vanished, witnesses to her sorrow, humiliation, and grief.

"I'd thought the stars favored our voyage," she said softly, fighting tears. "I carried every item of value left to me on this galley."

He leaned down, listening in silence.

"The Venetians stole it all away from me." Her sadness gave way to fury again. "And now I have nothing to barter with, nothing left to build good favor with the sultan of Egypt or anyone else. But I must do something!"

"The Venetians can be an unpredictable bunch. Captain de Naves has had his share of tangles with their fleets in the past. As have I." Captain Fordun picked at a splinter on the gunwale, worked it loose, and tossed it overboard. "One thing I've learned about Venetians is no matter what mischief they get up to at sea, they must answer for it at home. If you bring this matter before the doge of Venice, you can plead your case and seek restitution. It's their law, and they tend to see it through."

She studied him, astonished. "Would they actually give me what I'm owed?"

"It happens all the time. The more prestigious the injured party, the more likely the Venetians are to make the matter right. As you're a queen with powerful friends, I'd say the odds are in your favor. It would not be wise for Venice to scorn you in this matter, especially given all the witnesses to their admiral's outrageous tactics."

Charlotta nodded slowly, turning over the idea in her mind. "Venice. It lies due west, correct?"

"That's right, Your Grace."

He pointed at the western horizon, where a last flare of gold burnished the dark waters in the distance.

"A fortune teller told me that once night falls, I would find better fortune in the west. I had no idea what she meant until this moment. If I can get the Venetians to pay me for what they stole, my fleet can go to Rome, and I can ask for the pope's support." She stood taller, warming to the idea. "I am not a queen in exile. I am a queen with a kingdom to reclaim. I have no choice but to go to Venice and fight for what is rightly mine."

"I'll warrant Captain de Naves will approve of the idea, Your Grace. After what happened today, he'll not rest until he settles his grievance with Admiral Capello."

"As soon as the galley is ready to sail, we'll set a course for Venice, then. The doge will answer for their admiral's crimes against me." She faced him, fierce and determined. "I vow to you before God, the stars, and

Santa Maria, I shall get my gold back – and after that, my kingdom."

© Amy Maroney
*Oregon, 2023*

This story is based on true events. To learn more about Queen Charlotta, read *The Queen's Scribe*, in which Frenchwoman Estelle de Montavon navigates a deadly royal game of cat and mouse in the glittering medieval court of Cyprus.

## ABOUT AMY MARONEY

Amy Maroney studied English Literature at Boston University and worked for many years as a writer and editor of nonfiction. She lives in Oregon, USA with her family. When she's not diving down research rabbit holes, she enjoys hiking, dancing, traveling, and reading. Amy is the author of *The Miramonde Series*, a bestselling historical mystery trilogy about a Renaissance-era female artist and the modern-day scholar on her trail. Amy's award-winning historical adventure/romance series, *Sea And Stone Chronicles*, is set in medieval Rhodes and Cyprus.

An enthusiastic advocate for independent publishing, Amy is a member of the Alliance of Independent Authors and the Historical Novel Society.

'Amy Maroney has a gift of making the past come to life in a way that is relatable and engaging.' *Historical Novel Society Review.*

~ ~ ~

Website: **https://www.amymaroney.com/**
Buy Amy's books on Amazon:
US:
**https://www.amazon.com/stores/Amy-Maroney/author/B01LYHPXEO**
UK:
https://www.amazon.co.uk/Amy-**Maroney/e/B01LYHPXEO**
(Also available from other online stores or order from any bookshop)

# 12

## BETRAYAL

### BY CATHIE DUNN

**ROUEN, NEUSTRIA, EARLY JUNE AD 900**

The hall was buzzing with the sound of dozens of male voices. Night had fallen, and the air in the yard still held a chill that was well kept outside by the set of sturdy oak doors. Yet another kind of chill permeated the air in the usually comfortable hall. An outcry of rage, swiftly followed by calls for revenge.

Leaning back into her cushioned chair, Poppa sighed. Why did the constant disputes between Hrólfr and the pompous Robert, Margrave of Neustria – and newly rewarded with the ridiculous title, *Dux Franconum* by the Frankish king – have to ruin a day that had begun so peacefully?

In the early afternoon, she'd had spring flowers set out in vases across the hall, and even the floor rushes were fresh. Poppa delighted in making this hall as comfortable as her own in Bayeux.

This first day of summer had been so uplifting with its fulfilled promise of sunshine and warmth. She'd even enjoyed spending time outside, basking in the warming rays of the sun. The fresh air had done her good.

Now, the cold, harsh reality of West Frankish politics had brought her mood crashing down.

Poppa shifted her weight again, but the plump cushions could not banish the pain in the small of her back. She was so used to doing everything herself, as lady of her husband's hall in Rouen – and at home in Bayeux – but now that she was with child, her back was hurting, whatever she did. 'Twas a woman's fate, she knew, but one she wished to be over soon. But she knew she was only just halfway there. Not that she wished her child ill – far from it! The simple fact was that Poppa strongly disliked the limitations her pregnancy put on her. However, there was nothing to be done about it but suffer.

She winced at another twinge in her lower back, then picked up her goblet with shaky hands and took several deep draughts. The deep, red wine dulled her senses, and she let out a sigh.

After the evening meal was finished, Hrólfr had joined a group of his warriors at another table, their heads still together, plotting mischief against Robert of Neustria, no doubt, and Poppa found herself left to her own thoughts. With sadness, she realised that she missed Landina's kind help, but her friend's Norse husband, Sigurd, oversaw the defence of Bayeux, and after years of having rejected his repeated offers, Landina had finally agreed to wed him. As much as this pleased Poppa, the timing was most unfortunate.

When her head began to pound from the noise – or perhaps from the potent wine – she decided to go to bed. It would be quieter in her chamber, separated from the hall by a sturdy partition, and she would find it more comfortable. She rose and crossed the room to where her husband sat. Placing her hand on his shoulder, she leaned forward. "I'm retiring, Hrólfr. Tell me all about it on the morrow."

He nodded, his mind clearly on other matters, but he took her hand in his and squeezed it. "Rest well, my love. I'll be late, so don't wait up."

Poppa briefly shared a smile with him, then extracted her hand and waved at the gathered men. "I bid you good night."

To echoes of "Goodnight, Lady Poppa," she slid through the partition, and entered the small private chamber she called her sanctuary. With all the servants busy in the hall, she didn't want to cause a fuss, so she merely removed her overgown and slipped beneath the bed covers. Despite the day's heat, the nights were cool, and the warmth of the fur coverlets lulled her swiftly into a deep sleep.

"Hrólfr, wake up. Quick!"

Coming to slowly, Hrólfr blinked as he wondered what Knud, his trusted friend and seasoned warrior, was doing in his bedchamber. Knud and his men should be downriver, keeping the boundaries of Rouen safe from attack.

The room lay in hazy early morning light, and Hrólfr realised he hadn't had enough hours' sleep. He sighed and was about to close his eyes again and give in to the temptation of further rest when he was roughly grasped by the shoulders. Knud again? Was this a dream? Why were they fighting?

"Hrólfr, wake up! Rouen is under attack."

"What?" Suddenly alert, Hrólfr stared at the man crouching on the edge of the bed. Knud's hands were firmly embedded in his shoulders. "Knud? What in Odin's name are you doing here?"

Knud released him and rose. "Robert of Neustria is approaching the town walls with about two hundred men, or even more. I'm told they're hired mercenaries, from Burgundy."

"Keep your voice down!" Hrólfr heaved himself from the bed and grabbed his tunic. "Poppa needs rest. Let's talk in the hall."

"You don't understand." In the faint light, Knud's features looked agonised. The sense of urgency in his voice was unmistakable. "We don't have enough men to hold Rouen against such a large force. You must take Poppa away from here!"

"What, leave?" Hrólfr pulled the tunic on over his head. "No, I will join you and together we..."

"Listen, friend! Our men are spread across Neustria. Some are housed near the mouth of the River Signa and others in Bayeux. We cannot call them here in time to win against such a... a horde."

"But I can't just run away..."

"Hrólfr? What is going on?" Beside him, Poppa's face emerged from beneath the covers, and he softly swore under his breath. Could he truly take her away from her home?

Her eyes widened when she saw their friend. "Knud! What is the matter? Has something happened?" She half-sat up, covering her front.

"I'm sorry for the intrusion at this early hour, Poppa, but Rouen is under attack from Robert of Neustria."

"But how can this be? Surely, any group of men would have been spotted well in advance. How would they get close to our walls without us noticing?"

"My very question." Hrólfr had finished dressing and, crossing his arms in front of his chest, faced the old warrior.

"It appears they gathered to the south-east of Paris,

hidden away, and now they're approaching from the direction of Évreux. It's a straight route, and just enough daylight for them to see the road. But now is not the time to wonder how." Knud's voice held a hint of urgency. "Robert is after your head, Hrólfr. This time, he's serious, and that Frankish king won't raise a finger to help you. You wouldn't want Poppa to suffer the terrors of Burgundian mercenaries, would you?"

"Mercenaries?" Poppa gasped. "We must leave Rouen? Now?"

She stared at Hrólfr, and guilt flooded through him. She was with child, suffering physical discomforts, and now she had to travel, in a hurry.

"I'm sorry, my love," he said calmly, his mind made up. "We'll head for Bayeux."

"No." Knud shook his head. "That won't be far enough. My messengers roam Neustria for more tidings, but from what I've gathered so far, Robert's force is fast enough to sweep across the land unhindered, leaving a trail of destruction in their wake. They will catch you before you get there. Is that what you want?"

"Odin's breath!" Hrólfr's heart sank. "We should have been better prepared."

"Yes," Knud agreed. "Or you shouldn't have teased that pompous fool so much! But for now, it's best you flee across the water. I have ordered your *karve* to be readied and appointed a small group of our warriors to join you."

"What?" Poppa's voice squeaked. "Across water? But where?"

"Someplace where you are both safe, until Robert is distracted by other events." He grinned maliciously. "Then you can return and seek revenge."

"But... our people? I'm not sure the servants would want to leave. Many have families here in Rouen. If the mercenaries get into the town..." Her face paled, and anger surged through Hrólfr.

"He will pay for this." He clenched his fists, then his shoulders slumped. It was not the first time he had to escape the clutches of avaricious Frankish nobles, but never before had he had a wife and unborn babe to care for. Would a journey by ship even be safe for Poppa?

"He will, Hrólfr, but leave that part for another time. We must hurry. I'll wake the men in the hall, and your *thralls*." Knud gave a final nod, then left their chamber.

Tears rolled down Poppa's cheeks, and Hrólfr lowered himself on the bed, gently wiping the moisture away. "I'm so sorry, sweeting." His emotions in turmoil, he kissed her on the forehead, then stood again. "I'll organise the men and speak to the *thralls*. Without me here, they should be safe, if the gods are willing." He touched Mjölnir, snug at the base of his neck, then slipped the pendant beneath his tunic. "Someone will help you gather our most important things. One *kist*, Poppa. That's all we can take."

"But take where?"

"To the kingdom of the East Angles." With a sigh, he turned and left her alone. Poppa was strong. She would be fine.

*But the child? How would it fare?*

He shrugged off the uncomfortable thought and went in search of their *major-domus*.

Poppa's mind was whirling. How could Hrólfr be so thoughtless, taunting Robert of Neustria again and again, until the man was seeking revenge? And what about Knud? Had she detected a sense of guilt in his demeanour? After all, the warrior had been charged with keeping an eye out for potential attacks. His spies were everywhere. So how did Robert and hundreds of mercenaries manage to sneak up to the fortified town walls of Rouen?

Unsure whether to be angry or sad, she finally rose. Time was of the essence.

One *kist*.

She stared at their three large chests lined up by the wall. One held Hrólfr's clothes, and another hers. The third – sturdier than the others and secured by a lock – held their treasure: a stash of gold and silver coins, several beautifully decorated daggers, her mother's precious necklaces and gold bracelets, her gifts from Hrólfr...

How would she fit their garments for all seasons, weapons and treasures into one *kist*? It was impossible. She sighed and dug out her oldest linen gown, then slid into it. It was too big for her, so she knew she'd be comfortable on the journey. Poppa swiftly combed her hair, pulling out knotted clumps in her hurry, then tied it into a long braid before she covered her head with a simple veil. Then she tied the belt loosely around her hips and attached her pouch to it. It held only a small number of copper coins, her comb, a couple of narrow linen strips, and a tiny jar of marigold salve.

With a sigh, she raked through their clothes' chests, pulling items from each and throwing them on the bed. Robert's mercenaries would sack the hall if they got in. Without Hrólfr here, the place was of little interest to Robert, so perhaps they would be fortunate. She said a quick prayer as she knelt on the floor and prised one of the wooden slats loose, revealing a space that held a small square box. Opening it, she removed the key to their treasure chest and swivelled on her toes to unlock it. Footsteps rang loudly from the hall, and Poppa – sensing the urgency – removed a few less valuable items and hid them in the vacant space before securing the floor board again. Then she placed some of their clothes on top of the rest of their valuables until the chest was full to the brim.

It made sense to take their treasure. It allowed them to buy fabrics or food if needed. She remembered her pouch with needles and threads and stuffed it down the side of the chest. Her gaze fell on their cloaks hanging on hooks. Just as she rose to take them, Hrólfr appeared, followed by two of their household warriors.

"Are you ready?" His gaze roamed their chamber, and she blinked back the tears when she noticed a brief glint of sadness. "Robert is approaching the southern gate."

"Yes. We take this chest." She pointed at it and the two men slipped past Hrólfr and lifted it with a groan.

"Wait!" She quickly locked it, slid the key into her pouch, then sent them on their way. Facing her husband, she handed him his cloak. "Put it on. You'll need it on the boat."

He nodded and took it off her. "I... I'm sorry, Poppa." His voice was hoarse.

She placed her hand on his cheek. "I know, my love. Let's go." Throwing her own cloak around her shoulders, she grabbed her belt and pouch and hurried ahead of him into the hall without a backward glance at her sanctuary. She prayed it would stay untouched, but in these uncertain times, anything could happen.

With tears in her eyes, she bid their household farewell. As she'd thought, their *major-domus* and other servants preferred to stay in the only home they'd ever known, and several warriors were left for the defence of the hall. Before she had a chance to say any more, Hrólfr bundled her outside where he paused for a moment as the oak doors behind them were barred from inside.

From the direction of the southern gate, the sound of fighting reached them. Her breath hitched. "They've arrived."

Hrólfr bristled. "Knud will keep them at bay for as long as it takes. Come." He took her elbow and led her through the narrow lanes towards the Seine.

Moments later, they reached the *karve*. Poppa looked up and down the riverside, but it was the only boat she could see. Knud must have had all others moved, so Robert could not follow them. Usually, at sunrise, this area was bustling.

On each side of the hull sat a row of men on wooden benches, oars lined up in readiness. Hrólfr guided her across the plank and took her to the centre of the boat, where a flimsy, tent-like structure of rickety wooden beams and cloth awaited her. It barely reached her waist in height. Under the cover, she saw their chest was secured firmly. Beside it on the floor lay several cushions and two blankets.

Poppa snorted. "What's this?"

"Your home for the crossing. Stay under here, out of sight, and you'll be safe." He helped her crouch beneath the roof, then stepped back.

She raised her eyebrows. "One gust of wind, and this... thing will tumble all over me." Her mouth twitched, and she couldn't hold back a grin. How could she find humour when she was fleeing her home? She didn't know the answer.

Hrólfr gave a wry laugh. "It should hold firm until we've crossed the Narrow Sea, I hope..." He touched his pendant, and, with a nod, turned to join the men on the oars.

Poppa felt for her own pendant, his gift to her on the day they wed, which always lay nestled at the base of her throat. The familiar shape comforted her. In her mind's eye, she saw the five garnets that adorned the front of the delicate gold cross glint in the rising sun. And etched into the back of the cross: Odin's horns, delicately interwoven. It was a symbol of both their origins, and Poppa had never removed this most treasured piece ever since that long-ago day they were handfasted. How young she'd been!

The *karve* lurched forward as the men began to push her away from the river's edge. Over the hum of the oars, the sound of clashing weapons grew closer. Angry shouts reached Poppa's ears, but she did not dare emerge from her cocoon to see what was happening.

The young man rowing closest to her – someone she'd never met before, perhaps one of Knud's men? – met her questioning gaze, his expression grim. "The cursed Burgundians have arrived on the shore. Stay out of sight, Lady Poppa."

She nodded and huddled deeper into the cushions. A series of splashes told her of the mercenaries' desperate attempt at catching the boat with their spears, but she knew from the growing distance that even those could no longer pose a threat.

Soon, the *karve* was moving at a fast pace, leaving Rouen behind. Poppa watched the tension slowly leave the men's faces as they rowed.

How close had they come to disaster? A shudder ran through her body. If Knud had not raced to warn them, Hrólfr may be dead now. And what would have become of her? Poppa curled up on her side and draped a blanket over herself. Whatever would have happened – they had escaped, alive. But what of Knud and their men? How many of them would survive the marauding Burgundians?

Closing her eyes, she forced her mind to calm. A

kick inside her reminded her of what mattered most. Her child. She stroked her rounded stomach and calmed her breathing.

*We are safe. For now...*

Hrólfr swore under his breath as he kept pace with the other men on the oars, easing the boat into the centre of the river. He watched in horror as the Burgundian mercenaries spilled out over the riverbank, some urging their horses onwards to catch up with the *karve*. But thankfully, Hrólfr's men had pushed off just in time, and he could hear the attackers' voices rise in anger. Already, several groups veered off, down the narrow lanes into the centre of Rouen.

Their fury would know no mercy.

Fear for his friend's life mingled with the guilt he felt that he'd been unable to protect *his* town. He only hoped the inhabitants heeded Knud's warnings and stayed within. Though how safe they would be inside their flimsy homes was a guess. If Robert allowed the mercenaries to torch the town, it would be a massacre. Hrólfr wouldn't put it past the man. A plotter and schemer, Robert was dangerous and untrustworthy, despite his illustrious title. A thorn in Hrólfr's side for a long time.

Surely, King Charles would disapprove strongly of any such harsh measures taken against his people. After all, Rouen was a mainly Christian town within the realm of the West Franks. And whilst he may not stop Robert from seeking personal revenge, he would not permit his own people being killed in the process.

At least, Hrólfr hoped he wouldn't.

As they finally turned a bend and the wooden palisade that surrounded Rouen disappeared from sight, Hrólfr let out a long breath. Since his youth, he'd regularly faced dangerous situations – ambushes, battles, the lot – but never before had he had to ensure the safety of the woman he loved. And his unborn child.

Ironically, it was only last night, after hours of arguments with his men, that he'd taken the decision to approach Robert for a truce. King Charles wanted Hrólfr to push back a new attack by Danish raiders on the coast of western Neustria, and Hrólfr had no intention of looking over his shoulder and finding Robert stabbing him in the back whilst he dealt with the invaders. Instead, Robert and his Burgundians had almost managed to catch Hrólfr and harm his family. His fury grew with each stroke of the oar.

But as the *karve* edged further and further away from the attack, Hrólfr knew other dangers awaited them. The Narrow Sea was never reliable. Storms could spring up unexpectedly, and even sheltered in her small tent, Poppa was too exposed to the elements. A strong gust of wind would see the structure collapse. And she lay crouched, for lack of space. That couldn't be good for the babe.

*Please keep her safe...*

If Freyja would watch over Poppa, his young wife had nothing to fear. A smile played on his lips. Poppa was fearless anyway, the perfect match for the opinionated goddess. But with a child on the way, she was more vulnerable than before. Freyja would know.

*Protect her...*

Eventually, Dag tapped him on the shoulder and took his place at the oars, and Hrólfr stretched his long limbs. He scanned the land either side of the river, but apart from the occasional fisherman, he saw no one. He joined Ludo, an older Frankish warrior who was guiding the *karve* safely through the water, at the steering board. "We're making good time," he said. "I think we can slow our pace, to give the men chance to breathe."

Ludo nodded. "Yes, we should reach the mouth of the Seine by afternoon. What are your orders for our crossing?"

"We stop for the night near the small settlement just before the Signa reaches the sea. We stayed there a few weeks ago, during our recent search for Danes."

"Yes, I remember. A good idea. We can stock up with water and provisions there." Ludo squinted at the blue sky. "Not a cloud in sight. Let's hope it'll stay that way over the coming days and nights."

"It's our best hope, but the spring storms are never over until the summer's heat arrives."

"Hmm." Ludo's face fell.

Hrólfr slapped his back. "Trust the gods, my friend. Or your one God. They will carry us safely across."

"I'm sure you're right."

"I am." Hrólfr grinned, then left Ludo to concentrate on navigating another windy bend in the river.

He made his way to the tent and peeked inside to see Poppa lying curled up on the cushions beneath the covers.

"Lady Poppa has been asleep for a while, Hrólfr," Ragenard, who sat closest to Poppa's tent, whispered.

He smiled in acknowledgment. Not wishing to wake her, he watched her breathe deeply in and out. She needed the rest after such a disturbed night, as did the babe.

"Keep watch over her and call me if she needs anything."

"I will," Ragenard assured him as he moved with the oar.

With nothing to do, Hrólfr joined Ludo at the

steeringboard again and watched in companionable silence as the longboat wound her way through the dramatic scenery. Steep cliffs gave way to meadows and small beaches. Neustria's landscape was breathtakingly beautiful. He'd miss it. It was the only place he'd ever call home.

*I'll return. I swear...*

✤ ✤ ✤

The second day on their crossing dawned brightly as they moved through the water. The wind had picked up, pushing them north-eastwards.

The last two nights, Poppa had heard much talk about the kingdom of East Anglia. She remembered that Hrólfr had told her previously of the time he'd spent there, before he'd arrived in Western Francia and joined the siege of Paris. He always spoke warmly of Guthrum, the Danish warrior king who'd held East Anglia until his death a decade earlier, but Hrólfr's opinion of the current ruler was less encouraging.

They knew that Eiríkr, a Dane and king of the East Angles, led regular raids into West Saxon territories – actions which usually received brutal reprisals – and she considered his small kingdom far too volatile to be a safe haven. But it was their only choice, given Hrólfr was Norse, too. A Pagan. The West Saxons would kill him on sight, no questions asked.

There was no doubt that Eiríkr would demand her husband's service. The new king of the West Saxons, Edward, had already begun to build a reputation as a warrior, keen to continue his father's quest to drive the Danes from English shores and unite the kingdoms under one banner – preferably his.

And King Charles of the West Franks seemed to be impressed by him, from what she'd heard in Rouen.

Another reason they could not flee to lands occupied by Saxons. Charles should have come to her rescue, but most likely he'd hide behind a lame excuse. As a Frankish, Christian lady wed to a Norse Pagan, Poppa had not had it easy, as often her fellow Franks snubbed her. But she knew her Danish friends would defend her to the death. She prayed Knud and her servants were alive and safe. And for now, the quarrels between the ridiculous, preening cocks who called themselves kings faded into the background as the longboat cut swiftly through the grey water. Poppa sat leaning against the chest, her back hurting from lying on her side for so long. Soon, the heat of the rising sun and the steady rhythm of the movement lulled her into another sleep, and she gave in to the drowsiness.

A cry went up, and Poppa awoke as the boat bounced sharply. How long had she been asleep? She blinked, surprised at her wet face. The sun had disappeared behind dark clouds, and rain was spitting down at the poor men on the oars. The sail had been lowered, for risk of it ripping in the gusts. She huddled beneath her blankets, but they were already covered in a layer of moisture. A cry escaped her as the chest hit her between the shoulder blades when the *karve* crested a wave.

Hrólfr kneeled beside her, crouching beneath the dripping cover. He was soaking wet, but it didn't seem to affect him. Men!

He tied a handle of the chest to yet another wooden plank, then wrapped the blankets tighter around her. "This may not be much, but it'll protect you from the worst of the storm. We're close to the Kentish coast, but we couldn't even land here unless the sea calms."

"W... why not?" Her teeth chattered from the dampness seeping through her. She pulled the fur tighter around her. Where had summer gone?

"Strong currents lurk in the depths here. We must pass these cliffs and get to the shallow beaches." He caressed her cheek with cold, calloused fingers. "Also, this is still West Saxon territory, so going on land could be dangerous for us. Let me know if you need any help."

Poppa nodded. Her back hurt from the thump of the chest, but she dared not add to her husband's woes. He knew boats and the sea. She had to trust him. "I'll be well," she whispered, her voice hoarse. "Don't fret."

A moment later, and he was gone, no doubt to join the rowers, or do something else that was useful. Unlike her, stuck in here, unable to help. As her tiredness grew, she fought against it. No, she could not dare fall asleep in a storm. She might never wake up again.

Then another wave hit the *karve*, sending her high up, only to come crashing down again.

Poppa pulled up her legs and lay on her side. The jolting was making the pain in her lower back worse. She could not risk more pain – or her babe's life.

Her trembling hand sought her golden cross pendant, and she stared at it in wonder. The large garnet in the centre shone dark, fierce, as if angry at the elements. She enclosed the cross in her fist, closed her eyes, and prayed.

"Hrólfr, hurry!"

Balancing his weight in the rocking boat, he made his way to Ragenard. "What is it?"

The man pointed at Poppa lying draped over the *kist*. "She was sitting up, and then, suddenly, she collapsed." Ragenard hesitated. "I wanted to reach out but didn't dare let go of the oar."

Hrólfr patted the young man's shoulder. "It was the right thing to do, thank you."

He knelt beside Poppa and gently eased her back onto the cushions. Running his fingers over her face to wipe away the moisture.

"Odin's teeth!" He recoiled, then fastened his hand on her forehead. It was burning hot. "A fever." For the first time since they left Rouen, fear gripped his heart. They were still some distance from East Anglia's safe shores. He'd decided against landing in Kent, as the risk of discovery would have been too great. Instead, they rode out the storm. But now this! His breath shuddered.

"Hrólfr, do you have any dry clothes in that chest?" Ragenard asked. "She'll need to come out of those wet things."

Hrólfr nodded, a sense of embarrassment shooting through him. He had no idea what the *kist* held. "I'm sure there are."

"Then change her into something dry. I'll hold a cloak in place, so she's not exposed to our eyes." Ragenard called for another to take his oar.

"Where is the pouch?" Hrólfr's hands searched between the damp cushions and covers, found it, and extracted the key to unlock the *kist*. Opening the lid carefully, he pulled out a simple linen gown. Then he untied his cloak and handed it to Ragenard who stood behind him, legs wide apart for balance. Draping the cloak over the entrance to Poppa's small tent, the young man held on to the wooden frame, then turned his head away.

Hrólfr pulled Poppa's wet gown and shift from her, and swiftly replaced them with the dry gown. It was worse than he expected. Her whole body was on fire. Once he was done, he pushed the wet clothes and veil into a gap beside the *kist*, then locked it and slid the key into the pouch. Best not put it elsewhere, or he'd never remember.

He laid her out on the cushions, still curled up, her legs at an angle so no one would trip over them. Strands of damp hair had come loose from her braid, but this was the least of his worries. Apart from Poppa's marigold salve, they had no healing herbs with them, and everything on the boat was wet, even the blankets inside the flimsy shelter.

*Freyja, please help her. It's not her fault… it's mine!*

He touched Mjölnir then kissed Poppa's forehead. She was mumbling in her sleep, but the words were incoherent. He rose and took the cloak from Ragenard and threw it on the *kist*. "We must get onshore soon, or…"

"She's a fighter, Hrólfr." Ragenard took his place at the oars again. "Speak to Ludo. I think we may be close."

Hrólfr nodded. "Yes, and thank you for helping."

A wry smile on his lips, Ragenard blinked, then rejoined the others in their rhythm. "I'll pray for the lady…"

Hrólfr turned to join Ludo. "We must land, soon."

"So I've gathered. As it is, the currents take us close to the coast. If it calms soon, we'll be able to go ashore not far from here."

*And find a safe, dry place for Poppa to recover…*

**TEN DAYS LATER**

When the sound of voices reached Poppa's ears again, this time, they were no longer muffled. These were women's voices, and close by, it seemed. But she couldn't make out the words.

She wanted to speak, but her throat was dry. Slowly, she blinked. This wasn't her bedchamber in Rouen. Confused, she turned her head. She found herself in a small room, screened off by curtains. It only contained the bed she lay on, a small table, and a chest.

"Where am I?" She gave a hoarse whisper.

*The chest...*

She stared at the object, searching her mind for answers. This was her treasure chest, but how did it get here?

Then she remembered. Rouen. The frantic flight. The storm on the Narrow Sea...

She sat up, but a pain in her stomach made her groan loudly, and she lay down again.

The curtain to her right moved, and a young woman came in, muttering excitedly in a language Poppa didn't understand. Her gown was of a different cut than her own, and her hair was covered by a simple veil.

"I'm sorry, I don't..." Poppa's voice trailed off. What had happened to her? How did she get here? And where was Hrólfr?

So many questions, but if the woman didn't speak Frankish, how would they communicate?

"Ealswith," the stranger said, pointing at herself. "I am Ealswith."

Broken Frankish was better than none, Poppa supposed, and she gave her a shy smile. "I am Poppa."

"I know." Ealswith nodded. "Your husband... told me." She busied herself with something on the table, then approached the bed, holding out a clay cup. "You need to drink."

"Thank you." Poppa took the cup into her shaking hands and emptied it. The ale was cool, soothing her throat. "More?"

"Later. Drink in small... how do you say?"

"Measures. Yes, of course. But tell me, where am I?"

"In your new home."

"My new what?" She cocked her head. "Am I in East Anglia?"

"Yes, you are. Shall I fetch your husband? Or do you need else anything first?" The woman gently placed her hand on Poppa's forehead. She looked relieved. "Your fever... It has broken."

"I had a fever?" That explained her loss of memory. "For how long?"

"For over a sennight." Ealswith's expression darkened, and sadness entered her eyes. "We almost lost you. But our good herbs helped heal you. And God's mercy, of course."

A Christian. Good. "Thanks be to God." Poppa crossed herself. "Umm, there is something you may be able to help me with. I... I need to relieve myself, but if you'd rather not..."

Ealswith smiled. "Come, Poppa. Let's go in search of a private place, and then we'll tell your husband of your recovery." She helped her get up, pausing when Poppa's vision blurred. Moments later, they left the small building through a narrow door into a small, fenced off space. A garden. Her heart lifted. Beyond it lay a meadow filled with wildflowers. Poppa smiled, breathing in deeply. Already, she felt better.

After Ealswith had helped her to a screened off part of the garden, at the far end, and she had done what was necessary, the young woman led her back into the chamber, and Poppa sank gratefully into the bed and drew the covers over her. After only these few steps, she felt exhausted. Every bone in her body hurt.

A familiar movement brought her hands to her stomach. "He lives." A miracle.

Ealswith nodded. "Yes, your child is well."

"What a relief!" She closed her eyes for a moment,

stroking her stomach, enjoying the sensations. Then she watched as Ealswith refilled the cup with ale and handed it to her. "Where is Hrólfr?"

"Training our men."

That was certainly like him, taking over wherever he went. Poppa grinned. "And do they have much to learn?"

"Oh yes." Ealswith nodded. "We are simple folk, not warriors. But the king has called on all men of East Anglia to join his latest foolhardy endeavour." Her voice dripped with disapproval. "Your husband... he looks after our men, shows them how to fight."

"I see." Poppa drained the cup, then handed it back to the woman. "Would you let him know I woke up?"

"Of course. Now you must rest." Ealswith put the cup on the small table. "I'll return as soon as I've found him."

"Thank you," Poppa whispered, before a restless sleep took her.

The next time she woke, it had grown dark, and one solitary rushlight was casting the chamber in a warm gloom. How long had she slept for this time? Only then did she hear voices behind the curtains. Several male voices. One in particular stood out, as clear as if he sat beside her.

"Hrólfr?" Clearing her throat, she tried again, louder. "Hrólfr!"

Moments later, the curtain moved, and he stood there, gazing down on her as if in wonder. "Poppa, my heart." He crouched on the edge of the bed, and she shifted her hip to make way. His eyes never left her as he took her hand. "Thanks be to Freyja, you've recovered. In truth, I feared for you, and our babe." He kissed her gently, then sat back.

"Was it serious, the fever?"

"Yes. It lasted for ten nights. We were fortunate to

have been close to the coast by the time you fell into a deep sleep, so we chose to go ashore as soon as we could and looked for a settlement. That's how we ended up here."

"But how did you find a hut for us so quickly?"

He sent her a sheepish look. "Well, one of the village elders died recently, leaving neither widow nor children. And whilst the good people of this place pondered as to who should move in here, we came along and I, well, I paid them."

"You paid them?" She chuckled. "Good man."

"And then they helped us look after you."

Poppa smiled weakly. "That's how the world should work..."

"True." His eyes sparkled, and for the first time, a glimmer of hope rose in her chest – before his next words crushed it again. "I met King Eiríkr two days ago. As expected, he wants me to join him. And..." his glance went to the curtain, but all was quiet beyond, "it is not negotiable. He reminded me that we found refuge here only by *his* goodwill."

Poppa snorted. "He sounds like a nice man." She couldn't hide her sarcasm.

"He's no Guthrum, that's for certain. But the main matter is that you've woken up and the fever is gone. Ealswith is going to help you while I'm away."

Poppa held her breath. "And when will you leave?"

"The day after tomorrow." Hrólfr lowered his gaze. "I am sorry." He kissed her hand, but she withdrew it from his grasp.

"But... We need time to settle here. I don't speak their language, and I don't know anyone. What are their customs? Where will I get food from? What if there's something wrong with the child?" Exhausted, she let the tears roll and turned onto her side, her back to him. "What if you are killed?"

"I..." He gave a deep sigh and stroked her sweaty hair. "I'll return to you, Poppa. I sw..."

She held up her hand. "Don't make promises you cannot keep, Hrólfr! Only God knows our fate." She knew she sounded bitter, but her world had come crashing down, and she didn't know how to mend the broken fragments. "Go now. I need rest." Closing her eyes, she turned her face way from him.

She felt him stand still by the bedside, until, finally, his steps receded slowly.

"I'm all alone," she whimpered.

*What am I to do?*

Her breathing quickened, and her body began to shake. "What am I to do?" she asked out loud, but the question was met with silence.

A twinge in her lower back announced the return of the now familiar pain. This was just what she needed. Poppa tried to calm her breathing, but it now came in short, sharp burst. She rolled onto her back, and her body exploded in agony.

"Hrólfr!" she screamed.

Then darkness engulfed her...

© Cathie Dunn
*Southern France, 2023*

Read more about Poppa of Bayeux and Hrólfr (Rollo) the Viking in Cathie Dunn's latest release, *Ascent*, the first novel in a series about the forgotten women who forged the House of Normandy.

The story of their sudden flight from Neustria, which was a fact – although little is known of where they went and for how long – was not included in the novel, so *Exile* is the perfect place to share their journey in more detail.

## SHORT GLOSSARY

**Norse** – Frankish
**River Signa** – River Seine, the river running from near Dijon, in Burgundy, eastern France, through Paris and Rouen, to the English Channel
**Karve** – a smaller longboat, used for carrying goods and people
**Kist** – a chest, trunk
**Thrall** – a slave, servant

## ABOUT CATHIE DUNN

Cathie Dunn writes historical fiction, mystery, and romance. The focus of her novels is on strong women through time. She has garnered awards and praise from reviewers and readers for her authentic description of the past. A keen Medievalist, she enjoys visiting castles and ruins, and reading about battles and political shenanigans of the times.

Cathie is a member of the Historical Novel Society, the Romantic Novelists' Association, and the Alliance of Independent Authors. She also now runs **The Coffee**

**Pot Book Club**, promoting historical fiction authors and their books.

'...Beautifully penned for readers to easily get lost in.' *Historical Novel Society Reviews.*

≁  ≁  ≁

Website: **https://www.cathiedunn.com/**
Buy Cathie's books on Amazon:
**https://author.to/CathieDunn**
(Also available from other online stores or order from any bookshop)

# 13

# THE EXILED HEART
## BY CRYSSA BAZOS

### LINZ, AUSTRIA, 1639

Throughout Susanne's early morning ride, a vague but persistent discontent niggled at her. It hadn't been the fault of her horse, Freya, who was as sure-footed as ever on the hilly trails running between Linzer Schloss and Freinberg Mountain. Nor had she any complaints with her position in the imperial fortress, for although she had just reached her sixteenth year, she had her father's complete trust to oversee the household management in her mother's absence. As the emperor's governor of Upper Austria, Papa held everyone to a very high standard, including herself, and she relished the challenge. And yet the restlessness persisted, a worrisome itch under her skin, impossible to dislodge or assuage in any manner.

Deciding to cut her ride short, Susanne turned Freya back towards the fortress. In the valley below the castle, the Danube flowed around the town of Linz, nestled between the river and the foothills of a grey mountain range. Ice crunched beneath Freya's hooves and Susanne's breath misted in the air. It had snowed in the night, and the red clay roof tiles of Linzer Schloss were powdered white, muted like a dream. Overhead, a hawk cried out, soaring free on currents of cold air; the sound mirrored what Susanne felt – a lonesome cry, seeking some unnamed but vital need. She burrowed deeper within the folds of her crimson hood.

As she passed through the Rudolfstor entrance to reach the main courtyard, the ringing of Freya's iron-shod hooves bounced off the cobbles, echoed onto the stone-clad archway and mingled with the noise coming from the road behind. Susanne glanced over her shoulder. A coach and four were speeding her way, flanked by a guard of dragoons.

She hastened Freya into the outer courtyard, and the carriage drove past her towards the castle entrance. The plainness of the conveyance combined with the escort piqued her curiosity. Ornate carriages frequently arrived at Linzer Schloss with little fanfare, bringing those who sought to curry favour with her father, Count Kuffstein, while his star yet rose in Emperor Ferdinand III's constellation. Susanne and her father were here at the emperor's pleasure. Tomorrow, they could be turned from hearth and home at his whim. Their position, and her home, were only as secure as the emperor's goodwill, and her father never failed to remind her of it at every opportunity.

As the carriage rolled to a stop, a flurry of activity erupted in the courtyard. Her father's steward rushed out to greet the arrivals while a liveried footman hopped down from his perch to assist the passengers. First to emerge from the carriage was the emperor's general – a sharp-faced man who reminded Susanne of a crow. He adjusted the cloak that draped over one shoulder and said a few words to the steward before turning back to the carriage just as another man descended.

This stranger, Susanne had never seen before. A young man, he wore a woollen cloak the colour of the Danube under a summer sky. Light brown hair fell in thick waves to his shoulders; he was lean and a good foot taller than the emperor's crow. A modest hat was pulled over his forehead, shading his features. While the crow and the steward conversed together, the stranger studied the courtyard, his attention drawn to the dragoons positioned between the carriage and the Rudolfstor. Though he held himself proudly, there was a stiffness to his stance and a tilt to his chin that spoke of uncertainty.

Freya nickered, and the man turned his head and met Susanne's gaze. She felt a frisson of excitement, a sense of recognition even though she had never seen this man before.

The moment passed as quickly as it came. The crow hurried the stranger into Linzer Schloss, and the door shut soundly behind them.

When Susanne returned from the stable block, her flustered maid, Mathilde, pounced on her.

"Your father wants to see you." Mathilde whisked Susanne to her chambers. "He'll be kept waiting, but there's no help for it. You must change out of those riding clothes. He especially wants you to look your best. Praise be, you haven't picked up any bird's nests or foundlings this day." The riding cloak was tossed over a chair, a fresh lace collar was pinned to Susanne's modest bodice and a rope of pearls artfully draped around her neck.

Susanne barely had time to toss a handful of seed for her canary and give her pet rabbit a scratch before

Mathilde hurried her to her father's library. The maid melted away as Susanne crossed the threshold.

Instead of being seated at his desk poring over correspondence, Count Kuffstein stood before a window, staring down at the town of Linz. In his hand, he held a letter.

"Susanne, my Susanne. Where the devil is my daughter?" He bellowed over his shoulder before catching sight of her. "Ah, *liebling*, there you are." Tilting his head, he studied Susanne's appearance before a smile played across his distinguished face. He opened his arms and crushed his daughter in his embrace.

"We have a visitor, Father." A fact, not a question. Susanne had always been forthcoming with him.

"You miss nothing, that pleases me." He tweaked her chin. "Come and warm yourself by the fire." He offered her a seat and pulled a chair for himself. "We do not have a visitor, daughter, we have an opportunity. The Emperor Ferdinand has entrusted me to handle a delicate matter with a very special prisoner."

"The man who arrived this morning? Who is he?" She was careful to keep her expression demure, her attention fixed on smoothing the folds of her skirt. Her father need not know her interest. Count Kuffstein wielded such knowledge as a fencing master would handle a sword.

"A gift from the emperor," he said and lifted the letter aloft. Susanne recognised the imperial seal immediately. "He is none other than the brother of the Elector Palatine and nephew of the king of England."

Susanne looked up, startled, the events of a few months ago still fresh. An old dispute of power and land. The Elector Palatine had raised a mercenary army of English and Swedes and a few months earlier marched against the emperor. The clash had occurred in the north, at Vlotho, and God had smiled that day upon the emperor. The palatine's forces had scattered like fallen leaves, and yet there was one story that had grown to the proportion of a legend – how the palatine's brother had fought to the last man and came within moments of being killed. God had smiled on him too.

"Prince Rupert," she said.

Her father leaned back in his seat and folded his hands over his rounded belly. He nodded. "You are a clever girl. No one in Austria can match you for brains or beauty."

She flushed with pride. "He's a prisoner, then? What is to be done with him?"

"For what he and his brother dared, he deserves to be thrown into the deepest dungeon..."

Susanne's eyes widened, but she reserved comment.

"Do you not think so, Susanne?" her father asked, his brow arching. "He is a *Pfalzgraf* – a prince of the Palatine – and his rank has afforded him certain considerations, though there is a limit. Although the emperor admires the courage of this young man, the price of his freedom is allegiance. There can be no other way, for this man's father tried to usurp the imperial crown."

"Is he to be judged for the sins of his father?" Susanne asked. "The late emperor, after all, was restored to his rightful lands."

"A fair point, my child, but Rupert's brother raised a force to challenge the emperor as their father once did. The threat persists. It can end here, now that we have his brother as leverage."

"But surely, kindness will go further in mending

rifts? His courage has earned him this consideration, has it not, Papa?"

Her father looked at her reproachfully. "You are young and have a soft heart, daughter. He is not one of your needy animals. Trust me to guide our course, for have I not successfully negotiated treaties for the emperor? An impetuous young man will not be a problem." He tapped the letter against his knee. "I will not disappoint our Emperor Ferdinand. Although I have faithfully served him, there are those in the Privy Council who are envious of my success. They whisper in the emperor's ear that I, Hans Ludwig von Kuffstein, am not worthy of his trust. They would pull me down at the first opportunity." He rose and held out his hand to her. "Come, daughter, let's see what manner of man this young cub is."

Susanne's father did not throw their prisoner into the cellars as he had threatened, but the quarters assigned to him were on the third floor, in a bare and draughty room.

Count Kuffstein swept into the room while the guards remained outside, and Susanne received a better view of their prisoner. A travelling minstrel had once regaled her with tales about the French king's royal menagerie with the main attraction being a young lion. The minstrel had described the creature so vividly that the image of an impressive beast with a glorious mane lived in her thoughts for years. The lion had prowled his enclosure from one corner to the other, so the minstrel had said, muscles rippling with repressed energy. With Rupert pacing the mean confines of the cold, austere room, Susanne was reminded of the lion.

Rupert drew himself up proudly before Count Kuffstein. His youth surprised Susanne – he couldn't have been more than a couple of years her senior. But she saw something else, a vulnerability and the determined bravado of the unsure.

"My lord." Count Kuffstein presented Rupert with an elegant bow, one that he normally reserved for foreign dignitaries. The gesture was jarring in this dingy room. "I welcome you to Linzer Schloss. I am Count Kuffstein, his Imperial Majesty's governor of Upper Austria." He held out his hand to Susanne, urging her forward. "This is my daughter, Susanne Marie von Kuffstein."

"My lady," Rupert said with a stiff nod.

"My lord," Susanne returned coolly, before dipping into a curtsy.

Count Kuffstein rested his hand lightly on the pommel of his sword. "How do you find your accommodations?"

"If you seek to humble me, you do not know me at all, sir. I am a soldier who has made his bed on the ground alongside his men."

"They are indeed in the ground, so I've heard," Kuffstein said.

Rupert visibly winced at the reminder of the losses he had suffered on the battlefield; it did not go unnoticed by Susanne. "Nor have I forgotten."

Count Kuffstein walked around the room, making a show of inspecting the quarters. With the rough plank flooring, cobwebs draped from the ceiling, and cracked panes of glass, the room was not fit to house the meanest debtor. "It need not be this way. The emperor would be pleased to welcome you into the imperial family, under his protection."

"You must be mad," Rupert said, tossing his head back. Fire blazed in his eyes. "Align myself to the man whose father ruined my family and forced them into exile? My own father was a broken man when he died. He lost his lands – everything, and left my mother, a royal princess, a destitute widow."

"The fault lies with your father," Count Kuffstein said evenly. "He overreached and failed. Now your brother is stubbornly digging the same grave. I hope, for your sake, you have more sense."

Rupert glared back in mute rage.

"The emperor is not without sympathy for your plight," Count Kuffstein continued, in a more conciliatory tone, the one he used when wheedling concessions from beleaguered adversaries. "He has the highest admiration for your bravery, and it pains him to see you remain as a prisoner."

"Then release me," Rupert ground out before he started to pace again. "Ransom me and end this farce."

"The emperor will not agree," the count said, smoothly. "Instead, he offers you this – land to call your own, an annual income, and a title that befits your birth. You must also embrace the Roman Catholic Church."

Rupert snorted his scorn. "I will never be a papist. *Never*. To make such a pledge would make me an enemy to my blood. Though I am exiled from the land of my birth, I *refuse* to become an exile to my family."

Count Kuffstein clasped his hands behind his back and rocked on the balls of his feet. "With time to assess your situation, I trust you will come to a more pragmatic decision. I shall send for a priest to keep you company."

"Keep your Jesuit," Rupert spat. Then his gaze flicked to Susanne. "But if it's company you offer, I'd welcome other visitors."

Susanne's father glanced at her and then back at

Rupert. "Impossible. You are not in a condition to dictate..."

"Papa." Susanne stepped in. "Surely the emperor would not object to such a request?" Far from winning concessions, her father was only further antagonizing the prince. She sensed that Rupert would stubbornly fight to the death for his cause. Turning to him, she said, "If my father allows you the privilege of receiving other guests, will you admit a priest of his choosing?"

Rupert thought for a few moments, then he nodded. "I could agree to that."

"Very well," she said, pleased with her small success. "In the meantime, what can we do to make things more comfortable for you?"

Rupert glanced at the window. "Fresh air, the occasional hunt. An early morning ride would be welcome."

Susanne smiled. So he had noticed her in the courtyard. "You know we can't offer that. Are you fond of books?"

"As long as they aren't Latin or Greek. Paper and drawing materials would be most welcome, my lady."

A brave soldier and an artist, this man intrigued her. He posed a challenge, one that she was ready to undertake. "Consider it done."

Later that morning, Susanne strode to Rupert's quarters at the head of a small procession of servants carrying armfuls of linens, rags to stuff the draughty cracks, parchment, canvas, and inks, a stack of books from her collection, and a couple of musical instruments.

Her father had been outraged when he had seen what she had marshalled. "You would do well to remember he's a prisoner, not an honoured guest."

"Didn't the emperor ask us to take care of him? His bravery at Vlotho is proof that he will not be broken."

Susanne was surprised that her father did not see this. She ignored his displeasure and patted him on the cheek. Cradling her pet rabbit, Sofia, in her arms, she led the servants to the prince's quarters.

The guard on duty scrambled to his feet when he saw her and fumbled for the keys at his belt. He gave a sharp rap on the portal. "Susanne von Kuffstein to see you."

Susanne found Rupert at the window, with his blue woollen cloak drawn close about him. The sun had shifted on the horizon and it now slanted through the window and gilded his light brown hair. He nodded to her when he saw the servants filling the room with their burdens.

"I've brought provisions," she told him, absently stroking Sofia's grey fur. "Everything you've asked for and a few items besides. I see no reason to freeze you to death." To one of the servants, she said, "Yes, plug up the holes with those rags, and hang the drapery where you can." When she turned to Rupert, she added, "Peter and Paul will attend you." The two servants stopped unpacking the drawing materials long enough to bow to their new master. "They are good souls and will serve you well."

Susanne went over to the table to inspect the boxes of charcoal and pigments. She straightened the stacks of paper into an even pile. Rupert appeared beside her, and she sensed his nearness even before she looked up. It flustered her momentarily. Clearing her throat, she said, "I hope these supplies are acceptable?"

"Thank you." His smile was honest and unaffected. "This will keep me occupied." His attention shifted to Sofia, still cradled in Susanne's arms. "A strange companion, my lady."

Susanne smiled brightly. "She was a gift from an

uncle in Vienna who breeds them for their fur. I can't protect them all, but Sofia is safe here with me."

Rupert leaned in to get a closer look. His warmth and closeness filled Susanne's senses, leaving her feeling askew. When Rupert reached over to stroke the rabbit, his wrist brushed against her hand. He glanced up suddenly, an apology on his lips. Susanne felt the flood of red in her cheeks.

"I should let you be then," she said. "My father will be wondering what's keeping me."

Before she left, Rupert took her hand and pressed a kiss on it. "Thank you."

For the next week, Susanne held back from visiting Rupert, but he still managed to touch her day, even from his prison. Every morning, when she headed out with Freya for their ride, he was there, observing her from his third-floor window. It pleased and strangely unsettled her. While he was confined within four walls, she was free to enjoy the exhilarating ride. He was missing the early whispers of spring and the rich smells of thawing ground. She rode with a new awareness.

One day, riding through the forest on her way back to the castle, inspiration struck. Susanne dismounted, untied the red scarf around her throat, and fashioned a pouch. She searched the ground and gathered pine cones, mossy stones, bits of bark, and anything that looked interesting.

"He may enjoy drawing these," she told Freya as she used a fallen log to remount.

Susanne returned to the castle and as she passed through the Rudolfstor, she looked up to the third-floor window and saw him there. She evaded Mathilde and rushed up the stairs to the top floor with Sofia in her arms.

"Did you enjoy your ride, my lady?" Rupert asked, after greeting her. His attendants, Peter and Paul, kept a respectful distance.

"I've brought you something." Susanne untied the ends of her scarf and unfolded its contents on the table. "I found them in the forest."

Rupert picked up the items, one by one, then lifted the pine cone to his nose and inhaled deeply. "That is very thoughtful." Then his hand lingered on the red scarf, his fingers tracing along the fine weave. Susanne's cheeks grew warm. "It's a striking hue. Reminds me of you. I've never seen you without a bit of red."

Susanne's blush deepened. No one had ever noticed that, but he was right. Crimson satisfied a craving deep inside of her. "It's my favourite colour." His nearness was beginning to unsettle her, so she stepped away and drifted to a table covered in drawings: watercolours of drinking glasses, a composition with cutlery on a napkin, and the study of a window moulding.

Susanne picked up an unfinished sketch of a violin. The curve of the instrument's body was captured in exquisite detail. There was a sensuousness in the flow of lines that reminded her of her curves glimpsed in the mirror beside her bed.

"Do you like it?" His voice came behind her, startling her.

Susanne adjusted her hold on Sofia. "Very much, yes."

"I've only started on it this morning." Rupert scratched his unshaven jaw, drawing her attention to the dimple in his chin. How had she not noticed this detail before? "But I'm running short of inspiration," he admitted. "If you see a study of a chamber pot, you will understand it as a desperate cry for help."

Susanne laughed, and he smiled back. "What will you draw next? Perhaps the pine cone?"

"I was hoping to draw you."

Susanne thought he was teasing, but his expression was hopeful. "You could draw one of your attendants. Peter has a fine nose, or perhaps Paul's hands would do."

"I do poorly with noses, hands too, for that matter. Well? Will you take pity on me or shall I have them fetch a chamber pot?"

Susanne looked away. She longed to accept, but it was a foolish whim. "My father would not approve."

"I suppose he wouldn't." Rupert pointed to Sofia in Susanne's arms. "What about your rabbit? Surely, he wouldn't object to that? But you'll have to hold her still."

With a small laugh, Susanne said, "Why not? Mind that you flatter her, for she's quite vain, or I'll be offended on her behalf."

"I'll do my best," he said, placing a hand over his breast. He dashed off to position a chair by the window. "The light is good here."

Susanne settled Sofia on her lap where the rabbit snuggled in for a nap, while Rupert set up a table with his supplies and got to work.

It was a strange feeling to be the centre of his attention, Susanne thought. Even though Rupert was drawing Sofia, she felt the touch of his gaze on her cheek, her arms, and even her throat.

*I'm being too fanciful.*

As his charcoal scratched against the paper, she thought more about the caress of fingers against paper. The silence warmed between them, and the urge to break the spell gripped her.

"My father says you've been an exile since your infancy."

"Hmm." He held a pencil between his teeth as he made several sweeps over the paper with a stick of charcoal, then rubbed the edges with his forefinger.

"Is it not true?"

"It is." His lips quirked. "Few can claim that, I warrant. It usually takes a lifetime to work up to that notoriety."

"A sign that you're destined for greater things."

"Not if I remain a captive here."

Susanne lowered her gaze to Sofia and ran a hand down her silky ears and velvet back. "Pray, you'll come to terms with the emperor soon."

The silence stretched between them. Her mention of the emperor had cooled the mood, and she wished she could take it back.

After a few moments, he said, "Where did you ride today?"

Grateful for the reprieve, she answered, "One of my favourite trails, which strikes up the mountain." Then she told him of one section where the dark fir thinned out, giving way to a sweeping view of the river below. "I imagine this is the view hawks enjoy high up in their nests." Susanne became lost in her story, giving him details that she instinctively knew he craved to hear. *I will be your eyes; I will be your ears.* For a moment, she opened his cage through the seduction of her words. It would help him endure the days and months of his captivity ahead.

Then she realised that his pencil had ceased; he was quiet and his hands stilled. He leaned back in his chair, his hands resting on his thighs. "Thank you," he said. "Tomorrow, take another trail and tell me what you see."

Her mouth went dry. "Are you finished?"

"For now. I'd like to continue tomorrow. Will you return?"

Susanne nodded. "Show me what you've done."

"Not yet."

Rupert attempted to cover his drawing, but not quickly enough. The rabbit was barely defined – a few rough strokes formed a basic outline. But by far, his energy had gone into drawing her. He had captured her head, tilted slightly to the side, eyes dark and unfathomable. Braided coils of dark hair were fashioned like a stately coronet atop her head. Her expression was wistful, yet bold; curious, yet cautious.

Susanne was mesmerised. *Is this how he sees me? When did she become a woman?*

"Will you say something?" Rupert said.

Susanne bit her lower lip and the smile that threatened her. "You don't play fair. It was a rabbit you promised to draw."

Rupert grinned. "I'm a soldier. I will take every advantage even if it means I'll perish on the hill."

She could believe that. "Don't let my father see that or you will."

"Do you like it?"

She nodded, shyly. "You're very talented."

"Will you come and sit for me again?"

Something impish and wild nipped at her. "Here, take her," she said tucking Sofia in his arms, "so you may practise the proper method for drawing rabbits. I'll come back to see your progress."

Weeks of sweet breezes and approaching spring worked its magic on Susanne. After her morning ride, she would rush to visit Rupert. Under the indifferent scrutiny of his attendants, Peter and Paul, they conversed about books and art and the joys of horses. She felt herself unfolding like a flower under the sun, sharing her thoughts with him as she could never do with anyone before.

"I've always wanted a menagerie," she told him one day. "But not to display the animals for the entertainment of others."

"What would you do with them, then?"

"Offer them a sanctuary – a place they could thrive and be safe. It would have to be outside, somewhere sheltered." Susanne glanced up, shyly. "That sounds silly, doesn't it?"

"Sounds like the Garden of Eden," Rupert assured her, and she loved him for it.

The only shadow that was cast upon them came from her father, who maintained a presence like an ominous raven, reminding Rupert of the emperor's expectations. He mostly timed his campaign of converting Rupert for when the weather was fair, knowing the agony it caused a young man accustomed to activity and the freedom of the world.

After one day, forced to endure hours with the Kuffstein Jesuit, Rupert exploded in frustration and pitched a religious tome across the room. Susanne started from her seat.

Count Kuffstein's temper flared, and he strode across the room to Rupert. "You are the third son, with no prospects except for what fortune you can win for yourself." His voice held a hard edge. "You have always been an exile and will always be, destined to be forever dependent on the goodwill of your mother's family. What do you have except the life of a vagabond? With a simple pledge of allegiance to the emperor and the Holy Roman Church, you can have everything – land, title..." His gaze slid to his daughter for a moment. "You can have everything."

"I have not learned to sacrifice my religion to my interest," Rupert said, squaring his shoulders, "and I would rather breathe my last in prison than go through the gates of apostasy."

Count Kuffstein kept a stony silence, but Susanne saw a muscle in his jaw twitch and knew he was enraged. He gave a curt bow. "Very well. Daughter." He motioned to her. "With me."

Over the next week, Susanne's father jealously guarded her time. From morning to night, he kept her busy with never-ending correspondence and bookkeeping. Even her early morning ride with Freya had been curtailed, she couldn't even catch a glimpse of Rupert from the courtyard. She now perfectly understood Rupert's agitation with his confinement, for she had a taste of it too.

Rupert filled her thoughts every moment of the day – he was a fever that affected her thinking. She made more mistakes than usual, and her figures did not always balance. Susanne could barely sleep, waking up in the middle of the night and wondering what he was doing. Did he miss her as much as she missed him?

Finally, her opportunity arrived. Her father had been called away for business, and Susanne stole away to see Rupert. She worried that her father would have given orders to the sentinels who stood guard outside his door, but they admitted her without question.

Rupert greeted her, his appearance a little wild, unshaven, and bursting with restless energy. "I worried when you did not come. Did your father lock you away in a tower – does the fortress even have a tower?"

Susanne laughed, wanting to fling her arms around him, but there were Peter and Paul to consider, both beaming at her. "You needn't have worried." Her gaze swept the room and found a broken stool smashed in a corner and a large fist-sized dent in the wall. "Has a storm whipped through here?"

Rupert grimaced. "I can't stand it in here. I want to tear down the walls with my bare hands, to throw myself out of the window. What I wouldn't do to take wing and soar in the sky." He started pacing the room, reminding her again of the lion in the French king's menagerie.

"Perhaps I can bring you new books..."

Rupert turned to her. "I have a better idea – dance with me."

"What?"

"Dance with me," he repeated and held out his hand.

Susanne's eyes widened and she cast a discreet glance at Peter and Paul. The servants had been slouched on their stools, but now they sat to attention, all eyes and ears. To agree would be scandalous.

"We have no music."

Without releasing her gaze, Rupert motioned to his attendants. "Peter, Paul. Fetch your instruments and play us something suitable."

"My father will not approve, and well you know it," Susanne said. "Perhaps they can simply play us a tune? There can be no harm in that."

"Even if they're the finest musicians in Austria, I couldn't care less." His voice dropped to a caress. "It's you I have a wish to dance with, even if I have to hum the music."

His words caused a thrill, but still, she hesitated. Both servants looked at Susanne for approval. Finally, she gave them an answering nod. The two servants had always been loyal to her. She would have to trust them to keep this secret.

Peter and Paul fetched a violin and flute and settled

themselves on their stools before proceeding to ensure that their instruments were in tune.

Rupert held out his hand to Susanne again, and this time she took it. He bowed, a slight, almost reverential motion, and she dipped a demure curtsy in return.

Peter started to play the violin, setting a measured, lilting rhythm, and Paul joined in with his flute.

Susanne had had several dancing tutors, but dancing with Rupert was an entirely new experience. Although he held her hand lightly, she was attuned to his every movement – the leanness of his body; the warmth of his palm against her hand; the slight pressure along her arm as he guided her; of a discreet touch on her waist, guiding her direction in a delicate circle around him.

The movement complete, Rupert brought her towards him, raised her hand and gently kissed her fingers before leading her through another circle in the opposite direction. Bringing her towards him again he leaned forward and whispered in her ear, "You smell like sunshine and mountain air. You are intoxicating, Susanne." His breath, as he spoke, tickled her cheek and excitement coursed through her.

"I've never met a more clever, more beautiful woman." He backed away, walking her three steps forward, three back, and shepherded her through a figure-of-eight circle, bringing her, yet again, close, his hand holding hers, lightly, oh so lightly, before brushing his fingers, almost carelessly, against her breast.

He suddenly clasped his hands to either side of her waist and lifted her, swirling her a little to the side before setting her down and taking her hand again. Thus he swept her around the room, drawing her close, then moving away, their steps matched perfectly, his exquisite touch feeling like a burning brand. His hands every so often around her waist, lifting her high to left or right, his gaze locked into hers.

Her skirts swirled at her ankles as he spun her around and, for a moment, her heart soared... And then the dance was ended. He bowed and brought her fingers to his lips. They stood, so close, with Susanne and Rupert staring at each other, a foot apart, breathless and flushed.

"Peter and Paul," Rupert said, without tearing his eyes from Susanne, "put away your instruments and fetch us some refreshment."

The moment that the servants' backs were turned, Rupert drew Susanne into his arms and bent down for a kiss. Not a chaste peck on the lips but a passionate exploration of mingling breaths. Susanne revelled in her awakening senses. He released her when the servants reentered the room with plates and glasses.

Susanne stepped away, blushing; the look Rupert gave her was another kiss. She still felt the press of his lips on hers. Something had kindled in her, wanting to taste more.

They did not have an opportunity for another dance, but Susanne seized as many moments as she could find to spend with Rupert. She was careful to finish her work, and when her father was locked in his library, consumed by his affairs, she would hurry up to the third-floor room.

After one afternoon, that slipped too soon into early evening, she crept back to her apartments with the memory of stolen kisses. As she approached her father's library, she noticed his door was open. She tiptoed past, hoping not to draw his notice.

"Susanne?" he called out to her.

She grimaced. "Yes, Papa?"

"Come here, *liebling*."

Susanne pressed her hands to her cheeks, praying they weren't flushed before she stepped into her father's domain.

He was seated in a chair with a crystal goblet of red wine in hand. The flask was nearly drained.

"Yes, Papa, what is it?"

"The emperor is asking about my progress in converting Rupert." Her father set the goblet down on the table beside him and steepled his fingers. "He is receiving a great deal of diplomatic pressure to accept a ransom for the prince. His displeasure with me is growing, and the whispers from the Privy Council are getting louder. Everyone is questioning how it is that I can negotiate with a sultan, but one impulsive cub manages to stymie me. Have I lost my touch, they ask? The emperor wonders the same."

"He will not embrace our Church," Susanne said. "I am sorry, Papa, that you haven't been able to change his mind."

"You could."

Susanne frowned. "What do you mean?"

"You dance with him, you spend time with him, even cast foolish looks at him," his voice raised a notch. "Don't look surprised, daughter. Did you think you were allowed all these visits, with only a pair of half-addled servants in attendance, without my knowledge – without my approval?"

She blanched. Her stomach gave a sick lurch, and she clasped her hands tightly together.

"You care for him, I can tell. I've been told he feels the same for you. Encourage him a little. Smile. Dance a little more. It is not often that our goals are aligned with the needs of an emperor."

Susanne lowered her gaze and focused on her hands, clasped so tightly in her lap.

"You are the jewel in my crown, *liebling*." His voice softened. "Above all the others, you are my favourite, so I must look to your welfare." He cleared his throat. "There is a young nobleman in Vienna who may make you a fine match."

Susanne looked up. "I see."

"Or perhaps you may find a *better* one? For now, you will stay here in Linzer Schloss. There may yet be time for a betrothal."

"Thank you, Papa, and good night." She curtsied and hurried from the library.

It was only when she reached her quarters that she released a ragged breath and sank into a chair.

A special package arrived for Rupert from Vienna the next day. Susanne sat with her father in his library when the steward brought in a large wicker basket and laid it on the floor at Count Kuffstein's feet.

"What is this?"

"Lord Arundel, the English Ambassador, sends a gift for the prince, with his regards." The steward handed his master a letter.

Susanne noticed the basket was moving. As she drew near, she heard a series of yelps before a white fluffy head popped out.

"A puppy!" Both father and daughter exclaimed in unison, but while one sounded annoyed, the other was thoroughly delighted.

Susanne fell to the ground and found a squirming, wiggling puppy clambering on her lap. "What is this? Oh, you darling pup!" She laughed when his little tongue licked her nose.

"Lord Arundel writes that it's a breed of hunting dog. A poodle." He snorted. "Why should I indulge our prisoner, when he refuses the emperor's offer? He barely suffers our priest. He will not convert at this rate. Something must be done."

Susanne ignored her father's complaints. She held the puppy up to her face and nuzzled it. "He will love to see you," she whispered in his little ears.

" – betrothal."

Susanne glanced up at her father. "What did you say?"

"Nothing important. Only I wondered if this was a betrothal gift for the prince."

"Betrothal?" Her breath caught in her throat. "The prince is betrothed?"

"With Marguerite de Rohan, the daughter of the duc de Rohan." He sniffed. "Did I not tell you?"

Susanne's face was buried in the puppy's fur, so her father couldn't see her pale face. "No," she murmured, as lightly as she could. "I don't believe you did."

"The machinations started some time ago," her father said. "She is a Huguenot, but he would do better with a good Catholic wife, would you not agree?"

Susanne eased the puppy back into his basket and rose to her feet. Gathering the basket, she summoned a smile for her father. "I'll take this to the prince right away." Before he could stop her, she hurried out of the library.

Rupert didn't immediately notice her withdrawn mood, his attention stolen entirely by the puppy. His expression was a mixture of rapt wonder and joy. He lowered himself to the floor and welcomed the energetic puppy. Soon the two were playing together in a game of tug of war.

"Isn't he clever?" Rupert exclaimed over the puppy's antics.

Susanne watched as they got to know each other, but her father's words still stabbed her heart.

*Betrothed.* How foolish she had been choosing to forget that he could not remain here indefinitely. Naturally, he must have a brilliant match. It was the best way for his family to build alliances, and they needed them desperately. For now, he was at Linzer Schloss, but one day, he would leave.

"He'll make a fine hunting dog," Rupert said, now at her side, holding up the puppy. "Look at the size of his paws. Such a good boy. Boye. I'll call him Boye." Rupert laughed and then looked at her. He frowned. "Susanne? Is anything the matter?"

A vague excuse to brush away his concern was on her tongue, but the soreness of her heart spurred her onward. "My father says he is a betrothal gift from the ambassador. Shouldn't Mademoiselle de Rohan have sent him to you instead?"

"Betrothal?" Rupert drew back surprised. "By my word, Susanne, I am not engaged. I will allow, before my capture, enquiries were made, and Mademoiselle's suit was favoured by my mother. Until now, I haven't had an opinion one way or the other."

"Until now?"

Rupert glanced over her shoulder to Peter and Paul. Susanne stole a glance herself and found them bent over their tasks. Rupert touched her cheek and she turned to him. His warm brown eyes probed hers and he cupped her face in his hands. "I do not wish for an alliance with her, and I will not agree to it," he whispered. "Not when you are in this world." He took her hands in his. "You are my haven in a storm. You make me want to wish the world away."

Tears welled up, but Susanne blinked them away. She wanted to tell him about her father's gambit and the betrothal he held over her head, but she bit her lip and held her tongue. Rupert was passionate, he was impulsive. She didn't want him to speak the words that would ensnare him, words that he'd regret but would be too noble to take back. For she knew the price her father would demand of him, and she knew it was too great a price for him to pay.

Instead, she brushed her lips against his. "Let us not speak anymore of this for now."

Susanne tipped bird seed into her canary's dish. The little yellow bird hopped on the table, from one book to the other, favouring its lame wing until it reached its meal. Susanne propped her chin on her hand and watched the canary. She couldn't bear to see it confined, even though the cage her father had given her was generous and ornate.

Sofia hopped to her side, and Susanne lifted the rabbit to place her on her lap. Behind her, Mathilde folded clothes and tidied the room.

What should she do? Rupert needed his freedom, her father needed Rupert's capitulation. If her father could not shape Rupert to the emperor's needs, what would happen? Her father would be faulted for failing. Would they be sent away in disgrace? It would kill her father. Tears slipped down her cheeks.

Mathilde slipped her arms around Susanne. *Dearest Mathilde.* Susanne squeezed her eyes shut and leaned into the woman who had been with her since birth.

"Poor child," Mathilde said.

"You know?"

"I have eyes." Mathilde sighed. "There is no future between the two of you, forgive me for saying."

Susanne remained silent. It hurt her to see Rupert in pain, but it pained her to think that he would slip from her life. Was it so impossible for her to serve her father's ambition? Was there truly no possibility of a future together? The price of her hand would be the cost of Rupert's conscience and his family. He would be an exile to his family, and he would resent her for it.

*We do not belong together.* Her gut wrenched at the thought.

"You're right, Mathilde."

"What will you do?"

"Speak with him."

Mathilde gave her a final squeeze. "Courage."

Susanne climbed the stairs to the top floor, slowly. When she reached the outside of Rupert's door, she nearly turned back. *Courage. I must do this.* Before her heart was irrevocably crushed. *Too late.*

The guard admitted her, and Rupert greeted her with a smile, but it quickly faded.

"What is the matter?"

Susanne turned to Peter and Paul. "Wait for me outside." They looked at each other, startled, but they didn't argue. The door shut behind them.

"Susanne?"

She placed a hand lightly on his mouth to still his words and rose on her tiptoes to replace it with a kiss. His arms circled her, holding her close. Susanne committed to memory the taste of his mouth, the feel of his body against hers. She would have to remember every detail for the years to come.

Susanne pulled slightly away, her hands resting on his chest. "I care for you, please do not doubt that."

"I care for you too, but what are you saying?"

"I can no longer be here," she replied.

He searched her face. "It's your father."

Susanne shook her head. "Not really. The truth is that we can never be suited for each other. Neither of us can forsake our families. You've told me such wonderful stories of your siblings and parents. I feel as though I know them. They would never forgive you if you gave up your faith, and my father would never survive the emperor's displeasure if his daughter turned her back on him. There is more at stake than our wants and desires."

Rupert turned his head and looked away.

"You know I'm right," she said.

"I hate this." He looked up at the ceiling, as though searching for a miracle. Of course, there was none. His mouth twisted in a bitter smile. "You have managed to torture me more than your father could ever do."

"Rupert..."

He cupped her face and brushed a kiss on her lips. "Hush, never mind me. I want to rage, but I know you're right." He kissed her again, this time a demanding kiss that expressed the depth of his desire, frustration, and pain. His mouth slanted over hers, leaving Susanne breathless and reeling. She leaned into him and revelled in the feel of his body against hers. When the kiss ended, her lips felt tender and bruised.

Rupert pressed lingering kisses on her cheeks, her eyes, her nose. "You've been my bright sunshine, my love – my very love. You will always be in my heart." He touched his forehead to hers. "Will you give me a keepsake, my lady?"

Blinking back tears, Susanne untied one of the ribbons in her hair and pressed it into his hand. "Remember me."

"Always."

The next morning, the carriage waited in the courtyard to take Susanne to Vienna. She had told her father a lie, that Rupert had rejected her, and it was better if she were to spend some time with her aunt in the city. Count Kuffstein had been furious; the famed negotiator had been foiled and would now need to find a way to turn the situation to his advantage, while the man who was her father would do anything to shelter her.

A footman held the door open for her as Susanne crossed the courtyard. As she was about to enter the carriage, she paused and looked up at the third-floor window.

Rupert stood by the window, watching. Susanne drank in one last sight of him and raised her hand in farewell. He touched his hand against his lips and pressed his hand against the window pane.

Susanne turned her back on her first and only love and climbed into the carriage.

© Cryssa Bazos
*Canada, 2023*

## AUTHOR'S NOTE

Prince Rupert of the Rhine is best known for his contribution to the royalist cause during the English Civil War, but few are aware of the time he spent as a prisoner in Austria, where he fell in love with Susanne von Kuffstein. She was described in the Lansdowne M.S as 'one of the brightest beauties of the age, no less excelling in the beauty of her mind than of her body,' and Rupert 'never named her after in his life, without demonstration of the highest admiration and expressing a devotion to serve her.'

First love is fierce and bittersweet. I like to believe

that Susanne occupied a special place in his heart. Rupert never married – he rejected poor Mademoiselle de Rohan – and we do not have records of any other romantic involvements until much later in his life.

Rupert did eventually win his freedom after being imprisoned for two years at Linzer Schloss. The emperor, Ferdinand III, gave up on trying to convert this stubborn young man and only insisted that he promise to never take up arms against the empire again and make a public obeisance. When he met up with the emperor, who was hunting near Linz, Rupert single-handedly saved him from a wild boar attack and won his freedom in the most Rupert way possible.

## ABOUT CRYSSA BAZOS

Cryssa Bazos is an award-winning historical fiction author and a 17th-century enthusiast. Her debut novel, *Traitor's Knot* is the Medalist winner of the 2017 New Apple Award for Historical Fiction and a finalist for the 2018 EPIC eBook Awards for Historical Romance. Her second novel, *Severed Knot*, (in which Prince Rupert makes an appearance) is a B.R.A.G Medallion Honoree and a finalist for the 2019 Chaucer Award. *Rebel's Knot*, the third instalment of the standalone series, *Quest for the Three Kingdoms*, is a B.R.A.G Medallion Honoree and 2021 Discovering Diamonds Book of the Year. For historical articles about her research, visit her website **cryssabazos.com**.

'*Severed Knot* is an exciting thriller that takes readers on a wild ride! ... a truly unforgettable gem of a historic novel.' *InD'tale Magazine.*

Website: **https://cryssabazos.com**
Buy Cryssa's books on Amazon:
Amazon US:
**https://www.amazon.com/stores/Cryssa-Bazos/author/B072871QB3**
Amazon CA:
**https://www.amazon.ca/Cryssa-Bazos/e/B072871QB3**
Amazon UK:
**https://www.amazon.co.uk/Cryssa-Bazos/e/B072871QB3**
(Also available from other online stores or order from any bookshop.)

### ENDWORD
### by Helen Hollick

Back in the early summer of 2023, Annie Whitehead sent me a story to read, along with her disappointment that having written it for a particular reason, the story had been inadvertently misfiled and was no longer required. She now didn't know what to do with it. My response was immediate. I suggested an anthology with the theme of 'Exile'. I set about contacting a few authors who I have known well for many years, put the idea to them and received enthusiastic responses. The result? Well, you've just read it, (and I hope, thoroughly enjoyed the experience?)

It amazes me how one particular theme can generate so many different ideas – but then, all the authors involved are talented, successful writers with, between us, a wide range of writing experience, historical knowledge and expansive imaginations.

It has taken a good bit of hard work from us to compile everything – the actual writing was almost the easy bit – so on behalf of all of us I would like to say a few 'thank yous':

Thank you to:

Cathy Helms for designing the stunning cover, for formatting the text and for her assistance with the publishing process.

To Deborah Swift for her wonderful introduction.

To Annie Whitehead for taking the time to do a final proofread – and for being the reason behind the idea in the first place.

To the various editors of individual authors, and to the authors themselves – especially Alison, Loretta and Anna for their experienced 'eye' for spotting typos and bloopers, and finally, to *you*, the reader, for your continuing, enthusiastic and your very much appreciated support.

*Thank you.*

Helen Hollick
*Devon 2023*

# BEFORE YOU GO

We hope you have enjoyed these stories, please show your appreciation by leaving a comment or a review on Amazon or Goodreads – just a few kind words will suffice.

HTTPS://MYBOOK.TO/STORIESOFEXILE

## SOME FURTHER WAYS TO SAY 'THANK YOU'
## TO YOUR FAVOURITE AUTHORS

Leave a review on Amazon

'Like' and 'follow' where you can

Subscribe to a newsletter

Buy copies of your favourite books as presents

Spread the word – recommend books you enjoy to your friend and family

**The authors of EXILE thank you for your support**

Printed in Great Britain
by Amazon